THE FADE

Also by Chris Wooding

The Braided Path

The Weavers of Saramyr
The Skein of Lament
The Ascendancy Veil

THE FADE

Chris Wooding

GOLLANCZ
LONDON

First published in Great Britain in 2007 by
Gollancz
An imprint of the Orion Publishing Group
Orion House, 5 Upper St Martin's Lane, London WC2H 9EA
An Hachette Livre UK Company

A CIP catalogue record for this book is
available from the British Library

ISBN 978 0 57507 700 3 (Cased)
ISBN 978 0 57507 699 0 (Trade Paperback)

1 3 5 7 9 10 8 6 4 2

Typeset at The Spartan Press Ltd,
Lymington, Hants

Printed in Great Britain at Mackays of Chatham plc,
Chatham, Kent

The Orion Publishing Group's policy is to use papers that
are natural, renewable and recyclable products and made
from wood grown in sustainable forests. The logging and
manufacturing processes are expected to conform to the
environmental regulations of the country of origin.

www.orionbooks.co.uk

30

His knee breaks sideways beneath my foot, but I've clutched his head and cracked his neck before he really registers the pain. I let him fall and I'm gone as he folds to the ground, an emptied sack. Sometimes they give me a problem – an unexpected twist here, a swift parry there – but mostly it's just like disassembling dolls.

In the fighting-trance, I am separated. Oil on water. One part of me cold, clinical, governed by mantras and techniques familiar as breath. The other part is my terror, my anger, my bitterness, all mixed together into one nameless emotion that burns like the brightest fuel. The Cadre don't deny our passions; we harness them, and unleash them on those who would oppose our masters' will.

Around me is the noise: the roar of battle. We crash down the slope like a wave, two dozen of us. We wash around glittering crystal formations; we pass beneath arches of petrified sap. Blades of mineral grass crush like spun sugar beneath the soles of my shoes. I dodge past translucent protrusions sharp enough to open me like a bloody purse. Momentum pushes our charge to a reckless speed.

The air fills with the clatter of a shard-cannon. A man to my right is stitched across the chest and lifted from his feet, torn backwards as though pulled by elastic vines. The crystal forest erupts into puffs of glittering dust as it's punched by gunfire. I hold my breath. Inhaling that stuff would tear up my lungs pretty bad.

We'd hoped they wouldn't have time to traverse their gun. We'd gained the high ground and flanked them, and we thought the element of surprise would be enough. I feel sick as the forest is shredded around me and Eskaran soldiers are cut to meat by needles of stone.

Three heartbeats and we're on them. More Gurta are running up the hill to meet us, teeth bared, knives gleaming. The shard-cannon crew are firing through their own soldiers. The enemy are being cut down from behind, but they're still coming.

One of them singles me out, seeing I'm Cadre, seeing I'm small and slender and mistakenly thinking that makes me less deadly than someone like Rynn. I feint left and then launch off that foot, using the slope to get the height I need. He gets halfway through a swing before my foot connects with his jaw. I hear bone splinter. I touch down on his far side and keep running. I don't think I killed him but I don't care; someone else can do it. I'm after that gun. I hate guns.

Two heartbeats.

I glimpse the lake through the trees now. The water's bright, illuminated by phosphorescent plankton. Its light melds with the glow of the crystal forest. Patches of lichen glitter in the darkness far overhead, streaking the cavern roof.

One.

And suddenly the forest is smashing around me, the air crazy with the insectile whine of projectiles and the sound of breaking glass. The gun has been turned on me, and I'm coming out of the forest, right into its muzzle.

I break right and keep low, every new instant a miracle. Needles slice past, too fast to see. For a small eternity, I'm cupped in the hands of chance, life and death determined by the bucking of the shard-cannon, by obstructions and ricochets. Then there are no more crystal formations. The petrified white world of the forest peels back, and I've made it.

There's only six of them. Two manning the gun, four waiting, knives ready for the onslaught. They're yelling at each other in that foul dialect, everyone shouting orders, discipline crumbling. Just the sound of their fluting, trilling consonants makes something knot in my stomach. The old fear, the shame, the pain. I gather it and use it.

I'm first out of the forest, emerging a little way right of the gun. The pitiful wall of rocks they've built to hide behind doesn't slow me at all. I use it as a springboard, leaping over and among them. The gunners are my targets. I slash one across the throat, slicing through muscle and gristle with my shortblade. It's chthonomantically-treated obsidian: cuts through flesh like it was warm butter.

The rest of my assault force reach the emplacement moments later, by which time I've blinded the second gunner and broken his pelvis with my knee. The other Gurta can't touch me. Their strikes are slow, bodies declaring their intentions well in advance. I'm three moves ahead of everyone here.

The gun has fallen silent, its rotating barrel spinning to a stop. I get out of the way of the Eskaran soldiers as they come charging in. The Gurta put up a fight, but it's futile. They're taken down in moments.

When it's done, we count our losses. Three dead, one wounded, the rest covered in small wounds from flying splinters. I got off lightly with a few dozen scratches, nothing too serious. Could have been worse.

I hunker down on the wall at the far edge of the emplacement and look out across the lake while the men reorganise. There are Ehru out there, far from the shore, tentacles rising and waving and touching. They iridesce with colour, oblivious to the men dying nearby. I can't help but waste a few moments watching before I turn my attention to the troops below.

The main Eskaran force is forging along the lakeside. The enemy contests every step. Four hundred of us down there, all told. It's all to reclaim a tiny port called Korok which the Gurta took from us sixty turns ago. The Warmasters seem to think it's of critical importance, a staging point for bigger things, but I don't know about that. I just go where I'm sent. My fight is on the high ground, where the land rises to meet the cavern wall. We're meant to secure the terrain and take out the hidden guns that are butchering our forces on the shore. We're doing a pretty good job of it, so far.

I narrow my eyes and try to pick out Rynn in the chaos below. Big as he is, I can't find him. There's Vamsa, one of the Cadre of Clan Kessin, darting back and forth as she lashes the enemy with poison-tipped whips. I spot someone who can only be Jutti, the legendary Cadre dancer-fighter, identifiable by his acrobatic killing style. But no Rynn.

Our troops surge towards the Gurta earthworks, a fortified line of trenches and barriers, the last obstacle before the port. I hear the sharp pucking of shard-cannons and a swathe of tiny men fall to the ground. Two of our Blackwings fly overhead, their pilots strapped beneath the kite-like frames, propulsion systems scoring sparkling trails of energy through the darkness. They're dropping bags of explosives onto the Gurta, sending them scattering.

Our chthonomancers are hanging back, pooling their efforts, protected by a ring of heavily armoured crayl-riders. I watch a section of the earthworks heave and collapse, demolished by some invisible force, burying the enemy beneath tons of suffocating dirt. The Gurta might be formidably determined opponents, but their Elders will never match the rock-magic of our chthonomancers.

The Gurta defences begin to fail. I'm no tactician, but even I can see their cause is hopeless now. I feel myself smiling bitterly. Good. Let's see how this crushing loss squares with their insufferable sense of superiority.

Then I spot the rider on the slope, far down the lake shore, silhouetted by the dim glow of the crystal formations. Sitting erect in the saddle of one of those bat-like creatures they ride. He's holding up a spyglass.

But he's not watching the battle. He's looking out over the lake.

'Hoy! Belama! Where's your spyglass?' I call over my shoulder. The soldiers are angling the shard-cannon down at the Gurta earthworks. At this range accuracy is impossible, but at least we can stir up the defenders some. Belama slings me his spyglass, and I pluck it from the air and train it on the horizon. The cavern is colossal, like most of the caverns at this depth; I can't even see the roof, let alone the far side.

But I *can* see the ships. Sleek-hulled, sharp-nosed, slipping across the lake under the silent power of chthonomantic propulsion. Three of them, each capable of holding a hundred men or more. I look for the rider, but he's gone. It doesn't matter. I know what he was doing.

Waiting for his moment. Timing his attack.

And suddenly I understand what's coming. The ships will make landfall further up the shore, behind the Eskaran force, driving them towards the port and into the Gurta defenders. The rider will lead reinforcements down the slope and into our flank as we retreat.

We thought this was a lightly fortified target, of little importance to the enemy, but it's something much worse than that.

It's a trap.

The shard-cannon whirrs into life behind me, but I'm gone,

sprinting down the slope towards the lake shore. I tell myself it's because I have to report what I've seen to the Warmaster; but that's not what's uppermost in my mind. I have to find Rynn.

The Gurta earthworks are being overrun as I slip and scramble towards the water. The land steepens, thick with lichen and tall-stemmed fungi. I skid dangerously in my haste, battering my way through a clump of puffballs and leaving a cloud of spores in my wake.

The ground levels out as I reach the shore. Trampled moulds lie flattened underfoot. There are dead and wounded mixed among them.

The wounded are the worst. Dead bodies don't seem like people: some essential part of them has gone, leaving bags of meat. But the wounded are still aware, alive, screaming as they wave the stumps of missing limbs.

Some are being helped by comrades. Some aren't. I've seen enough battles to know that you can't care for everyone. You can't stay sane that way. So I race past the hurt and the dying, deaf to their cries. There's only one person here that I care about, and I dodge through the chaos of running soldiers to find him.

The whole force is moving forward, and I'm swept with them. He'll be near the front, leading the charge. He's Cadre; it's what we do. The soldiers look to us to inspire them, to lead. We are the elite, the heroes.

It's ridiculous, of course. We're not heroes. We're just very, very good at killing people.

I dart through the crowd. The soldiers are yelling themselves hoarse, rallied by the prospect of victory. Weapons are thrust in the air in triumph as they run: serrated blades, billhooks, compound bows of rootwood. I want to shout at them that they're mistaken, that the enemy has outmanoeuvred them, but it would be useless. I need someone in charge. Cadre don't call tactics, as a rule; we're there on the ground, in the thick of it. That's why the soldiers admire us, more than the Warmasters or the Division Leaders or the chthonomancers. We're like them. We fight with them, take orders like them, die with them.

I clamber over the ruin of the earthworks. Gurta dead everywhere. Insectile helmets cracked, armour slick with blood. Pallid skin flecked with black dirt. Smoke rising from craters, bits of people everywhere.

The fighting has begun again, this time among the buildings of the tiny port village. Korok has been a ruin since the Gurta captured it. Gravel paths wind between shattered buildings perched on a rocky hump of land. A few jetties project out into the lake. It's one of many similar towns in the Borderlands: joyless, functional, little more than a fortified trading post. They say it's valuable because it's the only place to unload heavy cargo this side of the lake, but I think it's a point of pride. The Gurta took it from us. We're taking it back.

I'm getting to the leading edge of the battle now, where the charge has feathered and spread out among the buildings. Archers are hidden in the ruins of the inn and the shinehouse. Its glow is feeble; the Gurta haven't recharged it, so the shinestone at the top of the tower is dying. The town is steeped in twilight.

I grab a soldier roughly by the arm as he runs past me. He whirls, angry at being handled like that. Then his eyes flick to the skinmark on my bare shoulder. The symbol for Cadre, encircling the insignia of my Clan. Suddenly he knows who I am.

'Who's your superior?' I demand.

He gives me a name. I don't care.

'Find him. Tell him to pull the men out. Gurta are coming from the lake and the high ground. They'll cut us to pieces when they arrive.'

I see the fear ignite in his eyes. His confidence in victory has been replaced by alarm.

'Tell him I sent you,' I add.

He runs to fulfil his mission, and so do I. It's unforgivable that I've just passed such an important message to a common soldier instead of taking it myself, but I've got other concerns right now. In a very short time the Warmaster is going to know about the ambush anyway. I have to warn Rynn. I have to be at his side when it happens.

I can't shake the terrible feeling I have about this. Like something huge and dark and infinitely, chokingly empty is rushing towards me.

I can't shake it, and I'm scared.

The buildings are made from dark stone and wood, low and ugly. They were put together with whatever was to hand: a shambolic longhouse; a grim inn; soulless administration buildings and warehouses. All shattered by the previous Gurta assault.

I skirt close to the walls; enemy archers would pick off anyone gung-ho enough to be running out in the open. As I watch, a soldier takes a shaft square in the chest. It punches right through him and halfway out of his back. I try not to think about the amount of force that must have taken. Gurta bows are legendarily deadly.

'Where's Rynn?' I ask a soldier who I find crouching in a doorway. He jumps out of his skin and tries to stab me, but I catch his wrist and shake my head, and he realises who I am. I repeat myself. He tells me. Everyone knows Rynn. He's hard to miss.

The thick of the fighting is in a yard between several of the largest buildings, just turnward of the docks. The Gurta have made their stand there, behind a barricade of rubble. Seems a stupid idea, to try and defend a position that's open on all sides, but a lot of things the Gurta do are incomprehensible. Even to me, and I know them better than most.

It's almost over when I arrive. The archers in the surrounding buildings have been taken out and the Eskaran swordsmen have gone in. Rynn towers over them, his enormous presence a rallying point for the troops. An axe in each hand, swinging left and right. He's not the fastest of the Cadre by a long shot, but there's something in his fighting style that makes him seem untouchable. He takes his swings with all the time in the world and still nobody gets close. The man's like a landslide.

It brings a smile to see him, just for a moment. Then I remember why I'm here, and the smile fades.

I go in. There's hardly anyone left for me to fight. The barricade has been all but overwhelmed. The Gurta are naturally small anyway, but Rynn dwarfs them, and they're afraid to engage him. I dart through the press of Eskaran soldiers and I've almost reached him when he spots me. A grin spreads, white teeth amid the bristling black of his beard—

—the next thing I know I'm on the ground and my ears are singing with a high, pure note. Sheer disorientation prevents me from doing anything more than blinking. I'm caked with something damp. Faculties shuffle themselves gradually into order and I remember a sensation like being slapped by a giant's hand. An instant of chaos, of flailing limbs and a bright light.

I raise my head. It feels like my neck muscles have been replaced by wood. Everything is stiff, everything aches at once, so much that I can't tell if I'm hurt or not. There's someone lying on top of me, his face on my chest. What's left of his face, anyway.

Suddenly my only desire is to stop that yawning, jawless thing from touching me. To get out from beneath the blank gaze of those dead eyes, which stare up, pleading, as if I could reverse what has happened. I push at the soldier, frantic with disgust. Scramble away backwards, bump into something else. I know it's a corpse, so I don't look. The shrill whine in my ears is making everything seem very far away and disconnected.

I get my knees under me and raise myself a little. The buildings are gone. The ground is strewn with corpses. One or two, like me, are stirring; but otherwise everything is still. At first, I'm not sure if I'm even in the same place as I was before the

explosion

and it falls into place in one cruel tumble. Why the Gurta were defending the yard rather than retreating. They booby-trapped the buildings. They crammed as many of us in as possible and then decimated us with explosives.

I can see our forces in the distance, falling into disarray. They daren't enter the town now, for fear of more bombs, and they can't retreat. Gurta reinforcements are charging down the slope towards them. The enemy ships are clearly visible now, powering towards the shore.

We've been outclassed. It's going to be a massacre.

And with that thought I remember why I'm here and not still up on the high ground. Fear drives me to my feet, and I stagger through the tangled carpet of limbs and bodies until I see him.

He's lying on his back, eyes sightless, his massive bulk emptied of that burning vitality that I've known ever since I was an adolescent. I can't even see a wound. But he's dead.

I have no strength in my body. Something is dragging me down and it's too insistent to resist. I sink on top of him, my head on his chest, but the heartbeat I know like my own isn't there. My eyes are fluttering closed, and I realise I'm hurt worse than I thought. I think I'm dying too. But that's alright. I don't want to be alive any more.

Rynn.
He's dead.
My husband.

29

I don't know where I am.

My eyes won't focus. There's a heaviness on my body, a great weight anchored to every muscle. Even the thought of lifting an arm seems an impossible dream.

It's dark in here, but there is a darker shadow looming over me. Big, broad, like Rynn. Sour smell: dried sweat, a wound gone bad, the breath of someone ill.

My mouth is dry. There's light in the corner of my left eye. I tip my head till I can see the jagged blur of it.

'ooo aakiii uuu?'

I swallow, but it does no good. It takes me a while to understand that the drone I just heard was a voice. I don't connect that revelation with anything. By the time it's formed, it's slipped out of my head. Keeping my thoughts together is like trying to catch live eels.

'omiii eee uuiiik'

The voice is deep, male, but there's something threatening in it and I don't know why. Everything's happening slow. He moves and leaves after-images of himself as he goes.

I take a huge breath suddenly; I can't help it, it's like I'm drowning and I need air. My head lolls away from the light and now I can't see anything.

I'm conscious of lying on something hard. Hard ground. As the man's weight shifts I realise that it wasn't only weariness keeping me down. He's sitting on my upper legs. His hand is on my shoulder. His other is on my cheek. Stroking it.

Things are tightening now, like a screw turned. A desperate energy is seeping into me from somewhere. I know I'm in trouble but I don't know why. My body tells me what my brain has yet to work out.

What's wrong with me? Something's wrong with me!

A tugging, my hips lifted, dropped, lifted again. Pulled upward by something wrapped around me. A slithering around my lower back, and the man casts something aside. I watch it go, my eyes crowded with ghostly trails in the aftermath.

It's my belt.

I can smell the sweat on him. Acrid. New sweat trickling over old; damp and unwashed clothes. It's hot in here, like an oven. I'm making little noises in my throat but I don't know what they are or what I'm trying to say.

I'm pulled downwards, but it's not down, it's *along* because I'm lying on my back. Bright alarms burst in my head and the tiredness in my muscles is pushed out by repulsion. I don't know why, but this is bad. I twist, but I'm pulled downward again, irresistibly. He's tugging at my thighs.

'y donnnee oo juuust lie still?'

He's taking my trousers off.

I begin to writhe, driven by some force, some primal thing that makes me kick and thrash even though I'm not exactly sure what's happening. My foot connects and there's a grunt. An instant later I'm hit by a slap that whiplashes my face back towards the light. White, fizzing stars crowd in around the edges of my vision.

There are other people here too. Shapes in the corners.

Why is nobody stopping him?

My senses are settling. I can almost see him now. One hand around the waist of my trousers, pulling at them while I buck my hips. He's trying to hold me down with his other arm. He's bigger than me, but he's clumsy and I'm getting less so by the second. Something about my clothing is foiling him and he can't get it off while I'm fighting, so he hits me again.

This time it doesn't faze me. I lash out. He recoils, holding his throat, wheezing. I don't think I hit him hard enough but it doesn't matter: he's hurt and I'm not half so helpless now. I get my foot to his chest and shove him. He's heavy, but there's no fight in him any more and he stumbles away, trips, goes down coughing. I can tell by the sound of his breathing that I didn't crush his windpipe, but he's going to have trouble speaking for a while.

My body feels connected to my brain again. Things are beginning to assemble themselves into some kind of clarity. I pull myself back, up against the wall, tugging my trousers up my thighs with one hand.

I push with my heels and somehow I sit up, though I almost faint doing it. The rock is damp and warm. I look for the man who was on top of me, but he's retreated into the shadows. I'm exhausted from the effort of moving.

Drugs. They kept me drugged. That's how I'm here.

Faint memories come swimming up like fish rising to nibble at the surface of a pond. I remember the sound of water and the creak of timbers, the rocking of a hammock. The weight of manacles on my wrists. I look at my hands and I can see the marks. Gurta manacles, toothed on the inside, that grip harder the more you struggle. I must have been a good girl. The cuts aren't deep. I still have my hands.

I remember the sound of their voices, laughing and shouting and joking. Sometimes talking to me in their own tongue. Jibing, insinuating. I hope I didn't reply. I don't think I did. Better if they don't know. Better if they think I can't speak their language.

There must have been a journey. I have a sense of time passing, a jumble of images. We went through caverns. Past crystalline outcrops and giant fungal blooms. The creaking of a cart beneath me . . . Yes, I remember . . . I was in a cage, on a cart. We travelled along roadways, the ground made even by chthonomancy, protruding rocks spread and flattened by Gurta Elders. I remember crossing a stone bridge over a chasm, the red glow and warmth of magma far beneath us. At one point we passed into a rockworm tunnel a hundred spans in diameter, streaked with phosphorescent algae still feeding on the residue of the ancient monsters millennia after they disappeared. I remember the sense of expansion, of coming out from the narrow, enclosing earth into that vast, cylindrical cavern, stretching away into darkness.

I remember them feeding me, and me eating, too drugged to realise they were drugging me. Splitroot or chamis oil, I bet, or some Gurta plant I've not heard of. Bastards.

I remember their faces crowding round me. Pale, slender, fine-boned, blue-eyed. Talking in that high, singing way of theirs. One of them had a dirty mask over the lower half of his face, and he was ministering to me. Examining me.

I don't remember anything else.

It's a prison. I understand that much, at least. A rough-hewn cave, irregular in shape so probably natural: Elders wouldn't make something this uneven. I count a dozen in here, though my vision hasn't quite recovered. They're pretty spread out, sleeping in corners or talking or just watching me. Some of them have little nests of blankets and rags that they're guarding warily.

It's hot. The heat comes from the walls. That means we're either very deep underground or we're near some geological kink like a lava channel or a steam fissure or something. Torchlight spills through a grille that's been fixed to the only obvious exit: a hole in the ceiling, twenty spans above me. Cross-hatched bars separate us from whatever is beyond.

I try to raise myself and suck my breath through my teeth as my back protests. Complaint noted. More gingerly, I lever myself into a less vulnerable position, and I wait to see if anyone else fancies trying anything. Nobody seems to want to. That's good.

My head is clearing fast as the drugs wear off. I should be applying my chua-kîn meditation techniques to speed the process – in fact, had I been conscious before they drugged me I could have negated most of their effects that way – but I can't muster the willpower. Something's nagging at me, something I should know. I wouldn't be able to centre myself in such an unquiet state of mind.

Then it comes to me.

Rynn is dead.

And I cry my guts out.

The time that follows is a blur. Sounds are dulled. My senses operate in a murky, smeared world of strangers and their strange activities. I feel like I'm dead. I wish I was.

They come with ladders, and one by one we climb from the pit. I climb, too. I don't have the strength to make decisions on my own.

The guards wear the same armour as the soldiers on the battlefield, moulded from hardened sap. It's a process we've never been able to figure out, but it provides an ultra-light and tough material, whitish with a faintly iridescent rainbow sheen, that fits tight to their narrow bodies. Slim carapaces to house their fragile flesh. Slender swords hang at their waists.

I climb the ladder and find myself herded onto the walkway at the point of a blade, to join the others from my cell. Outside the cell there is a cavern, sweltering and thick with shadow. The dark rock has folded into ledges and depressions, around which a complex and rickety wooden walkway has been built. Stairs lead down from a wide exit high on one wall. Heavy grilles of black iron mark the entrances to other prison chambers, some set into the floor like ours, others in the walls. I can see men there, fingers clenched around the bars, watching us hopelessly, their faces grimed.

I shamble like a sleepwalker. I speak to no one, and no one speaks to me, except when the Gurta guards bark their orders in broken Eskaran. There is a man with us, his throat bruised, staring at me sullenly. He is bulky with muscle and fat, his hair receding, two rings through his lower lip. Small eyes under a heavy brow, glaring.

They take us up the stairs and out of the cavern, into a series of wide stone corridors. Badly lit, weathered by time. I walk with my head down, barely noticing anything. We cross a room via a balconied passageway; beneath us, prisoners work mill-wheels to grind spores for bread.

Shortly afterward, we are brought to a halt by a large iron door. One of the Gurta unlocks it with a heavy key, and the door swings open. A blast of dry, scorching air billows from within, as from the belly of an oven, stirring my hair. Red light falls across us all.

We go inside.

The forge is a world of noise and sweat and fire. A seething landscape of molten metal, of clanking chains and pulleys, of pounding, oppressive heat. Great metal jugs spit and steam as their contents are poured. Dirty, glowing liquid slithers down trenches, flickers of flame dancing between the black patches on the surface. Men with hoods of animal hide and goggled eyepieces, brawny arms dripping, rake through the vats for impurities and wrench on hissing iron valve-wheels.

They put me to work on a device whose purpose I don't exactly understand. Another prisoner stands opposite me on the other side of a stone trench, through which a foul-smelling mineral slop flows, thick bubbles swelling and bursting on its surface. There is a kind of double barrier set across the trench, two heavy screens of cross-hatched metal. Our job is to slide them back and forth alternately, one arm pumping forward while the other pulls back, like trying to saw a log in two places at the same time. It's repetitive and seemingly pointless, and my shoulders ache and my back burns, but I do it anyway because I don't have the will to resist.

After the first shift I can barely raise my arms. The next shift I work twice as hard. I need the pain. I want it. Punishment for being alive.

The boy I work with is of a race I've never seen before, but I've heard stories. He's one of the Far People, a SunChild. Skin blacker than oil, irises so dark that it seems his pupils are enormous. He's slender and small, his hair hanging in tangles across his forehead. Seventeen or eighteen, I'd guess. His ears still haven't wholly healed from being clipped. The SunChildren cut the backs of their ears into fin-shapes as a rite of passage.

Ordinarily, I'd have been fascinated by him. I'd have wanted to know all about him: how he came to be here, where he was from, what strange customs he held. I'd always been the curious sort; I suppose that was why I found Liss and Casta such good company when others found their endless gossip infuriating. But my curiosity has withered, like all my feelings, to a blackened stump.

For his part, he doesn't say a word. I catch him glancing at me once or twice, but his gaze is quickly averted. Perhaps I see pity there, perhaps fear, perhaps nothing at all. But I'm thankful, at least, that he doesn't trouble me.

Our lives are measured by the clanging of an enormous bell, somewhere far above us. Each bell marks off three hours. Unconsciously, I count the strikes and match them to the rhythm of work and rest. Even through the haze of grief, I can't help but try and put things into order.

Gurta use the same system of turns, segs, hours and minutes that we do. We adopted it from them, after all. They use different terms, but the divisions are the same: two hundred and seventy-two turns to the year, the time it takes the mother-planet to circle its sun; ten turns to the orbit, or the time it takes our little moon to circle the mother-planet; one full rotation of Callespa counts as a turn; a third of that is a segment, or ten hours; thirty hours to the turn; ninety minutes to the hour. Deep beneath the surface, time is governed by the tides, the tug of the looming mother-planet.

I work, I eat, I sleep. Beyond the forge I see only a quad where they put us for several hours per turn, and a hall where we eat during breaks from the forge. I barely know where I am most of the time. I can't wake up out of this stupor and I don't want to, because without it I'll have to feel again. Instead, I lose myself in the push and pull of the screens, little caring that by being so zealous I'm making the boy work just as hard as me. He doesn't complain, and I wouldn't listen if he did. I wear myself out, savouring the agony of aching muscles. As soon as I rest, I sleep. There's no time for thinking.

Turns pass. I don't know how many. The others avoid me. They see the ruin in my eyes.

I know the faces of all twelve of my cellmates, and the names of everyone but the boy. We work with several dozen others at the forge, but at the end of each shift we're returned to our own cells. I notice who talks to whom, tracing their allegiances. The prisoners I've seen are almost entirely Eskaran males. I've seen no other women. It doesn't surprise me. I know how Gurta deal with foreign women.

We've a Khaadu in our cell along with the SunChild, and I've seen a Banchu and an Umbra and heard talk of Ya'yeen elsewhere in the prison. The Khaadu's name is Nereith. He has a wary friendship with Charn, the bulky man who tried to forcefully make my acquaintance while I was drugged to the back teeth. Charn's throat is almost back to its normal colour now. I can't even muster the passion to hate him.

Once, I'm woken briefly by the sound of tears. It's the boy. Everyone else is asleep, but the boy is crying quietly. It seems like a dream, and I'm coddled back to oblivion again; but the next shift, in the red light of the forge, I see the bruises on his face and arms. They're blue against the black of his skin, almost invisible. But I see them.

The same turn, someone is taken. We're in the quad when they come for him. I'm sitting on my own, as I always do, staring at the ground between my feet, my mind empty. I hear the scream, and look up to see a man I don't recognise being bundled away by guards, while others threaten nearby prisoners with pikes. There's no need. Nobody is going to his rescue.

'They'll come for you next, you sons of whores!' he's shrieking. 'You're all meat to them! They'll come for you next!'

The prisoners look away. So do I.

★

It's getting harder and harder to shut out the clarity. The haze that cushions me is tattering away. I fight to keep hold of it, but it isn't working. More and more I'm aware of things around me, of conversations. Old instincts are kicking in, subconsciously gathering information. I'm Cadre: I'm a spy, a warrior, an assassin, trained since childhood in the arts of subterfuge and combat and murder. I've suffered and suffered again, in ways that would crack the mind of someone weaker. But I'm recovering. And I can't stop it.

I have my own spot in the cell, where I curl up on the hard stone floor and find the blankness that is my only respite. But soon I'm robbed of even that sliver of peace.

For the first time since Rynn died, I dream. And when I dream, I dream of my family.

31

The graduation ceremony was a grand event, staged in the port city of Bry Athka on the turnward coast of the Eskaran Ocean. I hadn't been looking forward to it. Even as we arrived I was still hoping my son would change his mind and refuse his commission. It made me feel unworthy to think that way, but while I could feign happiness easily for the sake of others, I couldn't lie to myself.

Still, you can never get too many chances to dress up. Naturally, Liss and Casta had demanded that I premiere my outfit to them before anyone else saw it. They made politely uncertain comments, then took me out and bought me a riotously expensive alternative. Something in black and dark green, hugging me in all the right places. I'd allowed myself a little narcissistic pleasure in front of the seamstress's mirror while the twins drowned me in praise. Not bad at all, considering.

The hall was magnificent, its cream-coloured roof scalloped in gold and scooped like the inside of a clam shell. The sloping floor was broken up into tiers, enclosures and balconies linked by gentle stairs and crowded with guests. Colourful fungi grew from rockeries babbling with tiny streams.

Aristocrats hove this way and that, murmuring poisonous comments about their rivals and hunting for gossip. They glided from group to group, a slow dance of social manipulation, currying favour here and snubbing a former ally there. They wore elaborate headdresses, gowns made of jewels and exotic scales, tight uniforms and ripped, faux-poor attire. Most of them had been chthonomantically altered in some way: their skin coloured or patterned, pupils changed to crosses, breasts honed. Many were skinmarked with artful designs, safe in the knowledge that their chthonomancers could erase them when fashions moved on. And for each style there was a counter-style, like the Purists, who refused to wear any decoration and dressed in strict black clothes, with their heads shaved to give the appearance of receding hairlines.

Even Rynn looked halfway to respectable, though he clearly felt uneasy. Social events weren't his forte. He'd trimmed his beard and allowed me to pick his outfit. I'd kept it simple and subtle, out of mercy. He stuck by my side as if fearing I'd cast him adrift in the sea of eccentricity that surrounded us. He'd always viewed the aristocracy as unfathomably weird, and this display was doing nothing to alter his opinion.

I'd never found their little quirks threatening like Rynn did. They upset his sense of decency. For myself, I thought them rather charming, though I never let my fondness cloud my perception. It was easy to see the Plutarchs and their Clans as silly children with too much money, but the truth was that they played a different game to the rest of us, for altogether higher and deadlier stakes.

'Can you see him?' I asked my husband, who was taller than most people in the room.

'They're just coming out now,' he replied, his voice a deep rumble. He slid his arm around me as he said it and I leaned into him automatically. I didn't know whether he was sharing his pride or reassuring me against the nagging vestiges of guilt that I felt. Maybe he was thanking me for my decision not to oppose him on this. But in the end, I didn't care. There was a certain primal safety in his arms, in his smell and the warmth and the bulk of him.

Then, too soon, we were making our way down the tiers towards the semicircular stage at the end of the hall. Most of the guests were not overly interested in the ceremony, obsessed instead with gathering intelligence on their friends and enemies. Locating the best place to insert a knife and twist, I thought uncharitably.

I towed Rynn through the knots of gaudy conspirators. His hand was clasped anxiously to mine, and I could feel it becoming damp with sweat. My husband would throw himself headlong into two dozen Gurta swordsmen and come out without a scratch, but the thought of a formal ball drove him into paroxysms of fear. He didn't like things he didn't understand. He was a man of simple pleasures, uncomplicated, honest. One of the many reasons I loved him. After wallowing in the treacherous mire of the Veyan underworld or gliding through the immaculate viciousness of high society, I liked to come back to a man who said what he meant.

Liss and Casta intercepted us just as we'd found our spot near the front. By now I had become used to the latest changes the twins had wrought upon themselves, and they no longer shocked me. I was accustomed to Liss's deathlike pallor, her shrunken chest, eyes the colour of dirty water and hair like torn dishrags. Casta was easier to look at, fuller-figured, dressed in darkness and flame, her skin black as coal and her hair and eyes red like lava.

Liss detonated at the sight of me and I was buried under a smothering of kisses, which at least interrupted her delighted squeals momentarily.

'Orna, my love! We're so happy for you! Oh, you look wonderful in that dress. What a choice, what a choice. See? You can rely on us!' She darted a quick look at her sister. 'Aren't we happy?'

'Very happy,' said Casta, ever the more demure of the twins, who waited until Liss's assault was exhausted before placing a controlled kiss on my lips. 'Liss has been talking about nothing but the graduation for longer than I care to remember. Soon she hopes to be where you are, perhaps.'

'Oh, what wicked lies! See what words she puts in my mouth! I said no such thing!' She leaned in and whispered, her breath faintly rancid to match her attire. 'But I'm *dying* of envy.'

I laughed. The twins noticed Rynn and chorused their hellos before giving him a cursory kiss and ignoring him. Rynn was unfazed; he was watching the graduates lining up on the stage. He had an infuriating inability to concentrate on more than one thing at a time. Right now, he was only hazily aware that we existed at all.

'Do you think *my* child will join the Army?' Liss gushed. I didn't get a chance to reply; most of her questions were rhetorical. 'I hope not. Oh, I wouldn't send him to the war, not my precious one. I hope he's an artist or a poet or a sculptor, like Rynn's grandfather!'

I suffered a twinge of remorse at that. Liss had an uncanny ability to cause accidental wounds with her verbal flailing. My husband appeared not to have heard, which was a good thing. He hated his grandfather.

'I've decided it's going to be a boy, anyway, just like yours,' she declared.

'Won't the father have something to say about it?' I asked. I glanced at her twin, but Casta's attention had drifted elsewhere.

'Oh, men don't care about such things,' she said airily. 'He'll be too busy running his . . . textile mills or whatever it is he does. I *think* that's what he does?' She looked to Casta for help, out of her depth when dealing with something factual.

'He manufactures luxury rugs, among other things,' Casta told me with a tinge of weariness. 'Foolish industry when there's a war on, though against the odds he's doing very well at it.'

'Don't be jealous!' Liss pouted, then told me: 'She's so jealous.', like I didn't know.

Casta's eyes turned hard and I braced myself for an argument, but Liss was off again before things could turn nasty, crowing about an upcoming society ball I was going to miss because I'd be knee-deep in someone else's intestines on a distant battlefield.

I relaxed a little. I hated it when the twins argued. They always tried to drag me in as arbiter, and that was a dangerous place to be. They might have been my friends, but as the younger siblings of my master they also held the power of life or death over me. I wouldn't put it past them to use it in a fit of whimsy. I loved them both, but I was always just a little careful.

'There he is!' Liss interrupted herself with a kind of breathy, suppressed scream.

I turned to the stage and found my son, Jai, resplendent in the uniform of the Eskaran Army Officer Corps. I clutched Rynn's thick arm and felt myself melt at the sight.

Jai resembled me more than his father. His features were feminine, sensitive rather than blunt and broad, and he was slenderly built. But he had Rynn's wide, dark eyes and thick black hair, which he wore scraped back over his skull and glistening with oil. He'd always been small, even as a baby, for which I was deeply thankful. If he'd been Rynn's size he'd have broken me on the way out. Rynn's mother is wider than she is tall. You need specialised equipment for that kind of job.

Jai was staring fixedly ahead, the picture of rigid discipline, like the other graduates of the Bry Athka military school in formation alongside him. A hush spread as the Warmaster stepped onto the stage.

My grip tightened on Rynn's arm as the first words were spoken. He was really going through with it.

Oh, my boy. How had I let it come to this?

I caught up with Jai after the ceremony, but not before the Dean of Engineers from Bry Athka University did. He was already offering regretful congratulations by the time I arrived. Rynn had been stolen by a minor member of Clan Caracassa, eager to show off one of their Cadre. My husband was far more physically impressive than me, so he got to squirm while I ducked away and left them all to it.

Reitha stood with her hand resting lightly in Jai's. She'd only caught the end of the ceremony, having been delayed by her master in the study of the breeding patterns of some surface creature I'd never heard of. She gave me a conspiratorial smile as she saw me approach. We both knew what the Dean was like.

'Massima Leithka Orna,' he said. Bushy grey-and-black eyebrows ascended an ancient and wrinkled forehead. 'A pleasure, a pleasure to see you again. I was just telling your son – fine boy, fine boy – I was just telling your son that the military's gain is the University's loss. And a terrible loss, too. This boy's mind . . .' Here he paused to tap the side of Jai's head with a withered finger; Reitha barely suppressed a laugh as Jai flinched away. 'We must preserve a talent like this, we must use it for the betterment of our kind. What wonderful machines he might make! But youth will be obdurate, yes? Young boys will march to war.'

'Well, I know Jai is very flattered by the interest you've shown in him,' I replied. 'But I think his mind is made up. Besides, he's taken his commission now. The term of service is five years.'

Voids, just saying that made my stomach plummet.

'Bah! In this world, there's nothing that can't be done with a word in the right ear.' The Dean drew me aside and took a letter from inside his robe. 'If Jai should decide the military's not for him, we would be happy – *honoured* – to accept him into the faculty. This letter should open any doors that need opening.'

I tucked the letter into the sleeve of my dress, careful to ensure that neither Jai nor Reitha saw it. The Dean knew what he was doing. Jai would feel obligated to refuse an offer like that, but I had no compunctions about keeping hold of it for him. Just in case. Five years was a long, long time.

Impulsively, I gave the Dean a kiss on the cheek. He'd never know just how grateful I was for what he'd just done.

'Now, now,' he chuckled. 'No need for that.'

Reitha stepped over and took the Dean by the elbow, leading him away with gently irresistible force. 'You haven't met my master, have you, Dean? He teaches in the Faculty of Surface Studies. I must introduce you. You know, being a naturalist and being an engineer aren't so different . . .'

Jai's gaze followed his lover as they slid into the folds of the crowd. 'What did the Dean say?'

'He was hoping I could persuade you to change your mind.'

'Mother, please don't,' he said.

'I won't,' I told him. We'd had that conversation a hundred times.

'It's over, anyway. I made my choice. There's no going back.' He stopped, then said it again, staring into the middle distance. As if only now realising what he'd done. 'No going back—'

'Congratulations,' I said. The word felt too stiff, too formal. Clumsy.

He focused again and gave me a rueful look. His eyes wanted me to stop him but his pride wouldn't let it happen. He wanted me to make it all go away, like I could when he was a child. Begging my protection from something I couldn't protect him from. It dug into me like a spike.

Then he embraced me, and I held him. The uniform felt wrong on him, the fabric too coarse, too starched. But beneath it was the warm body, the blood and the heart that I made. You couldn't ever let that go. Not really. He was still mine, even though I felt I was abandoning him.

'Write to me,' I murmured.

'I will,' he said. 'I'll use the code. Then they can't censor my letters.'

I laughed, surprised. It had been years since we used the code he invented. A game between mother and son. Our little secret, one we never let his father in on. An echo from a childhood that felt like it was receding moment by moment.

'You still remember it?' he asked.

'I remember,' I said, then clutched him tighter, squeezing him to me. 'I remember.'

Later, I made my way out of the hall to a corniced balcony overlooking the ocean. Beyond the glow of the city, past the reach of its powerful shinehouses, waves tossed and swelled in the darkness. Out in the distance tiny clusters of lights floated, disembodied. Ships, making their way backspin towards Mal Eista or Jurew or Vect. The sea was rough, stirred by deep currents and a sharply switching wind, the breath of the earth drawn into stony lungs by enormous systems of convection and pressure which I only dimly understood. Constellations of luminescent lichen and algae streaked the roof of the immense cavern, far above.

Closer by, a pair of Ehru were signalling to each other in a cascade of colours, their tentacles hovering above the water. It was them I was watching, wondering about their language, their thoughts, their behaviour. There was a kind of romance in those vast, mysterious creatures. I admired their aloofness. The Ehru plied the seas and waterways of Eskara and lands beyond, but for all their obvious intelligence they had no interest in communication with our kind. The only contact they had was with the Chandeliers in the deep lakes.

Reitha told me she'd once witnessed several Ehru and two Chandeliers having a conversation, and the lightshow had been the most stunning thing she had ever seen, rivalled only by Callespa's nightly aurora for sheer overwhelming beauty. It made me think I'd chosen the wrong profession. Maybe I should have been studying to be a naturalist like her. Then I remembered that I didn't *have* a choice, and I remembered why, and my mood soured a little.

I heard Rynn join me on the balcony. He never could move quietly. That was why our masters sent people like him and Frask and Beltei to the front lines, to be the crushing head of the hammer-blow, whereas on the few occasions I was on the battlefield at all it was to conduct surgical strikes. I'm subtle, he's not.

'It's done now,' he said, a hand on my shoulder. He was wary, otherwise he would have put his arm around my waist. He treated me like a bag of snakes sometimes, never sure if something was going to find its way out and bite him.

'He thinks he's made it up to you,' I said, a slight edge to my voice. 'Whatever *it* is.'

'We made the choice long ago. So did he. Be proud of him.'

'I *am* proud of him,' I said. 'And I'm scared for him. He's going to war, Rynn. I know how the Gurta are.'

'And I don't?'

'Not like me.' I felt cheap for playing that card, but it had been a long time since it worked on Rynn anyway.

'The war will be over before Ebb Season. Not even the Gurta have the heart for it any more, and people are sick of fighting. It's bad for business.'

'It's good for some. Our Clan, for one.'

'What are you really scared of?'

Blunt enough to work. 'He's our *son*, Rynn,' I said. 'He's not like you or me. We're Cadre.'

'You can't protect him. He wouldn't let you.'

'But we could have stopped short of sending him off to a battlefield,' I replied acerbically. The rest didn't need to be said. *I* didn't want to let him join the military school. *I* didn't like the way his father pressured him. And *I* didn't do enough to prevent it.

'It'll be alright,' Rynn said, because it was the best he could offer. And then I felt his arms slide around my waist and his huge chest pressing against my back, and I sighed and relaxed into him.

'It'll be alright,' I agreed, softly. Because the alternative was too terrible to bear.

28

Each turn, after our second shift in the forge, they lead us to a small cave glistening with milk-veined stalactites, where hot water drizzles from the ceiling into a steaming pool. The men strip and sink into it with languid sighs and barks of approval. I sit on the edge, back against a stalactite, and savour the agony in my muscles. Better not to undress at all. I may have seen off one assailant, but I'm still the only woman among a dozen men who've been confined here for the Abyss knows how long. I'm not stupid.

Everyone still wears the clothes they were captured in, or in the case of those who were armoured, their underclothes. Most have dissolved into rags by now, so the prisoners work in a tattered motley or strip to the waist in the sweltering heat. The Gurta aren't concerned with prison uniform.

At least my clothing suits the temperature. I wear a sleeveless black top, to display the red and black skinmarking down my arms: the Cadre insignia on my left shoulder and Rynn's family sigil on my right, to indicate our marriage. Baggy black trousers end below my knee, with crisscrossed straps leading down to the sandals on my feet.

They took away the tools of my trade, though. The flash bombs, lockpicks, garrotte, throwing knives, all that stuff. And they took my blades, obviously. But I don't need blades to kill people.

I gather from the comments of the other prisoners that bathing is a blessing recently bestowed. Those who've been here longest say it's a privilege that's removed and restored with no apparent pattern. Randomness seems to infest our routine here. Sometimes we're led into the food hall but there's no food. Sometimes we have to work double or triple shifts at the forge. Once we were left alone in our cells for several turns, with silent guards dropping in bundles of spore-bread every so often as the stench became steadily more unbearable.

There's a hollow we use for a latrine in the corner of the cave, which they make one of us muck out with a shovel whenever they come to release us. The unfortunate chosen has to clamber up the ladder with a seeping sack of human shit on their shoulder, after which they're escorted away to get rid of it.

I've been lucky so far, and I've not been picked. Gurta have a strange attitude towards females. They treat their own women with an odd mixture of adoration and brutal repression. But as a foreigner, too old for enslavement, I should have been killed by now. Perhaps my Cadre status confuses them. They don't have woman warriors.

Whatever. I don't care what they think, as long as it spares me from hauling the contents of twelve men's bowels up that ladder.

There must be a purpose to this constant shifting of schedules. It occurs to me that I could simply ask another prisoner and see if they knew, but I don't want to break my silence. To do so would be to accept that life is still going on for me, and I have to keep living it. It's a step I won't be able to take back.

After the bathing they take us to the quad. We travel up through the guts of the building to get there, and things grow fractionally cooler. There are no more caves but corridors, cut from local stone without any of the frills and flourishes for which Gurta architecture is famed. I've no idea of the layout of this place; I was drugged when we came in. But from what I've overheard, it's garrisoned, making me think that we're inside a fort of some kind.

We're allowed to see very little. The corridors are tight and dark, and the glimpses we catch of the rest of the prison only show other prisoners engaged in slave labour, as we are. In addition to the forge there are kitchens, a laundry, a mill and a reeking tannery.

And then there's the quad, which is the part I find strange. Here, they simply leave us alone. It's open to the air; we can see the cavern roof and feel the stirring of the hot breeze. The walls are sheer and windowless for twelve spans or so, and then there's an inset balcony where archers wander, alert for trouble from the prisoners below.

There are other people up there watching us too, dressed in grey robes heavy with ornamentation. They are predominately old, their white hair yellowing with age, and some have their eyes hidden behind the round brass goggles they use to correct their sight when it begins to fail. Their Elders don't practise body alteration like our chthonomancers do; it's against their beliefs. They'd rather let their children die of entirely preventable conditions. Thoughts like that used to cheer me up when all else failed.

The prisoners gather and gossip and play games for exercise. Fights break out, unchecked by the guards. Then a ring of chanting men surrounds the combatants, goading them on. The quad is where many scores are settled. Here, we're allowed free rein as long as we don't try to leave. A man was beaten to death here not so very long ago. The guards did nothing to intervene. But a similar incident occurred several turns later, and this time they were quick to come to the victim's defence. It appears some of us are more valuable than others.

Rynn is dead. Jai is beyond my reach. From the depths of my grief, the distance between us seems unfathomable.

I'm in a prison, but not one made of walls and gates.

It's another period in the quad. The prisoners are in high spirits after their bath. They play-fight and tussle and tell jokes. Nereith and Charn murmur among a group of flint-eyed men; Nereith grins and I see his sharp Khaadu teeth, fang-like incisors for ripping meat. I sit, as I always do, against a wall. Left alone, as I wish to be. Sometimes I look up, a brief moment of animation; but most of the time I gaze at the flagstone floor, disconnected. I'm exhausted from the forge, too tired to think.

Bare feet shuffle into view. Skin deep black and shiny. I've heard that SunChildren secrete some kind of oil that helps them survive up there, on the surface. It gives a faintly bitter tang to his scent.

I wait for him to go away, but he doesn't.

'Help me?' he says.

It's the first time I've heard him speak. His voice is soft and clambers over the words awkwardly. Eskaran is not his first language, nor one he's accustomed to using.

I look up. His brow and lip are swollen, and he's holding himself awkwardly. He's wearing bruises under his thin shirt. Maybe a cracked rib.

Charn gets him in the quad, and on occasion in the cell. Likely it's because he's alone, and small, and alien. Nobody is on his side, so there's no fear of recrimination. He'll be bullied into a corner, hit rapidly several times, kicked when he goes down. It's done quick and neat, with no real malice. I don't think the boy knows why it's happening. I don't think even Charn knows why he does it.

'He is afraid from you,' the boy says. 'He speaks of you as Cadre. I have heard it. Fear is heard when he speaks.'

I look him over. There's something appalling about the sight, battered as he is. He's handsome, in a feminine kind of way: he looks like an obsidian sculpture. The bruises disfigure him, blasphemies against the clean lines of his face.

'Feyn is the name I have,' he says, when I don't reply.

I'm silent for a time. Then I hear myself speaking, as if from a distance: 'I can't help you, boy. Go away.' But what I mean is: I *won't* help you; stop intruding on my perfect misery.

His face is unreadable. Then he nods, as if he understands. I want to tell him that he *can't* understand, he's not old enough to know love as I have, the pain I feel; but there's no point. He walks away from me, holding himself.

I glance over at Charn and Nereith, and their gazes flick away from me. Our exchange has been noted.

Next shift in the forge I ask to swap with one of the coke-shovellers. Partly it's because I've become stronger, and the constant push and pull of the screens isn't gruelling enough. I want the extra punishment. But mostly it's because I can't bear looking at that SunChild boy.

The prisoner is happy to oblige. My job is pretty cushy compared to his.

There are six of us at the furnace, scooping coke into its roaring, smoky maw. One of them is Nereith, the Khaadu man. I ignore them all, putting my back into the work. The heat from the furnace draws sweat and dries it quickly. The faces of the men around me are grimy with black dust. They talk to each other as they shovel fuel from the pile into the hungry flames. They laugh and make crude jokes about their captors, they bitch about other prisoners, they reminisce about what things were like back home. They mock Nereith in a comradely way, calling him a cannibal. He shows his teeth and suggests how he might eat their mothers.

I'm getting stuck into the pile and am about to sling another shovelful into the furnace when the Khaadu grabs my arm.

'Not like that.'

I stare at him blankly.

He points at my shovel. 'Scoop from the middle of the pile, not the bottom. Your shovel is full of dust.'

I still don't understand.

'If you throw that into the furnace it'll ignite and blow back,' he says. 'You'll burn someone.'

Slowly, I turn away, shake off the shovel, take another scoop. This time my shovel is full of coke rocks. Nereith grunts in satisfaction and gets back to work.

I keep my eye on the Khaadu man. There's something about him. It's an instinct born of dealing with the dangerous, from aristocratic killers who murder by signing a contract, to fireclaw dealers with a blade and nothing to lose.

He's stripped to the waist; well-defined muscles; no fat on him. Entirely hairless, like all Khaadu, and his head is skinmarked with long red strips that follow the curve of his skull. Larger red strips run down his back. They're something to do with his social caste, but I've not met enough Khaadu to recognise his status. Their cities are far away from ours, through labyrinthine cave networks, Umbra-haunted fungal forests and sulphurous rock plains where poison gases leak from the ground. They don't visit Eskara very often.

But it's his teeth that draw the attention: long, sharp, fanged like a predator. Khaadu are a race of consummate carnivores. They prefer to eat their food still wriggling. The exception is when they eat their dead, or the bodies of their enemies. It's a ceremonial thing.

The Overseer makes his tour of the forge at the same time every shift. It's the only regular event we have. He emerges from his rooms, high in the smoky darkness, and descends to the floor, where he makes his way among us with an air of casual authority. He's a neat man, tall for a Gurta and straight-backed, his white hair swept back from his temples. It's impossible to stop his uniform from wilting in the heat but he does his best. The guards call him Overseer Arachi. He speaks good Eskaran when he tries, but he rarely talks to the prisoners. In fact, his inspection visits seem to be a matter of routine rather than anything else; I've never seen him actually *do* anything apart from tap bits of machinery and mutter about good, solid iron. The guards tolerate him and then call him names behind his back; they find his strutting comical.

The guards themselves idle about, bitching about this and that. We're not watched closely. Only the blacksmiths are well attended. In a forge where weapons are made, it makes sense to ensure no finished blades get into the hands of the prisoners.

This shift the Overseer has company. Four guards, and a man in heavy black gloves and a sooty smock, his lower face covered by a mask. I remember him, vaguely, from my drug-hazed induction to the prison.

They stop near me. The masked man indicates one of the coke-shovellers: a young man with lank brown hair. Two guards grab him; the others draw blades and push the rest of us back. The young man goes pale, then begins to scream. One of the other prisoners, holding a shovel, lunges to intervene; his companion bars his way with an arm. His jaw is tight with anger, but he knows it's suicide to get involved. There are a dozen more guards nearby, and they all have swords.

One of the guards clubs the struggling man with the pommel of his sword, stunning him into submission. He is quickly dragged away. The man in the smock sweeps us with his eyes and then departs after them.

I look at the Khaadu. He sees the question in my eyes.

'That was one of their chirurgeons,' he says. 'They're going to dissect him.'

Back in the cave, Charn beats the boy again. Nobody says a word. He's a big man, probably the strongest here, and in a prison men flock to strength.

I'm lying with my eyes closed, but despite the weight of exhaustion on my bones I can't find the darkness I need. The boy keeps me awake. First with his cries of pain as Charn punches and abuses him, and later with his muffled whimpers as he tries to stifle his weeping so as not to attract attention. Curled on the hot, damp rock, I try to stop myself thinking but it won't happen.

This was a bad turn. I gave up my solitude by speaking, and it was the boy who made me do it. What's worse, he was asking something of me. Asking me to help him. Why won't they leave me alone? I've got nothing and I don't want anything, because I know that to have and to lose is worse than not having at all.

The boy is crying. He's no child, almost a man in fact; can't he control himself? Can't he shut up?

Then I notice that I'm crying too. I only realise by the cool touch of saltwater on my cheek. I don't make a noise, but huddled in the dark of that prison pit, I'm crying.

I wait for my tears to run dry before I get up and walk across the floor towards Charn. One of his companions sees me coming and gets to his feet. Charn and another man follow. The others in the cave stir, shadowy rustlings in the corners: they're not used to seeing me move with purpose. In lieu of a name, I've heard some of them refer to me as 'the fade', after the dark apparitions that drift listlessly through Banchu corpseyards. If I had the heart, I'd laugh: the term is one I'm very familiar with, though it has a different meaning among those of my profession. But I'm not drifting any more.

The two men with Charn are shorter than he is, but both are stocky, and one of them looks quick. They're geared up for trouble. Charn has his arms crossed, a smirk on his face. He's not showing fear, but he's nervous. I can tell. Torchlight from above casts heavy shadows down their faces.

They're expecting a negotiation. A power show. Charn is the big man, he thinks I'm coming to him to talk terms. It's all about respect and power and face. But I'm not a man; I don't play man's games. So I beat the fuck out of them instead.

I take the quick one first. Rabbit punch just under his nose, stamp hard on his upper leg, dislocate his hip joint. The other man genuinely wasn't prepared for violence, so he's still barely moving when I backhand him across the face and put a knee in his solar plexus. He falls to the ground gulping air. I stamp on his lower back hard enough to snap a rib.

The other man has gone down on one knee, cheeks bloodless with the effort of suppressing a scream. For good measure, I kick him in the jaw, breaking it. I'm making a point here.

Charn licks his lips, takes a step back. He's scared that if he hits me

I'll hurt him worse, but he knows that the only chance he has is to get the first blow in. When he finally plucks up the guts to take a decent swipe, I catch his fist in my hand and nerve-punch his forearm. I've had the same done to me before, at the Academy. The pain is excruciating; it'll be dead and useless for several turns. His scream is embarrassingly high for such a big man.

I grab his nose between my knuckles and twist my wrist. Gristle crunches. He *really* screams now, flails away from me, falls to the floor clutching his face. That's for what you tried to do to me when I was drugged, I tell him silently.

And suddenly something comes swelling up and fills me, pushing the numbness aside, something harsh and bright and burning. Hate. But it's not directed at Charn; it's for myself. Because I failed to save the man I love. Because I let the Gurta take me. Because I wasn't good enough *again*.

I stand over the man who thought he could rape me. He's done. All the fight has gone out of him. My point has been well made.

He gets up onto his knees, so I hit him again. The first blow doesn't have a lot of conviction behind it, but it feels good. The second one is harder. He collapses, prone. So I kick him, hard, in the guts. He whimpers, flinches, moans. Doesn't even try to crawl away.

It's that submission that really unleashes me. The way he just fucking *gives up*, surrenders to me. Something breaks at the sight, and I lose control. I lay into him with fists and kicks, stamping on him, raining blows that are barely aimed. Spittle and gore fly from his lips; he yells and shrieks and cries as I batter him. I hardly hear the voices of the guards, shouting down at me from the caged mouth of our cave.

Then the boy puts a hand on my shoulder. The touch is gentle, letting me know he's not an attacker. It stops me more effectively than force.

'No more,' he says quietly.

I look at the bloodied mess at my feet. The hate has exhausted itself for now. I feel nothing.

The guards withdraw, content that the disturbance has ceased. They don't care enough to climb down and deal with it properly.

I step back to address the cave. My voice feels rusty from lack of use.

'Nobody touches the boy,' I say, and then I go back to my spot and go to sleep. The moans of the men I've just injured don't keep me awake like Feyn's sobbing did.

27

Next turn, the guards beat me half to death.

I'm eating in the food hall when they pull me away, spilling my gruel of spores and tubers. I hear them coming and I know they're coming for me, but I don't react. I let them take me.

The punishment is conducted in full view of the other prisoners. They pull me to the floor and pound me with short, vicious clubs. There are chua-kîn mantras and techniques that can block out pain or induce unconsciousness. I don't use any of them.

This is no less than I deserve. For Rynn.

The other prisoners are uneasy. Some have stood up from their benches and are being threatened by guards with swords. Angry cries are rising, abuse thrown at the Gurta. Gurta swear-words, learned for the purpose. Rough rootwood tables are pounded with stone spoons and empty bowls. The cooks have stopped stirring their cauldrons around the central fire and are watching.

The guards don't hit my face too hard, at least. I get to keep my teeth and no bones break. I'm thankful for that.

I'm mostly unconscious when they're done. I'm dragged by my arms, my heels dancing and juddering behind me. My mouth is full of the salt-metal tang of blood and my body is a blazing knot of agony. I drift in and out of awareness. Then suddenly I'm falling, there's nothing under me, and I'm shocked from my torpor by the slap and plunge of warm water. I flail, sinking, drowning . . . then I break surface, and my lungs find air long enough to throw up all the liquid I just swallowed.

I'm in a smooth-sided, circular pit, filled with brackish, vile water. Its stink is in my nostrils and all over the back of my throat. There's torchlight in the room above. Pale, narrow Gurta faces are watching me from the edge of the pit.

There are rusted metal rings set into the side of the pit just above the level of the water. I loop my arm through one. The torchlight disappears as the guards do. I hear a door close somewhere above me, and darkness comes. Eskarans have good eyes, able to make use of the smallest glimmer of illumination. But in the total absence of light, we're blind.

The pain settles in like damp, and swells. One eye is slowly forced shut by bruising. My cheek feels huge. The only sound I can hear is the lap of the water around me. In a moment of grim humour, I wonder if I've finally solved the mystery of where they dump all the shit from the cells. I actually smile a little, until the pain becomes too much.

Rynn always told me I had a perverse attitude. He was pretty fond of it, as I recall, even though it used to drive him mad at times. The more I'm ground down, the more defiant I become. I float, hanging loosely from the ring, and inside I'm laughing at the men who beat me. I'm scorning them for not killing me. There's nothing they can do that's worse than what's already happened. Fuck them. I'm not even close to breaking.

I can still hear the faint, dolorous clang of the bell, humming through the walls of the pit. By its tolling I estimate that I've been down here two turns, although I might have slept through it once or twice so I'm not sure. Sleep isn't so easy: I have to put the ring under my armpit to support me while I doze, but soon the circulation cuts off and I wake with my arm sparkling numb. The snatches I get are more frustrating than being unable to sleep at all. But this is all part of the punishment, so I endure.

They lowered a bucket of water a while ago. Clean water, not the filth I'm floating in. I drank as much as I could, puffy lips pressed to the rim of the bucket. They pulled it away before I was done, but it was enough to keep me going.

Eventually the lock clatters and the door creaks open. Torchlight appears overhead. Weak as it is, it makes my eyes tear and run to look at it at first, so I shade them with my hand and look away. A rope splashes down next to me, with a crude harness of belts attached.

~ Put it on ~ someone urges me in Gurtan. It takes me a while to process this simple command; slowly I reach over and pull it to me.

~ Put it on ~ they say again. I pretend not to understand at first, until they make hand signs. Then I strap myself in. It's not easy with a dead arm.

I hang on as they pull me up. I'm pathetically weak. It's an effort just to keep pushing away from the side of the pit with my legs, but if I didn't, they'd just drag me up anyway. When I get to the top, I'm lifted to my feet, unstrapped and marched out of the room at swordpoint.

They take me through a series of corridors I've not seen before. Some are panelled in rootwood from ancient mycora, or flocked with shredded bark from lichen trees. Small shinestones are set into the wall. The sight triggers a stab of nostalgia for the trappings of civilisation. I've become used to the grim, sweltering world of dank caves, bare stone rooms and growling foundries. Shinestones are an unexpected luxury here.

These corridors are better cared for than those I've seen so far, and better decorated. There are even some Gurtan flourishes on the lintels and sconces. Scholars whisper past in their robes, some quite young, fresh-faced. They don't seem the least surprised to have a bruised and exhausted Eskaran woman in their midst, soaking wet and reeking.

I'm led into a room in which a single shinestone lantern of wrought iron hangs from the ceiling on a chain. Against the walls are glass-fronted cupboards, drawers, a worktop crowded with alembics and alchemical devices and complex brass ticking things. Charts and books lie open. The air smells of old blood.

In the centre of the room is an X-shaped frame, tilted at an angle, with straps at every end. Standing next to it is the Gurta chirurgeon I saw the last time I was working in the forge.

It's a chirurgery. They're going to dissect me.

No.

And suddenly I'm fighting. Thrashing in the arms of my guards. Every fibre of my body is rebelling at the sight of that frame, where they'll stretch me out and cut the flesh of my belly with their knives. I stamp out at one of them and feel their ankle break beneath my heel. The man shrills, a Gurta cry of pain. I know the sound well. Then someone clubs me round the back of my head and I sag forward. *Fuck, that hurt.* I struggle but someone hits me again across the head again and I stop.

It's hopeless. Lack of food and the fact that I've been floating for two turns, barely using any of my muscles, has left me unable to fight against the three remaining guards. One of them is cursing me, sitting on the ground, holding his foot. The rest pin me while the chirurgeon looms closer, carrying a long, hollow glass needle in which an amber liquid glitters. I try to avoid it, but I don't have the strength. Nothing can stop the progress of that point. It sinks into my arm and peace spreads from where it touches me. I relax and keep relaxing until everything goes black.

This battlefield is scabbed with bloody pieces of men. The cavern roof presses low, shedding stalactites as it shivers with the rumble of explosions. The air is punctured with the dreadful rhythm of shard-cannon fire.

Yet I am unharmed. I fly on small, whirring wings, buoyed on the thermals from smoking corpses of Eskaran and Gurta alike. I pass over faces frozen in horror and shock, caked in mud and gore. I am blown towards my destination on a wind that smells of rancid meat.

Soon I see him. He is crouching in a crater, pressed close to the dead. They surround him, his departed comrades, their gazes blank and stunned. He is trembling. Tears have cut tracks through the filth on his face.

He is my son.

I fly to him, and he sees me. He reaches out to me desperately, but I am too small and too high, flitting.

'I am here,' I say. 'I have found you.' But the whispered voice that comes is gibberish. The message hides inside. A code. Our language.

'Where? Where are you?'

'I am coming to you,' I tell him. But then there is a great gust, and the wind turns against me with the bellowing heat of an oven.

'Where are you?' he cries, but I am being blown away, and my small wings cannot fight the fury of the wind. I struggle against it, but my efforts are all in vain.

'I am always with you,' I say, but now I am too distant to be heard.

I wake in a study, grander than anywhere I've seen in this place yet. Polished wood and shining metal everywhere. There are no windows, by which I surmise we're still deep in the heart of the prison, but there's a primitive air-circulation system dependant on convection.

I've been strapped into a chair, hands and feet secured. Sitting opposite me is a Gurta in late middle age. His hair is long and white with hints of yellow, tied in a ponytail. His beard hangs in two thick streamers from his cheeks, but his chin is bare. He's wearing a robe of red and silver, and his fingernails have been grown out and sharpened.

It takes me a few moments before I notice something else. I'm not wet any more. Nor can I smell the stench of that pit on me. I look down at myself. My clothes have been laundered. My skin is no longer dirty. I think they even washed my hair.

They stripped me and cleaned me up. I start to think about what else they might have done while I was unconscious, but I clamp the lid quickly on that. Better not to know. Dissociate. Nothing happened. Make yourself believe it.

It takes me a short while to realise that they aren't going to dissect me after all. What in the Abyss is this all about?

I wait for the Gurta to speak. To one side of his chair stands a complicated orrery in brass and gold, used for calculating tides and seasons according to the movement of celestial bodies. Only four are shown: those whose heat or gravity are strong enough to affect us, in our world deep beneath the ground. The two suns, Oralc and Mochla, blazing with stylised ripples of light; the mother-planet, Beyl, a vast, blank orb; its moon Callespa, tiny in comparison. Us.

The spheres are held up by metal arms attached to a dozen small cogwheels that force them to move in synchronicity. Beyl has almost reached the far side of Oralc. On the surface, the suns will be coming together in the sky. That puts us somewhere around the end of Ebb Season and the start of Spore Season. Up on the surface, the nights have lengthened to almost equal the days. If it's accurate, and I assume it is, then I can't have been here for as long as it feels.

The Gurta leans forward and harrumphs. His eyes are pale grey, washed-out, like those of a corpse. I hate his kind and everything about them. 'Please tell me your name,' he says in accented Eskaran.

I consider being awkward, but I decide it's better to seem cooperative for now. I need to know what he's after, and stonewalling him won't help.

'My name—' I begin, and my dry throat demands I swallow before I continue. 'My name is Massima Leithka Orna. I'm a Bondswoman of Clan Caracassa, and a member of Ledo's Cadre.'

'Ledo?'

'Plutarch Nathka Caracassa Ledo. Magnate of Clan Caracassa.'

The scholar's eyes crease a little more, a half-smile. 'My name is Gendak. I am a scholar, from the city of Chalem.'

'Now we're introduced.'

'I must apologise for the way you have been treated,' he says. 'It seems there was some confusion. You were not supposed to be harmed. Unfortunately my request was overlooked by my peers in their eagerness to punish you. I acted to protect you as soon as I heard.'

His apology doesn't exactly seem heartfelt. He's not sorry, not really. He just wants me to know it's not his fault. I wait for him to go on.

'Do you know why you were punished, Orna?'

'I attacked another prisoner,' I reply. It still feels odd to speak, and more so because of the swelling in my lips.

'That is not the reason you were punished. It is *who* you attacked that concerns us.'

'Charn? What's special about him?'

'He is a skilled blacksmith. We have very few here who can forge weapons. Charn is a valuable asset to us, and you have put him out of action for some time.'

'His arm will be right in a few turns or so. Be thankful I didn't break it.'

'It is *you* who should be thankful. Your punishment would have been much worse.'

I stare at him. He sits back, smoothes his whiskers. 'You do not interact well with the other prisoners. In fact, you do not speak with them at all. Why is that?'

'Why do you care?'

'I'm interested.'

I don't reply. I'm not falling for an evasion like that.

'You do not want to tell me?'

'Not until you tell me why you're interested.'

A long moment passes. All his moves are slow, considered. He lapses into immobility between sentences. But his mind is working, I see that. He's calculating me.

'It has been my life's work to make a study of you,' he says. 'Of your people. The Eskarans.'

'To learn your enemy is the first step to subjugating them.'

'Or to making peace with them,' he counters.

'Your kind don't want *peace*,' I say, bitterly.

'Nor do yours.'

That's true enough. Especially not Clan Caracassa. They've been making a tidy profit from the latest war, this last seven years.

Gendak stirs in his chair. Unobtrusively, I test my restraints, but I'm strapped in tight. I wait for more. 'There is a long history of antagonism between our people,' he says. 'Nobody living can remember a time when we were not at war or engaged in a precarious standoff. It has become accepted as the natural order of things. I do not think that is so. I think the key to making peace between our people is to understand one another.'

I'm not sure I believe what I'm hearing. 'You can't erase people's memories. Understanding is one thing, but too many people have been hurt by the war. There are too many grudges.'

'It has to start somewhere.'

His reasoning is sound, even if I don't agree. I don't think there can ever be lasting peace between us, and I wouldn't want there to be. I'd be happy to see every last one of them dead for what they've done to me. I'm remembering how they've been taking people away for dissection, how they beat me and threw me in a pit. How they killed my husband. Nothing can make me forgive them, ever. But my anger grew cold long ago. It doesn't control me.

'Your Elders say the destruction of my people is demanded by Maal's Laws. Wouldn't working towards peace mean defying them?'

He spreads his hands. 'Maal's wisdom was great. I am only seeking to understand you. How my studies are used – for war or for peace – will be out of my hands.'

'Does studying us include cutting us open?'

'There are other scholars who work towards other goals. Eskaran and Gurta physiology is very similar. You make excellent test subjects for new medicines and poisons, or as practice for our young chirurgeons. Gurta soldiers do not take prisoners as a rule. The only reason any of you are alive is because of your potential usefulness to us. When that usefulness ends, you will die.'

At least he's honest. And I don't miss the implied threat. Stay cooperative, or join the experiments.

'Your turn,' he prompts.

I pause for a time, thinking. 'I don't speak to the other prisoners because I don't care about them. I don't care what they have to say. I don't care about this place.'

'Is there anything you do care about?'

My son. My son, whom I'll never see again. Out there somewhere, fighting this fucking war.

'No,' I reply. 'There's nothing I care about.'

They put me back into my cell. The other prisoners watch me climb down the ladder. As I descend I can see Charn glaring through the muddle of bruises and cuts that constitute his face. His paralysed arm is in a sling. I can feel his hate, but it's impotent. Even battered as I am, I've sent a message to everyone here. Nobody will fuck with me now.

The ladder is pulled up and the grille overhead slams shut. I walk to my corner to sit down, saying nothing. As I go I notice the SunChild boy. He's watching me, like the others. As far as I can tell, he hasn't been harmed.

I don't know why that's important to me, it just is.

32

The city hid deep in the earth, far from the day.

It sprawled across the vastness of the cavern, innumerable lanterns and softly glowing windows crowding the swells and dips of the stony landscape. A plague of lights crept up the cavern's sides, and hung from the ceiling in clusters of stalactite dwellings, grim chandeliers of rock. Dimly reflective veins of metal and patches of ghostly, luminescent lichens shone like distant nebulae, occupying the void which the lights had not yet overtaken. Here in the endless dark, the tribes of Eskara had created a starfield, and they called it Veya, the Underhome.

I knew the city well: its plazas and alleys, its bridges and monuments, its bars and dens and secret societies. I knew where the pitmen brought their exotic beasts to fight for money; I knew where a person could sell a little of their soul for a skinmark of subtle power; I knew the cut-joints where they made dirty fireclaw potions for the dweomings in the slums. I'd visited the clubs where the aristocracy smoked and drank and made their deals. I'd walked through the sculpture-graveyards in the Greyslopes, their forms heavy with meaning, incomprehensible to anyone but the secretive race that created them. I'd watched a starving child give up his life in his mother's arms while she was too insensible to care.

The city cradled me. Here, among the many, I could be as alone as I wished or as involved as I liked. I stalked Veya like a predator prowling its territory, seeking to know every part. I investigated restlessly, sometimes silent and aloof, sometimes plunging into the society of others. To know the city was to have control over it.

The riverbank was bright and busy, even at this time, when most of Veya was asleep. Sharp-featured men and their elegant consorts sat in the forecourts of expensive bars, sipping from delicate goblets.

Courtesans haunted the tables of those men and women who dined alone. The air was full of the scent of cooking fish and the perfumed oil of the lanterns.

I leaned against the rail that separated the promenade from the steep embankment to the river. On the neathways side stood one of Veya's five shinehouses, casting its pale glow high and far. The dwellings of the wealthy coiled and bulged and slid along the water's edge. Some were fashioned like breaking waves, others as swollen seed pods or spiral columns. Stone and wood and ceramics blended into each other in a carefully planned tangle. The architects of Veya were nothing if not creative. This city was glutted with art.

I spotted my contact coming along the promenade. He had that look about him: a man who had mastered his territory, a man who knew the city. There was no need to swagger. People just sensed it, and deferred. Muggers chose other victims, not really understanding why. Merchants spoke to him as an equal, even though he was obviously not rich or important.

'Keren,' I greeted him, as he joined me at the rail.

Keren always looked battered and scruffy, as if he had just hauled himself out of bed. Somehow the fact that he didn't trouble about his appearance only strengthened his aura of weary dangerousness. Two small, implanted silver tusks protruded from just below his bottom lip. A thick head of shaggy black hair hung untidily over his face. His low forehead and grizzled cheeks were skinmarked with curving patterns.

'Orna,' he replied. He studied a freighter that was approaching from upriver, surrounded by a rippling island of light. It was being escorted by a half-dozen militia sloops.

After a moment, Keren made a vague motion towards it. 'Trade goods. Rumour is, Jerima Vem has twenty sacks of powdered bone-cane on there, out of his warehouse up in the Shivers. The den-runners round the Ashenpark are chewing their hands off wanting to get at it, but it's sewn tight. Vem's bribed or threatened every harbourmaster from here to Bry Athka.'

'I heard,' I replied.

He nodded. 'Makes you wonder. If he's moving that much bone-cane, how come everyone knows? Vem's not so careless with his information. Smells like a decoy to me. Or a trap.'

I looked sideways at him. 'It is.'

He grinned. 'What you know, Orna?'

'Vem's going fishing. He's after Silverfish.'

Keren barked a laugh. 'Silverfish? He thinks Silverfish would fall for something like this?'

'Exactly. Vem's intelligence network's a joke.'

'So how'd you find out?'

I turned my cheek to show the Bond-mark there: three diagonal stripes. 'Ledo's keeping Jerima Vem very sweet right now. Makes it easier for certain information to come my way from time to time.'

Keren grunted. 'Forgot. The marriage, right? Never could keep track of aristo politics.' He was already calculating how this information could be useful, who he could tell, what kind of leverage he might gain. 'What've they got against each other?'

'Vem and Silverfish? That I don't know. Silverfish has been plaguing Clan Jerima lately: interfering with shipments, leaking sensitive information, stealing from him, that sort of thing. Vem wants him off his back. So he came up with a tempting target.'

'It's *too* tempting.'

He pushed off the rail suddenly, and walked into the forecourt of a bar. The bulky guard – placed there to prevent the detritus of the street from sifting in – paid him no attention. Keren lit a cigarillo at a brazier and returned, wreathed in the sweet, cloying scent of smokevine.

We stood together in silence. As always, Keren offered a cigarillo to me, and as always I declined. I waited while he finished. Keren wouldn't be disturbed during a cigarillo, nor would he speak of anything important until he was done.

'Found your man,' he said as he flicked the butt away, sending it skittering across the promenade.

'Where?'

'Back streets off the Grand Plaza.' He gave me an address. 'This evens us up, okay? For the other thing?'

'We're even,' I agreed. We always played this game, tallying favours and debts. Some people wanted money, but Keren wasn't that way. He traded information for information, with anyone and everyone he could. He wanted to know it all. I respected that hunger.

We took our leave and headed in different directions along the promenade. I was glad to be alone again. I needed time to centre myself, to let all traces of sensitivity and sentiment bleed out of me. For what I intended to do, they would only get in my way.

The address Keren had given me was on the fifth floor of a building in a maze of narrow, knife-slash streets. Here, in the area around the Grand Plaza, dwellings were stacked high and pressed together hard. Balconies of wood and ceramic faced each other, close enough to jump between. Curved windows with webbed frames and tinted glass glowed green in the heights. Jabbered conversations and laughter swelled and faded, the voices of unseen couples wandering arm-in-arm, somewhere in the labyrinth.

I made my way up a zigzag stairway, passing alcoves in which doorways were set. At the top, I found the door I wanted. It was identical to the others, polished and set in a carved wooden arch. A bell tolled faintly in the distance.

Warm light crept beneath the door. Good. He was in. I pushed back my coat to expose the hilt of an obsidian shortblade, and knocked. There was a pause, and movement within.

The door opened. A middle-aged man, his body bulky and strong. Hired muscle. He went pale as he saw the Cadre sigil on my shoulder.

'Careless,' I said, and shoved the door open. I grabbed him in a nerve-claw, rigid fingers digging into the flesh of his throat, thumb driven under his chin. Wracked with paralysing agony, he could do little to resist as I propelled him roughly into the living area. There I threw him against a writing desk with a crash, scattering rolls of parchment and shattering a vial of ink.

There were four in the room, including the man I'd just assaulted. One was Ekan, the man I'd come to see: doughy, face run to fat, expression betraying surprise. The rest were thugs.

Ekan had taken precautions.

The two remaining thugs came at me from either side. One had snatched up an iron candle-holder as a club, the other had a dagger. I went for the knife-wielder first. The thug stabbed clumsily: a small-time heavy with an unlicensed blade. I slid inside his reach, grabbed his wrist and drove my knee upward into the elbow, inverting it with a wet snap.

I pulled the man across me as my next attacker swung, protecting myself with the body of my opponent. There was a dull thud as the candle-holder struck the shoulder of my unwilling shield. I wrapped an arm round his neck and broke it, tossing him aside, then sprang for the thug with the candle-holder.

He took another swing. I dodged it and punched rigid fingers into a nerve-nexus to make him release his weapon, then I headbutted him in the bridge of the nose. Didn't expect *that* from a woman. There was barely time for him to yell before I delivered a short, brutal punch to his solar plexus, winding him. He staggered backwards, doubled over and gasping for air.

The thug who had opened the door was back on his feet, lunging, hoping to take me off-guard. Not a chance. They were nothing but street-brawlers, pugilists at best. They had no defence against the subtler fighting arts. I dropped under the punch, caught his arm and used it to throw him over my shoulder. He might have been heavier than me, but weight can be used against you. The thug crashed to the floor hard, and I punched him in the throat, crushing his larynx.

I rolled off, coming to my feet, stanced ready for another attack. None came. I drew a shortblade, walked calmly to where the surviving thug was still gasping for breath, and cut his throat. Afterwards, I turned my gaze to the last man in the room.

'You know what this is about, Ekan,' I said.

Ekan was already on the verge of tears, half-insensible with terror. 'Listen . . . no . . . you don't—'

'I'm not interested,' I told him. 'You were warned.'

'We can go!' Ekan blurted, eyes shining with sudden hope. 'We can leave. You won't ever hear from us again!'

'You should have listened,' I replied. 'The Caracassa family takes a bleak view when people try to undercut their prices.'

'No . . . no . . .' Ekan was begging, eyes fixed on my blade, which was dripping spots of blood onto the floor. 'I'm just an apothecary, I'm . . . I'm just an apothecary! I need to make a living like everybody else!'

'You make it selling cheaper versions of my master's products,' I said.

'They were *my* products! My potions!'

'You copied them from us, Ekan. You know it. I know it. If I let you get away with this, I'll have a dozen more of you to deal with by season's end. I've got better things to do with my time.'

'Leave him alone!' shrieked a new voice: Ekan's consort, appearing in the doorway. A slight blonde woman, fiercer than her size would suggest. 'Leave him the fuck alone! '

I looked from the consort to the sobbing child hiding behind her leg, clutching at her gown. Eyes flitting between the dead men in the room and her cringing father.

'Don't swear in front of your daughter,' I said.

Her face twisted in hatred. 'Mindless bitch! Doing your master's bidding like a slave! He'll stop! He'll stop selling them!'

'I'll stop!' Ekan pleaded. 'We can leave. We can leave right now, nobody has to know!'

'I'd know.' I motioned at the little girl. 'Take her away. She shouldn't see this.'

There was a moment of balance. I felt the situation teeter and tip. Ekan deflated, and something died in his eyes. I'd won. He'd accepted his fate.

'Go,' he said to his consort. He was trembling. 'Go on. It'll be over in a moment.'

Biting back tears of bitter fury and helplessness, the consort retreated, pushing the child ahead of her. The door slammed, and the girl began to wail in earnest.

I pushed Ekan around so that he faced the desk, forced his fore-arms flat onto it. I swept aside the tally charts and accounts that he'd been keeping. That done, I stabbed my shortblade into the desk and drew out a thick strip of leather.

Ekan stared at it. 'What's that for?'

'Tourniquet,' I replied. I bent closer. 'Which is your least favourite hand?'

It was a long way to travel home on foot, but I walked everywhere if I could. I enjoyed the peaceful emptiness in the air, the roomy, quiet streets. The last bell of the turn had just sounded, the pause for breath before the city stirred again. Soon a new turn would begin, down here where there was no day or night, and the streets would begin to fill.

The Tangles were on the poleways edge of the city, up against the wall of the cavern. Here, dwellings were not built but carved into the gigantic roots of mycora, the immense fungi that grew on the surface, their discs spreading shade across the plains. Reitha talked about them often. Like much of the world above, their existence was only dimly comprehended by those races than hid in the endless passages of the underground. The surface was an alien place, of little interest to most. All they saw of mycora were the enormous root-systems that burrowed vast distances through the earth and rock. In the Tangles, the roots had broken through the cavern wall in a slither, and the rich had built their homes in them.

The Caracassa mansions were a mountain of dimly glowing windows, fashioned in many shapes, tracing patterns along the length of the roots. Ceramic domes and stubby towers rose from the cradling grey arms of the mycora. Small gardens and courtyards were carefully integrated into the organic flow of the structure. The whole edifice appeared to have been poured rather than built, a towering cone fashioned from points of light, imposing and beautiful in the dark.

The tips of two roots formed an enclosure at the base of the mansions, framing gates of solid brass, their surface rich with detail. They stood open, attended by four guards in red-and-black Caracassa livery, carrying double-bladed pikes. The guards knew me by sight, and let me pass with a curt acknowledgement.

I made my way across the enclosure, where gardens of crystalline plants and multicoloured fungi were laid to either side of a driveway. A small block of stables lay off to one side. Servants were cleaning a rickshaw nearby, preparing it for departure.

Inside, the mansions were warm and snug in contrast to the unwaveringly cool temperature of Veya. The corridors were large and tunnel-like, lined with polished panels of rootwood and dimly lit with lamps that hung from the ceiling. Paintings and objects of art were everywhere, including several of Rynn's grandfather's smaller sculptures. Red-robed handmaidens whispered past me, their faces hidden by veils. It was too late for much of the household to be awake.

I headed through corridors and up spiral stairways to my family's chambers. When I got there, they were in darkness. I went to the large round window that overlooked the living area, and gazed through the swirling metalwork to the city below. We were high up here, and the view over Veya was mesmerising.

I thought about what I had just done. My duties for my master were manifold, but intimidation and punishment were the tasks I liked the least. Still, Ekan knew the rules.

Potions – tonics for all ills, in a society whose people ran on chemicals – were a relatively small part of Clan Caracassa's industry. Their usual business was the manufacture of medicines and unguents tailored for frontline troops: healing salves, anti-infection medication, hunger suppressants, painkillers, rage enhancers. But even so, Ekan had to be stopped. His little racket might have been insignificant now, but there was no space for tolerance or conscience in my line of work.

I was Cadre. I was selected for this task because I was the best at it. It was my duty to serve. That was all there was.

I went into our bedroom. Something massive shifted in the shadows. Rynn turning over beneath the sheets. He mumbled something in a register too low for me to hear.

'It's me,' I said.

He woke a little more.

'Where've you been?' he muttered.

I walked over to the bed, shedding clothes as I went, and slid in beside him. He encircled me drowsily.

'Out,' I replied, but he was already asleep.

26

They put me back to work while I heal, pushing and pulling the metal screens through which that stinking mineral slop flows.

I'm working opposite Feyn again. At first I'm afraid I'm going to be greeted with fawning gratitude or pity; or worse, as the cause of my injuries, he'll inflict his remorse on me. But he does none of those things. He greets me with a shy smile, the first I've seen from him. Then he applies himself the screens without a word. He pushes when I pull, he pulls when I push. I go easy and let him dictate the pace. I don't feel the need to hurt myself any more. I hurt enough.

We've been at it some time when words start bubbling out of me. I can't be silent any more; it seems stupid to remain so uncommunicative. I'm *not* going to stop living and I'm *not* going to spend the rest of my life in solitude. I need to say something, anything at all. So I say: 'I have a son your age.'

Feyn's heavily lashed eyes flick up from the trough of grey slurry and regard me. 'What name does he have?'

'Jai. He's a junior officer in the Eskaran Army.' The thought inspires more fear than pride, but I've become used to that.

'May I ask, what name do *you* have?'

'My name is Orna.'

He's quiet. I go on. Now I've started, I can't stop. I'm a talker, and these few sentences have opened the gates of a dam. I want to *talk*.

'You're a SunChild,' I say baldly.

'Some name us the Far People. In my own language we are named *a'Sura'Sao*.' He punctuates the rapid syllables with a clicking noise at the back of his throat.

'Is it true you live on the surface? That you never go underground?'

He laughs. 'That is not true. We do live on the surface, under the sky. We hunt and are hunted by the animals there. We eat Callespa's plants, and we sometimes travel beneath its suns. But we must also shelter like you do, in caves and in settlements that we build.' He looks up to the roof of the forge, invisible in the fug that curdles up there. '*Goi'shew* is coming,' he says, his voice wistful. 'Soon my people will be on the move again.'

'*Goi'shew?*'

'The Season of Nights.'

'We call it Spore Season,' I tell him. 'Down here, the winds pick up and the fungi start multiplying. Mid-season in some places, the tides are thick with spores carried from across the sea.'

'I understand,' he says. 'I would like if you would correct me when I use your language badly. No teacher can copy talking to an Eskaran.'

'Substitute,' I say. 'No teacher can *substitute* for talking to an Eskaran. It means to put something in the place of another.'

A smile. 'I am learning already. I hope to be the first of my people to attend Bry Athka University.'

'Bry Athka? In Eskara?'

'Of course. Is there another?'

'You'll certainly cause a stir,' I tell him. He doesn't get it. I rephrase, slower. 'I mean, you will seem very unusual to us.'

'I see.'

'Many of us don't believe your people exist.'

He finds that hilarious. His laughter draws the attention of a passing guard, who snarls at him in Gurtan to get on with his work. Chastened, Feyn fixes his attention on the job, the smile gone from his face. But when the guard moves off, deeper into the black, hissing murk of the forge, he looks up at me, his lips curving wryly. I can't help smiling in response. It feels unfamiliar.

'We have a story about your people,' he says. 'Long ago, all people lived on the surface. Gurta, Eskaran, SunChild, Banchu, Khaadu were all one race, who we called *s'Tani*. It means "Old Men", in your language, but I am not sure if the translation means exactly what it should. The *s'Tani* were numberous—'

'Numerous,' I interrupt automatically. I shake my head at myself. 'Sorry. I'll keep quiet.'

'I want you to correct me.'

'We'll never get anywhere if I stop you at every mistake. I'll teach you properly later. Just go on for now.'

The boy is taken aback, so much so that he stops working at the screens and my rhythm is thrown. 'You will teach me?' he asks.

It's only by his reaction that I realise I just *did* offer to help him improve his Eskaran. And I meant it, too.

I'm starting to feel like me again. Something's dislodged and is working its way out, a mental splinter being expelled. Despite the pain of my injuries, I'm noticing that my limbs aren't so heavy any more. My senses feel more synchronised. No longer do I feel like a passenger in my own head, staring through fogged orbs at a world I've been removed from.

It feels wrong to abandon my grief, even the slightest bit. I *am* still grieving; I can't think of Rynn without a sensation like my chest being squeezed. But it's lost its power to destroy me. There's something else, slowly overwhelming my sorrow. I know it's there, but I can't put a shape to it yet.

And then there's Jai. Jai, somewhere on the front line. Jai, and a letter I have hidden in a drawer at home. A letter nobody knows about but me.

'Are you well?' Feyn asks, concerned by my silence.

'I'm fine,' I say. 'Yes, I'll teach you.'

'Perhaps I will tell you of the *s'Tani* later,' he says. He knows that my mind is in too many places right now, that I'm not listening. I'm surprised by his perceptiveness.

We work in silence for a while, and for the first time, I wonder what we're actually achieving with this constant push-pull of these cross-hatched metal screens. Breaking up lumps in the flow of slurry? Agitating the mixture so that it doesn't clot? I've never been a scholar, I don't understand these things. But I suddenly want to know. Because otherwise what we're doing is pointless. I didn't mind that before, but now I'm beginning to.

Gendak summons me again the next turn, considerately bypassing the beating and drowning warm-up this time. I'm led to his study with a knife pressed to my kidneys, escorted by armed guards. Once there,

I'm strapped into the chair again. The guards don't leave until they're certain I can't get loose. Even so, Gendak doesn't come too close. He sits some distance from me. Taking no chances.

'Why are you talking to me?' I ask him.

'You're unusual. A Cadre woman. It is not your custom to send women into battle.'

'Cadre are special cases. Sometimes they use us on the front line.'

'Are there many like you?'

'A few,' I say. I'm feeling less cooperative than I was last time. He's luring me with questions that he could easily answer himself. He's trying to make me relax, to trust him. Soon he'll start working towards more sensitive information. I decide to take control of the conversation.

'Where are the other women?'

'We do not take grown women. If they are young enough, those we capture on our raids are taken as slaves. We bring them up in our homes and they function as servants. We have many such servants here.'

That's interesting. I haven't seen any. I presume he means outside the prison.

'And if they're not young enough?'

'They are killed. Women are too much trouble to keep as prisoners. They incite the men to violence.'

'And me?'

'As I said, you are unusual. The soldiers did not quite know what to make of you. So you were brought here.' He cracks his knuckles absently. 'You are only alive now because of me. There are many who would prefer it otherwise. You have already caused us trouble.'

'So why not give me my own cell?' I wonder if this is an idea worth chasing. Less guards would mean an easier way out.

'If it was possible, I would. My influence is not great.'

We fall to silence again. I stare at him. Waiting. Let him talk.

'You must understand: our society visits the severest penalties on those who reject the Laws. Your clothes, your politics, your sexual promiscuity . . . by our culture, you are animals. There is no issue of cruelty. You are seen as beneath us.'

I recognise he's trying to be conciliatory and explain things from an objective point of view, but I can't help responding with venom.

'We don't *reject* your laws,' I say. 'They're not even worthy of rejection. The word of one insane Gurta counts for nothing to us.'

Gendak's face has darkened. Mocking their most revered leader really pisses them off. 'Only money counts to you. The wealthiest is the most powerful. That is the nature of plutocracy. Your society is ruled by merchants, not morals.'

'And yours isn't brave enough to question tradition. You follow the obsolete rules of the first person who thought to enshrine his morals in literature. How can people of such art and culture cling so tightly to something so obviously backward?'

He wants to snap back at me, but he knows I'm goading him. I see him swallow his words down, and his reply, though rigid, is not angry.

'What would you do with our women, were our positions reversed?'

'Who knows?' I say. 'They've a convenient habit of committing suicide rather than letting themselves be captured.'

'It is called *maazu*. They would rather die than allow themselves to be dishonoured. That is their choice. That is the nobility of the Gurta woman.'

'Very noble. I hear your people's coming-of-age gift to your women is a phial of poison, to be worn around the neck on a chain. So what happens if they don't choose to use it?' As if I didn't know.

'They would be cast out or executed.'

I raise an eyebrow and stare at him meaningfully.

'It is their duty to choose death rather than a life lived in shame,' he says.

'And who determines what's shameful?'

'The Laws,' he replies.

'Yes,' I say. 'And they tell you how to dress, how to conduct your rituals, how you should behave, what weapons you can carry, what words you should use and when, what kind of woman you should take as a partner . . . When did you people stop thinking for yourselves?'

'You have read the Laws?' he exclaims in surprise.

'A translation,' I lie. I read the whole thing in Gurtan. A litany of conditions governing all aspects of life, written by an ancient Gurta despot and enforced with brutal punishments. Maal's line lasted for twenty-five generations, until natural causes put an end to it. Each descendant ensured the people kept to the Laws. Over time, they became the blueprint for a society too sacred to alter or argue. The traditions are still upheld by the Elders and the Lawkeepers, and the punishments haven't got any less severe as far as I know. Trying to discuss the merits of Maal's Laws with a Gurta is pointless; to them, they're as necessary to life as the beat of their hearts.

He pauses for a time, studying me. I'm used to the pauses by now. I'll talk to him as long as I don't think he's learning anything from me. Maybe I'll learn something from him. Perhaps he really is interested in hearing my point of view, or perhaps he's searching for knowledge that they could use against us. I'm prepared to play for now. Besides, he's made it very clear that failure to cooperate would lead to a withdrawal of his protection. I doubt I'd be allowed to live long if that happened.

'Tell me about Bondsmen.'

'A Bondsman is somebody who has sworn a lifedebt to a particular Clan,' I reply, somewhat formally. 'Often, when a person borrows a sum of money from a Clan or otherwise asks for a favour, their repayment can be secured with service. If they fail to repay the loan or the favour in kind, they enter lifedebt. The severity of the debt determines the length of the debt in generations. My own lifedebt only applied to me. The most severe can last for seven generations.'

'Then your children are slaves? Do you *have* children?'

'No, and no,' I lie. I'm not telling him about Jai or Rynn. There are some things I don't want to discuss with him. 'Nobody forces you to take on lifedebt. You make the choice.'

'The child does not have that choice.'

I think of Rynn, how he was born into Bond, how angry it made him. 'Every child has to deal with the circumstances of their birth.'

'And how did you incur your lifedebt?'

'It was willingly taken, not incurred. Clan Caracassa did a great service for me when I was ten years old. In return, I swore my lifedebt.' I can't help sounding a little proud of it. I twist in the chair to show him my bare shoulder. 'This skinmark shows the Clan I'm sworn to. The one on my face means I'm a Bondswoman. No other Clan will employ me; not even minor merchants or labourers would risk it. Without Clan Caracassa, I'd probably starve.'

Gendak sits back and regards me with those pale, dead Gurta eyes. Some misguided romantics have called the Gurta elegant, fey, statuesque. I see only an unhealthy pallor, eyes like cataracts. I find their fluttering language not poetic but sinister and repulsive. People talk of trying to understand their enemy. I *do* understand them, and I hate them all the more for it. Rynn would say something eminently sensible, if he was here: *you see only what you want to see. You want to hate them for what they did to you.* That was true before he died, and it's doubly so now.

'It seems to me you have a system of indentured servitude, as alien to us as our ways are to you,' Gendak says carefully. 'We, at least, do not enslave our own kind. Perhaps, in the end, there is no right or wrong, only perspective.'

'No,' I reply. 'There's only history. Whoever wins this war gets to be right.'

The food hall is a rectangular stone chamber with nine long tables, surrounding a central fire where the prisoners' meals are boiled or grilled or spit-roasted. It's even hotter than the cell. I feel claustrophobic and restless. Aside from my little excursions to Gendak's study now and then, my life is a random sequence of forge-food-quad-cell. We see no other parts of the prison.

This turn we're fed a stew with fat spore dumplings floating in it, surrounded by chunks of gristle and fat. I'm not fussy. It gives me strength. For a long while I only ate because it was easier to do so than to refuse, but now I bolt it down. I talk to Feyn with my mouth full, waving my spoon around as I talk. I don't know what's got into me: suddenly, I have energy, and I *want* this food. I can actually *taste* it. Not that that's a good thing in this particular instance.

Feyn seems delighted by my transformation, and the fact that he has someone willing to speak to him. Both of us have habitually eaten alone and in silence until now. We're drawing gazes from the rest of the prisoners.

Encouraged by his interest, I talk about this place. I've picked up a lot from the conversations I've overheard from other prisoners. The guards don't trouble to be secretive, either. They assume their language to be incomprehensible to us.

Feyn has been ostracised since he got here, and he is remarkably ignorant about the prison. I wonder if he's simply not troubled himself to look for answers. He strikes me as strangely passive, given his situation.

So I tell him what I know. We're inside a Gurta fort called Farakza, on the edge of the Borderlands. The prison lies at its heart: the forge, laundry rooms, mills and so on. The academics are quartered nearby, and our cells are in the caves beneath the fort.

What I had learned from Gendak was common knowledge among the prisoners: they keep us alive to study us, to practice chirurgery, to use us as test subjects for their experiments. Gendak's attention seems benevolent in comparison to the horrors rumoured to await the most unfortunate: live dissections, agonising medical trials of new drugs, vile chthonomantic procedures that leave their victims warped and ruined. The Laws forbid Gurta to practice bodily alteration upon their own people, but it makes no provision for the protection of foreigners.

There is talk of an Elder coming to Farakza soon, the Gurta equivalent of our own chthonomancers. But whereas our chthonomancers wield no political power, their Elders are the custodians of the Laws, responsible for their preservation. They are the fists of Maal from beyond the grave, their authority unquestioned. It's through them that the words of one long-dead man still dominate the lives of an entire society today.

The prisoners are worried. Death is only death, but a living death is a terror beyond anything the chirurgeons could inflict. There is talk of pitiful, mewling things still chained in the depths from an Elder's last visit.

'It makes sense of things a little, a least,' I say to Feyn. 'The way they watch us in the quad, the way they keep on altering our schedule so we never settle. The way they wouldn't let us bathe for a long time. They're watching how it affects our moods; they're watching how we interact in our free time.'

'That would seem likely.'

'Studying us like insects,' I mutter. 'Give me a knife and ten minutes alone with one of those chirurgeons and I'll show them what a real dissection is.'

Feyn's eyes flicker away from me, made uneasy by my tone. 'They hurt you in the past,' he says. 'They are more than just enemies to you.' He has an uncanny ability to see right through me. He understands me with only the barest of clues.

'They killed my husband,' I say. And the words are out, over my tongue, past my teeth, before I can stop them. I've said it aloud. My throat closes up, too late to stop it, and my eyes prickle. I look down furiously at the table. Not going to cry.

He's silent for a long time and I don't look at him. Finally, he speaks. 'I see,' he says, and I think he does. 'But they did not kill your son.'

I look up at him. 'You don't know anything about my son.'

'I know you are not dead,' he replies, and he's so infuriatingly *certain* of himself that I want to jump across the table and throttle him. 'And perhaps you pretend that you are.'

'Who are you to say something like that to me?' I snap. 'You've given up! You just lie there and take it.'

'I have not given up anything,' he says. 'I am waiting. *You* have given up.'

I slam my hands down on the table in frustration, half-rising to my feet. 'I never fucking gave up!' I shout. And even though the prisoners next to me are staring, he's just gazing at me like a patient parent waiting for their child's tantrum to diminish. I feel stupid and embarrassed. I sit down again. Spoon some food into my mouth. Gradually conversation resumes around me. The guards relax.

I eat in silence for a time, thinking hard thoughts. Unforgiving thoughts. I've been shamed into looking at myself, and I don't like what I find.

I've been selfish. I held on to my misery for too long. I've been so wrapped up in Rynn's memory that I forgot who I was. Hiding, healing, cushioned by grief. But enough is enough.

I have responsibilities. I have duties. I have a life to get back to. I have a son who probably thinks I'm dead by now, but I'm *not* dead. I'm fucking Cadre. Nobody keeps me locked up.

Feyn watches me, and I know he knows what I'm thinking. Satisfied, he turns his attention to his food, leaving me brooding, burning, obsessed.

I'm going to get out of here.

25

They don't know who I am, these Gurta; they don't know the kind of precautions they should be taking. This prison can't hold me.

I'm more awake and alive than ever. I can't believe that shuffling, silent figure they brought into this place was me. I can't believe I was so weak. It makes me cringe to think of it.

I should have been trying to get out of here from the start, instead of wallowing in pain. My son is out there in the war somewhere. I know how things work: he probably hasn't even heard the news from Korok yet. He hasn't heard that his father is killed and his mother presumed so. I can't bear that he should think I'm dead. I can't bear that he should hear it from some official, in a dirty barracks in some forsaken hole in the Borderlands.

He doesn't know I'm still alive. And voids, I don't know if *he's* alive. But I have to get to him. It's the most important thing in the world to me now. I have to tell him he can come home. His father's gone: he died proud. But now there's no reason for Jai to stick it out any more. I have a letter at home that can get him out of the Army, and into the University. I want him to come back. To me, to Reitha, to safety. Before he gets himself killed.

Alert, I miss nothing. I memorise which guards bitch about which, who plays flip-chits with who. I know about money owed and money lent. I study the side-passages as we're marched from forge to cell to quad to food-hall. I construct a layout of this place in my mind and study it silently in the dark when I'm sitting in our cell.

And I start to see cracks in their security.

The guards are slovenly, safe in the knowledge that the prisoners are deep inside a garrisoned fort. As long as certain doors are kept locked, sealing the prisoners inside their own complex of corridors and cells, then they think escape attempts are futile. The perimeter of our prison section is tightly policed, but what goes on within is not. Guards do not take head-counts at any point. We swap jobs in the forge all the time, and nobody cares as long as the jobs are done. Prisoners often disappear, taken away by scholars. Sometimes they come back, sometimes they don't. It's possible to slip away and not be missed by anyone.

Despite the strict laws that govern them, Gurta are naturally disorganised. Discipline is imposed on them by society, so they have no need to foster it between themselves. It makes them a volatile people, their institutions patchy with feuds and infighting. Their army has suffered more defeats because of their basic nature than anything else. Their willingness to throw their lives away for their cause makes them fearsome opponents, but their inability to work together makes them sloppy.

I know these people well. I've escaped them before, I can do it again.

I begin to make my plans. The Gurta may be lax, but their confidence is at least partially justified. I'm forced to discard most options because I would be discovered within hours. Guards would notice an unlocked door, a missing key, and they would begin searching. I could evade them, maybe; but I don't fancy my chances of escape if the whole place is after me.

Besides, there's a complication. I'm not going alone. Feyn is coming with me.

I don't even want to think about why. Leaving him here would be to condemn him to death, but that in itself isn't a reason to bring him. There's a whole prison full of people in the same boat. And if I'd never come here, he'd still be being battered regularly, waiting for his captors to get round to cutting him up.

Anyway, I'm not responsible for the boy. That's the point.

So why do I feel that I am?

He's curiously evasive when I ask him about his time in Farakza. He speaks of past events in a very roundabout way, and tends not to refer to himself. Maybe he's over-modest, I don't know. But eventually I glean the facts by implication. He used to be a curiosity for the scholars here, but he made sure only to speak in his native language and to feign ignorance of Eskaran, to prevent them interrogating him about his culture. His people don't like to give up their secrets to outsiders.

The scholars tried to decipher his speech for a long time, failed, and soon left him alone to concentrate on more rewarding tasks. Obviously the order to keep him alive still stood, though he apparently wasn't so valuable that they would trouble to protect him from the beatings of other prisoners.

Well, all that is by the by. I need his help. The idea that I have requires more than one person. In fact, it requires a third member, too. Someone I'm not looking forward to talking to.

The man who tried to rape me while I was drugged.

Charn.

Other prisoners have been extending wary gestures of friendship. A tacit nod in the food hall here and there, a raised hand across the smoky forge. In the quad, a skinny Eskaran man with a deformed leg invites me to play a game he's invented, involving a series of grids drawn in dirt on the flagstones, using pebbles as markers. It has some serious flaws in the rules, easily exploitable; but for a time, I'm diverted, and I find that I'm enjoying myself.

His name is Juth, it emerges, and he's a publisher from Veya. He'd travelled to a village near the Borderlands in response to an intriguing letter from an author, promising a story unlike anything Juth had read before. While he was there, Gurta raiders sacked the village, having somehow got behind Eskaran lines. The author was killed, the manuscript burned along with the village, and Juth was captured when a blazing spar fell on his head and knocked him cold. He shows me the burns on his hairless scalp, beneath his cloth cap. Then he shows me the far more horrific ones on his back.

'My great regret,' he says, 'is that I read a portion of the manuscript before these barbarians came to destroy it. It was the most wonderful literature. I would rather have remained ignorant, so that I could pretend it did not matter that it is lost forever.'

Charn and Nereith mutter with their gang of cronies, casting glances my way. I doubt they have the courage to try anything, though I'm sure they would if they thought they could get away with it. But they're scared of me, and they're scared of Gendak. I meet with the scholar semi-regularly now, and that affords me some protection. If I were to be hurt, the Gurta might take an interest in my attackers.

Gendak's questions are gliding closer and closer to matters that I can't talk about. He wants to know about Ledo and Clan Caracassa. Things deeper than his usual sources can provide. Given the right motivation there will always be traitors willing to sell information to the Gurta, so anything that is public knowledge at home is safe enough to discuss. But he's feinting and probing, wanting more from me, retreating when I evade but always edging closer to his goals. I'm still undecided as to whether he's in it purely for knowledge, or if he's digging for secrets his masters can use against mine. Either way, we're going to come to an impasse soon. Things might get unpleasant then.

Feyn and I talk over my plan for escape, and we search for alternatives. For such a passive boy, he's fearless now he's decided we're getting out. His people are not afraid of death or punishment; in fact, their philosophy appears to involve not giving a shit about anything. He couches it in slightly more elegant terms, though I'm sure I'm only getting the outline and not a true understanding. They believe all connections are temporary, so to cling to them makes no sense. When someone is gone, they're gone. Live for now; the present is all there is. You can't know what will happen next, so why worry? Consequences are natural and inevitable. Just do what you feel you must.

The SunChildren, if he is representative, strike me as a very calm people, and yet they're impulsive too. I really think he was, as he says, just waiting. Waiting to die, or waiting for something to change. I was that change. I've offered him a possibility of escape which he didn't have before. Even if he had to push me a little to get me going.

So now he's decided that we're getting out of here, whatever the risk. The idea of dying in the attempt doesn't faze him in the least.

I like this boy. He's weird, but I can't help wanting to look after him.

'I need to talk to you.'

Charn tears a strip of meat off the bone and puts it in his mouth. They've been feeding us well lately, presumably watching what effect it has on our mood and work. He's making a show of being unconcerned, but I know being this close to him makes him jumpy.

He's sitting at a bench, Nereith opposite. The two men I injured the time I broke Charn's nose are no longer part of his crowd. They were taken away and never came back. I don't know what happened to them, and I don't really care.

'Food good?' I enquire of the Khaadu. He shows me his teeth in a disparaging snarl. Khaadu hate cooked food, and he's probably as nauseated by the slab of grilled hookworm on his plate as I would be if I ate it raw.

'You want to talk, talk,' says Charn. I'm leaning close to him, and I can actually feel him trembling with adrenaline.

'Alone.'

There's a long moment when he decides what to do, but ultimately he has to maintain the show that he's not afraid of me. He gets up, and we walk to a sparsely occupied bench. The guards watch us go, as do most of the prisoners in the food hall. We sit down, on opposite sides, away from the others.

The bruises round his eyes have almost faded now: only a sickly yellow pallor remains. He's much bigger than me, but he's chewing his pierced lower lip in agitation, rotating the rings with his tongue. Sweat beads his bald pate, but that's probably the heat in here.

'What?' he says, sullen and impatient. He feels I've won a victory by making him get up and come with me. Which I have.

'I need your help,' I say. It's not so hard; I'm not afflicted with an excess of pride, so there's nothing to swallow.

I expect him to laugh, but he doesn't. 'You need my help with what?'

I hesitate, just a moment. I have to risk trusting him. 'An escape.'

That gets his interest. He sits back, thinks. 'You cut me in on it,' he says. 'I get out too, or I walk away right now.'

'Just you,' I say. 'Nobody else. You don't breathe a word to anyone.'

He looks over at the table he's just come from. Nereith is watching us intently. 'Who else is going?'

'Feyn.' I see the expression on his face and add: 'Don't worry. He doesn't do grudges.'

He stares at me for a long time. Thinking hard. But he knows, as we all do, that sooner or later our time here will be up. And the end that awaits us is not a pleasant one. There've been insurrections in the past, but they always result in the prisoners being slaughtered. What keeps us in check is the futility of rebellion, the hard labour, the shifting schedule and the slim hope that somehow we will be liberated before our time comes. The prisoners try to make themselves useful to their captors, seeking to stave off their executions indefinitely. Men believe what they need to believe.

Charn's not stupid. 'Tell me the plan,' he says.

I lean closer. Our voices are quiet enough that nobody can overhear. 'The forge.'

'What about it?'

'Every shift, the Overseer takes a tour of the forge at exactly the same time. He comes through a metal door, high up on one of the walls.'

'I know it. I see him.'

'He locks it behind him, makes his inspections, then returns through the door and presumably locks it again.'

'Everyone knows that,' he says impatiently. 'What's the plan? Steal his key?'

'Exactly.'

He smirks, derisive. 'Think you're the first that thought of that? Some problems. First, the key's kept in his belt pouch, and he's always got a guard with him. If they catch your hand down his trousers, pardon the expression, they'll cut it off.'

'I can handle that. Next objection?'

Disbelief crosses his face. He's sceptical that I can dismiss the problem so easily. 'Alright then. Second and very large flaw in your plan: what happens when he gets to the end of his inspection, tries to open his door, and finds his key is gone?'

'They'll search everyone. If they don't find it they'll reason it's been hidden, and probably begin killing us until someone owns up or until they believe it's really been lost. Then they change the locks.'

'Exactly,' he says, in mocking imitation of me. It's not a very good impression.

'Unless it's back in his pouch by the time he gets to the door.'

Now he does laugh. Short, harsh. He wipes his hand over his face, hunkers closer. 'You want to steal the key off him, then put it back in his pouch before he completes his rounds?'

I hold his eyes, letting him feel my determination.

'And what happens in between these two highly improbable events?'

'You take an impression of the key.'

Suddenly he understands why I need him. But I see something else there too. The tiniest chink of hope.

'It'll never work,' he says. 'You'd have to get the key off him near the start of his tour, get all the way across the forge without being seen, get the key to me – you know the blacksmiths are most heavily guarded of all, right?'

'I know.'

'I can make an impression of the key without them noticing, that's easy enough. I can even get the key back to you. But for you to get across the forge *again* and put it back in his pouch?' He gives me a look like I'm insane. 'It'll never work. There's not enough time.'

'It can be done,' I insist. 'And if we fail, it's me who'll be punished, not you.'

'I'll be more than punished if they catch me with the key,' he mutters. 'They trust me. They know I don't misbehave. Taken me a long time to get them that way.'

'Then you've probably not got very long left,' I reply. 'Sooner or later, we're all going to go.'

He shakes his head. 'They need me. Any idiot can hammer a sword or make metal struts or shard-cannon barrels or whatever. But there's only two or three like me, who can make the proper stuff. Good swords, fine components, that kind of thing. I'm valuable to them.'

'So valuable that you want to stay here?'

'Shit, no. But valuable enough so I don't want to risk my position on a dumb idea like this.'

'You remember how easily I took out your friends?' I ask quietly. His face clouds. 'I'm Cadre. We go through training like you can't imagine to become the best at what we do. I'm a saboteur. Thief, spy, assassin, whatever needs to be done. I've been in and out of some of the most heavily fortified places in Veya.'

'I heard of you,' he says slowly. 'Nobody knew exactly what you did, but I heard of you.'

'This can be done,' I tell him, firmly. 'I can do it.'

He stares at me for a long time. Sits back, looks away: at the guards, at his cronies, at Feyn who is eating on his own. Nereith is still watching us with undisguised suspicion. Finally he flops forward onto his forearms, sighs.

'So I make you the key,' he says. 'What happens then?'

24

The first thing I do concerning my newfound and tentative friendship with Juth is to exploit it for a favour I don't intend to pay back. It feels bad, but I reason that if I fuck this up then having to bear the disappointment of a lame publisher is going to be the least of my worries. I think he'll understand.

Juth works in the salvage dump. Here, quantities of scrap metal scavenged from battlefields and left over from other construction jobs are deposited into a long trench, where they are sorted through for parts that can be reused. Then the trench is tipped up and the remainder slides into a mine cart, to be taken away and melted down.

The salvage dump is one of the first ports of call on Overseer Arachi's rounds. For my plan to have any chance of success, I need as much time as possible between stealing the key from him and returning it. If he completes his inspection before I get back, it's all over.

Juth is a pushover really; he's eager to please, and he sees my coming to him for help as an affirmation of trust. I ask him to swap with me for a shift, and to find someone to swap with Feyn too. It's not a big ask, really, though working the screens on the slurry-trough is much harder than sorting through the salvage dump. But it's only one shift. I tell him that we're hoping to steal some special components to trade with another prisoner. He points out that people who work the salvage dump are always searched on our way out; I tell him not to worry and give him a conspiratorial wink. I don't know where he imagines I'll hide these mythical components, but he accepts the story.

We're greeted at the salvage dump with a friendly wariness. Once we give them the cover story, the workers relax a little. They assume we know what we're looking for, give us thick gloves and let us get on with it. Feyn and I stand together at the trench, sifting through the tide of shrapnel and broken components, trying to appear busy.

The salvage dump is near one wall of the forge. Black, smoke-stained stone rears high above us. Behind me is a raised metal walkway that runs between the various sections of the forge, connected to them by short sets of steps. Every shift the Overseer comes strolling along, descends, admires this section or that, then returns and passes along the walkway to the next section. Nobody's quite sure of the purpose of these visits. Perhaps he's just fastidious, and sees these inspections as a duty he mustn't shirk no matter how little good it does. It'd certainly explain why he's so punctual.

I try to calm the anticipation building in me as I work. I'm *doing* something. Even if it gets me killed, I'm doing something, and that feels good. I begin to run chua-kîn chants through my head, curbing the hot swell in my chest that will make me do something rash. The chants, we are taught, are only screens to distract our conscious minds from the subtleties played out behind them, the true meat of chua-kîn learning that allows us to control our bodies. But I like them for themselves. They have a certain appealing monotony.

My heart slows, and the jitters subside. I notice that our neighbours have begun filling small metal bins with cogs, clockwork parts, pieces of piping and so on. I pay attention to what they take and start looking for my own pieces to contribute.

From here I can just see the Overseer's door through the black haze. It sits amid a strip of narrow, grimy windows, high above the forge, linked to us by a zigzagging flight of stairs bolted to the stone wall. I picture him watching us from his office, then turning back to his desk, tallying this and that, unaware of the plans being hatched by the prisoners below. I wonder what's beyond that door, and if it's even worth the risk to find out.

Then I see the door open, and there's no time to wonder any more. Arachi emerges, straight-backed, rigid. A billow of sparks fly up through the murk, carried on the thermals, obscuring my vision for a moment. By the time it's passed, he's descending. I didn't see where he put his key. I can only hope it's in the usual place.

Feyn catches my eye. He shows me a jagged shard of metal in his hand. I'm in no doubt he'll play his part. All we can do now is wait.

Sweat has dampened my hair. The pores of my face itch. Fresh sweat cleaning away old sweat. I don't know how long it's been since I bathed. I hate this heat. I want the cool air of Veya, the air chilled by the unforgiving endlessness of rock that surrounds it. I want Jai with me, in our chambers in the Caracassa mansions. He can use that wonderful, logical mind of his to construct devices that dispense potions, or which grind ingredients to a fineness hitherto unheard of. He can even make devices for war, if he likes.

It's a nice dream, but the reality is that my son has gone off to war for all the wrong reasons, and I didn't do enough to stop him. I've lost acquaintances, comrades and close friends to the battlefield or to the machinations of the Plutarchs, but I only really understood when I lost Rynn. And I can't bear that it might happen to Jai too.

Arachi descends to the bottom of the steps and my view is blocked by the machinery of the forge. He's meeting with his escort. A guard always accompanies him on his rounds, except when one of us is being removed. Then there could be three or four. I hope this isn't one of those times, or the plan will have to be abandoned. I've learned through long experience that, in matters of subterfuge, timing is everything. Patience is the highest virtue of the spy.

The man to my right hisses at me just as I'm about to drop some piece of scrap into the metal bin. 'Leave that, it's useless,' he snaps. I throw it back into the trench. My mind's not on my job.

I hear two sets of boots clanking on metal. Only one guard, then. I try not to look, but I can't help glancing up as Arachi approaches. His long white hair is brushed and waxed, and he's doing his best to look dignified in the withering heat of the forge. His collar is already damp and he dabs at his face with a pocket-cloth. The guard at his side is young, presumably saddled with escort duty because of his inexperience. He looks bored. Good. He'll respond well to some excitement.

Arachi and his escort descend from the walkway to our sunken enclosure, to get a better look at our work. Arachi is inspecting the salvage bins and murmuring approvingly about what valuable things we are finding, when Feyn screams.

There's something appalling in the alien way he expresses pain, high and raw and uninhibited. He stumbles back from the trench, one gloved hand clamped around his forearm near the elbow. The dirty white of the glove is already staining red.

He flails into my arms, babbling in the clicking dialect of his people.

'He's hurt!' I shout, as if it wasn't obvious. The other prisoners crowd close, trying to see or to help. I look at the guard and the Overseer in supplication. *You're the masters here. Will you aid your helpless subjects?*

It works. The guard wades in, suddenly aware of the need to assert his authority and impress the Overseer. I pass Feyn into the arms of another prisoner while the guard clears a way to assess the situation. In the confusion, it's easy to back up to the walkway and slip behind Arachi. He's watching the drama anxiously, presumably worried about how the accident will reflect on him. I wonder if he really understands that we're prisoners, and all headed for an unpleasant death anyway. He runs his little empire more like a factory than a forced labour camp.

The pouch hangs from his belt. He hasn't tied it properly.

The secret to picking a pocket is confidence. You have to be quick and light and sure. I've picked dozens of pockets and only twice been caught. My hand darts in and out of the pouch. The key is medium-sized, made of a sturdy metal and fashioned with an ornate grip. It disappears into my palm and I've moved away in moments. It's fascinating how much distraction can blind you.

I shove my way back in the group. Someone is wrapping a bandage torn from Feyn's sleeve around his arm. 'Get him to a chirurgeon, this needs sewing!'

'I'll take him!' I say, pushing through. 'Hoy! I'll take him. I know this boy.'

They relent, happy to let me take responsibility. They've probably worked the salvage dump for a long time now, and they're glad to be rid of two clumsy amateurs.

~ Find the duty officer ~ the guard says in Gurtan. ~ He's over near the smelting pits ~ When I look at him blankly, the Overseer repeats it in tremulous Eskaran.

I put Feyn's arm around my shoulder – we're about the same height – and start hauling him up the steps. He plays weak, in a swoon. Overseer Arachi steps back, faintly disgusted by the sight of blood.

We go up the steps and along the walkway until we're out of sight of the Overseer. Then we slip between two enormous flanks of metal, part of a giant system of sediment pots. Now that we're hidden, Feyn drops the swooning act.

'Are you alright?'

'I will not fail.'

'You cut yourself pretty deep.'

'It is not easy to be exact.'

There's nothing else to be said. Better be quick.

Between us and the blacksmiths are a labyrinth of trenches, the alleys of the forge. We keep to them as much as we can, running with our heads low to avoid the guards. We stop, crouch and wait for them to pass by, dark ghosts in the fiery murk, backlit by the yellow-white glow of molten ore. Feyn's wound is our excuse if caught, but they'll send us back the way we came in search of the duty officer. No ruse is going to get us close to the blacksmiths and Charn; there's no reason for us to be there.

We can't get across the forge without being seen, even given its size and the smoky atmosphere. Masked prisoners watch us with lensed eyes: the men who work in the most extreme heat, clad in flameproof hide. We run past another slurry trough like the one we work at, and a press that crushes metal into thin sheets with a deafening hiss. But the prisoners don't hinder us. Nobody here would report us to the guards, even if they suspected something was wrong. Hatred of the Gurta is the strongest common bond we have.

The blood has soaked through Feyn's bandage and is running down his arm by the time we come into sight of the blacksmiths. It's hard to tell how much he's losing: it doesn't show well against his skin in this light. But I'm getting really concerned now. It was he who came up with the idea of wounding himself as a distraction, but I daren't think about how I'd feel if he died for my plan.

So don't, I tell myself. *Get on with it.*

The blacksmiths work on a raised platform, in the looming shadows of the gigantic forge equipment. There are four of them, Charn and three others, each with their own anvils and hammers and water troughs. It's a prison joke that the blacksmiths are elevated above the rest of us, but really it's so the guards can keep an eye on them. They know how easy it would be to 'lose' a dagger here and have it turn up in the hands of a prisoner later.

There are two sentries posted, their pallid eyes sharp. I know them by name: Bal and Daquii. Bal is a quiet sort, mildly bullied by his peers; Daquii moans constantly.

Charn is obviously nervous, not concentrating on his work. He's a liability; I wish I didn't need him.

I pat Feyn on the shoulder to send him on his way, and he heads around to the other side of the platform. He clambers up onto a walkway while I sneak closer to Charn, keeping under cover as best I can. It's not easy; I'm exposed here. Then I hear Feyn yelling, crying for help. He's setting up a distraction using his wound, pretending he's just been hurt. The guards see him. Daquii hesitates, glancing at his charges; he's reluctant to leave the blacksmiths. But even a Gurta won't just leave a man to bleed to death.

Daquii runs down from the platform to see to Feyn. Bal moves to the edge to observe what's happening, but he doesn't abandon his post.

It's good enough.

Charn, recognising the signal, is casting about for me. I wave to him. He glances uncertainly at Bal, but I don't give him time to falter. I throw the key to him.

This was always the weak part of the plan, but there just wasn't any way to get close enough. It was always going to be risky.

In the dim light, Charn's catch is bad. The key bounces out of his hands, clatters to the floor. He drops and scrabbles it up. Bal almost turns back, but Feyn trips on the walkway and collapses just as Daquii reaches him, providing a much more interesting spectacle.

Charn is still dithering. I gesture angrily, and he gets to work. I don't know what he's got up there, some tray of soft metal or clay. I'm not certain. He was bleating about needing to keep it at the right temperature to take the impression properly. But in the end, he's remarkably quick. Two firm presses, one on each side, and the key is back in his hand.

Bal glances over at the blacksmiths, not suspecting anything, then turns back to the commotion below. I breathe out. One of the other blacksmiths, a shifty sort called Relk, is watching us with interest. It can't be helped. Charn checks the guards, throws the key back to me. I suddenly realise how difficult it is to see a small, dull metal object in a room churning with bright fire and smoke. Somehow I catch it anyway.

Then I'm gone. Feyn's done his part; Charn I can leave to do whatever he has to do to make that key. I have my own job.

Alone, I move faster. Back across the forge, racing, racing. The prisoners know something's up, but that doesn't matter. They won't give me away. It's the guards I'm concerned about. If I'm caught, they'll execute me for sure.

I see the guard on the walkway a mere sliver of a moment before he looks my way. It's enough time for me to stop dead and to throw myself flat against the metal wall of a mineral tank. He stares down the dark corridor between the tanks, wondering whether he really saw what he thought he saw, wondering whether it's worth clambering in there to find out.

Long seconds pass.

He moves on. I let out my breath. Prudence dictates that I give him plenty of time to vacate the area before I set off again. It's time I don't have. He's barely out of earshot before I'm scrambling up on to the walkway, down the other side. Heading for the furnaces, the last stop on Overseer Arachi's tour. We've wasted too much time. Maybe Charn was right, maybe it *can't* be done.

Then suddenly I'm there, and my heart sinks into my stomach.

His tour has progressed faster than I thought. He's just leaving the furnaces. I emerge from the shadows in time to see him walking away. The guard is following him, perfectly positioned to impede my access to his belt pouch. There's nothing left but a short and uninterrupted stroll back to the stairs. I can't get to him, short of running up and grabbing him. I'm frantic for some excuse, desperate, as every step takes him further away from me. But nothing's coming to mind.

That's when I spot Nereith. The hairless Khaadu, his body wet with sweat, shovel buried in a coke pile. He's seen me. Our eyes meet. Something there, but I don't know what. Then he pulls out his shovel and digs it into the coke dust on the edge of the pile, drawing up a big spadeful. Just like he told me not to do when I was working here.

He slings the coke dust into the mouth of the furnace, and it bellows flame. The searing cloud rolls out with a roar, and the workers fall back with cries of alarm, their arms shielding their faces. One of them is scorched badly. He falls, rolling on the ground, swearing in pain. The cloud of fire burns out as fast as it appeared, more impressive than deadly, but the commotion is enough that the Overseer and his guard notice it. The guard, pleased that he has something to do, rushes down to help. Arachi seems caught between wanting to lend a hand and maintaining a dignified aloofness. I can see he's tormented by this shift's disastrous tour. Two workers injured: it's a calamity for him.

He doesn't see me slide up behind him and put the key back in his pouch. It's far easier to put something into a pocket than to take it out.

The burned prisoner is taken away to be seen to. Angry words are exchanged, and Nereith fends them off with protests of his own. The Overseer mutters about new safety procedures and the guard is thinking of the stories he'll have to tell his friends when he comes off-shift. But I'm already gone, heading back to the salvage dump. No sense getting caught now, and no point waiting around to thank Nereith. He doesn't want my thanks.

He knew. He knew what I was doing, and he helped me, and that only means one thing. He wants in. And now he's earned it, the canny bastard.

It seems there are four of us now.

23

I forgot the most cardinal of rules in the spy game. Never underestimate anybody. Nereith was staring at us across the food hall the whole time I was talking to Charn. I thought he was seething with suspicion. The reality was much simpler. He was lip-reading.

The four of us sit in the shadows of our cell, facing each other, our hunched backs excluding the others. Faint light spills from above, casting shadows down the hollows of our faces. The rough walls of the cave drip with moisture. Everything smells of sweat and shit.

Charn holds out his hand, concealing what's inside. I take it. The cold weight of a key. I study it surreptitiously, keeping it shielded from sight. It's rough, but it looks like it'll work. A simple skeleton-key arrangement. There's no design on the bow and the blade is the tiniest bit out of alignment, but as long as the teeth are accurate it should be fine. And it's a pretty good job, given the circumstances.

'How did you get it out?'

'They hardly bother checking me. I'm trusted. I put it in my mouth.'

I flinch inwardly. That was a risk we didn't need to take. All it took was for someone to speak to him and we'd have been spitted. I'd told him to hide it in his buttocks. He found the idea offensive. Interesting how the idea of raping me seemed acceptable enough but even the suggestion of something tubular near his arse makes him get squeamish.

I let it drop. No point arguing about it. He got the key. I stash it in a secret pocket inside my trouser belt, designed for the purpose. Someone doing a casual pat-down wouldn't even feel it there. Besides, they don't bother searching lowly slurry-trough workers.

Feyn is a little weak, but his arm has been stitched up. I feel uneasy about exposing Feyn to the attention of one of those Gurta butchers. I don't want them to start getting ideas about seeing the insides of a SunChild.

'What we just did wasn't easy,' I tell them. 'If we keep our heads, we can all get out of here.'

'I'd like to know what you plan to do now,' says Nereith. His voice is very low, the chesty growl of a threatened animal.

'You'll know soon enough,' I reply. 'Before we go any further, I'd like to be sure who I can trust. The more people in on this thing, the more likely someone's going to screw it up.'

He takes the point. I'm deeply uncertain about him. He's got me in an awkward position: I owe him for saving the last operation, and he can make things very difficult for us if I refuse to include him. Some prisoners make bargains with the guards, trading information for favours. Anyone caught doing it tends not to survive very long, but desperation can make traitors of the most honourable men. I'm not sure about the Khaadu. I'm not sure what he'd do.

'I know about you, Massima Leithka Orna,' he says. 'And I know you've heard of Silverfish.'

That interests me. 'I've heard of Silverfish.'

'I haven't,' says Charn. He doesn't like to be left in the dark. Nereith makes a gesture to me, inviting me to tell him.

'He operates out of Veya, as far as I know, but he's got tendrils in all kinds of places. Very secretive. Nobody has seen him, to my knowledge. The only contact is through his lieutenants.'

'This man is a criminal?' Feyn asks, in his naïvely charming sort of way.

'Criminal, businessman; it's the same thing where I come from,' I reply. 'He's kind of a figure of legend in the Veyan underworld.' I look back at Nereith. 'Certainly a name you don't want to conjure with unless you mean it.'

'It's true that bandying his name around is unwise,' the Khaadu says. 'But I'm sure he would consider it worthwhile, if it helped one of his people escape from Farakza.'

'You work for him?'

'I gather information,' he said. 'Rather like you, Orna, though my methods are more passive than yours. I'm a spy, of sorts, in that I'm paid to keep my eyes and ears open. Silverfish needs to know what is happening in Khaad, as in the other regions of Callespa. I'm the one who finds out.'

'Then how did you end up here?'

'I was captured by a Gurta scouting patrol on my way to Veya. The information I carried was too sensitive to trust to a messenger.' He bares his teeth in what I assume is wistful regret. It's hard to tell. 'My news is useless now. I've been here too long.'

'What were Gurta patrols doing between Khaad and Veya? That's hardly near their battle lines.'

'They were a scouting patrol,' he repeats, deadpan. 'They were scouting.'

I study him for a moment. Deciding what to do about him. He takes the advantage.

'The way I see it, we have several problems. First is breaking out of the immediate prison section, within the fort. You've taken care of that one. I assume you intend to sneak up to the Overseer's office when he is on his rounds, and make your way from there?'

I nod. That much is obvious. 'We never see him arrive or leave except on inspections, even though our shifts change all the time, so we can assume there's another way out of there. From what I know of the floor plan, I'm fairly certain that it leads out of the prisoners' area.'

'Agreed,' he says. 'Then you face the next task. Moving around the fort without being caught. Even as renowned a thief as yourself could not manage that without foreknowledge of the layout or a disguise. Your skin and eyes would give you away. The only disguise that might work is that of an Eskaran slave.'

'One of their scholars told me they keep some here.' I almost say I've heard the guards talking about them too, but I stop myself. Habit keeps me from revealing unnecessary information. They don't need to know I speak Gurtan.

'They do,' he says. 'But you don't look like one. How will you get the disguise?'

'Laundry room. I'm working on it.'

'Let me do it. I know people in the laundry room. They launder the slaves' clothes with the soldiers'. If one goes missing, the slave won't dare to raise a fuss, in case they're blamed and punished for losing it.'

I'm faintly surprised. He's proving to be very useful. 'When can you get one in my size?'

'Next turn. Maybe the one after that. There are a several dozen slaves here, each with several sets of clothes. They dress their slaves well, as a reflection of their own status. More are arriving every turn in advance of the Elder's visit.'

He's thought this through. It suddenly occurs to me that he's been planning to escape for a long time, but the opportunity only came with me. I'm the only one with the skills and, more importantly, the *gender* to make this work.

'The Elder gets here in eight turns' time,' I tell them. I've learned as much from the guards. 'The whole fort will be in turmoil. That's when we leave.'

'But there's a problem with your disguise,' he says. 'They only take very young girls as slaves. So they can grow up in the Gurta way, learn not to be rebellious and to accept their position. Too much trouble otherwise.'

'I know that,' I say. 'What's your point?'

'The slaves speak Gurtan, that's my point.'

'I'll deal with it,' I reply.

'Not only that, but they speak a certain *dialect* of Gurtan. It identifies them as slaves. They have complex rituals, gestures: things that takes years to be taught. Even the greetings are formalised. Gurta love ceremony; they demand a lot from their slaves.' He rolls his shoulders, stretching his neck. 'They'll see through you in an instant.'

'I'll deal with it.'

He shrugs, decides it's not worth saying anything more. The warning has been given, and he doesn't have any better ideas. It's a risk we have no choice but to take. Getting out of Farakza was never going to be easy.

'What then?' Charn asks. We've already talked about this, but I think he just wants reassuring.

I don't have much reassurance to give. 'I scout the fort, and I find some way for the four of us to get out without being seen.'

'See, that's where the plan starts to come apart for me,' he says.

'We can't plan an escape when we don't know what's outside,' I say. 'We go step by step. I'll find a way. Then I'll come back for you, and we all go together.'

He snorts. *That's* the real crux of Charn's problem. He doesn't believe that I will come back. And if it weren't for Feyn, I probably wouldn't.

'You either believe me or you don't,' I say. 'Makes no odds to me.'

'I think you need us, besides,' says Nereith. Charn looks at him. 'After all, what happens after we escape? Are you going to make it back to Veya on your own? Do you even know the way?'

'I could find the way,' I say.

'But here we have a SunChild, whose people have lived off the land for uncountable generations and is an expert survivalist by birth; and you have a Khaadu who knows exactly how to get back to Veya from here, because he has travelled this way before in more peaceful times, when Khaadu and Gurta were not enemies.'

I hadn't even thought about Feyn's potential usefulness until now. It gives me a jolt of surprise. I'm usually so mercenary as well. It's very uncharacteristic.

'You remember the way?'

'I'm Khaadu. We remember *everything*.'

I don't give him the opportunity to gloat over my lack of knowledge of Khaadu abilities. I have a vague memory of Keren and I getting drunk in a bar, and his recounting some rumour about how the Khaadu had perfect recall. But in the same conversation he told me how they ate their own young if they were deformed or sickly. That was much more interesting.

'What about me?' Charn blusters. 'You'll need me too.' He's sore that Nereith hasn't counted him as an asset. The two of them have been tense since Nereith learned Charn was plotting an escape without letting him in on it. They're not so close any more, I suspect.

'You've done your part,' Nereith says dismissively, and that shuts him up.

I raise my hands to placate them both. 'We're *all* going,' I tell them. 'So let's work together. We'll concentrate on getting away from the fort for now.'

'I was awake on the way in,' says Nereith. 'They drugged me, but it doesn't work so well on my kind.' He hunkers forward. 'I only saw the main entrance, but I think it's the only one. I've never heard the guards talk about another.'

'Wait, you know Gurtan?' I ask.

'And Banchu, and Craggen, only in the Child's Tongue though: I can't make the booming sounds the adults do. I can understand a bit of Umbra if they're not whispering too quietly. And some Ya'yeen too, although that's trickier because you can't just memorise it. They keep changing the rules. Shifting meanings and all that shit; I can't handle it too well.'

'I'm impressed.'

'Don't be. It's easy for my kind. We only have to hear something once and we remember it forever.'

I find myself becoming faintly jealous of the Khaadu's natural advantages. They'd come in useful in my line of work. But then I remember laying my head on my husband's dead chest and hearing the stillness of his heart. Forgetfulness can sometimes be a blessing.

'There's two gates to get through on the main road,' he says. 'One at the entrance to the fort, and one before the bridge. I saw them searching an outbound cart on the bridge, so we can assume they always do that. Checking for contraband, I'd say.'

'What does this bridge go over?' Feyn asked.

Charn scoffs. 'How long have you been here?'

'I have not talked to other prisoners many.'

'Much,' I correct him. We've been having a few lessons in the cell, just talking really, but he keeps making elementary mistakes.

Nereith elaborates. 'Farakza stands on an island in the middle of a river of spume rock. You know what that is?'

'I do not recognise that word.'

'It's like lava, but it melts at lower temperatures, solidifies rapidly. The river around Farakza moves slow. On top is a kind of brittle crust, that breaks and moves as the river flows. It's been cooled by the cavern air and turned solid. Beneath it's still molten. Still very hot.'

'Is that why we are so hot in these lower places?' Feyn asks, indicating the cave around us.

'Exactly. These cells are underground, and we're surrounded by molten spume rock.'

I start to imagine the burning, sluggish flow oozing past beyond the damp walls of black stone.

'So once we're out, how do we get over the river?' Charn asks.

'This brittle crust,' I say to Nereith. 'How brittle is it?'

33

I returned from our family-vacation-cum-manhunt more restless than when I left. Jai was back at military school and Rynn had been tasked with bodyguard duty for an important official on a Borderland visit, so there was nobody to greet me on my return. Not that I minded; I do alone very well.

Ledo had told me about a particularly elusive apothecary called Ekan who was undercutting his business with cheap potions. I'd asked Keren to track the man down while I was away, and upon my return I found a message from him. He had something. I sent him one back, requesting to meet him later that turn.

While I waited for his reply I had time on my hands, so I wandered the Caracassa mansions restlessly, eager to be getting on with something. The matter of Jai's upcoming graduation filled me with unease, so I traced familiar routes, seeking old reminders, finding comfort in reminiscence. In time, inevitably, I came to the central atrium of the mansion, and to the greatest sculpture that Rynn's grandfather ever produced. His greatest sculpture, and his greatest mistake.

It was a circular courtyard, dominated by the enormous monument in the centre. The sculpture rose out of a round pool, from which stone channels led to ornamental fountains. Lush fungal gardens were arranged around the atrium, a profusion of yellow, purple, green and pink. I found I could identify them all, from the tiny sprays of puffballs to the different species of dwarf mycora, with their many-branched stems and flat caps spreading high overhead.

The discovery pleased me. Must have picked up their names from Reitha. I was getting to be quite the amateur naturalist.

There were people here, lounging beneath the arbours or walking slowly. Others sat on the elaborately wrought balconies that ringed the chamber, to provide a better view of Venya Ethken

Asta's masterpiece. The chamber echoed with the quiet susurrus of voices.

I traipsed idly along, enjoying the feel of the place. Paths were pleasantly lit by lamps. Powerful lanterns hung in the upper reaches of the chamber, their shinestones glowing, magnified manifold through glass shaped by master artisans. Light, like heat, could be controlled: by coloured panes, by angles, by the arts of the chthonomancers that ignited the shinestones and made them burn like miniature suns. It was as important to architects and designers as wood or stone or metal.

I found my favourite spot to contemplate the sculpture. It was a bizarre piece, shapeless and organic in form. Many types of stone and ore were fused together to create patterns which led the eye. Here, a bright red cluster of prismatic vanadinite; there, a long vein of blue-green chrysocolla. Bubbles of botryoidal malachite warred with scratches of silver and frills of celestine. And in among them, rarer minerals, raised from the depths of the earth where only the Craggens could go. At first sight it was ugly and chaotic, but its form had a mesmerising quality that drew viewers in. It was easy to become lost in the swirls and jags and curves. There was a puzzle there, a challenge hard to resist.

It meant something different to everybody, but to me it meant more than to most. Here were the shackles that bound the man I loved. Rynn was in Bond to Clan Caracassa just as I was. His grandfather, Asta, had borrowed the money from Caracassa to create this colossal piece for an eminent merchant; but when the patron was bankrupted by the machinations of the Eskaran markets, Asta found himself impoverished, all his money tied up in a half-finished sculpture that no one wanted. Caracassa claimed the life-debt for three generations, and his first task was to finish the sculpture he began.

Rynn was the last of his debt. I was only Bonded for the tenure of my lifetime. Had things been different, our son would have been born free. But that wasn't how it worked out in the end.

'Beautiful,' came a silken voice by my left shoulder.

'Disgusting,' said another on my right.

I turned with a smile. Liss and Casta, the twins. As opposite as day and night. They had both changed the colour of their skin since I had last seen them. Now Liss was as pale as her brother Ledo, ghostly and wan; but Casta was a deep grey-black, like coal.

'We missed you,' Liss said, and kissed me on the lips.

'I missed you too,' I replied, turning to receive Casta's kiss. 'Both of you.'

Liss was all in white, thin layers of gauzy fabrics drifting around her, shredded at the hems. She had contrived to look tattered, despite having spent a small fortune on the outfit. Casta wore black and red, and her hair was like magma.

'Now tell us about your vacation!' Liss cried.

'Rynn tells us nothing,' added her sister.

'We could make him, but where's the fun?'

My vacation. Ah yes. I'd barely got there before I'd been called away to Mal Eista to chase down and kill a man called Gorak Jespyn. The tricky fuck had been a nightmare to catch. I never did find out what he'd done to Clan Caracassa to deserve his fate.

Liss had linked arms with me and was tugging me away from the sculpture. She was already off on another subject. 'Have you eaten yet?'

'We didn't make it to breakfast,' Casta said.

'I'm hungry!'

'You're always hungry.'

'Well, now I'm *more* hungry. Did you eat?' This last was addressed to me.

I was laughing. I always enjoyed the twins' verbal onslaughts.

'What are you laughing at?' Liss asked, laughing too. 'She's laughing at us, Casta!'

'She's cruel,' Casta said, with a wry twitch of her lips. 'I always said that.'

'Is it true? Are you cruel?'

'No,' I replied, still laughing. 'No, I'm just glad to see you both.'

'There!' Liss said triumphantly to her sister. 'She's not cruel, she's happy.'

Casta slipped her arm through mine, so that each twin had one. 'I still say she's cruel.'

'Oh, I'm cruel,' I agreed. 'Cruel enough to demand your company for the next few hours.'

'That *is* cruel,' Casta said.

'And so impertinent!' Liss chimed in. 'When we're so important and she's just an . . . an errand girl!'

'Errand girl!' I cried in mock-outrage.

'Teasing, my love,' Liss said, kissing me on the cheek. 'Your will is our purpose. Let's go.'

We took a crayl-drawn rickshaw through the Tangles. The twins had a new favourite club called The Black Circlet, a broad, round building encircled by mycora roots. It stood above the main throughway of the Tangles, looking down on the traffic. On its far side, towards the cavern wall, was a lush garden of precious rocks and vines and waterfalls.

The club was frighteningly exclusive, but the twins were known all over Veya. We were ushered in and seated without having to say a word.

A robed handmaiden memorised our orders. I asked for a stimulant cocktail, as I'd snatched only a little sleep on my journey down from the subsurface: the lifts were uncomfortable and noisy, and I'd had too much on my mind. The twins, alerted, began to lay into me about how haggard I looked. I bore it all good-humouredly, and told them how vile they were, which they loved.

'Why don't you write to us while you're away? We could come and see you!' Liss demanded at one point. Casta watched me owlishly, interested enough to keep quiet for a moment.

'Why don't you write to *me*?' I countered.

'Ah, this and that,' Liss replied, as if that was an answer.

I felt momentarily saddened. It was true they bore a great affection for me, but I knew what they were like. They flitted from delight to delight, and out of sight was out of mind. My letters would go unanswered, not because they didn't care, but because they were utterly selfish. They would have been in paroxysms of happiness at hearing from me and then forget to write back.

'Well, you're here now,' Casta said, as our drinks arrived. 'That's all that matters.'

'I heard the news,' I commented, as the cocktail began to lift away the veils of tiredness from my mind and muscles.

'The news?' Casta and Liss said together.

'I hear you're to be a consort, Liss.'

Liss squealed and grabbed my hands across the table. 'Yes! Isn't it exciting? Casta hates him, of course. But she's just jealous.'

Casta said nothing. Liss seemed to have forgotten the unfortunate fate of Thulia Iolo, the last suitor that had dared to approach her. But then, she never really believed Casta had had a hand in that. She thought it was an accident. I suspected otherwise.

'So who is it?' I asked.

'Don't you know?'

'I have my suspicions.' I did know, but I also knew she wanted to tell me herself.

She laughed and squirmed, clapped her hands and giggled like a little girl.

'Oh, come on now,' Casta murmured.

'It's Jerima Dew,' Liss announced.

'Jerima Vem's son. Thought so,' I said. Clan Jerima: a powerful merchant family in Veya, into textiles and a little narcotics on the side. Strange choice for a match on my master's part. Clan Caracassa were members of the Turnward Claw Alliance, who were pushing for the continuation of the war against the Gurta. As a manufacturer of battlefield medicines, Ledo profited heftily from conflict. Clan Jerima were in the Folded Wing, who were agitating for peace. They were growing in power as people sickened of the war, but they were the natural opponents of the Turnward Claw Alliance. A Caracassa marriage into a Folded Wing Clan sent mixed signals to the allies of both parties.

I gave her my congratulations, but she became suddenly casual, examining her cracked fingernails. 'Anyway, Ledo thinks it's a good idea, so—'

I knew Liss too well to be wrongfooted by her mercurial temperament.

'What do *you* think?' I asked.

Liss shrugged and made an indefinite noise. 'But won't the ceremony be fun?' she enthused.

'The ceremony!' Casta hissed.

'She's just jealous,' Liss stage-whispered at me.

'You'd turn your back on your own sister!' Casta accused. I realised I'd made a mistake in mentioning the issue. Casta wasn't joking. The mood had turned suddenly ugly.

Liss appealed to me. '*She* goes where she wants! *She* leaves me lonely for turn after turn sometimes. But when *I* do something without *her* she won't have it! She's—'

'Don't try and get Orna on your side!' Casta snapped. 'She's not interested in your whining.'

Liss shrank. 'She's so mean, so mean sometimes,' she said, apparently to herself. 'I don't know how I stand it.'

'Oh, don't.'

'Well, you are.'

'It's yourself I'm saving you from.'

'You're not saving anything, and you can't stop me!'

'She thinks I can't stop her,' Casta said to me.

'She thinks she knows what's best for me!' Liss cried.

'It's been like this ever since she agreed,' Casta said, tossing her hair and glaring away across the club.

'She just can't bear to see me happy,' Liss countered.

'She won't *be* happy,' Casta replied, addressing thin air.

'Well, I won't be lonely any more when she's away,' Liss said, and then burst into tears. Casta, all ill feeling forgotten, immediately hugged her twin and kissed her repeatedly until her tears dried.

Even I was bewildered.

Food arrived and I ate, even though I wasn't hungry, because it was so expensive. Casta was somewhat subdued for a while, but she picked up again soon. It was clear that she still disapproved of Ledo's plan for her sister. Liss, true to form, was either oblivious or pretending to be.

Those two. They existed entirely in their own little world, like most of the Plutarchs and their families. Why was it that the people with power were the only ones licensed to act like children?

Sometimes the aristocracy scared me. I often wondered if we shouldn't be more afraid of our rulers than our enemies.

22

I wait for the next time that Gendak summons me, and we play the usual game of evasions, after which I'm sent back to my cell. He tends to call for me every three or four turns, sometimes later but never sooner. I won't be missed if I duck out for a little while.

The following shift in the forge, I make my move.

The forge is full of places to hide, and I'm an expert in putting myself where no one's likely to look. I swap work detail with someone who has a harder job than me – he jumps at the chance – and then don't turn up for it. There's a lot of workers stirring the sediment pots, enough that my absence goes unnoticed.

Instead I slip into the shadow of a vast, unused vat, chains hanging from it like the dangling fronds of a lichen-tree. From here I can see the door to the Overseer's office. The steps down are zigzagged, obscured to waist-height by a thin metal barrier acting as a banister. It's a small mercy, but I'm thankful for it. There's little chance I'd make it up there otherwise without someone spotting me.

I crouch in my hiding place, watching the nearby guards. They laugh and slander their companions, casting an eye over the forge now and then. I know these men: they're lazy. They really are too secure in their certainty that this place is escape-proof. Their over-confidence is my advantage.

The route to the base of the stairs is cluttered, providing easy cover. Once I'm sure it's safe, I scuttle over. Moving in quick hops, taking my time.

Sweat trickles down the back of my neck. The heat and noise press at me in waves. The screech and clank and holler, the stifling dry air.

I've done the best I can to keep myself clean since I bathed last. Nobody would believe I was a slave, reeking of the prison as I did. It's impossible to be truly clean in this place, but I got the worst of it off.

Of late, I've been bathing with the men in my underwear, scrubbing my clothes and hair, ignoring their hungry glances. For a long time I'd told myself that it wasn't safe to undress in front of the men, but I'd been lying to myself. None of them would dare touch me now. I just wanted to be dirty. Punishing myself. But all that's over.

The door opens, and the Overseer appears. He shuts the door and locks it, puts the key in his pocket. Down the steps he comes in his stately way, a small-minded man over-proud of his authority. There's a guard waiting at the bottom of the steps; it's the young Gurta who accompanied him on the shift when we stole his key. His boasting about all the exciting accidents he witnessed probably landed him with the position for a long time to come. He's regretting it now, I'm guessing.

They greet each other rather formally and move off, leaving the way clear. I scan the smoky landscape around me. A distant guard, not paying attention. No time better than now.

I hurry across the open space, crouched low, watching the guard from the corner of my eye. He scratches the back of his neck. For a few moments, I have that horrible feeling of exposure; I'm certain somebody is going to raise the alarm, someone I haven't even seen, and the game will be over. Then I'm back under cover, safe at the bottom of the steps, shielded from the forge by the metal barrier.

I climb the steps in a low crouch, moving with confidence now. This part is easy. Even if the key doesn't work, I have time to climb back down and take my place in the forge again. The only thing I have to fear is what's beyond that door.

At the top, I can't resist a peek over the edge. It's a stupid risk, but nobody will see the top of my head at this height and in this atmosphere. And it's worth it, just to see the seething, glowing panorama of the forge spread out beneath me, the thin, ordered rivers of molten yellow-white tracing among the hulking black monuments. For a moment, I feel superior: ruler of this place. I've beaten it.

Premature. I try the key and it fits the lock. But it won't turn.

I curse under my breath. Jiggle it, give it another try. It sticks. Now I'm getting worried. I try it again, with greater force. Still nothing.

For want of any better options, I reinsert, try it again, and this time it turns. Tumbling relief in my chest. Some problem with the marriage of key and lock, a misalignment. The key might be unreliable, but it does work.

I open the door a crack and look through. Nobody there. In I go, locking the door behind me. This time it obliges first time. I slip the key back inside my belt, and survey my reward: the Overseer's office.

It's underwhelming at best. Spartan, neat, and dim. Lanterns illuminate a room of bare stone with little ornamentation to speak of. There are scroll cases stacked in a cabinet, and a desk with a half-written letter on it. A row of dirty windows looks over the forge.

There are two doors. One is a supply cupboard, stocked with stationery, old file archives, and random bric-a-brac. Walls and floor are stone. No good. There's a cool draught coming from the other, cutting through the dull heat. That's my way out.

This place is musty and drear, and faintly sad. I briefly wonder what the Overseer's life is like behind his thin façade of dignity, whether he goes to his rooms alone, whether his life is as empty as his surroundings. Then I realise that I don't give a shit.

The draughty door is locked, but there's a key hanging on a peg on the back of it. This is trouble. I can get through, but unless I can lock the door from the outside and replace the key on the peg, they'll know I've been here.

I stare at the door, willing a solution to present itself. Speculatively, I try my key, but it doesn't fit. I take the other key down from the peg and unlock the door, open it a crack and peek out.

Beyond is a side-corridor of rough stone with dying torches choking in their brackets. It's not been cleaned for some time. That's good: a sign that it's rarely used. It terminates at the Overseer's door. There'll be little traffic through here.

I feel a pang of frustration. I could walk out of here now; I could disappear. Perhaps Arachi wouldn't notice the unlocked door. Perhaps.

No. You don't take risks like that. If Arachi raises the alarm, they'll find me, disguise or no disguise.

Besides, I still have to come back. I could leave Nereith and Charn without thinking twice. But I can't leave Feyn. Not if I want to get out of here with my humanity intact.

There has to be a way, but I'm not sure I'll have time to find it. And if I don't go soon, it'll be too late. The Overseer will return, and they'll catch me on the stairs.

I pull the door closed, search the desk and cupboards, looking for a spare key. Not happening.

I have to decide now. Turn back, or commit myself. And while I'm deciding, I notice again the annoying cold draught that chills the back of my neck.

The door to the corridor. There's light at the top. It doesn't sit well in its frame. I can fit my fingers in the gap between the stone and the top of the door.

I've got an idea. But I have to move fast.

I pick out a thread from the hem of my shirt, pulling it to a good length before snapping it off. Next I hurry to one of the lanterns, take off the glass bulb and soak the thread in lantern oil. I found candles when I searched through his desk; I steal one. He won't notice. As I'm tying the thread to the hollow O of the key's bow I move over to the windows and look through. Nobody can see me; I've spent enough time on the other side trying to peer through the shifting layers of smoke and grime to know.

The Overseer has finished his rounds. He's walking back towards the stairs.

I'm calm. Now my course is set, there's nothing I can do about it. I'm used to close scrapes, and I don't panic. You move quicker when you're composed.

Time is really short now. If this doesn't work, I'm finished.

I light the candle from one of the lanterns and then dart into the corridor, where I shut and lock the door. Holding one end of the thread, I push the key over the top of the door, in the centre: directly over the peg. Gently, I begin to lower it.

The smell of lantern oil hangs in the air. I can feel through the thread when the key touches the peg, but touching the peg and getting the fiddly fucking thing to snag are two different matters. The key is lying flat against the door, and the peg is protruding. The key needs to swing outwards, but I don't have any leverage. I grit my teeth, regretting the noise this is going to make; then I shoulder-barge the door. It sends the key swinging away from the rootwood. It clatters against the door on the backswing. An experimental slackening reveals that it's not caught on anything; I'm still holding its weight.

I try again. Align the key so that its bow is brushing against the peg;

barge the door. Still it fails to catch. I could do this for hours and never get a result, or it could happen next try.

Again. The Overseer must be near the top of the stairs now. The noise of the forge will drown out the racket, but as soon as he's inside, he'll hear.

Again. *Come on*, you whorespawn.

Again.

I almost barge it a sixth time before I realise that there's no weight on the thread any more. I let it out a bit, and the key stays where it is. It's on the hook. I've got it.

Yes!

No. A soft tread in the corridor, a rustle of clothes. Someone's heard me. In the office, there is the rattle of a key in the lock. I'm trapped.

But not caught. Not yet. I touch the candle flame to the end of the thread. The flame races up its length and goes out as quickly, burning it to nothing in a flash. It runs over the top of the door and turns the evidence of my achievement into floating motes of carbon. If any shreds of blackened thread still cling to the key, they'll be destroyed when Arachi picks it up.

I hear the door to the forge close and lock, the Overseer's groan as he stretches. The tread comes along the corridor with purpose now; somebody light, walking softly. They must have heard me barge the door. I have nowhere to go. So I snuff out the candle with wet fingers, stuff it into my belt, and I go *up*.

The corridor is just big enough for two people to pass each other. If I brace my feet and hands against the wall, if I stretch, I can climb up. But I need to be flat up against the ceiling to stand any chance of evading whoever's coming.

I brace my hands against the wall and throw my feet out, catching the opposite wall with one, then the other, until I'm precariously balanced above the ground. The rough brick bites into my palms as I walk myself, muscles straining, backwards up the wall until my heels touch the ceiling.

I'm spread-eagled at the top of the corridor, the walls just a fraction too far apart to make this easy. I'm undernourished and out of training. Not sure how long I can hold this.

The source of the footfalls appears just as I've stilled myself, locking my joints as best I can. It's a slave girl. An Eskaran. She's wearing a white dress, embroidered at the sleeves and hem with Gurtan devotional mantras: hymns to the wisdom of the Laws. Sixteen, seventeen at most. Willowy and pretty, her blonde hair tied in a complex bundle behind her head. She passes beneath me without looking up – it's amazing how people never look up – and knocks softly on the door. Four times, slowly, to announce herself as a slave.

There's a short delay, then I hear the key being taken from the peg and slipped into the lock. He hasn't suspected anything, but feeling relief is difficult as my arms are beginning to burn. I begin to run my chants through my head, settling into a light trance state, helping me ignore the demands of my muscles, hardening them in place.

The door opens.

~ I offer to you the apologies of my heart ~ says the slave in flawless Gurtan, making a quick gesture with her hand and ducking slightly. ~ Through my parents and my parents' parents, I am imperfect ~

It's ritual language. The Overseer dismisses it patiently. ~ The kitchens do not have any rock-bat, then? ~

~ Overseer Arachi, it has been retained for the honoured Elder's visit. I pleaded on your behalf, but they would allow me none ~

He smiles indulgently and cups her face with his hand. She's plainly distressed. All her life, she's been taught to serve a master race that she genuinely believes is superior. It's not punishment that scares her, it's the shame of failing.

Her servility makes me furious. Not at her; she doesn't know any better. I'm mad at *them,* the enemy, the people who made her this way. She's young and beautiful and she should be in Veya, or dancing with the boys of her village, anything but this living death. The hate is suddenly overwhelming, boiling through me, unstoppable. A feeling pent up for a lifetime that can flood endlessly but never run dry. It washes away my trance, and I can feel the hurt gathered in my joints, in my shoulders and lower back and all through my limbs. If it wasn't for the time spent working the screens on the slurry-trough, I don't think I'd have had the strength to make it this far. But I can't hold it . . . I can't . . .

~ What else do they have? ~ the Overseer is saying.

~ They have many cuts of lizard, Overseer Arachi. A supply cart arrived recently from the lava plains ~

~ Do they have fintail? ~

~ Master, they are preparing a stew of fintail and wrack-cap as we speak ~

~That sounds delicious. Bring some to me ~

~ For the love of Maal, I obey ~

She draws another gesture in the air with her hand, then bows and puts her palms over her face as if veiling herself. She leaves, pauses, looks back.

~ Yes? ~ the Overseer asks.

~ Master, I heard noises. As if someone was knocking at your door ~

~ Well, there is no one here now ~ he replies.

~ Of course. It is my mistake. Many apologies ~

With that, she departs. The Overseer stands in the doorway, watching her go. Maybe something lascivious there, maybe the affection of a man for a pet. I can't think. My arms and legs are trembling. Agony digs jagged claws into my shoulders, buttocks, thighs. My fingers are going numb and my hands feel like they're going to rip from my wrists.

Go inside, you bitch-fed catamite, or I'll come down there and kill you!

It's an empty threat. He dies, our escape is ruined. But it gives me the strength to hang on for the grinding, vast moments until he steps back and closes the door behind him.

I swing my legs under me and drop soundlessly to the floor. A dozen monstrous cramps hit me simultaneously, and it's all I can do not to groan as my tortured muscles howl at their abuse. But all pain passes, and this is no exception. I'm left panting and sore on the floor of the corridor, but I'm alive, and I'm *out.*

When I'm capable, I get to my feet and touch the folded package of servants' clothes, bound flat against my back, checking it's still there.

So far, so good. But we're a long way from freedom yet.

21

Fortune favours me. Overseer Arachi's office is buried among a small tangle of badly lit and narrow corridors. I try the first door I come to, eager to avoid the returning slave. It's a storeroom, piled with dusty sacks of spores, pots of dried spice and barrels of wine. There is a torch in the bracket, but it's unlit. Perfect.

I close the door behind me. The line of light around the edge is just enough to see by. In the near-darkness, I strip and undo the parcel of clothes. It's a red dress, made of light material, the sleeves and collar decorated with gold thread. I slip it on and adjust it. The fit is good. Nereith even had them spray it with scented water in the laundry room. Nice touch. It's a little crumpled, but it's been well folded and the material doesn't crease easily. Gravity should iron out the rest.

I have to keep a low profile wearing this thing. There are a lot of new slaves arriving in advance of the Elder's visit, so strangers won't be suspected, but if the slave who owns this dress should catch me, it's over. That aside, my presence should remain unnoticed. What other possible reason could an Eskaran woman have to be in a Gurta fort, unless she was a slave? Also, my age gives me a certain seniority which should deflect any casual probing from the younger girls. Since slaves are exclusively taken when very young, it will be assumed that I have been one all my life.

Disguises work, in my experience, because people are not naturally suspicious. The thought of a prisoner walking among them is too far-fetched to consider; but if I should draw attention to myself, then the ruse will unravel.

I have slippers too. As I put them on, I notice that my nails need clipping.

Suddenly I'm struck by an absurd stab of nostalgia. For the parties, the balls, the concerts of the aristocracy; for Casta and Liss and all their bizarre and eccentric friends; for the lights of Veya. Wearing something nice, being even partially clean, leaves me with a desperate longing for home and for the life I had.

I can't believe how low I've fallen, that the faintest of luxuries is so precious to me. I take a breath, steady myself. Better. I bundle up my worn and stained black clothes and hide them in a corner of the room, then I untie my newly washed hair and comb it out with my fingers. Should be passable, at least. Gurta dress their slaves well and they like them neat: a slave's appearance reflects on her master. I'm a little ragged, but it'll have to do.

I open the door and step out, my stomach fluttering. I adopt a confident bearing as I walk, putting purpose into my steps. I'm a slave on her way to do something important. Don't bother me.

I walk through cramped corridors of bare stone, lit by torches. I pass more storage rooms, disused and cobwebbed. This is a neglected corner of the fort, then, little visited. The Overseer's task must really be a thankless one if his office is back here. I wonder who he offended in the past, whose sister he dishonoured, which of the Laws he broke.

I come to a door at the end of the corridor. My intuition tells me that the fort proper lies beyond: I'm leaving the safety of these forgotten thoroughfares. I open the door, step through, and I'm immediately accosted with a sharp demand for attention.

~ Slave! ~

Though my heart jumps, the surprise doesn't show on the outside. I calmly halt and turn. There's a young Gurta scholar approaching me, long hair framing narrow, sly features. A velvet robe sways around his ankles. I suddenly remember Nereith's warning about the complex rituals of the slave girls, their particular Gurta dialect. *If you're caught, they'll see through you in an instant.*

I feel a quick tremble of panic run through me. Then it's too late to do anything about it, and I have to act.

I sketch the Form Of Abject Subservience with my hand, bobbing down a little on my knees and ankles as I do so. ~ Ruler Of My Will, I exist to meet your command ~ I breathe, eyes lowered.

He peers at me closely. ~ I don't recognise you ~ he says, but the tone is curious rather than suspicious.

~ I arrived only last turn, Master. It is my honour to attend the dignitaries arriving for the Elder's visit ~

His authority asserted, he dismisses my reply. ~ I sent one of your companions to fetch me fresh ink and paper. She hasn't returned yet ~ he says, indignantly. ~ My work can't be delayed like this ~

~ I am shamed by my sister's failure ~ I tell him. ~ I shall investigate immediately. You will not be delayed any longer ~

~ See that I'm not ~ he snaps, and walks away without waiting for the Affirmation of Obedience.

I head the other way. My pulse is gradually slowing. I have no intention of attending to his problem. He's simply impatient. Whichever slave he charged with the task would rather cut her own hand off than fail him; I've little doubt that she's already at his door, waiting for his return.

But my disguise worked. I'd hoped it would, but I'd still had grave doubts. Maybe I wouldn't remember the rituals, maybe my dialect was rusty, maybe things had changed in the twenty-eight years since my rescue.

Impersonating a slave isn't so hard when you used to be one.

Confident now, I begin to search. I've primed myself with the names of various scholars and dignitaries that I learned from the guards, so I can concoct false errands if anyone questions me. And I can always pretend to be lost: I am new here, after all. But I found out a long time ago that the best way to stay unmolested is to appear busy: most people won't interrupt you if they think you're in the midst of a task for someone else. So I balance my demeanour between stridency and submission, and I begin to scout out the world beyond my prison.

Farakza isn't the height of Gurta luxury. It's a fort: crude and bare. I've served in places of embarrassing opulence, towers in the sky like frozen paint-drop splashes, one within another, reaching higher and higher and dotted with lights. There, everything was marble; golden ewers glittered by the side of steaming baths; circular libraries rose, balcony upon balcony. I remember attending music recitals that made my skin prickle with the emotions they inspired. They have such an eye for beauty, these people; yet for every admirable aspect of their society, there's an ugly one. Cultured in some ways and backward in others. They both crush and adore their women. They write poems and lays of wrenching beauty and yet they are the most savage and brutal and callous people I've ever known.

For all that this is a functional place, some areas have been built with a little more elegance. These are the scholars' quarters: studies, bedchambers and tiny libraries. Here they're more given to flourishes: decorative panelling, smart cornices, fluted stone jambs. There are shinestones in sculpted brackets, held in the hands of stone Elders.

I start to see people in the corridors: scholars, guards, slaves. It's the slaves who worry me most. Running into the owner of this dress would be bad luck, but I'm afraid I might meet the *zaze*, the slave matriarch. As a new slave, I should be reporting to her for assignment and not wandering the corridors. If I'm stopped, awkward questions could be asked.

Safer to avoid the slaves altogether. I'll not stay in the dormitory, and I'll keep out of their communal areas. They'll assume I'm the personal slave of a visiting dignitary and that I sleep in their quarters, or even as their bed-partner. In a society where men's urges towards their own women are strictly repressed, Eskaran slaves are a valuable commodity. No laws of propriety apply. They can do what they like.

My first order of business is to explore the area around the Overseer's office. Getting the others out unseen is going to be the hardest part of this whole affair. Whatever route takes us away, it has to be quick and close. There's no disguise they can use.

Opening random doorways is a dangerous way to explore: slaves don't barge into rooms. So I'm forced to rely on observation, sticking to the less travelled routes, not straying too far. The difference in corridor styles – narrow and winding compared to wide and straight – leads me to believe that much of this fort has been built around an older structure. The older corridors form the shell of the prison, and they're dark and tight and will suit me well. The newer sections surrounding them are the domain of the scholars, and not too heavily trafficked. There's little need for guards here, and scholars spend a lot of time engrossed in their work.

Not too far from the Overseer's office, I find a door. Its very innocuousness attracts me. It's tucked into an alcove, small and hidden. I barely notice it as I pass. Behind it I find a tight spiral staircase leading down into darkness. Taking a lantern from its bracket in the corridor outside, I risk investigation, wondering what unlikely excuses I might give if anybody should catch me.

At the bottom is another door. Old and heavy and locked. I listen at it, and hear nothing. There's the faintest trace of light beneath it. I put the lantern aside and press my face to the floor to try and see under. Dusty. Nobody has been here for a long time.

Just for an instant, there is a breeze, soft and warm, like breath. Then it's gone.

I can't see anything through the crack. But that tiniest stirring of air against my face excites me. That's air from outside.

I hold the lantern up to the lock and examine it. It's basic and crude, made for a large and simple key. Give me two long hairpins and a little time and I can have it open.

Hairpins, then. I want to know what's behind that door.

Not long afterward, I find all the fresh air I want.

At the top of a staircase there's a doorway to a balcony. I hesitate for an instant before going through, weighing the dangers: a slave shouldn't be seen loitering. But there's no real choice in the end. Out there is the world that I have been shut away from, and shut *myself* away from. Gentle wind teases my face. I walk to the parapet and look out.

After so long hemmed in by the walls of the prison, the moment is magnificent. The cavern isn't anything special by normal standards – in fact, it's fairly barren – but I drink the view in all the same.

The balcony is on the flank of a tower, looking out over the battlements of the fort. Farakza stands on an uneven island of bare stone, scarred and rucked with age, in the midst of a slow river of spume rock. The ground around the fort has been flattened by the power of an Elder, stripping away the cover for two hundred spans. Anyone trying to cross that would be seen and killed. That presents a problem.

Manta-like shapes float on the thermals above the river, membranous wings stretched between rayed fingers of chitin, poisonous tails trailing. Beyond the river, scrub fungi and boilstone stalagmites have begun to reclaim the land. Hardened lichens grind through their mammoth task of breaking up solid stone into mineral-laden dust, and thorny plants rise on the river bank, leaching sustenance from the sluggish flow. I can't see to the far side of the cave: Farakza's lights are too bright. They drown out the faint glow of phosphorescent algae, the sparkle of tiny insects, the shine of plankton in pools.

The sense of space is exhilarating. I know Feyn would laugh at that, as one who lives fearlessly beneath the sky, but to me existence has limits: the roof of a cavern, the wall of a chamber, the length of a rockworm-bored tunnel. Existence is full of holes and passageways, drilled uncountable ages ago by vast beasts who have left nothing but their fossilised skeletons. This moon was hollowed by their industry. Long after they were gone, we descended, hiding from life above.

I'm assaulted by a strange feeling of claustrophobia. I feel trapped. I've *always* been trapped. Not by my surroundings but by circumstance. Enslaved at five, Bondswoman by ten, Cadre by seventeen and mother by twenty. I've prowled to the limits of my leash – I know every inch of Veya and I've been all over Eskara – but I'm always constrained. Loyalty, affiliation, duty: I hold them as virtues but they bind me like tomb wrappings.

Something like panic threatens. It comes fast, springing on me from nowhere. I want to get away. To scream and run in terror, in any direction, I don't care which. Not just from here, but from everything. My needs, my ties, my lack of choices. And even as I think that, I know that there's nothing I can do but continue on my course.

As fast as it came, it's gone. I'm left dizzied. Must be the excitement of being outside for the first time in I don't know how long. And yet I sense it's only lurking, not departed. My emotions have been unreliable since Rynn's death: they come in jags and spikes, shocking me.

I look along the battlements at the towers of Farakza. A few guards patrol the walls, but nobody's watching me. The fort is old enough that it's crumbling at the edges. It's brutal and functional and simple. It's seen wars. Right now we're far behind enemy lines, on the Gurta side of the Borderlands; but once this was a bastion against ancient invaders. Probably us.

I walk to the other end of the balcony as it follows the curve of the tower. Now I can see the shinehouse that rises above the fort. A narrow tower of stone, topped with a segmented bulb of magnifying lenses. Within lies a huge shinestone, pale light diffusing across the cavern, flattening the shadows to a cower. It's a small and basic affair, not like the five enormous, ornate shinehouses that illuminate Veya, but it does its job. It's a little dim now. The Elder will recharge it during the ceremony of his departure.

The yard below is more interesting. From where I am I can see a wide, flagged space directly inside the main gates of the fort. Buildings and stables crowd around the edges. A pair of chila are pulling a cart through the gate as I watch; they chirrup and toss their heads as they come. They've got pug faces with small, vicious teeth, brown sinewy bodies, long front legs that used to be wings when they were young. But they're strong, fast at a run and they stand shoulder-high to a man. I've never liked chila. They smell horrible and they remind me too much of enormous, land-bound bats.

The cart is met by guards, a few casual questions are asked, and then the yard-workers move in to unload the cargo. Suddenly, the yard is aswarm. Doors to storage silos are hauled open. Dainty menservants appear and begin to direct operations. The guards stand back and watch.

The preparations for the Elder's arrival are controlled chaos. I overheard two scholars talking about the other dignitaries who have arrived for the event: generals whose troops are drilling nearby, local Lawkeepers and so on. It must be an Elder of some importance, to generate this kind of interest. I'm almost sorry I won't be around. I'd have a go at killing him if I thought I could get away with it.

It would be so easy to leave here now. On my own, with this disguise, an escape would be child's play. I could bluff my way onto a carriage. Once beyond the river, disappearing would be simplicity itself.

But I daren't stay on the balcony any longer. An idle slave rouses suspicion. Reluctantly I turn my back and return to the closed-in world that, just for a few moments, I dreamed I was free of.

Finding something to pick the lock on my mystery door turns out to be harder than I thought. Hairpins are in short supply in a fort, and I've always found they're the only decent substitute for the specialised lockpicks I'd otherwise have with me. Slaves don't wear ornaments or make-up of any kind: they're supposed to be neat and plain. That leaves the Gurta women, and the only Gurta women here are the Entwined of the dignitaries.

I hear the tolling of the bell, louder here than below. By now my shift in the forge is long over, and no alarms have been raised. It seems I've not been missed. The tension inside me ratchets down a notch.

Buoyed by this, I decide to push my luck and talk to a slave. She gives me directions to the quarters where the dignitaries are housed. The arrangements are makeshift at best, and aside from a slightly increased slave presence, it's hard to tell the difference between this and the scholars' area.

I make myself look busy until I catch sight of one of the dignitaries leaving his room, his Entwined on one arm. He's middle-aged, muscular for a Gurta, hair plaited and sporting a white beard and moustache. A general, no doubt. The woman wears layered robes in an immaculate array of colours, and a fantastically impractical arrangement of jewelled flowers in her blonde hair. She goes masked, as they all do; the mask is white, brushed with yellows and pinks. Only her eyes are visible behind the veneer. Gurta women don't show their real selves in public, but they put a lot of effort into illusion.

Once they're out of sight, I slip into the room. The door isn't locked: there's no need. It wouldn't ever enter their heads that a slave would steal from them.

I walk past the open trunks of clothes and raid the vanity table. In a drawer I find an assortment of hair ornaments, including several sets of pins. I pick two simple steel ones, like slender knitting needles. If they're missed, then they're not valuable enough to suggest a theft.

I walk boldly out of the room just as another slave is coming in to tidy: the same blonde girl who I saw attending to the Overseer earlier. She automatically pardons herself and I sweep past without a word of explanation. I'm an older slave, even if I am a stranger. She defers, but I feel her puzzled look following me down the corridor.

I head back to the mystery door, taking care to avoid the Overseer's office nearby. The chances are slim, but he might recognise me from the forge. By the light of a lantern I borrow from the corridor above, I fiddle at the lock with my hairpins. It's clumsy work, and it takes me a while to get the bends in the hairpins just right, but eventually I hear the click I've been hoping for. Leaving the lantern at the foot of the stairs, I push the door open.

The room is unoccupied, and has been for a long time. Even with the warm draught slipping in through the broken window, there's a sense of desertion. Desultory cobwebs drape the faded junk pushed against the walls. Chipped clay crockery, ancient practice dummies for the soldiers, bits of disassembled furniture. A room where things end up, condemned to be forgotten by the hoarder who thought they might eventually have a use.

The window is narrow, but not so narrow that I couldn't get through it. It faces out into darkness, but when I peer closer I realise that it's the corner of a yard, hidden in the angle of the walls where no light reaches. The window has been shattered and a piece has fallen away. I open it and crane out. It's about fifteen spans from the ground. A person could drop that distance if they hung from their fingertips.

I can see out into the yard now, where torches burn and the light of the shinehouse is not impeded by other buildings. It takes me a moment to realise that it's the same yard as the one I was looking down on earlier: the yard in front of the main gate.

Now I've got a plan.

20

I sleep in my underwear on the stone floor of the junk room, so as not to crease my dress. I was never very prissy about comfort, even before I got used to sleeping in a cave, and my ribs and thighs have toughened from lying on my side on the hard ground. At least it's warm. The river of spume rock heats the cavern well; either that, or we're deeper beneath the surface than I thought.

I wake to near-total darkness. I had to replace the lantern in case it was missed, and I didn't want to bring light into the room for fear that it would be seen from the yard. I dress and arrange my hair by feel. Not easy, but the way it falls naturally is good enough.

I spend the time until my return making preparations. I've been counting the bells, even in my sleep. Simple awareness training. I have to hope they won't change my group's shift to work the forge, or I'll be noticeably out of place on my return. It's a real likelihood, given the randomness of our schedule.

I find a vantage point and spend most of the turn watching the comings and goings of the carts and wagons in the courtyard. The traffic is sporadic, but there's almost always one or two there, being unloaded or waiting while their drivers water their chila. They're in no hurry. The guards chat to the drivers, the workers chat to each other instead of unloading, everyone smokes. Small stacks of crates have accumulated, waiting for someone to take them away. I guess they're machine parts and weapons from the forge. Our work, ready to be picked up and taken to the front to be used against our people. I wonder what other prison industries they have going here.

By the time I leave, I'm satisfied that getting out of the main gate on a cart is possible. Nobody checks carts at the gate; they do it on the bridge over the river, where there's a wider thoroughfare. The yard is cluttered and carts are left unattended for long periods of time. I'm sure that, by the time the Elder gets here, this will all be immaculately ordered and clear, but until then, it's a mess. That helps me a great deal.

Of course, I remind myself, getting out of the gates is the easy part. Beyond them, there's no way to sneak through that flat area surrounding the fort, and stowing on a cart won't get us over the bridge. Also, how do I move my little group from the Overseer's office to the junk room without anyone spotting us? It's only a short way, but to make it there without coming across anyone at all? We'd have to be lucky. I don't want to rely on luck; that gets people killed.

As to that, I have an idea. It'll take a few more minor preparations, but they're not a problem. I consider stealing preserved food from storage and scrounging up some packs, but there's no point. We couldn't carry the extra weight, not with the route I intend to take. We'll just have to rely on what we can find as we go. That's Feyn's job.

I'd get a map if I could, but the opportunity just doesn't come and it's too dangerous to try. Still, I don't like trusting Nereith to see us home. Something tells me he could turn on us in an instant. His connection to Silverfish unsettles me.

Twice on my travels I have scholars or guards demanding tasks of me, and once a horny chirurgeon tries to commandeer my body for a while. Each time I beg them not to interrupt my task for General Daraka. I've no idea who General Daraka is, but dropping that name makes them back off fast. I'd heard the guards speak of him with fear and reverence in the forge, and it seems his reputation is well known.

I'm almost done when I hit a snag.

It happens as I'm emerging from the door at the top of the spiral stairs leading to my hideout. I've just shut it and walked away when I hear footfalls in the corridor coming towards me. I don't know how I know – it's the same intuition that tells you someone is going to cross the street and talk to you – but I get a bad feeling about them. It's too late to turn around and go back, too late to do anything without looking suspicious. So I keep walking.

It's a slave in a cobalt blue dress. She's a little younger than me, pretty in a curious sort of way, the kind of face that's interesting but you can't work out why. Taut with carefully suppressed anger. It deepens as she sees me, and I realise who this is.

~ That's *my* dress, you filthy thief! ~ she snarls in her masters' language. Slaves are forbidden to speak Eskaran even between themselves.

~ You must be mistaken ~ I reply calmly, but something is sinking inside me and it keeps on sinking.

She doesn't even hear me. ~ Ellya told me she'd seen a new slave scurrying around in my clothes ~ she says, her face close to mine. ~ Your master too poor to buy you something decent? What'd you do, steal it from the laundry pile? ~

I try once again, feigning surprise. ~ But this is *my* dress. Perhaps yours is similar, but I don't thi— ~

She slaps me. Hard. ~ Slut! Don't even try it. Take it off, *now!* ~

I don't move. There are tears in my eyes. She thinks it's because of the slap, or perhaps it's the useless remorse of a caught thief; she's wrong on both counts.

~ I'm sorry ~ I tell her.

~ It's no good being so— ~

I kill her. A single hard strike to a nerve point behind her ear, fast and vicious. She drops, dead before she's hit the floor.

'I'm sorry,' I tell her again.

I drag her body a few dozen spans to the door and pull her down the stairs into the junk room. I cry the whole way. Not for her, even though she was an innocent; and not for me, because I had necessity on my side. I cry because I'm so fucking frustrated and angry at this war, this endless war and the horror it brings. I cry because I'm in a prison where they dissect and experiment on their inmates while out there my son risks his life for a futile cause. And I cry because this woman didn't know any better than to be a servant of the race that kidnapped her as a child, and in the end I had to kill her for it. There was no possibility of bargaining. She'd have sold me out in a heartbeat.

I hate this world. All my life I've managed to ignore that, to shelve it away in the dusty recesses of the least-visited corner of my mind; but it's been with me ever since I was enslaved, and I'm not sure it'll ever go away. Since Rynn died, everything changed. Like everybody, I've always existed in a cradle spun from deceptions of my own making. They seem so flimsy and pointless now. Things are clearer as they fade. Simpler.

I have to get back to my son. That's all.

★

With everything ready and the body of the slave safely stashed in a chest in the junk room, it's time to break back into the forge and resume my role as a prisoner. I've fashioned a hook on a sturdy length of thread to fish the key off the peg for my return. I'm expecting it to be a whole lot easier than getting it *on* to the peg was. There won't be time to pick it, not with the crude tools I have to hand.

I head back to the Overseer's office. The dim corridors surrounding it are, as ever, almost empty. I play it extra careful though, just in case I run into the blonde slave who attends the Overseer. I guess that she's the Ellya who told on me. She recognised the dress when she saw me coming out of the dignitary's room. Best not to meet her again. I don't want to have to kill her too.

The next stop is the storage room where I left my clothes. I carefully refold my slave attire and leave it here, then pull on my gear. It feels filthy against my skin, but it's familiar. I've fought dozens of battles in these clothes, stolen gems and lives and secrets. Finally I tie my hair up with a length of black ribbon.

I'm back to my old self again.

A short creep later, I'm standing outside the Overseer's door, listening. It's a risk, but I can't think of any other way to do it. I know by the bells when the shifts stop and start, but without a pocket-watch it's hard to estimate when the Overseer will leave his office to make his rounds, and I can't chance missing it. If anyone comes, or if the Overseer comes out . . .

Nothing to be done. So I wait. He shuffles things about and coughs, occasionally opening a drawer. But luck is on my side and my timing is good. I've been there only a short time when I hear him unlocking the door to the forge. The growl and hiss of that choking, seething world swells and fades, and then he's locked it behind him and he's gone.

Now I have to get in. It turns out, unexpectedly, to be easier than I thought. I've just taken the hook and thread out of my pocket when habit makes me check the keyhole. He's left the key in the door on the other side. I almost laugh out loud. It seems our Overseer is more absent-minded than I gave him credit for. Quickly, I take off my shirt, slide it under the door, and poke the key through with one of my stolen hairpins. The key falls onto the shirt and I pull it back, the key with it. I open the door and I'm in.

The office is as drab as it was when I left it. I don't waste time. Locking the door behind me, I shuck my shirt back on and do it up, then take out the key Charn made and, keeping low, I open the door to the forge.

A billow of heat and dirty air greets me: the forge's welcome home. Suddenly I'm struck by the absurdity of giving up this chance of an easy escape. My slave's disguise won't be any use by the time I return. Sooner or later the woman I killed will be missed, Ellya will talk, and suspicions will be raised. But not for a while. If I go now, I can get away. It would be simple.

At the top of the metal stairs, crouching behind the barrier that shields me from sight, I very nearly turn back. Every sensible part of my brain tells me to do it, and listening to sense over passion has kept me alive in the past.

But I don't. I tell myself it's because I've made a deal, but that's not it at all.

Close and lock, stash the key in my belt, down the stairs. Staying low, unseen. I reach the bottom of the stairs and the only guards there are looking into the forge, watching the workers. It's a short dash to cover, and from there it's simple. I begin to recognise some of the prisoners and I know I've got the right shift.

Not long afterward I emerge from the shadows of the machinery next to the furnaces, where Nereith is shovelling fuel. He sees me, makes no reaction. Hands me an extra shovel. I get to work. None of the others say a word.

I'm back. But not for long.

19

Next time I meet Gendak, things get nasty.

I know that something's wrong when I see his face, even before I spot the chirurgeon standing in the room. There's another Gurta here too, older than Gendak, hair silver grey, skin dry and cracked around his rheumy eyes. He's dressed expensively, and regards me as if I were a particularly vile insect. A scribe lurks nearby, his quill hovering ready.

The guards strap me in tight, as always, but a dreadful sense of foreboding grows in me as they check my bindings.

This will be my last visit. After this, I'll be gone. The Elder is coming next turn; the guards talk about nothing else. I can only hope that chance isn't going to be so cruel as to stop me now.

Then it occurs to me. Maybe they know about the escape. But by then it's too late. I've been secured, and the guards have left.

~ They let their women fight and die in their wars ~ the old man croaks. ~ Disgusting ~

~ Very few, Magister ~ Gendak replies. ~ This one is exceptional ~

~ She is exceptional only in that her conduct is even more shameful than most of her kind ~ the Magister snaps.

Gendak is clearly cowed. His expression is uncertain, remorseful. He doesn't say a word, but he looks at me, and it's like he's begging me not to blame him for what's to come.

I don't like this.

The chirurgeon is preparing a spike. I can see through the glass that it's full of some kind of liquid. Those bastards have drugged me twice already; there won't be a third time. I begin to turn my mind inward, furling it closed, concentrating. A lifetime of discipline has given me exceptional control over my body, including the ability to resist and eventually neutralise most poisons. It's one of the harder techniques of chua-kîn training, but it's come in useful in my line of work.

~ Your methods are entirely too gentle ~ the Magister tells Gendak. ~ She has been playing for time ~

~ I was gaining her trust ~ he protests. ~ Such methods are slower but yield better results ~

~ Nonsense ~ he says. ~ She'll trick you, lie, betray you if she can. It's in their nature ~

Well, at least he got *that* right.

The spike is inserted into my inner elbow, and the drug spreads. It's gentle, insidious: it doesn't burn but it soothes. I can't entirely suppress the effects but I can stave the worst off as long as I keep my chants going. My body is working frantically to cleanse me, defying the drug's hold on my system.

~ Give it a moment to work ~ says the chirurgeon, as he leaves. ~ Then she'll tell you anything you want to know ~

So that's it. A concoction to loosen my tongue. Well, fuck you for not having the guts to just kill me, because this won't *work, and you'll never get another chance.*

Knowing what it is, I can concentrate on negating its effects. These kind of potions create a soporific blanket, putting the victim into a hypnotic and suggestible state. But my mind is anchored now, and though I feel like I'm floating in a dream, my thoughts are still clear enough to make out.

~ Ask her ~ the Magister demands of Gendak. The guards stand by, watching me closely.

He leans in, wets his lips, speaks. 'What is the name of your master?'

'Plutarch Nathka Caracassa Ledo, Magnate of Clan Caracassa, member of the Turnward Claw Alliance,' I slur. The words slip out past my teeth with frightening ease. I tell myself he already knows. This is only a warm-up.

'Explain your duties as Cadre.'

The scribe writes in the background; I can hear the scratch of his nib. I wonder what Gendak's getting at. We've been over all this. 'Whatever my master requires of me. Information . . . sabotage . . . theft. Assassination.'

'Did you ever act as his bodyguard?'

'Caydus or Jyirt are his bodyguards. But . . . sometimes I do it too. When they need . . . At functions and parties . . . he prefers the women there then . . . me and Vala and Quaday.'

'And you are loyal?'

'I'm a Bondswoman,' I say.

He glances at the Magister, then back to me.

'I'm going to say a name. You tell me if you have heard it before.'

I nod. My head lolls, not entirely faked.

'The name is Belek Aspa.'

The faintest tickle of recollection, but so distant that I can't hope to remember. I shake my head.

'You have never heard mention of this name?' he persists. 'Your master has never spoken it while you have been nearby? He trusts you, he would not fear to discuss secret matters in front of you.'

Now I'm curious. Enough to risk a query. 'Who's Belek Aspa?'

'I am asking the questions,' Gendak says.

And he does. He asks me directly about the size of the Eskaran forces, about my masters' intentions concerning the war, about chthonomancers and their Blackwings and how they power their craft, about Craggens and Ya'yeen and how they integrate with our society, about the mines and our technology and weapons manufacture. He asks me about our attitudes and beliefs towards the Gurta, he asks about fortifications in the Borderlands. He asks about the squabbles of the Plutarchs and the sway of politics. But I get the impression that the Magister lost interest the moment I said I'd never heard of Belek Aspa, and indeed he's soon obviously bored.

I'm grilled by Gendak endlessly, and I lie over and over again, giving him false locations, reinforcing myths, feigning ignorance. It's stunning what they don't know about us; almost as appalling as what the average Eskaran doesn't know about them. The scribe takes it all down. I enlighten them not one bit, and yet when they're finished they think they've gained the deepest of insights, a view into the heart of their enemy. The drug has been entirely cleansed from me by now, and my head is clear again.

The Magister leaves with a triumphant look at Gendak, and his scribe follows him. Gendak sits heavily in his chair, his pale grey eyes full of sorrow. We're alone. I'm not sure what to expect from him now.

'I did not want it to be this way,' he says. 'This was not my intention.'

I don't reply.

'I'm a good man, Orna,' he tells me, and there's a note of pleading in his voice. 'I'm a man of peace and learning. I wanted you to see that. I do not imagine you ever will, now.'

And still I don't answer. And I won't, either. Does he want sympathy from me? Understanding? Is he asking me to absolve him? Not going to happen. Because he might very well be a good man, he might have a noble heart and be learned and compassionate, he might have sons and daughters and he might love them and he might genuinely want to reach me; but he's still a fucking Gurta under all of that, so as far as I'm concerned, I'd like to bludgeon him to death with his own jawbone.

'You'll meet the Elder soon,' he says, almost to himself, as he gets up and makes for the door to let the guards in. 'You might consider that an honour.'

Perhaps he supposes I'm too groggy to remember his comment. Perhaps he genuinely believes I don't know what will happen. But I think this is his way of saying goodbye. I've heard the rumours. I know what kind of honour he means.

They're done with me now: they think they've milked me dry. I'll join the squalling freaks that the prisoners speak of, chained in the depths of the prison. One of the Elder's living experiments. A Cadre woman for him to play with.

Next turn, they'll come for me. If I'm not gone by then, I'll face the worst of all fates.

I'm taken straight from there to the food hall. They've recently started feeding us before our shifts in the forge instead of halfway through or afterward. Another one of their random and annoying changes meant to divulge some insight into our behaviour or metabolisms or whatever. I have no idea what their real purpose is, or if there's a purpose at all, and I don't care. By next turn I hope to never have to think of it again.

I sit with Feyn, as usual. He knows something's up. I tell him about the interrogation. Charn comes over and sits down, tearing at a hank of lichen-bread with his teeth. A moment later, Nereith also joins us, sensing a conversation he doesn't want to miss. Their new closeness with Feyn and me has been noted by their companions.

'Time we cleared a few things up,' Charn says.

'Like what?'

'Like you haven't even told us the details of this plan of yours yet, and the Elder's coming next turn, and that's our time, right?' He's been worrying at this particular subject ever since I got back from my trip outside. Every time I put him off it frustrates him more. 'You think we ought to know what we're doing, since you're asking us to risk our lives?'

'I'm not asking you to do anything. Stay if you want,' I reply.

'You know what I mean,' he snarls, poking a finger at me. 'Take me, for instance. Surrounded by guards. Can't even go for a piss break without an escort. How you planning on getting me out of there without anyone noticing?'

'It's covered,' I assure him.

'You *said* that, so why the secrecy?'

I fix him with a level glare. 'Because there's four lives here at stake, including mine, and I've lived for a long time by not trusting anyone. Now I'll tell you all what to do just before next turn's shift, and it'll all run smoothly.'

'You believe that one of us would betray the others?' Feyn enquired.

'Could, not would. I'm not taking the chance.'

'And yet we have to trust *you*,' Charn sulks.

'I'm the one with the plan,' I tell him equably.

He gets up and goes back to his own table, where his welcome is muted. They're not so fond of him any more.

Nereith glances over at him, and back to me. 'I'm very interested to hear how you intend to solve that little problem he just mentioned.' He grins. 'Unless, of course, you're not.'

'You're not solving it?' Feyn asks me.

Nereith explains. He likes to show off how smart he is. 'It's impossible to get Charn out the same way we're going. As a blacksmith, he's too well guarded. He served his purpose, and now we're leaving him behind.'

Feyn looks at me, black eyes calm. The Khaadu's got me.

'This turn the fort is in chaos,' I tell Feyn. 'Last-minute preparations.

By the time the Elder arrives, most of the chaos will be over. We're not going to wait until the next shift. We're going now.'

'You really are quite ruthless sometimes, Orna,' Nereith says, a hint of admiration in his voice.

'Shouldn't have tried to rape me, should he?' I reply with a shrug, and go back to my food.

34

Heat, shadows, hard breath. He pushed against me amid a shifting landscape of bedclothes. The little whimpers I made had long ceased to be fake. I'd given him one climax already but I was building unstoppably toward another, and this one would be the real thing. This bastard knew what he was doing. I hated him for that. I hated him for making me enjoy it.

We came to a gasping, shuddering halt together, and I held him close so I wouldn't have to look at him. He stroked my hair as I shivered in his arms. Afterward, there would be the ugly wash of guilt, the poisonous self-hatred. But for now, just for this moment, there was only exquisite post-orgasmic sensitivity and the feel of his thin, muscled body against mine.

Thankfully, he wasn't one of those that liked to hold their women as they slept. Alcohol and sex combined to put him out only minutes after we finished. I lay next to him for an hour until I was sure he was deep under, then I slipped gradually out from beneath the covers.

The chill air of the city settled against my skin, raising goose-pimples. Slats of light, thrown from the nearby shinehouse, stretched across small piles of discarded clothes. It was near the end of the third seg, and the streets were quiet beyond the shuttered windows.

Naked, I padded across the room and out into the corridor beyond. The apartment was silent and still. Expensive sculptures stared blindly into the gloom. I found the door to his study, opened it and went inside.

He had carelessly left the files I needed in an unlocked cabinet. Perhaps he thought the guard on the apartment door was security enough for him. Perhaps years of being the accountant to a crimelord had made him think of himself as untouchable. Well, whichever: it saved me looking for the key, or going back for the lockpicks hidden in the heels of my designer shoes.

One thing I liked about accountants: they were meticulous. They kept records. They liked to know where every last scrap of money went. Take a safehouse, for instance. The kind of place where a crimelord might hide somebody. Safehouses cost money. It didn't take me long to find three addresses in the city. My target was staying in one of them.

I headed to the bathroom, flushed the toilet, and then returned to bed. I'd rather have left then, but I didn't want to do anything that would make him in the least suspicious of me. I was just a woman he picked up in a bar. He'd probably want to fuck again when he woke – he seemed like the type – and I'd act the obliging slut once more. Then I'd be gone, leaving promises to call on him, and I'd never see him again unless it was to cut his throat. I'd dearly have loved to do that. Not for making me cheat on my husband. But for making me *like* it.

It was always cold in Mal Eista. The city had a bite in the air. The light possessed a sharper edge than in Veya, chill and bright. Steam rose from vents and lakes and lungs.

I sat in a café, sipping at a mug of hot, syrupy sweetroot, eyes unfocused as I swam in thought. I was wrapped up in a fur-lined coat and hat, warmed by a nearby wrought-metal brazier. Beyond the forecourt, the alley was crowded with shoppers. Restaurant windows glowed with firelight; inside, men and women talked animatedly over their meals. Lichen-trees stood stiff and skeletal in rows. White bats darted across the rooftops of stern, imposing apartment blocks.

I'd spent too long here, tracking this man. It was beginning to feel more like home than Veya did. The brief time I'd spent with my family in the subsurface caverns seemed a lifetime ago, but the resentment at my situation had not faded one bit. Unworthy as it made me feel, I was bitter at being sent here. I knew it was my duty to obey the Clan in all things, but I didn't have to be glad about it. I wanted to be with Rynn and Jai.

The annoying thing was, I didn't even know who to be angry at. My orders were generally delivered on behalf of the Clan, not from any specific person. It made evading the blame easier if I should screw up. But I had a pretty good idea.

None of the lesser Clan members had the authority to command me. The twins wouldn't have paid for me to go on vacation only to send me off on a mission the very same turn. At least, I didn't think so. That would be odd, even by their standards. So it could only have been Ledo.

But I couldn't resent my master. A Bondswoman didn't do that kind of thing.

My instructions concerning my target were very clear. Kill him in his sleep if possible. If not, do it from a distance. Make it quick and definite. Don't mess around. I didn't usually get orders that specific. Often they left it to my discretion as to the best way to get the desired result. I wondered what he had done to Clan to incur their wrath, and why they were being so careful about specifying a quick and quiet kill. But in the end, it wasn't my place to ask.

He was a small-scale merchant named Gorak Jespyn. A man who'd made some wise investments and wiped them out with some unwise ones. I wondered if he owed the Clan money, but I'd found no indication of that; and besides, killing someone wasn't the best way to get them to pay you back. Even if he'd fallen on hard times, experience had taught me that people possess an amazing resourcefulness when faced with sharp objects and the threat of losing certain valuable extremities.

No, it was something else they wanted him for, but I had no idea what.

The other mystery was Jespyn's connection with Sladek Dev. Jespyn was staying at the pleasure of Mal Eista's premier crimelord in return for I-know-not-what kind of favours. For someone so insignificant, he had a lot of powerful people interested in him. I'd been after him all over the city, trading favours, leaning on people for information, digging and digging. He'd cost me a lot of time. I wanted to take it out of his hide. But that was idle fantasy. I'd play the good girl and just kill him straight.

I replayed the events of the previous turn in my mind. The casual meeting, the seduction, the sex. I wished I could tell my husband that the easiest way to get inside someone's place is to be invited. That a man's guard is at his lowest when he's in bed with you. That what I did was necessary, *unavoidable* even. To get the information I needed, without alerting anyone, I had to let him fuck me.

But you didn't have to like it, I heard him reply, and I had no answer to that. I didn't want to. I just couldn't help it.

He didn't deserve someone like me. Someone so honest shouldn't have to suffer a wife whose world is wrapped in lies. And though my heart had always been his and his alone, my body had often been given to others. If he knew half of what I got up to in the name of our Clan, well . . . I didn't know if he could still love me then. I believed he knew that too. That was why he never asked.

Times like this, I made myself sick.

The accountant wasn't a person to me. He was just a fade, like many fades before him. Ghosts. Immaterial, insubstantial, unimportant, nameless. A fade was someone you went through to get to someone else. A slang term in the trade. Sometimes you had to do them favours, sometimes blackmail them, kill them, pleasure them; but in the end, they were only a stage on your journey to get something else done, a puppet to be used and then discarded.

Some fades, like the accountant, it was necessary to forget. Because when this was done, I was going back to my husband, and I would make love to him in our bed. By the time that happened, there wouldn't be a trace of the accountant left in my mind.

Just a fade. Like all the others.

Money always made my job easier. A man with nothing could disappear without a trace, but the richer my enemy, the harder he had to work to conceal himself, the more fronts he had to defend. Money left a trail.

It was kind of like the place where Gorak Jespyn was hiding. Rich people bought big houses. Big houses had a lot of potential entrances, and a lot of places to hide. You could fill them with guards, but you'd never cover everything.

Sladek Dev was rich. Even his safehouses were mansions. Good news for me.

The information I got from his accountant was solid. Less than three turns after I kissed him goodbye, I found the man I'd been tracking.

*

The heating pipes clanked and creaked in the high-ceilinged corridors of the mansion's upper floor, fending off the chill of the city. Shinestones cast a flat light across a floor of black stone sparkling with bright mineral veins. Huge rootwood beams spanned the corridors overhead, holding up smaller support beams that fanned out towards the peaked roof. That was where I hid, crouching in the shadow, listening to the footsteps of the approaching guard.

As he passed beneath me, I threw a looped length of chain down over his head, pulled it tight and then slid off the other side of the beam. The chain was still wrapped around my hands, turning the beam into a gallows. I dangled suspended in mid-air, my body providing enough weight to lift him two spans off the floor. He clawed at his throat, gasping, eyes bulging. He saw me hanging next to him, scrabbled at me weakly. I pushed him away with my feet. The gaze that met mine was pleading, panicked, helpless.

It wasn't a nice way to go.

His fight for life didn't last long. His muscles went slack, and pungent urine trickled from his trouser leg. I let go of the chain and dropped to the floor, and he fell in a heap.

I didn't like the necessity of killing the guards. It felt messy. I'd rather have tried to get to Jespyn without alerting anyone. But I considered it prudent to take out the three men who patrolled the upper floor, at least. Just in case Jespyn turned out to be tricky and managed to get off a cry for help. I didn't like the idea of three armed guards finding me standing over a dead body.

Besides, it didn't hurt to send a little message to Sladek Dev. A playful nip at his flank to remind him that it might not be wise to shelter a fugitive from Clan Caracassa, whatever the incentives. Because next time we might do something a little more drastic, and a little closer to home.

I stashed the body quickly and retrieved my bow and quiver from where I'd left them, hidden in the beams. The other two men would be at the door to Jespyn's chambers. I'd watched this place for half a turn before I made my move, and they always kept two on the door while a third one patrolled. It was a similar tendency towards regular patterns that made it so easy to cross the courtyard and scale the mansion wall unseen.

I peered around the corner of the corridor. Sure enough, there they were. Two dark-haired men with swarthy features, muttering to each other and laughing with the casual ease of long-time friends. The nearest one drew out a pair of cigarillos and gave one to his companion. I nocked an arrow as he brought out matches.

They both leaned in together to light their smokes from the same flame. I stepped out, aimed, and shot the nearest one through the back of the head. The force of the arrow threw him forward so that he butted his companion in the nose. It was almost hard enough to knock him out, but not quite. He recoiled, his face bloody and slack with shock. I shot him through the chest before he had the chance to recover.

I stepped over the bodies and listened at the door, wondering if Jespyn might have heard the noise of falling bodies. Probably not. By my reckoning, he was asleep, and had been for several hours.

For wrecking my vacation. For taking me away from my family. For making me betray my husband.

I opened the door quietly. If Jespyn was still asleep, he wasn't waking up again.

18

I'd already made arrangements for myself, Feyn and Nereith to work the salvage dump for this shift. A few favours, a few promises. Easy enough. Juth, the publisher with the deformed leg, helped me out again. I tried to swap with him and he was curiously resistant to the idea, but he helped me get three others to swap instead.

He works alongside us at the dump as we wait for our moment, sifting through the debris with gloved hands, pretending to know what we're looking for. Feyn seems absolutely calm, and Nereith is doing a good job of hiding his feelings, but I'm wound up so tight it's hard to breathe. This time I'm risking more than myself.

I calm myself with silent chants and try not to notice that Juth is giving me plaintive glances. He suspects something's up. I knew I wasn't going to be able to get three of us onto the salvage dumps without raising some eyebrows, especially after our display last time we were here.

I keep a lookout for Arachi descending from his office. This will be the last time, I tell myself. The last hour of my life I spend in this sweltering, dirty air, pounded by the percussion of the hammers, the clashing of chains and the hiss of burning metal plunged into cold water. I'll get out of this place and I'll get Feyn out too, or I'll die trying.

I see the door at the top of the stairs open, and a thrill like a physical jolt runs through me. We're on.

The next few minutes are an agony of suppression. Only Feyn seems not to care. I suspect his philosophy runs along the lines of *if anything goes wrong, it goes wrong; why worry about it?* But nothing is going to go wrong. I tell myself that, and I've almost started to believe it when the Overseer and his guard come striding along the walkway behind me. Then:

'Take me with you,' Juth whispers.

I swear inwardly. I knew it. I pretend not to have heard, hoping his courage will fail and he won't ask again. He's a timid sort; it might happen.

'Take me with you,' he says, loud enough that Nereith looks up.

I stop work and stare at him, cold.

'You're getting out, aren't you?' he persists.

There's no point in lying. Very shortly, the three of us are going to disappear, and everyone at the salvage dump is going to know what's going on. There were already rumours that I'd escaped before, but Nereith spread a story that I was being kept for observation by one of the scientists, and my reappearance seemed to corroborate that. After all, what kind of lunatic would break out of a prison only to break back into it again?

When we make our move, nobody here will say anything. It's us against them, and anyone who overtly takes the guards' side will find their continued survival a very unlikely prospect. I've no doubt that Charn might put a word in the right ear, secretly, when he realises that we've left him here to die; but I plan to be away from Farakza before this shift is over. By the time Charn realises we've cheated him, we'll be gone. He'll only know when the alarm goes up at the end of the shift. One person can go missing without raising suspicion. Three? The only woman in the forge, the only SunChild and the only Khaadu? No chance. We're all too distinctive to go unmissed by the guards for long.

'I can't,' I say to Juth.

His narrow face firms in determination. 'You can!'

'You're lame,' I reply. 'You'll be a burden. You'll get us killed.'

Nereith is following the conversation closely. Our voices have dropped, but he's lip-reading. Feyn is glancing towards the Overseer and the guard, who is coming down the steps from the walkway to carry out his usual inspection.

'I could tell him,' Juth says, indicating the Overseer. 'I could tell him right now.'

'I could kill you in such a way that it'd look like a heart attack. No one would notice.'

'A dead slave? You don't need that kind of attention.'

Normally I could spot a bluff from a man like him, but I'm too wound up and he's too nervous and agitated. Threatening him was stupid; it's only firmed his resolve. The next decision has to be made fast and I just don't know.

'Don't do this,' I whisper. 'I take you or you tell, either way you kill us all. Don't get involved.'

The Overseer is surveying the workers now, making approving noises. Then he notices us. It's impossible not to. We're making no noise, but the tension of the stand-off is visible and palpable.

There's a desperate pleading in Juth's gaze. He knows this is his only chance to avoid a horrible death. A man with a lame leg won't last long in here. The weak and the unusually strong are first on the list for experimentation. He's not a bully by nature but fear has forced him to adopt the role.

Then he sags, and the fevered light in his eyes goes out. I turn back to the salvage dump, and so does he. The Overseer watches us for a few moments more before deciding not to dirty his hands with prisoner squabbles. He moves on, the guard trailing behind him.

There's nothing I can say. No thanks would be enough. Juth is letting us go, and his last faint hope goes with us. That's not an easy thing to give up. I've seen people go mad clinging to that final glimmer of self-preservation. I've seen people die and take everyone down with them. It takes courage to accept the inevitable.

Nereith and Feyn are both watching me. We're ready to go. I'm about to give the signal when Juth grabs my arm. He pulls out a tattered, sweat-crinkled envelope from inside his shirt and pushes it into my hand.

'Please,' he says.

I glance at it and slip it inside my top. The address is in Veya. I don't ask how he obtained the paper. By the looks of it, he's been carrying it around for some while, hoping to find a way to get it to the outside. He must have always known he had no chance of making it himself.

'I will,' I tell him.

'Deliver it by hand. Promise me.'

I feel I owe him that, and Veya is where I'm headed eventually anyway. So I promise. Then he lets me go, his fingers trembling. I wish I could save him, but I can't.

I pull off my gloves, scan for guards, and motion to the other two.

They down gloves and we walk calmly out of there, across the walkway, into the red shadows of the forge machinery. The other workers watch us go, and I know in their hearts each of them is either cursing us or wishing us good fortune.

Getting to the foot of the stairs is easier than it was before. I know where I'm going, and both Feyn and Nereith can handle themselves. Feyn has natural camouflage and he's utterly silent; Nereith isn't trained in stealth but he's certainly not clumsy. There's a certain grace about the way he moves.

There aren't any guards in sight as we make the short dash between the machinery and the stairs. I feel a slackening of tension in my gut as we slip into the cover of the waist-high metal barrier obscuring the steps from the forge. We hurry up the stairs, crouched low, and when I reach the top I pull out the key that Charn made and it turns first time. Little things like that give me a good feeling. We can do this.

Once inside the Overseer's office, I shut and lock the door to the forge. Nereith and Feyn take in the dingy room with the same faint puzzlement as I did the first time I was here. The key to the other door is on the hook again but I don't have time to mess about with threads and candles like before. I'll have to leave the door unlocked and the key in it. He's left it there before, so maybe he's absentminded enough to think he forgot to turn it. Hopefully he won't notice until he leaves at the end of the shift anyway. The plan's not as neat as I'd like, but that's the way it has to be.

I scout out the corridor, check it's clear, then lead Nereith and Feyn to the storage room where I left my slave's clothes. I open the door slightly, slip in, then let them past after. I'd left a clay shard where it would be shifted by the opening of the door. Nobody has been here while I was away.

'Stay here until I get back,' I tell them as I dress hurriedly in the dark.

'Where are you going?' Nereith asks.

'Creating a diversion.'

Suitably attired, I head out into the corridors. I'm not nearly as confident as I was last time I was here. By now the girl who originally owned these clothes will have been missed, and undoubtedly Ellya will have told the other slaves she was last seen storming off to find me. This dress is dangerous now. I have to avoid the other slaves if at all possible, and hope I don't bump into any Gurta who knew my victim well enough to care about her disappearance.

It's a short distance, and the only person I see is a guard, who doesn't even glance at me. My luck's holding.

I find a linen room I'd selected on my last excursion. This is where clean sheets and blankets are stored after drying. Shelves of fabric line the walls, awaiting pickup by slaves. The Gurta are fastidious, obsessive about cleanliness and elaborate ritual, and that means having people to look after them. They've used slaves, of one stripe or another, since their histories began.

The shelves are only half-full when I get there, but it's enough. All the slaves are out cleaning the rooms of the dignitaries. I walk in, take the lantern down from the wall, smash it on the floor at the foot of a set of shelves and walk out again with the fire already beginning to catch on the bed sheets.

My journey back is as unhindered as my journey there, and it's with some relief that I return to the storage room where Feyn and Nereith are waiting. I strip and pull on my travelling clothes again, then tie my hair up with a thin blue scarf. The time for deceptions is over; I'll stand or fall with these two. There's a certain comfort in that.

'What will happen?' Feyn asks, and it takes me a moment before I realise he means: *Now what?*

'We wait. Sooner or later somebody's going to notice that I've just set one of the rooms on fire.'

A distant scream, exquisitely timed, and Nereith actually starts laughing, which sets us all off. We keep it muffled, but we really can't help it. It's that slightly hysterical laughter you only get when you're scared out of your wits. There's nothing like it.

Then we hear footsteps outside, racing, and we all hush at once.

The footsteps recede quickly. Someone is ringing a bell. Another pair of runners pass by our door. People in the corridors between here and the junk room where I stashed the slave's body are rushing to the summons. Everyone helps in a fire, slaves and guards and scholars alike. This is my way of making doubly sure that our short journey is made unobserved.

We wait in the dark, as still as the barrels and jugs and coils of rope that hunker half-seen all around us. We wait, and wait, and when we hear no more footsteps, I say: 'Now,' and we're gone.

I'm a veteran of breaking into and out of places, but the way it's done is by not taking chances, by being prepared. The parts of this plan that kill me are those in which I have no option but to put my head into the fanged mouth of chance. And we haven't even got to the *really* dangerous part yet. That waits for us outside.

Two guards burst through a door into the corridor right in front of us.

I knew it. Fucking typical.

It takes a moment for them to register that there are three escaped prisoners loose in the fort, but they go for their swords quickly. Still, I have the advantage of surprise. I was already running at them when the door opened. The first only just has his hand on his hilt when I drive the heel of my palm into his nose, spearing the cartilage into the front of his brain. His stunned gaze empties and he crumples.

The second guard pulls out his sword and takes a slice at my neck, hoping to take my head off. It stirs my hair as I duck, then I grab his outstretched arm at the wrist and punch into his armpit, between the iridescent armour plates of hardened sap. Hit a Gurta hard enough in the right spot and you can stop their heart. My aim is good, and I've got a lot of hate behind that strike.

I stare down at their lifeless faces, their pinched features white, cheekbones tinged with blue. Two for you, Rynn. It's not even a start.

'I see your reputation was not exaggerated,' Nereith says dryly, as he grabs hold of the wrists of one of the dead guards. 'Let's get these bodies out of the way.'

We put them in a storeroom, barely bothering to hide them. We don't have time. Nereith takes up one of the swords, but I tell him to leave it. The extra weight could make the difference between life and death, if we get as far as the river. He obeys without complaint. I'm not sure he knows how to use a sword anyway.

The last section of the dash is unhindered. Doors slam distantly, voices echo down the corridors, but we reach the spiral stairs without incident and head down into the thick darkness. The junk room is as I left it, though the air is faintly putrid with the scent of over-ripe decay. The slave in the chest is beginning to go off. Feyn notices it instantly, looks towards the chest and then back at me, a question in his black eyes.

I shake my head. Don't ask.

The drop from the window isn't a problem for any of us. This part is as safe as it gets. Due to a trick of the fort's construction, it's dark enough that we can't be seen from the yard: a convenient fold in the architecture, shadowed from the shinehouse that rises above the fort.

We gather against the wall, hunkered low. Ahead of us is the yard, scattered with piles of crates and sacks, busy with workers. A storage silo yawns on the far side, fed with cargo from the carts. The men yell bawdy jokes at each other, the answers returning in chorus since they've all heard them many times before.

'I'm going to get closer,' I tell Feyn and Nereith. 'Come after me when I give you the signal.'

With that, I scamper along the wall. With my black clothes and dusky skin I'm almost invisible. A quick rush to the cover of a netted heap of boxes gets me a good angle on the activity. There's a covered wagon nearby, its tailgate hanging down, half-loaded. Sheaves of metal rods are being slung into it with little care or delicacy. Behind them are several tied crates beneath a loose tarp. More slave-made weaponry and machine parts, on their way to the Borderlands? Perhaps.

A cart is just being let in through the gate. For a short time I watch and wait, observing the lax rhythm of the labour. Seeing where they go, who they stop and talk to, when the best moment would be to make a run. I'm thankful that they leave their carts at the edge of the yard, to make space for other traffic. There's a lot of peripheral clutter. If not for that, we'd never even get near.

I wave at the others and they scuttle, low and quiet, to my side. We're well hidden here, as long as nobody decides to look behind the crates. And we're beyond the point where I can even consider the possibility of failure. There really is no going back.

'That one?' Nereith asks, peering around the side of the boxes at the wagon.

'Good as any,' I say. We can make it in a dash. With luck no one will spot us. I've been relying far too much on luck lately, but in the absence of preparation it's the best thing I have.

It's all about expectations. Nobody expects three escaping prisoners to stow away on a wagon. I doubt half of these Gurta even know there's a prison inside Farakza. As long as we're not seen, we have every chance.

'Ready?' I say to Feyn, because he's first to go. I have to be last. I have to pick the times.

Feyn nods. I look out and around. The wagon obscures most of the courtyard; the loaders are heading back to the warehouse.

'Go!'

And he's off, running low to the ground, not looking anywhere but at his destination. It's a matter of instants but the time stretches like putty. Then he's up on the tailgate, disappears inside, gone as if he was never there. The chila tethered to the front of the wagon murmurs, tossing its furred head. But no alarms. No cries.

'Go!'

Now it's Nereith, and he's a little slower. Those seconds scrape by like fingernails on slate. I'm not watching him, only the warehouse door where two workers have stopped and are talking.

I look back, and Nereith is gone. He's made it.

My turn. I keep my eye on the workers. They're looking over at the wagon now, and one of them is heading back.

Then I hear a grunt from the chila, and someone very close by hollers to one of his companions: ~ Move it! I'm getting old just watching you, you lazy *molchon* ~ Many Gurta insults are untranslatable; they have a wide and colourful variety.

I skirt around the boxes to find the owner of the voice clambering into the chila's saddle. He pulls on his gloves and picks up the reins. Getting ready to leave.

My ride is about to depart without me.

I race back along the boxes, just in time to see a scar-faced Gurta approach the rear of the wagon. He takes hold of the tailgate, swings it up and locks it. ~ No more ~ he calls to the driver. ~ Let's get going ~

The driver cries a command and snaps the reins. The chila takes the weight of the wagon and begins to lumber forward. Just as it begins to move, the scar-faced Gurta hops up on the tailgate and climbs inside, pulling the flaps closed behind him.

I break cover and sprint. It's barely travelled six spans, but the extra distance has opened up a terrifying view of the courtyard. I can't tell if any of the workers witness my dash. It doesn't matter, because if I get this wrong I'm dead anyway. I vault up on to the tailgate, thrust aside the flaps and lunge in.

The scar-faced Gurta is bent over as I come at him, occupied with tying some metal rods together. Of the stowaways there's no sign. He turns at the sound of my approach, his face shadowed in the gloom of the wagon. I rush him in the cramped space. Shock registers on his features. It's the expression he dies with.

I try to muffle his fall but he knocks rods into a noisy tumble. ~ Everything alright back there? ~ the driver calls jovially. I freeze. Waiting. The wagon rolls onward.

Silence. Silence. And still silence.

I let out a breath. The driver probably thinks he hadn't been heard, and he doesn't care enough to persist. We're still moving. I don't dare shift the body for fear of making more noise, so I creep to the back where I find Feyn and Nereith hidden behind some crates, under tarp. Nereith's calm façade is paper-thin now. He knows how close that last one was.

I hunker down with them, and we cover up and wait. Moments later, we hear the driver call out. ~ Good luck tomorrow, friends! I envy you the honour of meeting an Elder! ~

I think of the 'honour' I would have suffered, had I met him. I can't help a shiver.

~ Good journey ~ the guards call back. They're separated from us by nothing but the hide that covers the wagon.

We never even slow down. Past the gates, past the walls, and out of Farakza. My heart is punching at my gut. I can't believe we've got this far.

But there's one more obstacle before we're free. And it's the worst of them all.

17

Peering through the hide flap of the wagon I get my first glimpse of Farakza from the outside, as we bump and jolt away. The walls seem enormous from here, and though they're crumbling at the edges and battle-scarred, they don't look like they'll be coming down anytime soon. The fort crouches in the centre of its rocky island, solid and unadorned in contrast to the Gurtas' usual delicacy. It's built of the same black stone as the island, its interior buildings speckled with lighted windows.

The shinehouse at its centre is the highest point, casting the shadows of the watchtowers outward, splaying dark fingers across the island and the river beyond.

Feyn and Nereith join me at the back of the wagon, moving carefully to avoid disturbing anything. I can practically smell their adrenaline; even Feyn is excited now. As we are carried further from the walls, the oppressive weight of the prison lifts from me. Suddenly I feel more alive than ever. I feel unstoppable.

The guards on the battlements are watching the wagon as we go, eyes drawn to the movement. The ground has been chthonomantically flattened around the fort, to provide clear ground for archers to take down any troops that approach the walls. But beyond that, the island returns to its usual state: scrubby crevasses and thin ridges, a pile-up of stone crushed together by some ancient subterranean peristalsis.

'If we get no further than this,' Feyn whispers, 'then what you have done is wonderful.'

His words and his tone provoke a flood of warmth. Without thinking, I reach out and gently clasp his upper arm. 'We're going much further than this.'

He lays his hand on top of mine.

'What about him?' Nereith asks quietly. He's looking at the corpse of the man I killed. There's a strange hunger in his gaze, and I realise he hasn't had anything palatable to his kind since he's been here. Now he's faced with a fresh dead body, blood still cooling in the veins. Nereith wants to eat him.

'Pick him up,' I say. 'Carefully. Keep it quiet.'

'We're throwing him out?'

'In a few minutes we'll be at the bridge. You want them to find a dead body inside?'

'The driver will realise he's not here.'

'They won't raise the alarm for one missing worker. If we're lucky, the driver will go back and look for him.'

'The guards can see us from the walls,' Feyn points out.

'There's a dip in the road. I saw it from the tower balcony. We'll be out of sight for a short time. That's when we get off. Now help me.'

Nereith and I manage to lift the body off the metal rods with only a small amount of noise. If the driver hears, he doesn't care.

The terrain has become rocky again by the time the wagon tips into a slope and the road rises behind us, blocking our view of Farakza. Then we push open the back flaps of the wagon and drop him out as gently as we can. The dull thump of the corpse hitting the road is barely louder than the creaking of the wheels.

The three of us follow him, dropping to the road as the wagon climbs out of the dip and heads towards the bridge. Our driver is none the wiser as to the passengers he carried.

The road is simply a smoothed path, scattered with pebbles. The island stretches away to either side, its black skin pleated and folded in innumerable valleys and gullies. We've been carried past the flattened zone by our wagon, and now we're free to slip along the hot, secret kinks in the land. I motion to Nereith to lift the corpse, and we hide it.

'Follow me,' I tell them, and they do, though Nereith casts one last hungry look at the body before he abandons it for good.

The terrain provides good cover, but sharp rocks catch at my clothes and score my skin. Fungi caps suck themselves back into their stems at our approach. There are chi-rats here, their huge eyes red points in the gloom. They scuttle away with a clicking of claws and chitin armour as we approach, dragging their segmented tails behind them. It's not the little scavengers that worry me, it's the larger predators that follow them. But though we hear haunting wails in the distance, we're not troubled by anything bigger than vermin.

I take us away from the road and the bridge towards the river, heading for a point where our crossing won't be observed. We can hear the crack and grind of spume rock as we get closer.

It's here that our escape stands or falls. The part I couldn't plan for in the slightest. We make it over, or die trying.

The rock gullies give out onto the lip of a cliff. I look down and there it is: a river of spume rock, scalding, the heat pushing against me.

This is never going to work, I say to myself, but it has to. There's no choice now. My heart sinks as I think of the task we have ahead of us. It's so much worse than I thought.

The river is a jigsaw of stony plates, crammed together, sliding inexorably past us. The slow-moving, brittle surface floats on the sluggish, viscous liquid beneath, tugged along by it. Spume rock hardens on contact with air, turning crisp and black; but underneath it's molten, hot enough to kill through proximity alone. The surface creaks and snaps noisily, and every so often a plate splits and a geyser of steam blasts into the air. The river glows with its own red light, shining up through the cracks, lighting our faces from below.

But there's more. We're not alone here.

How anything can live and thrive in this kind of environment is beyond me, but Reitha has told me of many species, not least the Craggens, that exist in environments far more hostile than this. I'd already seen the spike-rays from afar, hanging on the thermals, dipping and banking in the semi-dark. Their manta-shaped bodies end in deadly, barbed tails which they use to impale their prey before carrying it off to be eaten.

But now I can see why they've gathered. The near wall is a cliff, dropping about thirty spans to the river. And it's covered in tarracks. Six-legged things, the size of an infant, built like spiders but armoured like crabs. They're squat and silvery. In place of a head, there's only a bulge at the junction of their thick limbs. The pointed tips of their claws are strong enough to punch a hole through a breastplate, and their acidic venom dissolves internal organs, causing an agonising death. I should know; I've employed it once or twice.

The venom is not their only defence, however. I read about tarracks, back when I was studying poisons. They can stun their prey with some kind of energy charge, paralysing victims long enough to inject them. The naturalists don't quite know how it works, but they know its effects well enough. A big tarrack can knock out a full-grown man.

They're using the heat from the river to foil the spike-rays' thermal vision. The spike-rays know that they're here, through some other sense that I can't explain, but they can't quite find them. This is a nesting-ground. Sticky pods adhere to the crevices in the cliff-face, incubating the tarracks' young within. To even get to the river, we'll have to climb through.

Nereith looks down, his bald head trickling with sweat. 'I assume, knowing as I do of your unparalleled experience in these matters, that you accounted for the possibility of lethal wildlife?'

'I thought I'd send you in as decoy, then we sneak past while they're eating you,' I reply.

'Very enterprising. I wondered why you'd had me along.'

I stare at the river, trying to think my way round this, but I can't come up with anything. Then I pick up the heaviest rock I can find and heft it over the edge into the river. Two spike-rays swoop at it, reacting instinctively, alerted by the motion; at the last moment, they bank away, realising it's not prey.

The rock lands on one of the plates of solidified spume rock and cracks it a little. But the plate holds. We watch as the rock is slowly carried away from us.

'Think it'll take our weight?' I ask Nereith.

'I think so,' he replies. 'You two are lighter than I am. I should go last.'

I give him a look. 'Don't fancy being the decoy, then?'

'It was your idea,' he replies with a fang-mouthed grin.

I look over at Feyn, who has hunkered down next to us. 'I will go first,' he says to me. 'You are more heavy.'

'If ever you get to Bry Athka University, Feyn, remember this: *never* tell an Eskaran woman how heavy she is.'

Nereith guffaws, but Feyn only gives me a puzzled smile. He doesn't get it.

'*I'll* go first,' I tell him. He nods, and in those black, black eyes I get the impression that he understands something I don't. He has a curious way of making me feel like I'm always learning something he already knows, like he's seen right through me and he's waiting for me to catch up. Patient, indulgent. The longer I know him, the older he seems. He might have the body of a youth, but he has a calm wisdom belonging to someone three times his age.

I edge to the lip of the cliff.

'Wish me luck,' I say, seized by an inappropriate playfulness in the face of what's to come.

'Khaadu don't believe in luck,' says Nereith.

'What is "luck"?' Feyn asks.

I shake my head. 'You two are useless.'

I start to climb. In ordinary circumstances, I'd be down this cliff in a couple of minutes, if that. It's an easy surface: solid handholds, an abundance of places to wedge my feet. I'm used to climbing sheer walls. This is simple.

But the tarracks tense up the moment I set foot on the cliff face. They stop their slow creeping. They know I'm here. So when I descend, I do so very deliberately. No sudden moves. If I alarm them, they'll go for me.

I climb sideways for a short while, to avoid a pod right below me. The tarracks move back, keeping their distance. They don't quite know how to deal with me yet. I can hear the clattering of the spike-rays overhead, calling to each other. They've noticed me too, and are similarly confused.

Shit, I hate this. I can't remember the last time I felt so helpless. All I can do is hope that either the spike-rays or the tarracks decide not to kill me. When I die, I want it to be my choice, or at least my fault. I can't stand this feeling of having no control, trusting my life to a bunch of animals.

The heat is becoming desperately uncomfortable. My back is slick, clothes clinging to me. Out of the corner of my eye I spot one of the tarracks quivering, doing minute and rapid press-ups. I'm no expert on animal body language, but I'm pretty sure that isn't good.

I want to be here even less than you want me here, I tell it silently. *Leave me alone and I won't bother you.*

The tarrack takes a few experimental steps closer and resumes quivering. Testing me.

'Back away!' Feyn says from above. 'This is his . . . his—' he fights for the word, and hits on the right one '—his *territory*.'

I begin moving to the side. It brings me dangerously close to another pair of tarracks who have positioned themselves between me and their pod. They start to become as agitated as the first, and my aggressor, emboldened, takes another few steps towards me.

'I'm *going*, you persistent little fucker!' I snap at it. The effect is negligible.

I keep climbing down. There's nothing else to be done. Maybe if it thinks I'm leaving its domain it'll—

Two of them come for me at once, as if at a signal. One from each side. I look down, desperate, but I daren't drop. Not onto that surface. The river glows forbiddingly beneath me.

'Stay still!' Nereith cries. Instinctively I press myself against the rock, and suddenly there's a blast of wind and something large thunders past my head. One of the tarracks is ripped up and away, trailing like an anchor from the tail of a spike-ray. The other one has stopped dead, about a span from my shoulder.

'Forgot about them, didn't you?' I murmur spitefully, dredging up a seam of defiance.

The remaining tarrack quivers next to me. I can smell it from here, dry and musky, and taste the metallic tinge in the air that surrounds it.

Something clicks and thumps down the cliff-face to my right. A large stone, dropped by Nereith. The tarracks all freeze again. He's trying to create a distraction.

My aggressor isn't buying it. Slowly, slowly, it creeps forward. I can't do a thing as the first of its armoured limbs presses onto my shoulder blade, and it walks three of its legs onto my back.

I fight down the urge to throw it off. The touch of the tarrack appals me. It's straddling the nape of my neck, supporting its weight with the three legs still gripping the rock. I gather in my increasing panic, begin my chants, slowing my heart, relaxing my muscles. Better play dead, or I'll *be* dead.

For a long, long time it stays there, unmoving, trying to decide what I am. I'm barely breathing. My chants cycle relentlessly in my head, but I find I can't concentrate on them. I'm thinking of a conversation I had with Jai, long ago, just after he'd failed the tests to become Cadre. I'm thinking I wish I'd done things differently, that I'd been stronger back then, said the right words. Maybe, if I had, I could have died in peace now, knowing that Jai was safe and happy. But I can't die with things as they are. And that makes the fear so much more bitter.

The tarrack moves, shifts its position so that it's over my head. One leg is still resting on me, ready to plunge if I should move. My eyes are squeezed shut. I can feel the weight of it, its underside pushing against my hair. Something's moving against my scalp, something underneath the body of the tarrack.

Mouthparts.

The realisation comes an instant before pain stabs through my skull, a white-hot blaze of heat. Wetness trickling onto my shoulders. It's *bitten* me.

And still I don't move. I might have reacted spasmodically if I weren't half-buried in a trance, but when someone trained in the chua-kîn arts plays dead, you can stick a sword in their arm and they won't even twitch.

I wait for the second bite in dreadful anticipation. Sweat is running into the bite wound, mingling with the blood, stinging. The tarrack is still again.

Come on! Do it, if you're going to!

But it doesn't. Instead, it steps off me, moves away a little. I make no outward reaction, but inwardly I'm sobbing with relief. I suppose it doesn't like the way I taste.

'Orna! Are you hurt?' Nereith calls from above, as loud as he dares. But as he leans over the edge, he dislodges a small shower of pebbles, which bounce and scatter down the cliff face towards me. I see the tarrack tense, feel the air suddenly tauten and the fine hairs on my arms stand up. Then there is an almighty *snap* and my body bucks like I've been kicked, and the last thing I realise before I lose consciousness is that I'm going to fall, and I'm going to die.

16

I can hear someone calling my name amid the din in my head. The blackness is total and it's burning hot. As the ringing in my ears starts to fade, I can make out the voice, and for a moment I really believe that it's Jai calling. I'm dead and he's coming to me like the fireclaw visions of a dweoming.

Then my eyes flutter open.

I'm flat on my back on the surface of the river. The heat is excruciating. I've been carried a short distance on the flow, and I can see Feyn, halfway down the cliff, making his way through the tarracks. He looks over his shoulder, sees me raise my head. The whole scene is red-lit from beneath, lending everything a surreal aspect, making me wonder if I really woke up at all.

'Orna! Do not move!'

Then my predicament really hits me. I turn my head a little and I see the cracks that radiated out from my body when I hit the surface. Even that slight shift in weight makes something crumble under my shoulders. Through the pain I can feel the tug and crunch of the river. This plate isn't going to last much longer.

Gingerly, I try to pick myself up. Something gives beneath me.

'Stay where you are!' Nereith cries, from where he's standing at the top of the cliff. 'He's coming to get you!'

But I'm being carried away from Feyn faster than he's descending, and anyway the heat is too much to stay still. There's a loud crack and my mind is made up. I push with my heels and elbows and roll to the side as the plate splits apart and a geyser of steam blasts into the air. The plate tips and bucks wildly; I cling to it with my fingernails, pressed face down. Burning hot shards of spume rock pepper my back and hair.

Gradually, the new plate evens out. It's holding.

I can't lie here for more than a moment; the heat is too much. I get to my feet. I'm not as careful or as delicate as I'd like, but I can't bear being spread flat on that surface any more. The rock tilts uneasily, but it holds.

I look back at Feyn, checking he's okay. Nereith has begun his climb now. The tarracks seem to have decided that we're not a threat as long as we stay away from the nests.

I begin to walk, spreading my weight. The far bank is just a slope, ragged with hardy lichen scrub. All I have to do is get to it.

The surface gives frighteningly with each footstep, letting me sink just a little. I'm light-headed; I can taste salt on my tongue. Dehydrating fast. I've got to move quick, but each time I put my weight down I'm convinced the plate is going to shatter and pitch me into the boiling sludge below.

The river is busy with rifts, moving apart and pushing together as the plates jostle for space. I have to jump them, even though the impact could crack the surface. The first is the most terrifying. I ride my landing down to one knee, absorbing it with my thigh muscles as best I can.

The plate stays firm.

Back on my feet, and I'm glancing up at the spike-rays, who are taking a worrying interest in these strange beings in their territory. I'm big prey for a spike-ray. There's no way one of them could lift me. But it might not stop them trying.

Feyn has reached the river, untroubled by the tarracks, and is beginning his crossing. I daren't think about him now. I have to concentrate on myself.

Over another rift, then out into the centre of the river, arms held to either side. I've got good balance, but the uncertain footing makes me want to simply run and hope for the best. The heat, the red glow from beneath, the protracted threat of imminent death – it's like being trapped in a nightmare.

Then I see one of the spike-rays begin a plunge. It comes down lazily but with purpose, heading for me, not caring whether I've spotted it or not. Almost nonchalant as it tries to kill me.

I tense, digging my toes into the treacherous crust. It'll come at me with the tail, in a stabbing motion; I watch as it curves, predicting the moment . . .

Now.

I jump aside and roll, clearing a rift with my jump, hitting the ground shoulder-first and coming up in a crouch. I finish the manoeuvre facing the spike-ray as it swoops back up into the sky, not in the least fazed by its lack of success. Then the ground shifts beneath me, and it's only because I'm in a ready stance that I move fast enough to avoid being cooked by a steam jet. Still, I land too heavily, and have to hop aside again for fear that the shattered ground beneath me will collapse like the last.

I can't stop myself hurrying now. I'm dizzy from the heat and I'm worried other spike-rays will follow their companion's example. The bank isn't far. A few solid-looking plates give me good landing spots, and I've got the measure of the tipping. Moving at reckless speed – although progress is still slow – I cover the second half of the river, buoyed by my own momentum.

The plates at the river's edge are a little more broken up, so I slow down again for them; but finally, with a last jump, my feet hit solid ground. I collapse amid the tough lichens, hugging the earth, and then scramble up the slope, away from the heat.

When the temperature is bearable again, I look back. Feyn is almost two thirds across, and by his face he's as frightened as I was. Nereith is behind him, making his way steadily. If we'd been carrying packs or wearing armour none of us would have stood a chance. Even the sword that Nereith wanted to take from the dead guard might have made a fatal difference. Suddenly I realise why this river makes such an effective moat for the fort.

But I've done it. I was right. I've got out, and I can get them out. As long as they don't stumble now . . .

I'm so fixed on watching Feyn that I don't see the spike-ray come for him until it's too late. It flies low over the surface of the river, and by the time I notice it I doubt my shout will help. But Feyn reacts fast to the warning, and with blind trust. Without even knowing where the danger is coming from, he throws himself forward. The spike-ray swings past him like an axe, its tail stabbing. Feyn arches his back with a yell as it scores across his ribs.

My hand goes to my mouth. He staggers forward, and for an

instant I think he's going to fall, but then his head seems to clear. He checks for other spike-rays, and he's back on track again.

I don't take my eyes off him the rest of the way, demanding that he make it, as if by sheer force of will I can make his steps light and keep him from plunging in. Only when I see he's within reach of the shore do I allow myself a breath of relief.

I head downstream to meet him; he's been swept a little further by the current than I was.

I bundle him up the slope, my hands coming away red with blood. His thin shirt has been sliced through and there's a long lash across his ribs, but when I pull off his shirt and examine it, I realise it's not bad at all. Some blood, already dry in the heat, but little real damage. It'll heal as long as there's no poison.

'Does it burn?' I ask him, feeling around the wound for a barb that might have detached. 'How do you feel?'

'I feel weak,' he said. 'The heat . . .' He turns over so he's sitting on the slope of the riverbank, and in his expression I can read all the terror of the past few minutes. I have my chants, he has his philosophies, but in the end we're both the same and we're both scared rigid.

I kneel down next to him and put my arms around him, gathering his head into my collarbone. A moment later, I feel him return the hug, hard, as if clutching me is the only thing to stop him from being swept away. I can smell the bitter oil on his skin, feel his pulse through his forehead and wrists.

I miss my son. I miss him so badly.

'Hoy!' calls Nereith, and I hear him crunching up the riverbank from downriver. He crouches down next to us, panting, and grins. 'Where's *my* hug?'

I can't help laughing, because if I didn't I'd start to cry and I don't have time for that shit right now. Nereith is watching the spike-rays, but they've lost interest. We look back across the river, where Farakza glowers in the dark of the cavern, its shinehouse a beacon of pale light.

Nereith slaps me gently on the shoulder. 'Good job.'

A slow clang rings out from Farakza's bell tower, pulsing over us.

'End of shift,' I say quietly.

But the bell rings again, and again, and my heart and guts begin to squeeze tight. Not yet, not *yet!*

When Nereith speaks, he's saying what we all know. 'That's not the end of the shift,' he says. 'That's an alarm.'

35

The lift from Veya to the surface wasn't built for comfort. It was a tall circular chamber of grimy black metal, with three levels stacked one on top of the other, connected by stairs. Each level was filled with seats in concentric circles, facing a central column which housed the enormous screw that the lift travelled up and down. By controlling geothermal pressure in the shaft, the chamber could be made to ascend or descend, slowly turning as it did.

I sat and listened to the screech and groan of metal on metal. The lights, resting in coiled iron sconces, dimmed and brightened fitfully without ever dispelling the gloom. They were a relatively new invention, powered by the motion of the lift itself. I didn't trust them. They seemed permanently on the edge of failing.

We rode the upper deck, of course. Though it was still too loud for easy conversation up here, it was the best available. The lowest level was a nightmarish swelter, where the heat from the shaft pulsed through the floor of the chamber. Our short vacation was Liss and Casta's treat, a moment of suspicious generosity on their parts, and they never did things by half measures.

'You must go! We insist! Spend some time with your family!'

'Our brother works you too hard. You and Rynn both. Between one thing and another you're hardly ever together.'

'We know how it hurts you.' This was Liss, fawningly sympathetic.

'We'll pay for everything.'

'Oh! Won't it be fun?'

'It's the least we can do for one so close to our hearts.'

I accepted, naturally. Turning them down would have led to consequences I didn't want to deal with. They got Rynn pulled from his escort duty – guarding a powerful friend of Caracassa, more for show than anything else – and persuaded Jai's tutors to give him a few turns' leave from military school. Then Jai asked if he could bring Reitha, and we said of course, and the twins said of course. So we were four.

I watched my son and his lover as we sat in the lift, surrounded by the din. Jai was fascinated by the lights. He hung on every sound, trying to understand the lift's mechanisms. He had such a wonderful mind, mystifyingly ordered and logical, endlessly interested in the way things worked and how to make them better. It was a compulsion; he couldn't stop himself tinkering with any device he laid his hands on. Our home in the Caracassa mansion had been full of disassembled lamps and clocks and spring-loaded toys until he went away. Without them, the place felt bare.

And yet, when Reitha touched his arm and leaned in to talk to him, I saw the other side to my son. The way he softened, the look in his eyes when he laughed. He worshipped and adored her. Beneath that rigid structure of thought there was an ocean of feeling. He was a sensitive child, prone to crying when young. Never really the physical sort. He learned to fake it around his father but nobody was fooled. Jai was always my child rather than Rynn's.

The lift stopped several times on its journey to disgorge passengers and to take on new ones. It took hours to get to our stop, near the top of the shaft. Most of the passengers emptied out here. It was a small cavern, a junction from which a half-dozen tunnels led, and we walked into the middle of a bazaar. There were a multitude of hawkers, who had set up stalls beneath the glow-lamps in anticipation of the crowd. They sold the eggs of rare animals or offered cakes and drinks; they provided transport or sought to recruit labour; they displayed precious minerals from the surface. Some sold paintings of the night sky: depictions of the aurora, or of the mother-planet Beyl looming over the horizon, all purple and black streaks. Little groups of people waited to welcome associates or family. Militia crayl-riders patrolled the stalls, holding obsidian-bladed pikes. The air was stuffily warm and dry; the cavern echoed with voices.

Reitha fairly dragged Jai to the pens, where crayl were being sold for domestic use. I liked crayl. They were wonderful beasts of burden and tireless mounts, and if trained well they were also vicious and formidable fighters. Native to the surface, they were nevertheless well adapted to life underground. They spent Red Tide Season sheltering from the endless day in the subsurface cave networks that riddled Callespa, only emerging onto the surface when the nights began in Ebb Season.

Reitha was an animal-lover; it went with her job. She petted the crayl in the pens, and they turned their muzzles to nose her hand. I stood by her and joined in. She offered me a smile. I knew she valued these moments when she felt we made a connection, however small. Like Jai, she was sensitive, and she could see how I felt about my only son being taken by another woman, no matter how well I tried to hide it. She wanted me to like her, and I *did* like her, but nothing was going to erase that faint primal jealousy.

I wasn't an animal person by nature, but it gave me a faint thrill to touch them. They were several times my weight and easily capable of ripping me apart. Shaggy four-legged beasts, high as my shoulder but able to rear up to twice that height. Retractable claws like knives. Broad, flat muzzles with wide nostrils, and small eyes buried under fringes of thick fur. The merchant nearby watched us closely, while pretending not to. He had already decided we weren't going to buy, so now we were just a nuisance.

'She appreciates them, I can tell,' Jai said to Reitha. 'She has an attraction to anything hairy and brutish.'

Reitha gasped, appalled at his cheek. She brought out a wicked streak in him which I was rather fond of. I aimed to clip him but he dodged away, laughing. 'And slow, too! What's the Cadre coming to?'

'You're very cocky for someone who can still be beaten up by his mother,' Reitha said, swatting his arm.

'She'd never hit me. I'm Ledo's property. It's more than she's worth to damage this chassis.'

I wasn't rising to it any more; I was too preoccupied with the animals. Jai gave up teasing, content with a victory.

'What do you like about them?' Reitha asked me, genuine interest in her tone.

I looked over at her. Small, even features, brown hair, dusky skin unlined by age or care. Intelligence in her eyes. I always admired her daring, her determination to work on the surface no matter what the risks. It had warmed me to her immediately.

'I like that they're survivors,' I replied, after a moment's thought. 'Not too many animals made it through when the tribes went underground. But these held on. They're tough. Adaptable.' I thumbed at the ceiling of the cavern, indicating what was beyond. 'I like that they can live up there.'

She smiled again, wider this time, and went back to petting a crayl that was butting her arm.

I left them alone and joined Rynn, who was casting a critical eye over a rack of swords on another stall. He had one out and was turning it over in his hand.

'That's a good choice! All of these are forged from the finest metals, mined near the surface!' the stall-holder was enthusing. He was young, and hadn't yet learned to spot a disinterested customer. He'd noticed the Cadre emblem on Rynn's shoulder and was desperate for the prestige of selling a blade to him. 'You can't get this kind of thing down below! You could plunge this into a Craggen's shoulder and it wouldn't break!'

Rynn put the sword back and turned to me without even acknowledging the seller's furious efforts.

'Are we going?' he asked. Impatient to get on, as ever. He wouldn't relax until we arrived at the hotel.

'Give them a while,' I said, taking his arm and leading him away.

'I'll sell it to you for half price!' the stall-holder shouted after us, flailing now.

'It'd still be too expensive,' Rynn murmured under his breath.

The lift ride had made him cranky. I found him adorable when he was in a grump, but I'd long since learned not to show it. It somewhat undermined his gravitas when his wife told him how cute he was when he was angry.

We walked idly around the stalls, looking at this and that.

'You think he's happy?' Rynn asked suddenly.

'With her? I think he's in love.'

'I mean, at the school.'

I thought about that for a moment. I knew the answer, of course; but I had to choose my words.

'He did it for you, you know,' I said eventually.

A pause. His eyes roved, like they always did when he was on the spot. He wasn't comfortable talking about things like this. 'I know,' he said.

It was only two words, but it was a momentous admission from him. A chink in the armour. I saw at that moment a chance, no matter how slim, to change his mind. I didn't want our son at that school. But by the time I'd realised that, he was already there. And I couldn't go against both my husband's wishes *and* my son's. Jai would protest till his dying hour that he wanted to be an officer in the Eskaran Army, and he'd hate me for robbing him of the chance.

But all three of us knew it was not what he really wanted, and all three of us knew why he was doing it.

We stopped and bought enamelled cups of liquor, then sat on a low table outside the stall. Rynn was still inwardly squirming. The cavern bustled with life. We were surrounded by the smells of cooking and cakes and the jostle of sellers and buyers and animals. But amidst all that, we were alone, in a little island to ourselves.

'Jai is strong,' I said slowly. 'But not in the way you think of strength. He's driven, he's ambitious, and he's got talent. If we give him his head, he'll be a great engineer, or an architect, or an inventor. He'll be a great man.' I leaned across the table and wrapped both my hands around one of his. 'I can see that. His tutors see that too. But he doesn't. He's too busy trying to please you.'

Rynn sipped the liquor, thought about that for a time. The struggle in him was plain in the frown on his face. He was a simple man, and I wouldn't have had him any other way. He wouldn't have been the man I married without his temper, his gruffness, his unwillingness to socialise and the fact that he'd never danced with me since our wedding. But he had stubborn cut deep into his bones, and getting him to reverse a decision once it was made was like trying to divert an ocean.

'It was his idea,' Rynn said. 'The school.'

'Of course it was. He wanted to prove himself. He was fourteen years old, and he wanted to get your attention. You'd barely said one word of encouragement to him since he failed the Cadre tests.'

'You're making this my fault,' he said.

'No, it's my fault too,' I said. 'But it *is* a fault.'

'He won't back out now.'

'He won't do it because he thinks it'll be a worse failure in your eyes than if he'd never started. Make him feel it's okay and he will.'

'I don't want him to,' Rynn murmured, clutching his thick beard. It was something he often did when agitated.

'I know,' I said, quietly. 'You want a son who's a warrior. Someone feared and revered: Cadre, like us. But Jai isn't a warrior and he never will be, no matter how hard he tries to make himself one.'

Rynn was silent for a long while, but I was used to that. I knew better than to bombard him with further pleas. It would only make him annoyed.

'How can I make him believe I don't mind him leaving the school, when I do?' he said eventually.

And there was the problem we'd never be able to get over. Rynn was honest: utterly, entirely straight down the line. He was literally incapable of deception. He didn't understand how it worked. Jai would see through him unless Rynn absolutely believed in pulling Jai out of that school. And he just didn't.

'Try,' I asked. 'For him.'

'I'll try,' he promised, and he *would* try; but right then we both knew he'd fail.

Later, we ambled through a sea of golden lichen stalks, our hotel behind us, a ridged brown dome rising among a forest of dwarf mycora. The mycora this close to the surface grew twenty or thirty spans high, which was still tiny compared to the monsters that grew in the sunlight. Some sprouted shelf-like discs and had flat or inverted tops; some had rounded, helmet-like ends and were brightly coloured. Some were like enormous anemones; others hung in translucent veils. The variety was endless.

I was walking with Reitha and Jai, admiring the scenery. Colourful fungal blooms waved in the gentle wind; small chitinous animals darted around the thick mycora stalks. Streams wound over rockeries of mimetite and amethyst and snowflake obsidian. Gau-gaus jagged through the air, their strange cries echoing their names, quick flurries of scale and tail and wing. We watched them pick the insects out of the sky with their small, needle-toothed jaws.

But what set this place apart from other areas of natural beauty down below was the light. There was a quality to it unlike any other. I had seen grottoes lit by luminescent fungi and translucent, glowing stalagmites, greens and blues in breathtaking harmony. I had visited a Ya'yeen installation where shinestones and flame refracted through gemstone lenses to create light patterns so beautiful I almost cried. But at home, light was muted, controlled, refracted and maximised. Light was our life. If ever it was entirely gone, we were lost.

This place glowed with the wild light of the world: the crazed, maddening, lethal fire of the suns. It was hard on the eyes, but it stirred old, old instincts, a cocktail of fear and desire. We had once lived in that light and been betrayed by it. Somewhere inside, deeper than thought could go, I wanted to feel those rays on my skin like my ancestors had. To turn my face up to sky and stand naked to the day.

Only naturalists and explorers and cartographers ever got to go up there with any regularity. It wasn't the kind of place that the untrained should wander in. But occasionally there were military skirmishes on the surface, and they were getting more frequent as the war dragged on. The generals on both sides were realising that a tortuous journey through bottleneck caverns underground might easily be circumvented by going over the top, if only they could learn to deal with the dangers. War on Callespa had always been a three-dimensional affair.

Rynn had stayed in the hotel; he had little interest in our excursion. If he felt the same pull as I did, he didn't show it. I had never been up to the surface, though I had been close several times. I didn't know if I had it in me to stand beneath a roofless sky, but I couldn't deny that I had a desire to find out.

We saw animals on our way, roaming free. Slender quadrupeds with long, delicate legs, covered head to foot in beige chitin. Squat things with domed silver exoskeletons that looked like smooth rocks when they retracted their feet and hid. Reitha pointed them out to Jai and named them. They were surface-dwelling species, made to weather the intolerable light of the suns.

I had drifted off into a peaceful daze, lulled by the scenery and the temperature, when Reitha cried out ahead of us. She had been following a small, hopping creature which rattled its carapace noisily whenever she got too near.

'Come here and see this!'

Jai responded to the delight in her voice. He was smiling even before he saw what it was. If it made her happy, it made him happy. I'd never seen him so besotted.

Reitha had found flowers. Small, delicate flowers, nodding in the breeze. They were huddled at the foot of a green and grey mycora. Tiny insects were flitting between the white cups.

'Can you believe it?'

I really couldn't. Flowers. I'd never seen them growing wild.

'They must have just enough light here to survive, but not enough to kill them. Do you know how delicate that kind of balance is?'

'They're beautiful,' Jai said, and by the reverence in his voice I knew he meant it.

'They've held on somehow,' she murmured.

It was hard to beat that, but Reitha and I had a surprise in store for Jai. Like me, he had never been to the surface; but unlike me, he had never even been near it. So when we were done with the flowers, we took him to the edge of the hotel grounds, where a sheer cliff dropped away, overlooking the chasm-fields. And there we showed him.

There was daylight here. Raw daylight, cutting down in blazing white beams through the cracks and fissures in the roof of the cavern. Sharp islands of illumination moved slowly across the floor and slid up the walls, inching their way over vineyards and fields and irrigation channels. Hundreds of men and women in sunsuits worked the vast expanse of cropland that had been cultivated at the bottom of the chasm. They kept to the shade, staying clear of the direct sun, tending fruits and other foods that could only be grown in ambient sunlight, but were too fragile to survive the unshielded rays for long. The air was heavy with drifting motes, feathery spores that glowed furiously in the light and suffused the atmosphere with a dreamlike haze. And it was warm: not the warmth of a fire or the warmth of deep, grumbling magma but the warmth of a star.

Jai was stunned. Not only by the scale of the chasm-fields, but because he had never seen the light of the suns until now. I watched him as he laid eyes on true light for the first time in his life, and I saw the tears gather and his throat close. There was nothing that could prepare you for it: millennia of instinct suddenly awakened by the sight, like a dam-burst inside. We were built to live beneath the sky, and our bodies remembered.

Reitha smiled and hugged herself to him. She appreciated his sensitivity, and I loved her for that. Maybe, just maybe, she could give him the confidence to step out of his father's shadow.

As if summoned by the thought, I saw Rynn striding over from the hotel, waving at me. There was another man with him.

'Stay here,' I told them. 'I won't be long.'

I headed back to meet Rynn and the newcomer half-way. By the time I got there I had already resigned myself to what was to come. He was a Caracassa man.

'Clan Caracassa requires your services,' he said, without preamble. It was the standard phrase they used. Never mentioning which *member* of Clan Caracassa required my services. No need to give away unnecessary information. A wise habit in the cut-throat world of the aristocracy.

I looked at Jai and Reitha, standing together, arm in arm in the glow of the light from the chasm-fields, lost in the vista. I really wanted this time with them, with Rynn. I really wanted it, and now I was being robbed, and that was the way life was.

I turned back to the agent, my eyes flat. 'What's the job?'

'There's a man in Mal Eista. His name is Gorak Jespyn. Your masters want him dead.'

15

We hear the ululations of the raka. The caverns foil sound, jagged walls fracturing the echoes, making it hard to pin-point their distance. But the Gurta are behind us, with their hunting-beasts, and they're coming fast.

'The blood,' Feyn says, panting as he climbs. All of us know it but none of us wanted to say it. 'It is me they are following.'

It didn't take them long to equate the three missing prisoners with the disappearance of the yard-worker. Or maybe they found the bodies of the guards we hastily stashed, or the Overseer discovered the door to his office was unlocked when he'd locked it earlier, or Charn ran to the guards when he realised we'd double-crossed him, or someone smelt that poor slave girl I left rotting in a trunk. Considering how sloppy the whole operation was, it's a miracle we made it out.

We're still in the cavern where Farakza lies. We've a good head start, but the Gurta are relentless and I knew the moment they hit upon Feyn's blood-trail they'd be unshakable. Even though the wound isn't bad, it's going to keep reopening until he gets to rest. Without weapons, outnumbered, we don't stand a chance if they catch us. I'm the only warrior here; I don't rate my chances against six or seven armoured monsters, each three times my weight, with beaked muzzles that can shear through bone.

The only choice is to run, but I know Gurta: they'll never give up the pursuit. It's a question of whose strength fails first. And it's likely to be ours.

We clamber along paths carved long ago by underground cata-clysms, water erosion, magma flows and the efforts of geophagic fungi, lichen and stone-burrowing insects, which, given millennia, can eat through anything. On Callespa, life evolved beneath the ground long before it appeared above. Rockworms the size of cities cored the crust of the world while the surface was still a poisonous, unformed wasteland.

Following a faint breeze, I find us an enormous lava trench, long cold, running out of the main cavern. We take it, reasoning that it will slow the raka: four-legged creatures don't deal with steep, uneven trench-side rock as well as we do. But I'm not sure any terrain is likely to slow our pursuers for long.

We clamber over black stone, making our way up a slope of sharp edges and horn-like overhangs. Colourful minerals have grown in the wake of the flow, in bubbled humps and great crystals. It's hard to see here, but a distant crop of raw shinestone provides a dim glow. Around it have grown photovore lichens and tiny plants, some of them with a luminescence of their own to attract insects. Light multiplies in the dark.

Feyn is struggling. His eyes aren't as good as ours, and the roof of the trench oppresses him. I can see it in the way he hunches his shoulders. The trench must be forty spans high and three times that wide, but it's still crushing him.

'Stop,' Feyn says, and we stop, chests heaving, looking back at him.

'It is me they are following,' he says again, his face bearing an expression of helpless honesty. 'I will go another way.'

Nereith turns to me. It's what he's been thinking for some while. I know he's already agreed, but he's waiting to see what my reaction is.

'You go,' I tell him. 'I'll go with Feyn.'

'No!' Feyn protests. 'Go with him. You will not be followed.'

I ignore him. 'You can find your way back?' I ask Nereith.

'I told you I could,' he replies. His eyes flick from me to Feyn and back again. 'What do you think you're doing?' he asks me.

I don't answer that. He wouldn't understand.

The raka howl somewhere down the trench. Nereith shakes his head in despair. 'I hope you make it,' he says, but it's empty. He already believes we won't.

He heads along the slope at an angle, but before he gets five steps I say his name one last time. He gazes back at me inquiringly.

'I have a son,' I tell him.

'I know.'

'How?'

'Massima Leithka Orna, married to Venya Ethken Rynn. I hadn't heard you had a child, but considering the state you were in when you arrived, I guessed someone close to you had been killed and I assumed it was your husband. In light of events since—' he looks at Feyn, '—I put two and two together.'

Of course. With a Khaadu's memory, it's not so surprising, even if I find myself resenting his insight.

'Last I heard he was stationed at Caralla,' I say. The words don't come easily. They have to be forced through a knot in my throat. I don't know why it's so difficult to talk about Jai. 'If you could tell him . . .'

Tell him what? *Your mother was alive last time I saw her, but by now she's probably not?* Tell him I love him? I'm not entrusting that to Nereith. Abyss, I don't even know if he's heard his father is dead yet.

I just want to see him. The words will come then, I'm sure of it.

'Tell him there's a letter,' I say. 'There's a letter, from the Dean of Engineers of Bry Athka University, in a drawer in my room. Have him send someone to collect it. If I don't make it back . . . he needs to know about the letter.'

'I'll pass near Caralla,' Nereith says. 'If the Gurta haven't taken it yet . . . well, I'll do what I can to get there.'

I smile sadly. He turns away, pauses, turns back.

'Should you reach Veya . . . should you ever come across a problem without a solution . . .' He trails off, his face grave. 'Remember who I am.'

I remember alright. He's one of Silverfish's men. And he's offering to be a contact for me: a connection to the faceless legend of the Veyan underworld.

In all the years I've spent trawling the murky depths of the city, trading information and digging out secrets in the service of my master, I've never even got close to Silverfish. He's a whisper in the dives and cut-joints, his name steeped in paranoia. A ghost of the alleyways.

I've run across his trail many times, though. His secretive network of operatives wields enormous influence in the underworld, but unlike the other gangs you never know who's working for Silverfish and who isn't. There's a good deal of doubt as to whether Silverfish exists at all, or whether he's the mythical head of an organisation without a leader. Nobody knows. I have to admire that.

And now here's Nereith, telling me he can put me in touch, if ever I have the need. If ever I make it home.

It's as close to a thank-you as I'll get from him, I suppose.

He begins to climb down toward the bottom of the trench, branching off in a different direction from us. I watch him depart with the feeling that I'll never see him again, and there's a small part of me that regrets it. I respect him. I wish I'd known him longer.

'Ready?' I say to Feyn.

He nods, but he holds my gaze for a long time, and I just can't tell what he's thinking. 'We will not escape them this way,' he says.

'No,' I say. 'We probably won't.'

'Then we must go where they will not follow.'

'There's nowhere they won't follow us. They'll chase us till they drop. It's the Gurta way.'

'Will they follow us to the surface?'

I don't know how long it is before we find an upward-slanting channel. I know that we're both light-headed and weak from exertion and hunger, and I know every muscle in my body aches from climbing and running. If only we could find water we'd stand a chance of throwing them off the scent, but there's nothing.

We're in the trackless barrens of the Borderlands, a webwork of inhospitable caverns and chasms that have separated Gurta and Eskara for as long as our civilisations can remember. A war-torn, disputed wilderness crawling with troops and bandits of all kinds. Neither side wants it but neither will let the other have it. Why is it only now that I can see how utterly ludicrous that is, in the face of the thousands upon thousands who die over this wasteland? I suppose I never had to care until now. I hadn't known what it was to lose someone to the Borderlands, to be faced with the threat of losing another.

Feyn has gathered several clumps of fungi that he pronounces edible, and we chew them whenever our hands are free. They're vile and bitter but he assures me that they're safe.

'A SunChild must be sheltered from the sun, like you,' he says. 'When the Season of Days is, we are in the high caves. These grow there, like here.'

I trust him, because I'm not going to make it otherwise. I have to fight to keep the fungi down, but it eases the worst of the hunger.

We take the way up, following the breeze. The upward tunnel becomes a shaft, ten spans across at its widest part, a slanting, near-vertical crevice. Water trickles down its folds. Feyn tastes it, pronounces it clear – though clear of *what* I don't like to ask – and we drink.

The Gurta are close. As we haul ourselves up the teeth of the shaft, I'm comforted only by the fact that the raka won't be able to make it up an ascent this steep. The soldiers will have to follow on their own. If we can get ahead of them, we can lose them.

I want to lie down and sleep and not care if I never wake up again. But I've come so far. I'm not stopping now.

I have to slow my pace for Feyn, but his endurance is surprising. Perhaps his kind are tougher than they look. I'd thought him fragile, because he's so slender and passive, and because he wept when he was beaten. But then I remember how he never complained or flagged at the slurry-trough. He comes from a race of travellers who live in a world deadlier than mine, hardened by generations of life on the surface. He's strong enough.

I don't think about how far we have to go. I think only of the next handhold, the next shelf, the next upward lunge. I concentrate on the tapping of the water as it runs from pool to pool, trying to solve its rhythm. I think of the way the chaotic surface of the pools reflect the light of the phosphorescent patches that have grown beneath them, and how its eddies and impacts have never stilled for thousands of years. I meditate as I climb, and reality becomes elastic.

The pain in me dims. It's only physical pain. I've known much worse.

The shaft begins to switch back on itself as we near the top, broken by some ancient quake. It tightens dramatically, so much that we can barely fit through. I'm worried Feyn will freeze up in there. Claustrophobia's not unheard of even among my people; it must be worse for his.

He takes a deep breath, lets it out, and squeezes through the fissure. I don't know what keeps him going, but though he's as tired as I am he's showing no signs of giving up.

The fissure takes us up almost a hundred spans before it widens again suddenly. I clamber out to find Feyn heading away along a sloping tunnel. It's the back end of a cave, wide enough for six men abreast. Cracked bones and a rotted nest of scrub attest to an animal that once lived here, but it's abandoned and empty now.

'We are close,' Feyn declares, his voice numb with weariness.

We follow the thin stream to a spring bubbling in a hollow in the stone. I catch up with Feyn as he drinks.

'Can you smell the air?' he asks me, and I can. It's warm, arid, unfamiliar.

We travel on. The cave splits into other caves, and we're forced to choose carefully. We can hear creatures calling to each other in the depths. Deep booming sounds, like Craggens but without the suggestion of language and structure.

Some time after, still following the breeze, we find a short vertical ascent. Feyn struggles up it first, and when I get to the top I find him sitting on the floor next to me, his thin ribs heaving beneath his ragged shirt.

But there's something else. I sense it even before I see it. About thirty spans ahead of us is a corner, and the stone at the end burns with white light.

Daylight.

I shield my eyes, which are blurring with tears. Dazzling after-images make it difficult to see. A primal, irrational fear uncoils within me. To be so close to raw daylight terrifies me. I'm afraid it will somehow flood in and consume us. I start to regret letting Feyn talk me into this course of action.

'Now what?' I ask him.

'Now we wait.'

'You brought us all the way up to the surface and now we *wait*? That's your plan?' I demand of him.

'Yes. We wait until the sky becomes dark.'

'There are Gurta right behind us, Feyn! They'll be here in minutes!' I turn away from the light, searching for a way out of our predicament. I can't believe he's done this to us. I can't believe I trusted him. 'Let's go back. Into the caves. They can't track us without the raka.'

'They are too close behind us.'

He's right. There haven't been any branches off this tunnel for quite a way. We'll only end up running into the Gurta and hastening the inevitable. But still—

'You don't want to *try*?'

He shakes his head.

I want to be furious, but I can't manage it. I want to keep struggling, but his calm is infectious. I can't stand that we're so fucking close and we've been thwarted. I want to keep running, out into the sun or onto the swords of the Gurta, and yet his acceptance of the end cools me. Shrill hysteria and urgent demands seem out of place now. I'm too tired.

I sit down next to Feyn. For a long time, neither of us says anything. I'm the one to break the silence.

'We could hold them off here. At the top of this cliff.'

Feyn gives me another one of those parent-child looks, as if to say: *now is that really true?* And it's not. I could have held them off back at the fissure, but they'll be through that by now. There'll be archers to cover the Gurta climbing up the cliff, and they'll kill me the instant I show my face.

'You never finished your story,' I say.

He makes a quizzical noise.

'The *s'Tani*. The Old Men, when we were all one race.'

'You remembered,' he says, and gives me that heartbreaking smile of his. Voids, it's beautiful when the boy smiles.

He settles himself and begins. When he speaks, it's like a teacher to a pupil. I recall his ambition to be the first of the Far People to attend Bry Athka University, and I see for the first time that he might make a good Masterscholar.

'A long time ago, there were the *s'Tani* and the *a'Jaka'ai* – the underdwellers, whom now you know as the Umbra, the Craggens and the Ya'yeen. They grew in the dark, but the *s'Tani* grew beneath the suns. They walked naked under the skies, and the touch of the light was warm.

'Then the suns grew cruel. The sickness began, and in anger the *s'Tani* blamed each other. Instead of one people, they became many people. They went underground then. The Gurta, the Banchu, the Khaadu, and the forty tribes of Eskara whose names you still carry long after the blood has been mixed.'

'It's not mixed so much,' I tell him. 'You can still see the bloodlines.

Rynn was Venya, they're always built like crayls, with broad faces. Fentha still have red hair and eyes. Nathka have beautifully proportioned features.'

'And yours? You are of the tribe of Massima.'

'Small, hair very black, brown eyes, dusky skin – I'm a typical Massima. Besides, we cheat. A child can take the tribal name of either the mother or the father. We pick the one most suitable.'

'Your son?'

'Massima,' I say. 'He was never a Venya. Go on with the story.'

'The people went underground, but some would not give up the sky. They called themselves *a'Sura'Sao,* which you call the Sun-Children. They hoped to endure the sickness, to become . . .' He waves his hand, searching for the word.

'Immune?'

'Yes. Like other sicknesses, we thought some would resist it. Many would die, but the survivors would be strong forever against it. And they said "We will show our brothers and sisters that we should not hide from the light. It is better to die here than live down there. They will remember us, and they will come back, and we will bring them here to live beneath the sky." '

'Didn't work out that way,' I say, looking out over the edge of the wall. I can hear Gurta voices in the distance, jabbering at each other. Gurta never could shut up. Suicidally tenacious yet hopelessly disorganised.

'Many died before we realised that the sickness was not like other sickness,' he continues. 'And it was getting worse. But we learned how to live, for we would not go below. And we waited for our brothers and sisters to come back, so we could show them.'

'But they never came.'

'They came back, but by then they had forgotten us. We greeted them and they slaughtered us. They saw savages and they were afraid.'

'Was that us? The Eskarans?'

'We do not recall. Back then, we did not know the differences between you. So then it was decided. We would let you make your own learning. You did not deserve help from us.' He makes a gesture that approximates a shrug. 'We visit only the most remote places of your people, to trade for what we need. But we do not stay long.'

'Ignorance equals division,' I say. 'Welcome to the world.'

'You know this, and you hate the Gurta anyway.'

'I have a right. They killed my husband. They enslaved me as a child.'

'There is more,' he says. 'They have done other things.'

I don't know how he surmised that; his talent for perception is frightening. I nod, but that's all.

'And yet you admire them.'

'Yes!' I snap at him. 'Yes. Who wouldn't? I've lived among them. They have culture and poetry and wonderful things, devices and songs and stories that can pull your heart from your chest. And yet they're stuck in this ancient prison of laws and rules that means we'll never see eye to eye, we'll never stop fighting. We'll only ever understand them when our scholars are picking over the bones of their once-mighty cities, and then we'll lament the loss of a great culture, feel terrible about its destruction and then pick another fucking fight and go do it again!'

I realise I've raised my voice and the Gurta can probably hear me. Feyn has a way of prodding sore spots. I'm almost certain he does it on purpose.

'I detest having to acknowledge the good points,' I say, quieter. 'Hate should be clean, in and out like a blade. You can't let yourself admire your enemy or you lose the will to kill them.'

Feyn looks down at the ground between his knees, his manner thoughtful. 'We have a saying. The translation is: Hate is like fire. If you embrace it, it consumes you.'

I almost make a scornful comeback and then stop myself. Pithy sayings are all very well, but good advice that you can't take is just irritating. *Stop hating*, he says. So simple. And while I'm doing that, I'll change the day to night.

The thought has barely crossed my mind when the light from outside begins to dim. Disbelief makes me doubt my hold on reality.

'Ready to go?' Feyn asks, getting to his feet.

I can only gape. The world is darkening before my eyes.

'What is it? What's happening?' I ask as I stand.

'Halflight,' he says.

'You knew? All this time underground and you still knew when halflight was coming?'

'It is life and death to us,' he says. 'It is instinct.'

The release of a bowstring reaches me a fraction of an instant before the arrow arrives, but that time is long enough for me to pull him down. The arrow skims close enough to part the hair on the side of his skull. An explosive curse comes from the darkness of the cave behind us.

We run. The light is dying as we plunge towards it. A second arrow ricochets from the cavern wall, rattling at our feet.

We round the corner at a sprint, and with that, we race out of my world and enter his.

14

The cave mouth opens a short way up a barren mountainside. At the foot of the mountain is a great flat stretch of scarred yellow-brown rock, which terminates suddenly at the edge of a sheer cliff. Beyond it is a sunken basin, bordered on all sides by steep escarpments and distant peaks.

Mist hangs thick in the basin, broken by the caps of colossal fungi. Mycora. The Caracassa mansions are built into the roots of one of these, many thousandspans underground. They emerge from the drifting vapour like humped islands, or tower above it, swollen discs spreading outward from their massive stems. The jagged tips of sandstone pillars are dimly visible down there, hazy shadows in the whiteness.

And above it all, the sky. The terrible sky.

The horizon is dominated by the colossal presence of Beyl, the mother-planet, looming before us as we burst from the cave and begin to slide and scramble down the mountainside. She's a vast orb of black and purple and green, banded with darkly glowing clouds of poison, flickering with storms the size of continents. She dwarfs our little moon, so massive that she snuffs out the risen sun. The last vestiges of the sun's light are dwindling as her enormous bulk slides across it.

Halflight. The false night brought on when the mother-planet eclipses one or both of our suns. But it won't last long: further along the horizon, the sky is brightening, heralding the arrival of another sun. A second dawn is coming, and if we're not under cover by then, we'll not live to see another.

I can't think straight. My mind is a mess of conflicting fears and instincts, foremost of which is the sheer *wrongness* of being outside. The idea that there is nothing above me, an endless emptiness, forever . . . I feel like I might just float into the sky and disappear. My body is seizing up with fear. It senses the day, lurking in sullen abeyance. It knows how slender the window of night is. It knows what will happen if the sun catches us in the open.

Escape. It's all there is. It's all I can allow myself to consider. If I think about anything more than skidding down this treacherous mountain slope, I'll fall apart. My body is burning with exhaustion: our short rest has done little to redress the rigours of our flight from Farakza. The Gurta are behind us, promising death as surely as the suns. Only Feyn can deliver me. This is his world. I have to believe in him.

We reach the bottom of the slope as the Gurta emerge from the cave. They have the altitude to put us within the range of their bows, and though the distance should make it an impossible shot, I've faced enough Gurta archers to know that impossible doesn't apply.

'Feyn! Don't run straight! Zigzag!' I shout at him. He's a little way ahead of me, having taken the lead on the way down. He's heading for the mist basin, the only feature of the landscape within reach of a sprint. Eerie crackles and piping noises began to drift up from below: the first soloists of the night chorus, tricked by the eclipse.

He starts to jink left and right randomly, as do I. We lunge and brake and throw our weight in different directions. I'd feel ridiculous if I didn't know it was our only chance of avoiding their arrows; and moments later I'm proved right. A shaft fires past my ribs and misses me by inches. Three more clatter around us, but none as close as the first. The last one falls some way behind. We're gaining distance while they stand still and fire.

I risk a glance back. They've resumed the chase. I call to Feyn and he understands: he breaks into a straight sprint again, and I follow suit.

The wind is picking up, stirred by the drastic drop in temperature. The air is cool and bone-dry. The sky is filled with stars, uncountable stars, and stroked with feathery strands of bruise-coloured cloud. Beyl's skin prickles with auroras, phantom tentacles thrashing over her flank at the point where she swallowed the sun.

The flat shelf of land is bare and blasted, hard stone pounding my soles through my shoes. My vision has narrowed to a tunnel, and I keep Feyn square in its centre. He's racing towards the mist basin as if he intends to fling himself off the cliff when he reaches it. Maybe he will. Maybe it's better than the alternative.

Glid larvae are dispersing before us, absurdly peaceful, floating down from the breeding grounds on the mountaintops. They ride the switching winds, using their membranous hoods as parachutes, fat grub-like bodies curled beneath, heading for the sea of soupy mist.

I can't think about them. I can't think about anything. Hysteria is threatening and the moment I let it in it'll shatter me.

Feyn alters course. He's seen something. I try to spot it but I can't, so I simply follow. We're heading for a hump of rock on the lip of the basin. Nothing makes sense over the scream of my senses telling me to fall to my knees and dig at the earth with my hands, to get back underground. I can feel the impending dawn, the insidious rise of the second sun over the mountains, and I know how an animal must feel as it hides from the gaze of a predator. The terror of that blazing eye will surely kill me, even before its light does.

The arrow hits me with the force of a hammer, punching through my shoulder in a nova of agony. I manage to stagger a dozen more steps before my balance deserts me and I fall on my face. Shock starts to settle in but my training won't let it. Subconscious defences, built up over many years, dam the flood. Teeth gritted, I start to get up as another arrow skips across the stone to my left. What kind of range do these bastards have, anyway?

Then Feyn is there, pulling me up, and we run. The arrowhead is sticking out of the front of my shoulder and it grates against my collarbone with every step, but I can still feel my arm and I can flex my fingers. I want to be sick.

Ahead of us. A fissure in the earth, a split in the hump of rock on the edge of the mist basin escarpment. That's what we're running for.

The sky to our left has turned purple-blue, dazzlingly rich. The tips of the mountain peaks are limned in fiery brightness.

Another arrow skitters past us, falling short. They must know what we know. Because as I watch the world bleaching before the dawn, I realise that we aren't going to make it. And if we don't, they certainly won't.

We're still a hundredspan from the fissure when the edge of the second sun clears the mountaintops.

Sunrise.

The world goes white. An awful, seething white, tinged with a burning blue. Shadows are smashed into cracks and crevices. The rocks and pebbles at my feet are thrown into sudden and sharp relief, every detail branded on my vision even after I shut my eyes. And with the light comes a prickling heat on my skin, the deadly glow pushing against me, scouring, pummelling.

Sheer primal panic claws at me like some frenzied beast trapped inside my ribs. I hear myself scream but it doesn't feel like me. My arm is thrown up in front of my face and I don't know which way is forward any more. My heart wants to burst; it beats so hard that I feel it's about to split. I stagger, flailing, shrieking.

Feyn, shouting at me. I can't hear the words. Somehow, I'm running. Sunlight surrounds me like flame. I'm stumbling through an inferno, my skin shrivelling at its touch.

I know nothing but the need to get out of the gaze of that cruel blue star. My lungs ache and my head swims. I fall, but Feyn has me, dragging me on.

'Keep going!' he cries, and I understand this time. 'Keep going!'

Then, shadow. Wonderful shadow. Somehow the fissure has swallowed me, somehow enfolded me in its protective sheath of dense rock. I'm crammed inward, borne on by Feyn. The arrow in my shoulder catches against the rock and the pain almost makes me pass out, but it's pain and it's real and I hold on to it. I'm barely aware of my surroundings, only that we are crushed together, sandwiched between stone, and Feyn has his arms around me, holding me close to him.

The Gurta are screaming. The sound comes to me through the haze. Somehow I raise my head, pulled by a savage need to watch them suffer. Consciousness hovers just close enough to permit it.

My eyes adjust quickly, bringing more detail with every passing moment. I see them fall to the ground, pawing at their faces, their high-pitched cries raw with desperation. Their pallid cheeks blister and rupture, oozing. Their movements become spastic as their brains scramble with sun-madness. Hair comes away beneath their hands. They scratch at the skin of their arms, tormented by furious itching, and the skin rips under their nails, wounds seeping with blood that instantly cooks black. Gore and bile drool from their noses, their mouths, and stains the crotches of their armour. Their cries become strangled, their white eyes yellowing and turning blind. One by one, they collapse and are still, but the deadly light of the sun is relentless, corrupting them. They boil with foulness from the inside out.

I can't take my eyes away from them. Mesmerised with horror. There's no satisfaction in this. Even they don't deserve this.

It takes some time before they cease to draw breath, by which time they are charred and sundered. Were it not for their armour and clothing, it would be hard to tell what they once were.

Gradually, I come back to myself. My skin is burning, itching. My shoulder is pulsing with pain where the arrow rests. I'm exhausted almost to the point of collapse. But overwhelming it all is the relief, the pure and incredible relief of shadow after light.

I'm alive. Even if only for this moment, even though I know in my heart that I've been sentenced to death by the touch of the sun, I'm alive. The sensation is dizzying. I feel desperate, eager to touch and taste and see and experience every tiny thing. Swept up, carried away, I have no idea why I do what I do next but I do it anyway.

With my good hand, I grab Feyn's head by his hair, tip his mouth up to mine, and I kiss him, hard.

The moment – and it's only a moment – is strange. There's no beard and his lips are so thin and soft, not like Rynn's. There's the taste of him, foreign, not like any Eskaran I've ever kissed. Everything is unfamiliar, and everything is wrong, and even before I notice that he's not responding I know it was a mistake but I still couldn't help it.

He pulls gently away, his hand between our lips. His eyes are sad, brimming with that soulful and fatherly understanding that I hate so much.

'No,' he says quietly.

It's not long before the sickness sets in.

Feyn allows me a short rest before we move deeper into the fissure. I could stop here and sleep forever but we have to get the arrow out of me and find a safe place before I'm too weak to stand. The fissure – the legacy of a long-dried stream – is wide enough for us to squeeze through and Feyn is confident it will take us to the floor of the basin, but I know that I'll never make it down with the arrow sticking through my shoulder so we break off the head and I pass out for a few moments. Then he breaks off the flight, which is worse, because I stay conscious.

I've become suddenly very cold, mentally as well as physically. Logical. No time for despair. One foot in front of the other. Survive.

Feyn is right; he'd read the land well. The fissure runs down to the sloped sides of the basin. He doesn't seem any the worse for the brief exposure to sunlight, nor does he waste time on sympathy for me. Every fibre of my body wants to give up. Everything seems pointless now. But he just won't stop.

The bottom of the basin is marshy and dank. Thick creepers straggle out of scummed pools to wrap around the trunks of lichen trees. Huge fungus-flowers sit like veined and spotted cauldrons, enticing in unsuspecting insects. Gnarled mycora roots arch overhead, long chains of algae hanging from them. The hoots and cackles of the animals are loud. I catch sight of something slithering rapidly along the arm of a lichen tree, but it corkscrews away before I can identify it.

The mist is thin down here, like a grey membrane across our sight. Above us is a bright haze of blinding cloud. I can only assume that the mist protects us to some degree, or that the uneclipsed sun hasn't risen high enough to shine directly down into the basin. Either way, I just don't care any more. I stagger, limbs like stone, following my dark guide through the murk.

One foot in front of the other.

Survive.

Feyn finds a shelf of dirt and rock high up on a slope, overhung with vines like a curtain. He checks it expertly for signs of occupation, scans the surrounding foliage, and then ushers me inside. I'm shivering. I want to scratch myself to relieve the awful itching but I can't stop thinking of the Gurta, how their skin came away beneath their nails. Will that happen to me? Maybe Feyn knows. I daren't ask.

I slide under the low roof of the overhang and lie down on the soft, loamy soil. It smells of freshness and moisture and a vegetable kind of scent that I don't recognise. My eyes are beginning to sting and water. My shoulder is going numb where the length of arrow is lodged in it. I'm afraid, not of the pain that I believe is coming, nor the horrible death that will follow, but of my helplessness to prevent it. The waiting is always the worst.

Feyn checks me over swiftly. His expression is remarkably unconcerned. At first I find it reassuring, but later I realise that it's just his way. I know what he's thinking. If I die, I die. Nothing can be done. He'll move on. The SunChildren don't really do mourning.

'Stay here,' he says, with a swift grin.

'Was that a joke?' I ask weakly, through parched lips. 'You'd better keep me alive if you want to learn some better ones.'

'I will do what things I can,' he says, and then he's gone, disappearing through the curtain of vines.

I sleep. Even through the pain in every part of me, exhaustion demands its due. Feyn returns with water in a funnel-shaped fungus bloom, and he makes me drink even though swallowing hurts like blazing fuck. Then he positions himself behind my head and gives me a stick to bite on. I know what's coming but neither of us say a word. The stick tastes like dirt, bitter and acid. I nearly bite through it when he pulls out the arrow shaft.

He salves and dresses the wound with ripped sections of his shirt, then makes me eat a sweet paste folded inside a bland-tasting mushroom the size of my hand. He grinds up some spores and spreads them on my exposed skin, which calms the itching a little. He has the quiet, efficient manner of a physician, and I submit because I have no choice. Never in my life have I felt so bad, never in the depths of the worst illness in all my turns.

'It is done,' he says.

I look up at him, my eyes asking the question that my lips won't.

'It will pass within three days, or it will not pass,' he says. 'Your skin is not like mine. I do not know if the sickness got deep.'

'What if it did?'

'Then you will die. There will be very much pain. I will make poison for you, if it is that way.'

I cough feebly in surprise at his bluntness. 'Do you know what the Eskaran word "tact" means?'

'It means "to lie." Is that right?'

I smile. It hurts my face. 'Yes, that's right,' I croak, and then I go back to sleep.

13

Time is slippery and unreliable. I wake and sleep and it's hard to tell the difference. Fevered nightmares curdle with the hallucinations that cloud my eyes when they're open. Sometimes I'm aware of the shelter of the rock, of Feyn sitting next to me and talking. Other times I'm flitting through a world of horrors, bewildered, consumed by pain. Moments of lucidity float like windows on a sea of delirium.

Faces from my past loom up at me, distorted. Master Allet, Aila, Keren, Chorik. Someone saying a name, over and over. *Belek Aspa.* Voids, where do I know that name from?

At some point I feel my stomach clench and its contents come rushing up my throat to fill my mouth. Feyn is there to clean my face, but afterward he makes me eat again, and I throw it up again, which clears my head a little. He makes me eat a third time, and I keep it down.

I can sense large things moving about in the undergrowth beyond my bunk of stone, soil and vines, but whether they are real or not I can't tell. Insects creep on the edge of my vision and crawl up my arms and into my hair. Feyn tells me they're just the pricking of my nerves given shape by my tortured mind. It doesn't help.

It's impossible to get comfortable. Moving is a torment as my bones seem to grind against each other. The sickness crawls beneath my skin, fighting to burrow deeper while my body struggles to cast it out. It's a black, oily, vile thing, a taint in my veins.

Somehow, in amongst it all, I find the lucidity to begin a chant. At first it comes brokenly, in bits and pieces, but in time the phrases link up, form a chain and hold solid. I sink into a shallow trance. I have to drive out the taint. It's the only way I'll make it through.

If I die now, I'll never see my son again.

*

I surface from a dream of knives into a state of suspicious clear-mindedness. My body aches but my thoughts feel like mine again. It's night outside my shelter, and the mist basin is raucous with sounds of life. Something enormous and wet slurps through the fungal underbrush beyond the layer of vines that protect me. A small crab, its shell polished as a mirror, is sidling through my den, segmented eyes watching me. It's cool and dark, and a hissing wind scours the land.

Feyn is sitting cross-legged at my feet, listening to the cacophony outside. He turns and looks at me, sensing me wake.

'I feel better,' I say, quietly.

He shakes his head. 'It is how it happens. The worst is coming.'

My momentary hope collapses. 'What's the worst?'

'My people call it . . . the translation is "Shadow Death".'

I don't much like the sound of that.

'Long in the past, we thought we could beat the sickness by facing it,' he continues. 'Many went out into the sun, to test themselves. Many died. But those who did not die, they became changed.' He pokes the steadily approaching crab with a stick of petrified lichen-tree and it scuttles away from him. 'Even now, some want to test themselves. Some take the risk, to make Shadow Death.'

'You were exposed,' I say. 'Out there. You caught the sun too.'

He shakes his head. '*a'Sura'Sao* have skin that protects us, like the animals who walk in the day. We can stand in the light for a short time. It depends which sun, what time of day, many things. One sun is stronger than the other.'

I sigh, and relax a little. That news relieves me of a tension I didn't realise I had inside me. I manage a smile. If I die now, at least I did this. At least I got him out.

'The ones who make Shadow Death and survive are stripped of all things,' he says. 'They are made new.'

'How?'

'It is in their eyes and thoughts, and in the things they speak. They have been to the end and returned. Only Shadow Death can do this.'

'How long will it be?'

He brushes his hand through my lank and stinking hair. 'Soon.'

And yet I feel better than I did before, as if I was already on my way back. A cruel deception. I shift my weight and settle.

'Talk to me,' I say. It comes out more pleadingly than I intended. 'Talk to me until it comes.'

'What should I talk of?'

'You,' I say. 'Tell me about you.'

He seems uncomfortable about this, and I suddenly begin to understand why I know so little about him, even after all we've been through together.

'Our way is . . . not to speak of our own histories,' he says. 'We believe that now is the only importance. Others may tell our tales, but for us to speak of our own, it is . . . not polite. It is boastful.'

'There's nobody else to tell me,' I say, gently insistent. I need something to keep my mind off what's to come, but more than that, I want to know about this person that I've risked my life for, whom I've dragged from a Gurta prison for no sane or logical reason I can think of. I deserve that much. 'Will you do it? For me?'

He drops his eyes. 'I will tell you,' he says. 'But if you survive, you must never speak of my boastfulness.'

He's perfectly serious. I treat it with the gravity it deserves. 'I won't say a word.'

So he talks. He talks of being born into a coterie, which I learn is the best translation of their name for a clan or a group. He talks of the travelling life, of hunting and herding when the nights come. He talks of storing food for the retreat to the high caves during the Season of Days, when the suns are on opposite sides of Beyl and so Callespa is bathed in permanent light, except during the brief periods of halflight when the mother-planet shadows us. He talks of the ways they have come to live beneath the suns, and how they exist on the hostile skin of our moon.

Then, when he has evaded the issue long enough, he talks about himself. A quiet, shy child, living in the shadow of his brother. The elder sibling was a hunter, a fighter and explorer. Handsome, strong and capable, he attracted the admiration of the young people of the coterie. Feyn was slight and not inclined to physical pursuits, but he was fiercely bright and a voracious learner. He spent his time with the elder folk of the tribe, or listening to the debates of the Pathfinders. He tells me that the Pathfinders are an elected triumvirate who lead the coterie.

As he speaks, I begin to see a life of quiet alienation, a boy wise beyond his years who could not engage with his peers, even in the small world of the coterie where everyone knew everyone. He walked with the Loremaster – the coterie's teacher-of-wisdom – instead of hunting with the other boys or practising his crafts. Comfort came in learning, and in the company of adults who wouldn't mock him or force him into unwilling competition.

Books were a rare commodity in the travelling life, where portability was vital, and most knowledge was carried in the heads of the Loremasters, whose apprenticeship involved memory techniques that gave them Khaadu-like recall. They were living libraries. But occasionally books were found or traded with distant outposts, and made their way into circulation among the coteries of the SunChildren. The Loremaster of Feyn's coterie had one such book. An Eskaran novel called *The Light In The High Tower*.

Feyn's obsession with this strange language, its alphabet and structure, became all-consuming. He pestered the Loremaster to teach him what he knew of Eskaran, but was disappointed to find the Loremaster's knowledge woefully incomplete, for he had only learned a little from another Loremaster called Siaw. He had intended to decode the book, but he did not have enough of the language to make it possible. It was wasted on him.

In his early adolescence Feyn left his coterie and joined another, taking the book with him as a gift. SunChild coteries meet occasionally in great fairs during the Season Of Nights, he says, and it's not uncommon for members to swap groups. Some did it for the change, or to find new friends or partners, or to get away from someone they disliked. Feyn did it to travel with Siaw.

Under his tutelage, Feyn began training to be a Loremaster, and he learned Eskaran. Though Siaw's own knowledge was imperfect – picked up from sporadic contact with Eskaran traders on the fringes of society, the source of what few tales we have of the SunChildren – he knew enough to show Feyn how to read his book.

I've never heard of *The Light In The High Tower*. By Feyn's account it seems to be a cheap romantic novel, of the kind you might find circulating among the handmaidens in any aristocratic court. I don't have the heart to offer my opinion. To him, it's a stunning piece of literature, a window into a society he can only imagine. To me, it sounds like something I'd use to wedge a door open.

'I became excited by an idea which said: *go underground*,' he tells me. 'I wanted to go to this place, Bry Athka, where the book speaks of. They have a University, a great place of learning. That is true?'

'It's true. My son went to the military school there.'

'You have been to the University?'

'A few times,' I say, not mentioning that my longest visit was to murder a respected academic who was about to publish his treatise on the dangers of foreign conflict to a merchant society. Caracassa's enemies would have wielded it over the Turnward Claw Alliance for years to come if it reached general circulation. He'd been repeatedly warned, but he was too stubborn to listen. I wasn't proud of myself for killing an old man for what seemed such a small thing, but neither did I feel guilty. I was under lifedebt: I was Ledo's weapon. Conscience was a luxury I gave away when I skinmarked my cheek with the sign of a Bondswoman.

Then he tells me the story of a girl, who treated him kindly and whom he fell in love with, but who would not accept him in the end. Her heart was with the hunters, not a quiet Loremaster-in-training. Knowledge and learning did not keep a girl warm at night, or make her feel safe.

It was an achingly familiar story. I almost began to tell him how my son had gone through the same thing more than once, but I felt it would cheapen Feyn's experience, and by the way he spoke of this girl, the wounds were still fresh.

So he left that coterie and travelled alone for a time. It was a dangerous thing to do, but SunChildren sometimes took such journeys of self-reflection. Feyn felt he had to examine himself and decide if his life was on the right path.

'My sorrow drove me away,' he says. 'I felt I had no worth. What worth was it to read a book? What worth was it to know the words of a society I would never be with? Tradition had kept the *a'Sura'Sao* at a distance from the Eskarans. Our meetings with your people were brief, and in far places. So I decided I would meet with the Pathfinders of many coteries at our next gathering and persuade them that I should go to Eskara and learn your ways, and teach you of us.' His eyes come alive at the thought. 'I would go to the University at Bry Athka and return an explorer! Braver than any hunter!'

'You did this for a girl?'

'At first I thought that was true, but it was not for her. It was to be done for me.'

'What happened?'

'When I had made to decide, I travelled to meet a coterie I knew of. We travel certain routes, you understand? We leave markers and trails for *a'Sura'Sao,* who know how to read them. Our lands are full of secrets for our kind, hoards of food and equipment, buried sunsuits, maps to hidden places. It is necessary for us to help one another to survive. I could pick up their trail and follow.'

'But you never got there.'

'I could not catch them before . . . mmm . . . you call it "big wind"?'

'Hurricane,' I say. I remember Reitha telling me about the storms that sometimes engulfed our moon, blanketing all the known lands and probably far beyond, laying waste to anything not hardy enough to stand up to them.

'Yes. It comes sometimes at a certain time of year. I took shelter in the caves, and I had many supplies, but it blew for seven days and it did not seem as if it would stop. So I began to think . . . now is the time I must go underground. Why should I ask permission? The Pathfinders might say no, and then my life is worthless.' He's fidgeting now, embarrassed by his impatience, ashamed.

'So I went underground. Gurta caught me. They took me to Farakza. I think they had never seen a SunChild, so they thought I was a . . . freak?' I nod as he looks to me for approval of the word. 'But the scholars know I was a SunChild. Otherwise, the chirurgeons would cut me up. So they try to learn my language, but it is not easy, and I think they forgot about me.'

'You were lucky,' I say.

'What is luck? This is twice time you said it.'

I'm about to reply, but suddenly it feels as if the world has plunged away from me. My head starts to pound, my body feels simultaneously lighter than air and heavy as lead. It feels like an attack, like poison flooding through me. Feyn sees it.

'It is beginning. The Shadow Death.'

I can feel the pain growing, rising, inexorable as the dawn that did this to me. I grab Feyn's hand and hold it tight.

'Don't leave me.'

'One way or another,' he says, 'you soon will be free.'

There's a stabbing like a rusty blade in my guts which drives the breath from me. All sense flees in the oncoming panic. I can't face what's coming. I crush his hand as if I could break the bones there, lessen the pain by sharing it. Feyn sits and watches me as my vision clouds and my body arches and delirium clamps icy fingers around my head.

I'm dying. Nothing can stop that now.

'Jai, I'm sorry . . .' I mutter through clenched teeth, and they're the last words I'm capable of saying before my throat begins to seize.

Of all the final thoughts I could have had, why an apology?

36

I never was very domestic, but I liked to try. Every so often I was seized by the urge to be like a storybook mother, the kind of strange being that relished cleaning and cooking and ensuring that the cupboards were full. The urge never lasted long, and usually ended in a vague suspicion that I was the victim of some vast conspiracy, that these people only *pretended* to enjoy their lives in order to fool me into copying them. I just didn't have the temperament. It all seemed so pointless.

But still the urge would come back, and when I awoke this particular turn I was seized by a feeling of immense gratitude towards my husband and son, for no other reason than that they existed. In thanks, I would make them an elaborate breakfast. Just because.

Rynn ambled dozily out of the bedroom to find me cursing at the stove, surrounded by piles of chopped spores and attending to several spitting pans. He wandered over to the huge round window that dominated our living-space, yawned and scratched himself as he looked out over the Tangles from our vantage point high up in the Caracassa Mansions. His little routine. Then he came over to me, slid his arms around me from behind, and all my frustration faded away for a moment as I melted into him with a murmur of pleasure.

'Smells like another disaster,' he rumbled in my ear, voice deep from sleep.

It was a risky ploy, but this time it made me smile.

'You'll shut up and like it,' I replied, turning to kiss his grizzled cheek.

He gave me a squeeze and disengaged. 'Make me extra. I don't know when I'll get to eat this turn.'

'Your will is my purpose,' I said, with a flourish.

'That's the spirit, wife!'

Any reply I might have made was forestalled by a particularly violent eruption of oil from one of the pans, making me flinch and suck my breath in through my teeth.

'Watch that pan,' Rynn said helpfully as he slumped down on the settee. He wiped the back of his hand across his eyes and groaned. Waking up was a dreadful experience for him. It took him most of the turn to get over it.

I went back to my cooking. Voids, how did people find satisfaction in this?

'When do you have to go?'

'On the tenhour. They'll pick me up out front.'

'You have any idea how long?'

He made a negative grunt. It was a stupid question anyway; he would be as long as it took. He'd only received the message late last turn. The usual thing: *Clan Caracassa requires your services.* This time he was acting as an escort for a trainload of medical supplies heading for the Borderlands. That was as much as either of us knew. No doubt there would be several other Cadre on board. Maybe it would be a straight there-and-back job, or maybe it was a cover to move them to the front so they could be employed on some secret mission or another. We both knew the score. It wasn't our place to question.

In two turns' time I was also being sent away, and I hadn't even been told my destination yet. They just said I was needed. *Clan Caracassa requires your services.*

'I'll square it with the minder before I leave,' I said, and felt suddenly sad. It took some of the momentum out of my temporary drive towards good motherhood. The Clan provided somebody to look after Jai while we were away, of course; but I worried that his solitary, introverted nature was our fault. So much of his life was spent under the care of nannies and minders. Would he have been more vivacious, more playful, a happier child if his parents had always been around? Or would he have turned out this way no matter what?

'There's another one of your little notes here,' Rynn said, as I tipped a pile of diced mushrooms into some egg mixture. Perhaps it was just weariness, but I thought I heard a slightly disparaging edge to his voice.

I walked over and took it from his outstretched hand. 'Found it behind one of the cushions.' he said. He wasn't looking at me.

I returned to the stove and read it while watching the breakfast with half an eye. The content was fairly banal: a short summary of what Jai had done at school the previous turn. But the real message was hidden inside. It was written in code. *Our* code, the secret language that existed between Jai and I.

I had a dream last turn. I was in a battle. I was fighting the White-skins. There were explosions and shard-cannons. I was scared and I hid in a hole, but the White-skins were coming. Then a moth came, but the moth was you. And you said something, but it didn't mean anything. Then I realised you were talking in our code. And you said you were always with me, but you were being blown away by the wind and you couldn't stay, so in the end you weren't with me at all.

I read the note again while the omelette stiffened in the pan. No telling how long ago he'd written it. I couldn't remember the last time I'd looked behind the cushions of the settee. But then, I did recall one morning when he'd woken up agitated and more distant than usual. He wouldn't talk about it then. Perhaps this was the reason.

He'd taught me the code on the condition of absolute secrecy. Of course I agreed to his terms. I was pleased that he wanted to share this with me alone. It made me feel special to be singled out this way, and proud that he had come up with something so clever. It was an impressively complex system for a twelve-year-old to devise.

Ever since, we had been leaving notes for each other around our chambers. Usually they were entirely pointless, phrases and poems and little stories that meant nothing out of context. As we got better, the notes got longer, and so did the coded messages beneath.

At first they were simple phrases, created only for the satisfaction of having the other decode them: *How are you this turn?; My name is Jai, what's yours?; There is a hole in my shirt. Please fix it.* Later, we actually started to make meaningful communications through the notes. He would write long letters about things he wouldn't say verbally. As if the medium of code had opened a channel through the defences he had erected around himself. *There's a girl in my class I really like . . .*

Rynn had asked about the notes, of course, but I told him they were just a game we were playing. He wasn't convinced. He pretended not to be bothered by it, but I could see he felt annoyed at being excluded. He felt he was being laughed at, perhaps.

It gave me a small and uncharitable sense of triumph to see his reaction. Cheap, but there all the same. Maybe if he'd been more understanding with Jai when he was ten, he wouldn't be shut out of our son's inner world now he was twelve.

It was only natural that Jai should choose me for his partner in this. I had always been the one who encouraged his inventiveness, whereas Rynn had barely praised him at all these past two years, since he failed the Cadre tests.

Jai came out of his bedroom as I was dishing out breakfast, arranging it so as to best conceal the burnt bits. Mushroom omelette, roasted sporebread, kebab of black bat, and a bowl of spicy stew. A jug of sugar water stood in the middle of the table, and three ceramic mugs. I'd done my best, but somehow the result still ended up far less impressive than it had in my imagination. Once again, I had decided that this perfect domestic wife act just wasn't for me.

'Ah! He emerges!' Rynn grinned. It was meant to be a bluff greeting, but Jai took it as a dig. It was the kind of misunderstanding that was becoming more and more frequent between them.

'It's not *that* late,' he said, looking at the brass clock on the wall.

'Come and sit down,' I told him, with a smile. The sight of him in his morning robe, dark hair in disarray, brought back a surge of that grateful warmth which had inspired me to cook in the first place.

He took his seat. Rynn had already begun to eat. He had quite an appetite, and he wasn't fussy. I loved that about him.

'Your father has to go away again,' I said as I sat down. Jai was loading up his plate. He paused, looked inquiringly at Rynn.

'That's right,' Rynn said, between forkfuls. Then he slapped Jai on the shoulder. 'But you're a young man now, eh? You'll cope.'

I caught the wince that crossed our son's face, before his expression fixed into the reassuringly grave frown of a boy acting a role beyond his years. 'Of course. It'll be, what, a few weeks? Voids, I'll be fine.'

'Don't curse.'

'Sorry.'

'I'm sure it won't be that long,' I said. 'One of us will be back pretty soon, I bet.'

He gave me a quick little smile. *It's alright, Mother.* But the smile didn't reach his eyes. He couldn't quite hide the disappointment.

I watched the two of them as they ate. Rynn oblivious, comfortable with the silence. He never spoke unless he had something to say. But Jai was all coiled up, wanting to speak but not daring to, knowing that he wouldn't be understood. He was palpably awkward around his father, and I suffered when I saw him that way almost as much as he did. He was so desperate for the approval that had been withdrawn from him, but he didn't know how to get it back. Just being near Rynn was torment, and yet being away from him was worse, because then there was no possibility at all of redemption.

Rynn was only aware of it because I'd told him. But he didn't know what to do, either. Jai was too smart to fall for false compliments or feigned encouragement. Rynn was too honest to give them. Jai couldn't deny that his truest desire was to be an inventor, not a warrior. Rynn couldn't deny that his son – the only child we would ever have – didn't match the image of manhood that he'd dreamed of. Between the two of them, they were at a stalemate.

Jai took a breath to speak, but he was interrupted by a frantic rapping at the door.

'It's Liss,' he said. Rynn groaned.

I got up, knowing that Jai had guessed right. The second barrage of hammering proved it. Nobody else ever assaulted our door with that kind of agitation.

'What's that woman want now?' Rynn said.

I cast him a sharp look. *Don't disrespect our masters in front of our son.* He fell to his plate again, grumbling. 'More trouble than it's worth knowing those two,' he muttered around a mouthful of omelette. He'd long forgotten that the only reason we had a son at all was because of the twins.

I opened the door and Liss threw herself into my arms, wailing. She was in a particularly flamboyant fashion phase, her thin frame swathed in layers of bright colours and her hair dyed green and orange. Thick red and yellow makeup had run down her cheeks.

'Hello, Liss,' Rynn said, deadpan, as if her melodramatic entrance was the most normal thing in the world. Jai suppressed a laugh.

Liss threw him a haughty look, sniffed, and wiped her eyes,

smearing her makeup further. 'Let's go elsewhere,' she hissed. 'I have a deadly and terrible secret!'

I was worried about her, a little; but this last line, delivered with absolute seriousness, almost made me crack up. I turned it into a cough instead. She was so ridiculous sometimes, it was easy to forget how dangerous it was to offend her.

I didn't need to ask where Casta was. Liss was only ever seen alone when Casta disappeared on one of her periodic absences. The abandoned twin was more than usually woeful and lachrymose during those times, but she was doubly excitable when Casta returned.

'We're having breakfast,' I told her, though the protest had little force. As a Bondswoman, I was at her beck and call. I was just hoping she'd understand and put her own crises aside for a moment.

She didn't. 'Never mind them. Come on! There are lives at stake!' She took my hand and tugged me towards the corridor outside.

'I'll see you when I get back, then,' Rynn said. Cold.

I was suddenly angry at him. What right did he have to take that tone? As if *I* was responsible for Liss's shitty timing. As if *I* had ruined things.

But I knew what he was thinking. He disapproved of my friendship with the twins. He thought I should have made an effort to distance myself from them. And this was the result. Hence, my fault.

I didn't trouble to reply. I'd only have said something snappy. It hurt me to leave this way. We were both passionate people, and that meant we had our arguments; but we always resolved them before we went to bed. Now I would be replaying that last comment over and over the whole time we were apart, constructing arguments, imagining what I'd say when we next met. I should have just been able to forget it, but I never could. I hated the idea that he'd scored a point on me without giving me the chance to defend myself.

And what was worse, I hated the idea that he might die with this faint thread of poison hanging between us. If he was to die, I wanted it to be with the absolute certainty that I loved him.

I followed Liss out into the corridor, glaring at her back. The good mood I had woken up with had soured. I felt a failure as a mother and as a wife.

This had better be good, Liss.

I tried to ask her what was wrong, hoping to get it over with quickly so I could get back to my family. She hushed me. 'Too many ears and eyes,' she said, and wouldn't be drawn further.

She took me high up into the Mansions, to her chambers, blind to my obvious impatience. The twins' rooms were embarrassingly opulent but messy, an uneasy fusion of Liss's extravagance and Casta's more restrained personality. She led me by the hand past the door guards, through the reception rooms with their gaudy curtains and pools stocked with bright fish and eels, into the bedroom where the twins slept.

The enormous bed was in disarray, and Liss's clothes were draped over any place that would serve as a hook or a hanger. Casta's influence was evident in the carefully organised ornamental figurines that populated the bedside table and window sills. Shinestone lamps of coloured glass gave the place a cosy ambience, although there was still a faintly creepy tinge to the room. Something to do with the idea of the two of them sleeping together.

Liss threw herself down on the bed and I perched next to her. 'So tell me,' I said. I could still catch Rynn outside the Mansions if Liss's latest problem could be dealt with quickly.

She rolled onto her side and gazed at me hard. 'I received a letter,' she breathed.

'And?' I was annoyed, and it slipped into my tone.

'You're not *listening* to me!' she snapped, and then her head slumped down on the bed and she sulked. 'You don't care.'

I took a steadying breath, composed myself. Being thorny wouldn't help my cause. Better to just go with it. 'Forgive me,' I said. 'I didn't mean to be curt. I just have a lot on my mind.'

'You hate me,' Liss accused, lip trembling.

'No, I love you,' I said, stroking her hair. It was hard to stay mad when she looked so pathetic. 'We're friends, aren't we? Aren't I the one you come to when Casta's away?'

Liss sniffled and nodded. She was like a child: infuriating, selfish, but ultimately innocent. She didn't think about other people; it wasn't in her nature. She didn't know any better.

'Tell me what was in the letter.'

Suddenly animated, she flung herself upright and drew out the letter from inside her dress. She presented it to me proudly.

'I have a *suitor*!' she declared.

I blinked. *This* was the cause of the tears? She certainly didn't seem too sad about it now. I took the letter.

'Open it!' she said. 'It's from Thulia Iolo. He says he wishes the pleasure of my company at his mansion in the Rainlands!'

'Well, that's good,' I said, reading. I looked up. 'Isn't it?'

'Yes! He loves me, he loves me! And I love him!'

'You do? Have you met him?'

Liss waved that away. 'When two people are meant to be together, they just know.'

'He's certainly a rich man,' I mused. 'Good political match. I can't see Ledo objecting.' I managed a smile. 'I'm happy for you, Liss.'

Her face clouded with dread. 'Oh, but you don't know, you don't know. You don't know how Casta gets.'

'How does she get?'

'Murderous! Murderous angry!'

'She doesn't know?'

'No! No, no, no! How could I tell her?' She was pacing around the room now, agitated. She opened the door and peeked out in case Casta should be listening. Once certain that we couldn't be overheard, she became courageous. 'And why *should* I? She goes away and never tells me why, but what about me? If *I* want to go away, she forbids it! If *I* want to have a husband, she says she'll do terrible things! Just because *she* hasn't got a suitor. Who could love her?'

She cringed and then ran to me, clutching me for protection. She'd gone too far and was afraid that her sister would somehow know. 'I'm sorry, I'm sorry. I didn't mean that. You know I didn't mean that, don't you?'

'I know you love your sister,' I reassured her. 'And she does, too.'

'Where does she go, when she goes away?'

'Perhaps she's looking after Clan business. After all, if something should happen to Ledo, she'll become Magnate.'

Liss snarled. 'She always acts the older sister. Older by a few minutes! That's all! If I'd come out first it would have been different!' Then she became maudlin. 'She doesn't keep any secrets from me. Not from me. Only this.'

'Will you go to the Rainlands, do you think?'

She nodded. 'I'm ruled by my heart, Orna. Nobody understands the love that I feel. I'm helpless in its grasp.'

'And will you tell your sister?'

'Never!'

But I knew she would. Liss was too weak-willed to keep a secret from Casta. I wondered if Liss's fears about her sister were founded in anything factual, or if she was just overreacting. Certainly, Casta was possessive. But dangerously so? Who could say?

Thulia Iolo was either very brave or very ill-informed.

Then Liss was away on another tack, rhapsodising about how she felt like a woman at last, now that she was the object of a great man's affection. My hopes of seeing Rynn before he left dwindled to nothing. I settled in and resigned myself to a long session of counselling. The needs of a Bondswoman were secondary to the needs of her masters and mistresses.

Once, my life had been simple. So very long ago. Once there had been a farm, a mother who cooked wonderful meals and a father who was invincible and would never let anybody hurt me. Once we told tales by firelight and I didn't have a care beyond what games I would play with my little brother. Once the White-skins were only a story to frighten children into obeying their parents.

I wanted those times back. I wanted a world that was straightforward and clean, a world where I didn't have to kill anyone and nobody tried to kill me and I could be a mother to my son and a wife to my husband.

But that world, if it existed, had passed far beyond my reach.

12

We're moving.

It's the first thing I notice, even before I open my eyes to see the soft bed I'm lying in. The blankets are of a downy material I don't recognise. A curtain of furred hide surrounds the square bed, sealing me into my own small world. Music is coming from beyond, wind instruments cooing over the sporadic pluck of strings.

That's when I realise I'm not dead.

I don't try to stir myself. I just stare at the ceiling, where arched beams support a curved wooden roof, and think of nothing. I don't feel relieved, or happy, or thankful. Just peaceful. So I lie there for a long time, listening to the music. The air is cool on my face. Tears creep from the outside corners of my eyes, trickling down towards my ears. I don't know where they're coming from, but they come anyway.

After a while, I try to work out where I am. It's some kind of room, and big; I can tell that by the acoustics. But the sensation of movement puzzles me, a gentle and irregular up-and-down swaying and the occasional bump from below. It doesn't feel like water, so we're not on a ship. It feels like we're travelling over land, but the room sounds far too big to be any kind of wagon or cart.

My fingers brush against my thigh and I feel an unfamiliar fabric there. Stirred by curiosity, I raise the blankets and look down at myself. I'm shocked by how much effort it takes to hold them up. My body smells of scented oils, delicate and bitter.

I'm wearing a pale green slip, dyed with angular patterns along its length. It's the patterns, more than anything else, that put the whole picture together for me. I remember seeing similar patterns at a bazaar in Veya, on artefacts that were being sold as genuine SunChild merchandise. I had been sceptical, and doubly so when I saw the outrageous price. But now I wondered.

I'm with the SunChildren. Feyn has brought me to his people.

I lie back. The insidious tingle on my skin has gone. The agonising pain and delirium seems like a nightmare, fading in the face of wakefulness. I've passed through the Shadow Death.

Eventually thoughts begin to intrude, and the fragile tranquillity I felt begins to come apart. Thoughts of Jai, of Rynn, of our escape from Farakza. So I raise myself on one trembling elbow, and I part the hide curtain a little.

I'm in a small hall, made of varnished rootwood or something similar. My bed is one of four, occupying the corners of the room. The other three have their curtains drawn back and are empty. Patterned hangings decorate the walls, low tables beneath them. One side of the room is evidently a food preparation area of sorts, with a small metal stove, a chopping surface and knives and plates gently rattling in their racks. Glass globes set on heavy stone bases glow from within, and several large areas of wall are covered by flaps of thick brown hide. I guess that they work as windows when they're open, but it's a little chilly and they've been fixed shut.

There are six SunChildren here, sitting in a circle on a large mat in the centre of the room. Three men are playing instruments, the other three – an old woman and two small girls – are watching. I'm surprised to see that one of the wind instruments – a kind of flute fashioned from a reed – is being played by Feyn.

Their skin is uniformly black, and both men and women wear their hair in oiled ringlets. They're small and willowy in stature, wearing robes of unfamiliar weave, something like silk. Each robe is stitched with the most marvellous designs. Some show sun-rays and landscapes and animals and people, evidently depicting a story. Others are more abstract but no less beautiful, with bold, jagged shapes and curling embroidery. The craftsmanship is dazzling.

I watch Feyn play for a short while, before one of the children notices me and points, exclaiming excitedly in their percussive tongue. Feyn breaks off from the melody immediately, puts down his flute and hurries over. The others dissolve into chatter, and the old woman has to physically restrain the children from running towards me.

Feyn pushes back the curtain, his dark eyes sparkling. 'Welcome back,' he grins, and that makes me smile too.

'So that was the Shadow Death, hmm?' I say. 'Don't know what all the fuss is about.'

He laughs, almost hugs me, hesitates, then does it anyway as best he can with me lying down. The others in the room make celebratory cries, a high *yi-yi-yi*!

'You have been spared by the suns,' he says.

'No,' I reply. 'I *beat* them.'

Feyn turns back to the others and chatters off a rapid string of syllables, punched with the back-of-the-throat click that characterises their language. Relaying what I just said. The others break up laughing, and one of them slaps his upper arm repeatedly in what I take to be appreciation of my comment.

'Is this your—' I begin, then realise I've forgotten the word he used.

'My coterie? Now it is.'

'How did you get me here?'

'I made a signal,' he replied. 'I will show you how, when you are strong again. They followed my signal, and they found me.' He strokes my hair tenderly. 'I had to leave you several times, to climb out of the basin and tend to my signal. Each time I was afraid something would find you before I returned. It is not good to be helpless in that place.'

'You did fine,' I say, and I lie back on the pillows. 'You did fine.'

Suddenly I feel light-headed, and I have an overpowering urge to sleep. I'm weaker than I thought. Feyn understands, of course. He runs his fingers along the line of my jaw, touching me like a lover, and then retreats and closes the curtain behind him. I can hear the children's frantic questions and Feyn's patient answers, fading away as I fall into the plush folds of oblivion.

I wake and it's bright. That gives me a shock. I know that light. It's daytime.

Feyn is lying in bed next to me, his thin shoulders rising and falling in slumber. I'm mildly surprised by that, too, but it pales in comparison to the proximity of the suns' light. And yet we're still moving. These people travel during the *day*?

At first I don't dare move. Instinct tells me I should burrow under the blankets and hide. But whereas before I would have panicked, after passing through the Shadow Death it seems ridiculous. Gradually I calm myself. The brightness is coming from outside the curtains, but it's not strong enough to be direct sunlight. Before I can think myself out of it, I part the curtain and look.

The room beyond is deserted, and the other three beds have their furred curtains drawn. The hide flaps on the walls burn with white light: the sun is beating on them from the outside. There are two on each flank of the hall.

I look for a while longer. The light in the room doesn't seem to be threatening. I couldn't say why, but the hide flaps have robbed it of its danger. Still, I don't trust it enough to leave my haven, so I let the curtain fall closed again. It's only then I notice what's on the inside of my wrist.

I stare at the symbol, bewildered. Two chevrons pointing toward my hand, shot through with three vertical lines. I rub at it with my thumb. It's been skinmarked: painted in with dye and then chthonomantically bonded so that it will never fade. Back in Veya, we have dweomings who do this kind of thing, or chthonomancers for the rich. The Gurta have Elders, that could do it if body modification wasn't forbidden by one of their many fucking stupid Laws. It seems that the Far People have their own way of tapping rock-magic, then. Interesting. I wonder what the symbol means. Given what I've seen of these people, I doubt it's anything but benevolent.

Just being awake tires me out. The warmth of the suns has raised the temperature in the hall to a drowsy heat. I nestle back into the covers and slide close to Feyn. His back is to me, so I fit myself against him, my arm across his ribs. His fingers sleepily entwine with mine, but I know by the depth of his breathing that he hasn't woken.

I lie against him, his thin body unfamiliar. Rynn was bulky and hairy; Feyn is slender and smooth. I think back on that kiss and I still don't know why I did it. I can't even bring myself to be hurt or embarrassed by his rejection. I was exhausted and frightened and right then I wanted something to take away the pain. Someone to touch me kindly, someone to need me. Because my husband was gone, and my son was so far away.

And yet I can't help wondering what he's doing in bed with me. Is it the custom of his people to share beds? Were they short on space? Or is it something else? Something more?

And is that what I want?

I'm appalled at myself for even thinking about it. Liss and Casta would have paroxysms of joy if they could see me now. The boy is my son's age.

I don't let him go, not straight away. I tell myself there's nothing erotic in it. It's just the *comfort* I need. The feel of another person. If I believe that, I can stay this way a little longer.

But in the end I can't. I can't keep Rynn out of my head. All the times I slept with other men in the service of my Clan, none of them felt as wrong as this. Because Rynn is dead now, and because this boy isn't a fade like the rest were. My husband looms larger in my memory than he ever did in my life. I feel disloyal for even contemplating the absurd possibility of being with Feyn.

I draw away from him, away from his warmth. Voids, the thing I miss most is being held by my husband, the feeling of protection. I miss feeling like a little girl, safe from the world in daddy's arms.

In that moment, it hits me that I'll never be held by him again, and I quietly cry myself back to sleep.

It's night when my eyes open, and Feyn isn't there. The motion of the hall is more noticeable now, bumpier. I hear the SunChildren talking and the sound of rapid chopping. I smell food and I realise that I'm ravenous. I've lost a lot of weight during my convalescence.

At the first twitch from the curtain, the children come running over to look at me. I smile at their wary fascination. The old woman bundles them away, scolding, as Feyn comes over with a plate of food. It's a kind of warm mush of sugary pulp with seeds and other, less identifiable things mixed in.

'You should eat,' he says, though I need little prompting.

'With my hands?' I ask, noting the lack of cutlery.

'That is our way,' he replies.

I'm fine with that. I scoop the mush into my mouth. It's way too sweet, but I could stomach just about anything right now. When I'm finished, I ask if he's got any more.

'Too much will make you ill. Be slow,' he says.

The food has woken me up, and I look about, suddenly restless. 'We're still moving,' I say.

'Yes.'

'Where are we?'

Feyn offers his hand. 'Do you think you can stand?'

I push the blankets off. 'I can try.'

He helps me up. I get a dizzy rush, but it passes. I walk carefully across the room, with Feyn at my shoulder steadying me. The men murmur greetings, to which I reply with a nod. We go over to one of the windows. I see that the hide flaps have been pinned back, revealing inverted triangular holes with no glass in their frames.

I look out, and then I understand.

The palette of the night is haunting greens, faint blues, ethereal purples. It's brighter than I would have thought: the stars that pack the sky spread a cold glow across the broken surface of the rock plains. Distant thunderheads mar an otherwise empty horizon, flickering from within. The landscape is desolate and alien: rock formations rear up like monsters breaching a petrified sea. In the distance, mountains slope into rugged peaks, forested with mycora and lichen trees and foliage I've never seen before. A distant flock of flying creatures soar on membranous wings over the canyons that cut the plains.

I have to step back quickly, staggered by a sense of vertigo. That eternal glittering nothingness overhead threatens to overwhelm me. But I remind myself that I have a roof over my head, and I make myself go back, dragged by the wonder of the world beyond the window. And as I stand amazed, the terror begins to recede. My body and brain are starting to understand that I'll come to no harm. Old, old instincts are asserting themselves again. The instincts of my ancestors, who lived and died beneath a ceiling of stars.

I had dismissed the possibility that this moving room was being pulled like a wagon, simply because it was too big. I was wrong. They're being pulled in chains of five or six: wide, low constructions with rounded roofs covered in some kind of reflective black carapace. Charms and totems dangle from overhanging eaves. Each carriage in the chain is built on a stout wooden platform, below which several sets of enormous rollers turn slowly, grinding over the stony ground.

But it's the creatures at the head of each chain that make me catch my breath. I know them immediately. They're called gethra. They were Reitha's particular field of interest, and she never tired of talking about them. Her dream was to study the gethra herds once she had qualified as a naturalist. Suddenly I can see the fascination. I've never in my life beheld any land animal so colossal.

They're like moving pieces of the landscape: almost featureless humps, rising out of the earth. Long, segmented tails drag behind them, armoured in the same dusty, scratched black stuff as their shells and ending in a wide fan that brushes over their trail as they lumber forward. Every other part of them is hidden, but I know that beneath that canopy of armour, massive crablike legs move steadily in sequence, working together to haul their tremendous bulk. The carriages are attached by a complicated series of chains and ropes, some attached to bolts driven into the gethra's shell, some disappearing underneath.

As I stare, I realise I shouldn't have been surprised that the SunChildren can travel during the day. Their whole society has depended on foiling the deadly touch of the suns. They have methods I can only guess at, special techniques for sunproofing material and access to resources unknown to the world below. Creatures like the gethra have adapted to life under the suns and evolved protection from their light. No doubt the SunChildren have copied nature's designs over the millennia. With all that time to learn, and the advantage of superior intelligence, is it any wonder that they have mastered the suns as well as the animals have?

'Where are we going?' I ask Feyn.

'Turnward,' he says.

We're heading towards Jai. Turnward of Farakza is the Borderlands, and beyond that is Eskara.

It's as if he's read my thoughts. 'In several days' time, we'll pass near a cave network that will take you down into the Borderlands. The Pathfinders have agreed to divert the caravan a little way to take you there.'

'And you?' I ask, turning towards him.

'I will stay. I have spoken with the Loremaster of this coterie. I understand now I was foolish. There are reasons why my kind must be . . .' he struggles '. . . aloof?' I nod my approval. He's really getting good. He smiles and continues. 'I will study further on Eskaran, because I know more now. Then perhaps I will travel to a far away outpost, where there are Eskarans, and I will learn more. When I am older and more wise, I will speak with others at the gatherings, and seek to be sent to the heart of your lands.'

I feel an uneasy mix of sadness and relief at his words. I know he'll be safe, and that's what counts; but it's an unexpected wrench to realise that I'll be leaving him behind and that I'll never see him again. Perhaps he knew it would be that way. Perhaps that's why he didn't return my kiss.

Stop thinking about it. It can't happen.

I turn over my hand to show him the sigil on the inside of my wrist. 'What's it mean?' I ask.

'It means you are a friend to the SunChildren,' he says. 'It means you belong to a coterie. Only a few outsiders have ever been given this gift.' He looks over at me with those huge black eyes. 'It means you can stay. If you want.'

I stare through the window at the panorama before me. Beautiful, frightening and strange. A world without limits. A new start. Voids, I can't deny that it's tempting. More than tempting. There's a great desolation in me and I'm yearning to sever my ties to its source forever: from my masters, from my life, from all the memories of Rynn.

'You said, just before the Shadow Death took me, that one way or another I'd be free,' I murmur.

'Yes,' he says, and that's all.

I think about that for a time. It's an attractive idea. To stay here. Cut loose. Never look back.

But an idea is all it is, a fantasy, like my dreams of a peaceful life. Because there's still Jai. He's still down there. I've not come this far to stop now. It was my son that got me out of that prison, and it's my son who'll keep me going.

'I wish I could, Feyn,' I say, and I mean it. I really wish I could. But all my choices were made long ago.

II

At first I spend much of my time in bed, but as my strength returns I'm up and about more and more. During the days we're confined to the carriages. Then the SunChildren sleep or talk or play music. They practise whittling, weaving, fletching and archery; they hold mock-battles, cheered on by their peers. They don't seem to fear the light as long as the hide flaps are secured shut over the windows, so I don't either.

The occupants of the carriage are very curious about me and about the world below, and I spend a great deal of time answering questions back and forth through Feyn, who acts as our translator. It's clear that Feyn is some sort of hero to them now. Not only can he speak the language of the underworld with apparent fluency, but he has gone into the depths and come back alive. He's allowed to speak of what he saw and learned but not what he did: that would be boastful. A person should only be judged on their interactions with the judge, not on past glories or disgraces. Strange custom, but it's kind of sensible in its way, and if it's the strangest thing I encounter during my time on the surface I'll be very surprised. So I fill in the story, with Feyn translating.

I learn their names and forget them instantly. My attempts at copying their language meet with politely mystified smiles. I can't nail the click that they make to punctuate their words, and they can't understand me without it. Languages have never been my strong point. Even when enslaved to the Gurta, surrounded by their language every moment of every turn, I was a slow learner and I suffered for it.

When night falls, the SunChildren are set free. The men slip out of their soft robes and into their sunsuits, scatter from the carriages and head to the stables in the last carriage of the chain. From there they emerge on whip-lean, chitin-armoured steeds called *scha'rak*. These animals are long-limbed and apparently eyeless, but they run at frightening speeds and have no difficulty in navigation. The men disperse ahead of the caravan, searching for good spots to stop. The women emerge and stretch their legs while the children play alongside the enormous, grinding rollers that support their homes. The gethra move no faster than walking pace, but I note that nobody strays too far from the caravan, and several men on *scha'rak* stay behind as outriders, watching for danger.

I'm something of a celebrity among the coterie, and upon my emergence Feyn and I are surrounded by women and children. They're remarkably restrained: they don't mob or pester, but simply walk beside us, talking between themselves and occasionally asking questions through Feyn. The children are having a harder time controlling their excitement. I suspect that only obedience to their elders is stopping them from poking me to see if I'm real.

I find it rather endearing that they're so oblique in displaying their interest. I ask Feyn whether they're doing it so as not to make me feel uncomfortable, but he looks puzzled and tells me that's how the SunChildren are.

I don't know exactly what it is I feel as I stroll beneath the naked sky. It's like trying to chase a memory I'm not certain I dreamed or lived. It's the kind of deep-seated, unquestioning sense of belonging that I associate with home and family, back in the dim and distant past when I was very young. I'm afraid of the sky, a threatening intimation of latent agoraphobia, but my fear can't get a grip on me. I'm beginning to understand what Feyn meant about people who've survived the Shadow Death being different. When you're on your second life, you really don't sweat the small stuff.

I can't help drinking in the land. I'm stunned by its scale. Much of it is blasted and bare, scoured by the murderous gaze of the suns, but life is not so easily beaten. It hangs on, defiant.

Gargantuan mycora tower over the bleak plains, cracking through solid stone. Feyn tells me how tiny animals live in their stems and caps, hunted by larger predators that come from elsewhere, which are in turn hunted by the SunChildren.

But in those places where the suns can't reach, the canyons and ravines and basins, that's where the action is. We pass oases that swell outward from the tiniest underground springs. Geysers and boiling swamps cloak distant lowlands in a sheltering mist, ghostly in the starlight. Sometimes whole hills are colonised by mycora, providing a roof beneath which more fragile flora can grow.

Feyn gives me a spyglass and shows me where the animals of the upper world scuttle and wing. The night is alive with movement. I see strange bats trailing luminous tendrils from their jaws, which lure in the insects they eat. I spot quick, barrel-bodied things that slither from holes dug in the earth. I see a cluster of photovores, who live off nothing but the day's light, their bodies transparent and crystalline. They softly glow in the darkness as they clamber along the rock faces: lumbering, clawed things, safe from predators inside their gem-like carapaces.

On the cliff-tops, lashers trail sticky tendrils from the mouths of their protective pots, giant anemones against the starry skyline. The wind drags their deadly limbs out like streamers, waiting for some airborne meal to blunder into them. Distant two-legged predators with long, sinuous necks lope menacingly over the high ground, lowing at the rising moon. They have blunt, skull-like faces, and they follow the caravan at a distance. These are *ki'kay*, according to Feyn. Opportunist killers, apt to sneak into unguarded camps and run off with a child. The hunters take them out if they get too near, but their meat is foul.

Feyn describes how each animal has armour or reflective skin, hibernation techniques or behaviour patterns that allows it to prosper in this merciless world. Most hunt at night and burrow or hide when the dawn comes. A few, like the gethra, can suffer the suns with impunity.

It's an undiscovered country, and yet I feel I've been here before. The echoes of my ancestors, resounding over thousands of generations. Were we really ever meant to live underground? Did these people have it right all along, refusing to yield to the suns? Was it an act of bravery that led the tribes of Eskara into the darkness, or was it cowardice?

Not my problem. I'm an assassin, not a historian.

We stop in a shallow dead-end canyon, where small, tough plants have taken hold around the edge of a scrubby dried-up water-hole. The caravan is broken down to form a barricade and enormous bales of feed are brought out for the gethra. The men circle restlessly and then ride away to hunt, leaving a few guards as before. The women busy themselves building up fires, mostly with materials from a storage-carriage.

I wish I was strong enough to go with the men, but I haven't fully recovered yet, and I don't much rate my chances of riding one of their mounts. So I'm left with the women, the elderly, and those like Feyn who earn their place in ways other than by their prowess in the hunt: the Loremasters, the Mystics, the Pathfinders and suchlike.

I'm surprised by how much these nomads bring with them; I always had the impression they would live entirely off the land. But as Feyn explains, in a barren world nobody can guarantee that resources will be there at every stop, so they stock up when things are abundant and use those stocks when they're not. Their carriages are mobile houses, stables, storerooms. I'm beginning to think of this as less of a caravan and more of a moving town.

We watch as the coterie's Mystic enacts the ceremony of drawing the water. He's bald and thin, with every visible inch of his skin covered in designs. He wears heavy robes that seem too large for his frame. The ceremony consists of him sitting cross-legged at the edge of the depression and burning various herbs in pots, making gestures and intoning words in the language of the SunChildren. The others treat it with great gravitas. It all seems a little unnecessary to me.

Still, there's no denying that it works. Water begins to pool at the bottom of the depression, seeping through the cracked mud, and before long the waterhole is filling again. As long as the Mystic keeps chanting, the water keeps rising; but it's a slow process, and after a while I get bored. It's not as miraculous as Feyn seems to think I'll find it. We have chthonomancers back home who can do stuff like this as a party trick, and without all the chanting. At least I've solved the mystery of who put the skinmark on my wrist.

Later, Feyn and I sit together on the porch of one of the carriages, drinking fruit juice. It's an expensive commodity down below because of the scarcity of fruit, but here they have it in abundance. Fruit grows in the low, sheltered places – the mist basins, the shaded canyons, in the mycora forests – and the SunChildren gather it as they desire.

'Why do they wear their suits at night?' I ask, motioning towards one of the scouts, who is prowling about on his mount nearby.

'Sometimes those who hunt are trapped by a large beast, or injured. Then they will not return before dawn. We are not careless where the suns are concerned.' He takes a sip from his cup. 'Also, they are our armour. Animals are dangerous here. Usually they stay away from gethra, but gethra are slow and they do not eat other creatures. Some, like the *ki'kay,* try to get into the camps.' He scratches his arm and makes a noise that indicates he never really thought about it much. 'It is tradition. Warriors wear sunsuits.'

'And you?'

'I am not a warrior.'

I study the scout. He's draped in a beige cloak and wearing a voluminous cowl. Beneath that he wears plates of rigid hide over a flexible undershirt and trousers, heavy boots and gloves, and a ceramic mask with a tinted glass slash for a visor and slits for breathing.

'How long can one of them survive in the sun?' I ask.

'Depends. On time of day, how strong the suns are. In your time . . . three hours, maybe. Four or five at best. Maybe two if both suns are high in the sky.'

But I've stopped listening. 'Three *hours*?'

He looks at me mildly. 'Yes.'

I'm stunned. I had no idea it was even possible. 'The best sunsuits we have give you one hour at most, and that's with armour so thick it's completely impractical.'

'Yes,' he replies. 'That is why many of my people think it is not good to mix with you. You would learn our ways, and you would learn them fast. And then you would come up here.'

'Your people are very wise,' I say, with not a little bitterness.

'But I think that the people below will come anyway. We should know you, and let you know us, and in that way we would both be ready. But we will not teach you our secrets. You would have to find them for yourself.'

'Some public-minded citizen would torture them out of you, I'm sure.'

'No. For we send only people like me, who do not know the secret of the crafting. And if just one of us was harmed, all of us would disappear. When you emerged we would be waiting for you. And not as friends.'

I'm silent for a time, until he adds: 'Others feel this way too. Not many, but some. With what I know I may be able to make it this way.'

'Don't trust us,' I say. 'Don't trust anyone. If you let us get stronger than you up here, if you let us take the advantage, it'll be over. We'll crush you.'

'We know this. Your kind are war-like. You need to fight or your society does not work.'

'Voids, that's a depressing thought,' I mutter. 'How the fuck did we come to *that*?'

'Civilisation is a stampede,' he says, looking away. 'Hard to steer. Impossible to stop. Destroying everything in its path.'

The hunters return soon after, dragging the corpses of several creatures with far too much scale and fang for my liking. The creatures, each twice as long as I am tall, are swiftly skinned and cleaned, then brought to the women to cook over the fire. The men are ebullient, laughing and celebrating. I move down to the fire with Feyn, and we sit silently in the warmth and the light, watching the life of the coterie.

Just for now, just for the short time I'm spending in the company of these curious people, there's no weight on me. It's the first time I can ever remember feeling this way. I'm not responsible for anyone here, and I'm beholden to none. Nobody knows where I am. My master and Clan probably think I'm dead. I'm floating, adrift, and it's wonderful.

I look up at the boundless sky, dense with stars. A dull grey moon, a sister to Callespa, is visible high above us. I don't know its name and I don't care to ask. Let it remain unknown.

Sometimes, that's the greatest gift you can give.

We travel for several days more, our pace slow and steady, and I concentrate on regaining my strength and putting back the weight I've lost. I begin to work my way through chua-kîn exercises in the carriage. The children sit and watch me, rapt, as I force myself to endure the punishing regime of movements and stances, while the old woman stitches torn clothes and the men play games of chance with Feyn.

At night, when I'm not sitting with the others, Feyn educates me about SunChild signs. I've given up trying to help the women with whatever they are doing; it only ends in me getting good-naturedly shooed away. I watch the men enviously each time they ride out on the hunt, wishing I had time to learn how to ride one of their skeletal mounts. But I don't, so I learn other things instead.

Feyn shows me the way that rocks can be arranged to indicate a waterhole nearby, or how certain marks point to a stash of food and weapons and sunsuits. He tells me how to spot the trail of a caravan, even long after the ferocious dawn winds have scattered the traces. He teaches me how different coteries have different signs, often marking a well-used trail or spots they frequently return to, so that other SunChildren can find them. In a nomadic culture where people rarely gather, it's necessary for them to be able to locate each other should the need arise.

'This is how this coterie found us,' Feyn says, indicating a thorny vine hiding amongst a group of similarly mean-looking and robust plants.

'This vine?'

'We call it—' he begins, then stops. 'You will not remember. But you should remember what it looks like. This vine is life to us.'

I turn it over carefully in my hands. Thick, fleshy and sharp.

'Cut several coils of that vine and leave it in the sun for a day. Then collect it at night and burn it. The smoke it will make, it smells very bad.'

I look up at him. 'I don't understand.'

'If it is burned in the right place, it will carry very far. For someone who can read the wind, it is easy to find. It means you need help. They will come. The *scha'rak* smell even more further. They can trace you.'

'They can *track* you,' I correct him. It's become a habit now, even though it seems pointless, knowing how little time we have left together. I wish I could stay with him, just to talk, just to make his task of mastering Eskaran easier.

No, that's not the reason. I just wish I could stay with him. Saving his life committed me somehow, and his saving mine just drove the hooks deeper.

I can't decipher my feelings concerning this boy. I've turned it over and over in my mind, but I can't find an answer that satisfies me. I protected him in prison, I risked myself to go back for him when I could have escaped far more easily alone. Now we're sharing a bed, and even though there's no more touching since that first day I awoke to find him there, the proximity unsettles me. I feel tugged towards him; it's an effort of will to keep a gap between us under the covers. Even the thought of it inspires a poisonous feeling of guilt, of *wrongness*. Every day I find myself wondering why I don't just ask to move beds, to sleep with the old woman or the children. And yet I never do.

What is he to me? A surrogate for Jai, for a mother who misses her son? A replacement for Rynn, for a wife who's lost her husband? Both? Was it just that I needed to save somebody, to make up for those I couldn't in the past?

Or is it simply that he represents a way of life to me, this SunChild world, a place utterly apart from obligation? A place away from the war, away from the conflict that killed the man I love, away from roofs and ceilings and walls. It's a harsh world, but it's a life with more freedom than I've ever had. Is it because he's a new start?

I tell myself he's too young, far too young, but under this canopy of stars it doesn't seem to matter.

I don't know what I feel. But I know I'm too tangled to make smart choices where my heart is concerned, and he knows it too. Rynn's death is too fresh, and my mind is on my son. I wonder, if not for that, would things be different? Is he holding back because he knows I need time to make sense of this? He's so difficult to read.

One thing's for sure. The goodbyes are going to be tough.

Memory is an awful thing. A journey can seem like a lifetime while you're on it. One perfect turn can stretch like a season. But when it's over, and you look back, it seems like the whole thing happened in the beat of a heart. It's gone and can't be brought back.

The caravan waits at the crest of the rise against a purple-blue sky. The aurorae of impending dawn are just beginning to stroke the horizon. The wind is rising, blowing my hair about my face. At my back is a cave: dry, unremarkable, crooked. It will take me home.

Feyn stands with me. The others have already retreated inside the carriages, but he doesn't seem in a hurry. He assures me that he knows the dawn, and it won't catch him out.

I've said my farewells to the rest of the coterie. They were very kind. Several of them pointed to the mark on the inside of my wrist and made encouraging gestures. I didn't need Feyn to tell me that I was always welcome among them. Their simple generosity makes me feel vaguely ashamed of my cynical Veyan attitude towards friendship. In the city it's not given freely, it's subject to conditions and it can shatter with a single blow.

They've loaded me up with a pack full of food and given me shortblades to replace the ones I lost, back in another life. They're beautifully crafted, and undoubtedly valuable to a people who probably have to trade for all the metal they obtain.

'I wish you would come with me,' I say, though the unselfish half of me hopes he will refuse.

'I wish you would stay,' he replies.

'I have a son.'

'I know.'

That hangs in the air between us for a time.

'Do you think he will come with you, if you find him? Do you think he will turn his back on war?'

'Yes,' I say, then: 'Maybe. His father is dead now. You can't reason with a memory. Maybe he'll decide to stick it out, in Rynn's honour. I don't know. I just have to talk with him.'

'And will your master let him do it?'

'I persuaded him before. I can do it again,' I say, though I'm not one-tenth as sure of that as I sound. 'Ledo's sisters are my friends. They'll help me. And I have a letter from the Dean of Engineers at Bry Athka University. Ledo will see the sense in it.' At least, that's what I hope. Ledo's been known to be as whimsical as his siblings when the mood takes him. You can't be sure of anything where the aristocracy are concerned.

He studies me for a long time, his black eyes roaming my face. 'Who are you doing this for?' he asks.

'What does *that* mean? I'm doing it for him, of course.'

He stares at me for a long while before his gaze falls away.

'I came back for you, too, Feyn,' I say. 'I could have got out of Farakza on my own.' I realise belatedly how harsh that sounds. I'm annoyed at him for implying that finding my son is more about me than Jai. But I don't want our parting to be this way, so I soften the edge a little. 'It's how I am,' I say quietly. 'I don't think like you. I don't have your philosophies. I can't just cut loose.'

He nods reluctantly, then brushes his oily black hair away from his eyes. The wind is beginning to moan on the cliff-tops, and the air is full of the hiss of rustling dust.

'The dawn is coming,' he says. 'I have to go.'

I can feel something shrinking and dying inside me, and it's so terrible I can't bear it.

'I wish you luck,' he says, with an uncertain tone to his voice. He's still not sure what luck is. I laugh and put my arms around him.

'You're learning,' I tell him quietly, and then he holds me back and we become very still for a little while. I feel the pulse at his neck against my own. I'm never going to see him again.

'I have to go,' he says once more. The sky is lightening fast. He glances at it, then back at me, and though there's a thousand things to say we don't say any of them because they wouldn't be enough.

'We will pass this way again, at the season's end,' he says. 'After that, I cannot say.' Then he turns and runs towards the carriages, and I start walking into the cave, tears in my eyes.

Down, down, away from the killing dawn. The world I know opens its arms to me, and darkness clasps me to its chest.

37

'You're pregnant?'

I looked at Rynn, my eyes hard. Daring him to follow through on the shock and horror in his tone. Daring him to imply it was my fault.

He was normally oblivious to non-verbal cues – my husband didn't do subtlety – but he got this one. I saw him swallow the words he was going to say.

'This is bad,' he murmured.

I knew it was bad, but I still chose to take his words the wrong way. I was nineteen, scared and furious and spoiling to take it out on somebody.

'I'm glad the thought of our having a child brings you such joy,' I spat at him sarcastically.

'Don't be stupid, you know that's not what I meant,' he barked back at me, and I shut up. That was why I loved him. He didn't take any of my shit.

He stood immobile, framed against the circular window that looked out over Veya from the heights. Our rooms in the Caracassa mansions were lit with soft lanterns, throwing low shadows across the polished rootwood floor.

'How?'

'Well, when a man and a woman like each other very much, they—'

'Voids, Orna, I'm not in the mood!' he snapped.

I was stung. Foolish of me. I dealt with my fear by joking, but he didn't. He used anger. And he was terrified.

'I was sick,' I murmured. 'You remember? Sometimes the potions don't work when you're sick.'

He remembered. The illness took me out for twenty turns. It's not easy for a man like Rynn to go that long without sex. The moment I felt up to it, he was at me with breathtaking fervour. We should have waited till my body was back in balance.

He glanced at me from under his heavy brows. Determining whether I was blaming him. I wasn't.

'We have to tell Ledo,' he said.

'Yes,' I replied, but I had gone cold at the thought.

'Do you know what—'

'I'm keeping the baby,' I told him.

'That's not your choice,' he said.

I looked away from him, crossing my arms. Mind made up.

He stormed across the room, a shadowy hulk of rage. Grabbed my arm, thrust one thick finger at the symbol on my left cheek. Three diagonal slashes: the Bond-mark.

'Do you really know what this means? Do you? It means you're *property*. It means you're Ledo's to do whatever he wants with. How do you think he's going to react when you tell him?'

I pull away from him. 'He'll tell me to get rid of it,' I say.

'And if you refuse?'

My voice is smaller. 'He could execute me.'

'He *will* execute you *both*,' Rynn corrected. 'He could execute you just for getting pregnant. He could execute me too.'

'He wouldn't. He wouldn't waste two of his Cadre that way.'

'Are you sure? Are you sure of anything where the aristocrats are concerned?'

'He wouldn't,' I insisted.

Rynn calmed a little, stepped away. He walked to the window and looked out. After a long silence, he said. 'You're his property, as I am. You've already proved yourself one of his best. You'll be out of action for whole seasons. Even after you're back, will you ever take the same risks again? Will your mind be on the job, or on our child? Will mine?'

It was a speech of exceptional length from my husband. Usually he chewed matters through in his own head, not aloud. He must have been really scared if he felt that he had to share it with me. This wasn't something he could handle alone.

'I'm not giving it up,' I said again.

'He'll kill you, Orna. There's a process. We should have asked permission. Our first duty, above all others, is to serve him.'

'I swore myself into Bond when I was ten,' I said. 'Don't tell me about loyalty. He won't execute me because I'm too good at what I do.'

'He'll execute you if you disobey him.'

And he was right. What use were Bondsmen if they were not utterly obedient? Death was the inevitable consequence of rebellion for the Bonded. And still, it didn't seem to make a difference to me. The threat of what might happen had paled in comparison with the threat of not having this child. I saw the logic of the situation – voids, it's not as if I hadn't thought it through myself a hundred times – but it didn't seem to connect with the process of choice. It just didn't *matter.*

Even while contemplating the possibility of my own execution, I had been drifting into fantasies. A baby, a place of our own. Rynn coming home from his work, something mundane and boring and safe, me staying at home, learning to cook, trying out my culinary experiments on my hungry husband. I dreamed normality, the life of the Veyans that ran shops, shuffled papers in banks, bid in the auction-houses. The simple life, where husband and wife were never apart for more than a few turns and nobody had to die.

But fantasy was all it was. We could never be other than Bonded. Rynn could never have a job other than the one given him by Clan Caracassa, and they would never consider it because, like me, he was so good at what he did. I would never be allowed to be a mother, because what use was that to Caracassa? Our children would not be Bonded. Rynn was the last in a three-generation lifedebt and I had only sworn my own life away, not that of my children.

They would make me give up the baby. But I couldn't do that.

'Do you want me to get rid of it?' I asked him.

His back was to me. I saw him tense slightly. Then he exhaled a long breath. It was the question he had been dreading.

'If we get rid of it now, Ledo doesn't have to know,' he said slowly. 'Then we can ask him for permission. If he grants it, we can try again.'

'I know that,' I said. 'Do you *want* me to get rid of it?'

He sighed again. Rynn was very careful with making definite decisions, because once made he almost never went back on them.

'No,' he said. 'I want us to keep it.'

Tears welled up in my eyes. I blinked them back. 'Can we run?'

'If there's no other choice.'

'You mean it?'

'I said so, didn't I?'

He did mean it. A life of poverty and probable starvation, of being rejected by society, eking out a living on the borders of Eskara. Nobody would trade with us or give us jobs. Our friends in the Cadre would devote their lives to hunting us down.

Better than nothing.

'First we talk to Ledo,' he murmured. 'See what he says. Agree with whatever he orders us to do. Then we run, if we have to.'

I could barely speak. There wasn't room for air in my chest with the utter and total love I felt for this man.

'There's another way,' I said quietly. 'Casta and Liss.'

He turned back to me, a frown on his face. 'Ledo's sisters? You barely know them.'

'They like me. Especially Liss.'

'You think you can ask them for a favour like this?'

'If anyone can persuade Ledo to be lenient, it's them.'

He thought about this for a time.

'They're aristocrats. You can't trust them,' he said.

'I don't have to trust them to manipulate them.'

I asked them to meet me in the sculpture-graveyards of the Greyslopes. It was exactly the kind of dark, sinister place that spies meet in cheap novels, which is why real spies never met here. But I knew Liss wouldn't be able to resist the breathless romance of a clandestine meeting, and so I played to her expectations. The atmosphere was important.

I had met the twins for the first time not long before. They had come to my rooms and invited me to join them for a drink with that uniquely threatening friendliness that can only come from people with the power to have you killed. I went along, of course. Maybe they had a special task for me. After all, as the younger sisters of Ledo, I was beholden to them as much as him, unless their plans conflicted with Ledo's interests.

It turned out they had no such task in mind, though it took me an hour to work it out. I finally established that the reason was simply that Liss was fascinated by me because I was a spy. Ledo had mentioned my name in connection with a particularly daring (and lucky) theft I had made on Caracassa's behalf, and Liss had latched onto the idea and become obsessed. Now *she* wanted to be a spy, and she demanded that I recount my most dangerous exploits, my life, my techniques. Casta sat by and listened quietly while Liss grilled me.

I felt uncomfortable talking about sensitive matters, and avoided them when I could do so without being caught; but I didn't have the option of refusing her. I did, however, try to impress upon her the importance of secrecy, to which she slapped her hand across her mouth and mumbled something through sealed lips. It was hard to believe that the lesson had sunk in very far.

I was left bewildered by the whole affair. Soon after, they called on me again, and this time we went out and got drunk in a club and we never spoke of matters of subterfuge once. Liss had apparently decided that being a spy was boring and that she wanted to be an explorer on the surface instead. She was now stuffed with facts about life above, which she excitedly repeated to anyone who would listen. I was to learn, when my son started dating Reitha, that they were mostly fiction.

Still, whatever I had done, they had decided that they liked me. For a short period of time, they treated me like a friend, or perhaps a pet. It was difficult to tell with them whether I was an amusing project or someone for whom they had genuine affection. They made me uneasy, but I played along.

Then they seemed to forget about me, and that was that. It wasn't appropriate for me to call on them, and I wasn't sure I'd want to anyway. I liked them a little, but they were hard to warm to and whimsical by nature. I could never feel safe with them. We were from different worlds, and theirs ruled mine.

It had been several seasons since we had last spoken. I wondered how they would react to my mysterious summons, or if they would react at all. *Meet me in the Greyslopes at the 27th hour*, read the message. *Beneath the Bleeding Coil.* Simple, direct, urgent. If anything was guaranteed to make Liss clap her hands and squeal in delight, it was the promise of a secret meeting.

So I waited in the midst of the sculpture-graveyard. The Ya'yeen had built this place, and many like it, in memorial to their slain siblings. They dealt with evolution by always birthing identical twins, one of which was given away to another family. When they reached adulthood, the twins were seized by an overwhelming and unstoppable drive to seek out and kill the other. In this way the stronger and smarter survived; the weaker was immortalised in sculpture by the victor.

The Bleeding Coil was exactly as its name suggested: an enormous, uneven coil of metal and minerals, riddled with tiny pores through which murky yellow Ya'yeen blood dripped into a receptacle at its base, where it was drawn back up by some kind of pressure differential. That, at least, was how it appeared. The strange world of the Ya'yeen was steeped in meaning, every thought percolated through their bizarre world-view which said, as far as I understood, that *everything* meant something. The way a dropped piece of food fell, the path of a bat, the shape of a cavern, the way the streets of Veya were laid out. Their brains were wired for nuance, texture, subtlety. They saw things that nobody else could. Whether what they imagined was actually *there* was a question I didn't care enough about to answer.

When I looked at the Bleeding Coil, I saw something ugly and powerful that I actually quite liked. But to a Ya'yeen, the sculpture was a message delivered through the shape of the coil, the location of the pores and frequency of the drips, the position within the graveyard, the way the dim light of the nearby lamp fell on it, the donor of the blood the sculptor had used. They found us endlessly confusing, because we were a people who could live our whole lives without doing anything that meant anything at all.

I waited in the quiet, cool darkness, surrounded by dozens of sculptures of varying levels of incomprehensibility. The Greyslopes were built where the ground slanted upward to meet the cavern wall. The place took its name from the colour of Ya'yeen skin. They clustered here for reasons they could never quite explain in a way anyone understood.

I could see out across the city to where the River Vey cut through the ocean of lights. Stalactite dwellings hung in the darkness above the Shivers, delineated by the glow of their windows. A sudden breeze fluttered my hair. I thought of the life growing inside me, and I swore I would do everything to ensure that my child would be born, so that they too could stand and marvel at the beauty of the world.

The twins were late, but they came. Liss was bundled in a hooded cape of deepest black, Casta in a moulded suit of light, bronze-coloured armour that hugged tight to her body. She carried a narrow sword and a whip at her waist, while Liss wore a diaphanous dress that barely concealed her newly buxom figure. Since I had seen them last, Liss had grown breasts, hips and lips, all of formidable size. Her pale skin was tinged a light blue and her hair, beneath her hood, was black and tied in coils on either side of her head. Casta's hair was spiky and blonde, and her eyes were entirely white in the nut-brown frame of her face.

Liss hurried up to me and clutched my arms with anxious fingers, kissing me swiftly and nervously on the lips. 'Oh my love, what has happened? What is it?'

'Maybe she's asked us here to kill us,' said Casta, always the more morbid of the two. But she came up to me and kissed me anyway. 'Nobody would know.'

'We've been terrible to her!' Liss gasped, as if that proved Casta's theory beyond doubt. 'Terrible! No wonder she wants to kill us!' She tore open her cape to further bare her already semi-bare breasts, head thrown back dramatically. 'Do it, my love! A blade in my heart! We deserve no less!'

Casta's hand was on her sword, as if she actually thought I might do it.

'I haven't called you here to kill you!' I cried, before their delusion could get out of control.

'Oh,' said Liss, sounding almost disappointed. She lowered her head slowly. 'Do you like my new breasts?' she asked conversationally.

'Don't they hurt your back?' I asked.

'She had the muscles strengthened to cope with the extra weight,' said Casta with a bored tone, staring off down the paths of the sculpture-garden. 'I hate these things. Ya'yeen are idiots.'

'Aren't you furious?' Liss asked, as she closed her cape and spared me further sight of her chest.

'About what?'

'We forgot all about you,' said Casta. 'We do that.'

'But you remember me now, right?' I asked uncertainly.

'Oh, we could never forget our dear friend Orna!' Liss gushed. Talking to these two gave me a headache.

'You want something,' Casta stated. I guessed she was looking at me, but it was hard to tell as she had no pupils or irises.

That was my cue. 'I'm in trouble,' I said, and my eyes filled with tears that were not entirely faked.

Liss melted. She flung her arms around me – no easy task with the obstructions between us – and burst into tears. 'Oh, what can we do?' she cried. 'How can we help?'

'You're pregnant,' said Casta.

That was some deduction, given the evidence. But I buried my head in Liss's shoulder and whispered 'Yes.'

Liss pushed away from me, holding me at arm's length, and cried: 'But that's wonderful!' She looked to Casta for support. 'Isn't it?'

'She didn't ask permission,' Casta said, her voice steady. Evaluating me.

'It was an accident,' I said.

'But you have to keep it!' Liss said, then to Casta: 'She has to keep it!'

'She *wants* to keep it. That's why she's come to us.'

'Oh.' Liss was catching on now. She glanced around the sculpture-garden, searching for sinister eavesdroppers. It was deserted but for a few bats chasing ragged circles above us.

'Will you help me? I have no one else to turn to,' I pleaded. I knew the idea of helping someone in trouble was an easy sell to Liss, but Casta was tougher. I got the impression she was not convinced by my tears.

Liss made appealing eyes at her twin, thoroughly on my side. But Casta was giving nothing away.

'This child,' she said. 'It means a lot to you.'

'It means everything.'

'What if our brother says no?'

I opened my mouth to answer, and shut it again. My intuition told me something was amiss here. It felt like a test. I knew what I *should* say, but somehow I knew it would be the wrong thing. Casta needed convincing. She needed the truth.

'I'll keep it anyway,' I said. 'No matter what.'

Almost as soon as the words had left my mouth, I regretted them. If they told Ledo what I'd said, he'd have me imprisoned. Our chance for escape would be gone.

I heard Liss suck her breath in through her teeth. I waited, my eyes locked with Casta's blank ones. There was no telling how she would react to that kind of defiance from a Bondswoman.

'We will speak to Ledo,' Casta said slowly. Then she turned and walked away without another word. Liss was torn between her twin and I for a few moments; then she gave me an apologetic glance, kissed me swiftly and hurried after Casta.

Ledo received Rynn and I at his table, where he was taking his morning meal: strips of boiled fish in a fruit sauce. He looked spectral, dressed in a white brocaded robe only marginally paler than his skin. A thick mane of braids and twists hung around his face. Jewelled bands and interwoven ribbons of red and blue in his hair were the only hint of colour about him, except for the bleak blue of his irises: the natural colour of the Nathka tribe.

'My beloved Orna,' he said, his voice soft. 'My heart swells to see you.'

'It's an honour to sit at your table again,' I replied.

'And Rynn, equally beloved; I trust your endeavours bear sweetness?'

My husband's awkwardness was excruciating to witness. Ledo had picked up the watery, over-emotional manner of speaking which had become stylish in society of late. Rynn didn't quite know how to respond to it, so he mumbled something about what an honour it was, clumsily following my lead.

He invited us to join him at the table with an airy sweep of his hand. The table was carved from mycora, as were the rounded walls of the room. Most of the Caracassa Mansions were built of the stuff, cut from the enormous roots that spilled through Veya's cavern wall and into the Tangles.

Two bodyguards stood nearby: Caydus and Jyirt. Both of them carried enormous curved blades. Caydus was hulking, ruddy-skinned, with a mane of bright blond hair, while Jyirt was bald and had a cadaverous look about him. I knew them both slightly. They were not concerned: we were part of Ledo's Cadre, the inner circle of the Plutarch's most trusted retainers. If he was safe around anyone, it was us.

Handmaidens appeared, bringing breakfast platters of bread, succulent spores, flaked fish and expensive fruits from the chasm-fields near the surface. I was famished, but I knew I wouldn't be able to eat anything, just as I hadn't been able to all last turn. My stomach felt too knotted to manage food. It didn't stop Rynn, however, who went for the plates before I nudged him to remind him that the Plutarch was served first. He retreated, blushing.

'Will the twins be joining us at breakfast?' I asked, to salvage the situation.

'The twins do as they will, accountable only to each other,' said Ledo, with the shallowest of smiles. I didn't like his tone.

The handmaidens served us in silence, then retreated from the room. Ledo had become grave, and it chilled me. I had no idea what the twins had said to him, or if they had told him of my defiance in the sculpture-garden.

'When you married, I gave my permission with a gladdened soul,' he said. 'Some said that for two of my Cadre to be so joined in love would weaken the both of them. That a man could not give himself to combat if he had given himself to a wife. A woman could not use all her silken wiles if she feared to betray a husband.'

Rynn shifted uncomfortably and cleared his throat. That aspect of my craft was never spoken of, ever. There was no way I could explain to him the kind of steely hatred I felt for myself when I slept with other men. Nor would he ever be convinced that it was utterly necessary in some cases, because the surest way to a man's secrets was through his bed. Being a Bondswoman meant loyalty to the master above all. Even my husband.

'But I believed in you,' Ledo said. 'And you rewarded my trust. You have become valuable as the rarest of jewels to me.' He bit into a fruit, chewed, then held it up before him and examined it. 'I wonder, will a child diminish you the way they thought your marriage might?'

He didn't appear to be asking us, but rather himself, so we kept quiet. Rynn ate, trying to make as little noise as possible.

Ledo put the fruit down and lowered his eyes. 'Disappointment aches in my stomach like the voids,' he said heavily.

'I swear, we didn't mean for this to happen,' I said. 'We would never intentionally conceive without your approval.'

'Your loyalty is not in question, Orna. But there is precedent to consider. There are others in my Cadre who may also desire children. What soothing words will I have for them?'

I had nothing to say. There was no defence that would convince him.

He sighed and sat back, steepling his fingers and tapping his index fingers against his teeth. 'You will continue to work for me as a spy until your condition prevents you,' he said. 'You understand, I am sure, how the lush bloom of pregnancy can be exploited to lower suspicions in the society of men and women. I will arrange someone else for the more physical aspects of your work.'

My breath was trapped in my throat. I could barely believe what I was hearing. Rynn continued eating, gazing hard at his plate. Food offered the only safety in the room for him.

'The child will be crèched as soon as it is reasonable to do so,' he continued. 'If I see the quality of your work diminish even a little, Orna, your child will be taken. Rynn, my words brush you also.'

Rynn looked up at him briefly, then back at his plate.

'Thank you,' I whispered. 'You won't regret your decision, Magnate. We will—'

'The child will also be Bonded to Clan Caracassa,' he interrupted. 'Standard lifedebt, for a single generation. It shall not pass to their offspring, but they shall be mine as you are.'

My relief curdled in my mouth. No, no, no, this was too cruel. Our children were supposed to be free, to choose their own paths in life. Rynn had wanted that even more than I. Rynn, who had never known anything but Bondsmanship. Rynn, still paying for his grandfather's mistake even now. Abyss, they were meant to have the chance at a normal life even if we could not.

I almost protested. I almost forgot who I was and who he was and how much we owed him for allowing this. I almost forgot how much I owed the twins for persuading him.

'You're very generous, Magnate,' Rynn rumbled next to me, and I shut my mouth before I could say what I wanted to. He had seen it coming and headed me off. Every once in a while, he saw right into me.

I swallowed down the bile, took a breath, and said: 'We are grateful for your mercy.'

Ledo nodded vaguely and returned to his breakfast. Rynn took my hand beneath the table and squeezed it hard. And with that, we had saved our child's life by giving it away.

10

Caralla lies on the edge of an immense lake inside a cavern so large that its dimensions can barely be guessed at. Still, it's easy enough to find. I just follow the explosions.

It's been several turns since I left the surface. Time is meaningless when you have no sun and no kind of timepiece, and it's only by my body rhythms of sleep and wakefulness that I can gauge it. That, and the fact I started my period the day before I left Feyn, and it's all but over now.

A fleeting memory makes me smile. I'd had to beg some towels off the SunChild women, translating through Feyn. He was more embarrassed than I was. I'm pretty earthy about that kind of stuff. Just biology; nothing to be ashamed of. I've seen too many people's insides to be shy about my own.

It took me a while to orient myself underground, but I'm not too bad at stone-reading and I have the innate sense of navigation that all but an unlucky few of Eskarans possess. Chthonomancers say it's all about sensing lines of magnetic force, a method we've evolved in lieu of any other way of determining direction underground. They have it down to an art. For people like me it's just gut feeling. Stone-reading is all about knowing how to understand the flow of the rock, the accumulation of different minerals and so on, to predict where caverns and tunnels have formed. Basic survival techniques.

Eventually I found a landmark I recognised: a crystal mountain growing out of a small lake. I was near the front lines, in the middle of the Borderlands: almost exactly where I wanted to be. A Chandelier was hanging beneath the water, flashing restlessly while long-limbed glass spiders stalked the periphery of the cavern. I wished I had time to stay and watch the show – trying to decipher the Chandeliers' language of light was addictive and hypnotic – but I had to move on.

By the time Caralla comes into sight I'm on full alert. I find a spot on the edge of a promontory, high above the lake and concealed by ragged mineral outcrops. There I hide, and watch.

Below me, across the gently phosphorescent expanse of the lake, I can see Caralla. It's an enormous cliff-fortress that has been a defensive linchpin of the Eskaran Army ever since I can remember. The fortifications crown the cliffs and spread all the way down the overhanging face to where a harbour hides behind protective seawalls. Shard-cannon emplacements bristle everywhere, powered by chthonomantically charged battery-packs. Hundreds of lights speckle the black rock, and the fortress is topped by two shinehouses like horns, spreading their cool radiance across the cavern and far out over the water.

There are ships on the lake. A dozen of them. Slim, black, their sails furled as they run under the power of the Elders on board. Every so often, one of them hurls a volanite ball from one of its cannons: chthonomantically-charged rock, pulsing with energy, which detonates on impact. Caralla has been scarred by the bombardment, but its core still holds strong.

Further along the lakeshore, I can see the rapid flashes of smaller shard-cannon emplacements. Over there, amid the sharp rocks and narrow, fungus-choked defiles, the foot soldiers have engaged.

Is he in there? Is my son among them?

No. I can't think that way. I need to move, to distract myself. My side of the lake seems relatively quiet, so I start to head around to the fortress, skirting the cliff-top.

As I get closer, there are signs of what has passed here. Gurta and Eskaran bodies, many stripped of their armour and weapons, lie dead and rotting. Abandoned and burned-out gun emplacements, blast-patterns from bombs. The battle here is long over, and the Gurta were driven back. Whatever assault they are making now, it's happening on the other shore.

I'm creeping through that dank, blasted world when I hear a steadily growing sound, like the dull bellow of flame, getting louder, building. I look up in time to see a blinding mass of light gathering out of nowhere in the heights of Caralla. An enormous prism, surrounded by huge mirrors, becoming bright as the suns as it's energised by a dozen chthonomancers at once.

I'm dumbstruck. They've got a pulse-lance.

A bolt of energy screams forth from the prism, with a sound that splits my head. It punches through the dim air and connects squarely with one of the Gurta ships, annihilating it in a rain of splinters and spray. Then silence falls, the light fades, and all is as it was, except for the flaming wreckage floating on the surface of the suddenly choppy waters.

For a moment I just gape. I've never seen a pulse-lance in action before. It's pretty impressive. But devastating as it is, it will be hours before the chthonomancers are rested enough to charge that thing again. The Gurta have taken a blow, but they'll keep coming. Time is short.

Further along, I identify myself to the Eskaran forces that are holding a line along the cliffs. I'm touched by the reception I receive. They break into spontaneous cheers as word spreads of who I am. I had no idea I was so popular.

'We heard you were dead, in that fucking disaster at Korok,' one of them grins. Korok: the town which took my husband's life.

'What happened? After they ambushed us, I mean?'

'It was a slaughter,' says another soldier, through gritted teeth. He spits and wipes his forehead. 'They knew every move we were making. It should have been an easy take, but they knew everything. Someone sold us out.'

A chill trickles into my blood. I look at the first soldier, a dirty-faced blond man. 'Is that true?'

'It's a *rumour*,' he says, with a pointed glance at his companion.

'What about the others?' someone asks. 'What about Rynn and Jutti and Vamsa? Did they make it?'

And somehow I'm steel when I say it. 'Rynn is dead.' I see the disappointment on their faces. He was a real hero to them. 'Jutti and Vamsa . . . I don't know.' They were Cadre, famous fighters both. Jutti with his acrobatic, flamboyant style, Vamsa with her poison whips and equally poisonous tongue. I didn't know them well.

Someone punches the questioner in the ribs, reminding him that he's talking to the dead man's widow.

'Where have you been?' another man asks.

'Away,' I reply, suddenly out of patience. 'Can someone take me to whoever's in charge?'

'Warmaster Vask,' says the blond soldier. 'Come with me.'

We head through the troops, eventually reaching a road that leads to the crest of the fortress. There is little traffic, and the sounds of combat are distant. We walk until an empty delivery cart passes us, heading our way; then we hop aboard and let the driver take us.

'What's happening here?' I ask.

'Just a lull,' he says. 'They want this place badly. We've heard there are Gurtan reinforcements on the way. Lots of them. They're just keeping us on our toes until then.'

'What about us? Anyone coming?'

'We don't know. There's talk of a big push, to break the Gurta lines once and for all, put them on the run. Nobody knows where or when.'

'You believe it?'

'There's always rumours,' he says, hands clasped between his knees. 'Good for morale. But this time . . . I don't know . . . seems more real than usual. The Warmasters are up to something.'

I nod absently, watching the road disappear behind us. 'Do you know a young officer by the name of Massima Leithka Jai?'

It takes him a moment to work it out. 'Your son?'

'He was stationed here, last I heard.'

He makes an apologetic face. 'I'm sorry. There's so many here.'

'Doesn't matter. Vask will know.'

'They say . . . they say you can find out anything,' he murmurs. I look back at him. 'Can you find out the truth?'

'You mean, can I find out if there's a traitor?'

He nods, unsure if he's been too presumptuous.

'I'll find out,' I say. 'Don't worry about that.'

Relief spreads across his face, and after that we travel in silence.

'Warmaster Vask!'

I fall into step alongside him as he hurries through the stone corridors of Caralla, messengers and underlings flitting around him, delivering news and taking orders.

'Who are you?' he asks, not looking at me. He's a slender man, gaunt and with black hair slicked to his skull. Hard-eyed and sharp-featured.

'Massima Leithka Orna, Cadre to Plutarch Nathka Carac—'

'Caracassa Ledo, yes,' he interrupts. 'I don't need your service history. Come to help?' He makes a sharp turn down a corridor and his entourage follow smoothly.

'I'm afraid not, Warmaster; I'm on Caracassa business.' Which is a semi-truth, since I'm trying to take Jai away from the front lines and that's Caracassa business, in a way.

'Shame. We could use you.'

'Warmaster, I need to find an officer who I believe was stationed here.'

'Who?'

'Massima Leithka Jai.'

'Your son?'

'That's right.'

He signs something thrust into his hand, barely looking at it, without breaking stride. I have no idea where we're going, but I get the impression that he has to keep moving because the moment he stops he'll be swamped.

'I can't help,' he says.

'Finding him is vital to Caracassa affairs,' I lie.

He's not taken in. 'Vital how?'

'I can't tell you.'

'Of course you can't.'

'Warmaster!' I snap at him, and my tone brings him to a halt. His entourage freeze, knowing I've overstepped my bounds. He turns on me with a cold gaze, then takes me by the arm and propels me through a door. 'In here.'

The room is somebody's office: a thin, elderly man and two clerks. Vask orders them out and they scurry, leaving us alone, shutting the door behind them. I open my mouth to speak but a volanite impact shakes the room and robs me of the words.

'Listen, Orna, I really *can't*,' he says, and his tone is not angry as I would have expected, but confiding. 'Army administration is in disarray. Communication has always been bad, but since they announced the upcoming offensive—'

'So it's true?'

'It's true. It'll be huge. They call it Operation Deadfall. I trust you know better than to let that information leave this room?'

'Of course.'

He sighs, sits down on the desk. Tired, harassed. 'The Plutarchs of the Turnward Claw Alliance – Ledo among them, I might add – have started classifying all kinds of records. They're keeping troop movements under wraps while they reorganise, to minimise security leaks. They're also doing it to mask the casualty rates.'

I don't like the sound of that.

'One way or another, a lot of people are going to die,' he says. 'If we do this and we fail, they can't let anyone know the scale of our losses.'

I curse softly. That's how the aristocracy work, alright. I know Vask is being straight with me and I appreciate his trust, but my boy is out there somewhere.

'I need to find him,' I say. Desperation is edging into my tone. 'Is there anything you can do? You're a Warmaster.'

'I can only petition a Plutarch to provide the information. Someone like your master. With all the bureaucracy involved, it'd be quicker if you did it yourself. I assume you can?'

'Yes,' I say bitterly. 'Yes, he'll see me.'

'I wish I could help, Orna. I hold the Cadre in highest regard. You have no idea what you do for the men. They fight twice as hard when you're fighting with them.'

I manage a smile at that.

'He could be anywhere along the Borderlands,' Vask says. He's seen that I'm still thinking about alternatives. 'We've had troops swapping in and out of here all season. I'm telling you, you won't find him by looking. Go back to your master.'

He's right, and I know it. Abyss, it's too cruel. To get here and then to leave empty-handed, when every turn wasted is the one that might get him killed.

Sharp claws of panic scramble my guts. I feel so helpless it makes me sick. Isn't there any way I can stop this? Isn't there anything I can do *now*? If Operation Deadfall goes ahead, and the rumours about Korok are true, my son will be sent into the jaws of a massacre. Never mind the thousands of others who will suffer; I only care about one of them.

If the rumours about Korok are true. *If* there's a traitor. Those are questions I need answers to, and fast.

Suddenly, I'm against the clock. And though it seems absurd to be heading away from the frontline instead of searching for Jai, I know that Vask is talking sense. The quickest way I can get to Jai is to go home and see Ledo. Only he can help me.

'The men are talking about a traitor,' I say, a tinge of desperation in my voice. 'That we were betrayed at Korok. Aren't you worried about Operation Deadfall being compromised?'

'There are always traitors, Orna,' he replies. 'And there are always rumours. Maybe we were betrayed, maybe we were just outsmarted. But that's for the aristos to deal with. Until I hear otherwise, Operation Deadfall goes ahead.'

He makes for the door, reaches for it, stops. Then he turns back, a faintly puzzled look on his face.

'There was a Khaadu, came asking for your son only a few turns back.'

'Nereith?'

'That's him. I sent him on his way. Khaadu might be allies, but I don't trust them that far.'

Wise of him, I suppose, since Nereith actually works for Silverfish. 'Is he still here?'

'Could well be. Ask around. He's hard to miss.'

And with that he leaves, returning to the waiting gaggle of attendants, and I'm left alone with my hopes turning to ashes in my heart.

9

The rain is unending here. Sometimes it falls in a fine mist, sometimes a lashing spray, but it never stops. The lakes that sprawl across the enormous cavern – one of dozens that comprise the Rainlands of Eskara – are constantly evaporating with the heat of the magma flows below. The steam rises, condenses on the cooler cavern roof hundreds of spans above, and then returns to the lakes in droplets. Phosphor trees nod in the haze: tall, branched lichen formations with heavy globes of light hanging from their branches, casting a pale illumination throughout the cavern.

I sit in the doorway of the boxcar, one leg dangling off the edge, watching the world speed past me. The blood-warm rain soaks me, and I let it. The rapid clacking of the tracks has become a metronome, counting time away. I'm going to Veya. I'm going to see Ledo.

Nereith sits in the shadows, out of the rain. But for a few crates of documents and some damaged but salvageable weaponry, we have the space to ourselves. They even provided some mildewed bedrolls. Other carriages are full of wounded, on their way back from the front, but there weren't enough to fill the train. I'm not sure whether that's a good or a bad thing. At least the wounded are still alive.

I can see a village in the distance. It's an island of light in the rain-mist, an uneven heap of hanging lanterns amid the lakes. It lies mainly around the base of an enormous, gnarled mycora root, which bursts from the ground and bends upward to the sky. Most of the dwellings are built from huge seed pods. They stand upright on stilts, windows lit brightly and smoke wisping from their tapered tips. Others, like the communal longhouse, are stone or treated wood. Still others cling to the lichen trees or the flanks of the root. The whole village seems to have been grown rather than constructed.

'Sankla,' Nereith says idly. It takes me a moment to realise he's identifying the village. 'Not too far now. Another turn or so.'

I stir from my reverie, glance at him despondently.

'Be patient,' he says. 'If you do this, you have to do it right. Ledo should be in a good mood, at least. You have that on your side.'

'Why do you say that?'

'Clan Caracassa has been steadily losing out on business for a while now,' he says. 'Couple of other clans have set themselves up as competitors in the medical supplies trade, and they seem to be doing it better than Caracassa.'

I know that; it's my job to know. I don't see where he's going with it, though.

'Those suppliers don't have the output capacity that Caracassa does; they're not so well established. This big military push that's coming up, Caracassa will do very well out of it, I should think. Their competitors won't be able to meet the demand, but Ledo will. I should think it'll pull his fat out of the fire, so to speak.'

'How do you know about the offensive?'

He gives me a look. He's certainly not wasted any time getting back in the game.

'He can spare one officer, I'm sure,' Nereith says, knitting his fingers behind his skull and leaning back against the wall of the boxcar. 'Question is, *will* he? After all, Jai is a Bondsman. He's been trained for war at Clan Caracassa's expense. He chose his path and you approved it. Why should Ledo listen when you tell him that it was a mistake?'

'He's a gifted engineer and an inventor. He'd be better serving Caracassa that way.'

'Away from the front line.'

'Yes, away from the front line!' I reply sharply. He's needling me and I'm rising to it. I can't help it. I'm too raw right now.

'You think Liss and Casta will help you out again?'

I can't believe my ears. Is there anything this Khaadu *doesn't* know?

He shows me his fangs. A Khaadu grin. 'I work for Silverfish,' he says. 'I didn't just walk off the street and get the job, Orna. I got it because I earned it.'

I let my questions drop. 'I can't be certain of anything with those two. Nor with Ledo.'

'So what if he says no?'

'I'll find a way!' My tone is getting more irate.

'If you'll permit the observation of an uninvolved bystander,' Nereith says, stretching lazily, 'the fact that you're getting angry suggests you're afraid to have your plan called into question. And that suggests that you haven't thought about it very hard.'

'Voids, Nereith! I've thought about nothing *but* the plan since Farakza.'

'No,' he says. 'You've thought about saving your son. You've thought about the end but not how you're going to get there. You're papering over the cracks with blind hope, and that – forgive me for saying – is beneath you. You're not being rational.'

I pull myself up, out of the rain. Sodden, I stalk to one end of the carriage, slick my hair back from my face, furious. Trying to think of a comeback that will beat him. Thing is, there isn't one. He's got me pegged.

'This is all I've got,' I say at last. 'This is what got me out of Farakza. This is what kept me running when I might have given up. It's what got me through the Shadow Death.' I slump against the side of the carriage, knees drawn up to my chest. 'He's my son, and I'm his mother. Of course I'm not being rational.'

Nereith is silent for a time. Then: 'Do you think he'll thank you?'

'I don't know. I know he doesn't want to be there. I know if he's back in Veya he could be near Reitha again.'

'You do realise he could be dead already?'

'Yes,' I say through gritted teeth. 'I do realise that. And until I find out for sure, I won't stop looking.'

Nereith considers me a while. 'Would you really defy your master to get your son back? You, a Bondswoman?'

He doesn't need a reply. It's in my eyes. Nereith just watches me, weighing me with his gaze. I get the sense that I've just been evaluated.

'My offer still stands,' he says. 'When all else fails, come to me. Silverfish can help you.'

'For a price.'

'Naturally.'

It's tempting. But I really don't want to get tangled with Silverfish. Not until there are no options left. Abyss knows where that would lead.

'I'll keep it in mind.'

Away from the village, the dark gathers in. Distant clusters of phosphor trees draw the wildlife like oases in a desert; luminescent lichens float in pools, entangling and consuming the fish that are drawn to them. Predators hide in the undergrowth, waving glowing stalks above their mouths, enticing curious victims. In a world of eternal dark, the best way to attract prey is to offer light.

We're following a river which churns and spatters alongside the tracks, beneath the slow sparkle of glowfly swarms. Bats flit this way and that, snatching the insects from the air. Dark, heavy shapes lurk in the water, bright eyes peeping out.

'I have a question for you,' I say, out of nowhere. 'Belek Aspa. Ever heard that name?'

No hesitation from the Khaadu. 'He's a Gurta Minister. Right up there with the High Elder himself. Smart politician, by all accounts. Why?'

'Just had the name rattling around my head. Couldn't think who he was.'

'Right,' says Nereith, suspicious. But he doesn't pursue it any further.

A Gurta Minister? That was the name the Magister used during my last interrogation in Farakza. Asking me if I'd ever heard it mentioned by Ledo.

I don't like what that implies.

38

The Academy was all I'd known for four years now, ever since I was accepted at the age of ten, the same age I swore Bond to Clan Caracassa. The cavern that housed the Academy complex was the limit of my world; I wasn't allowed to leave it, and I didn't want to. I'd suffered enough of life outside to last me a long time.

The Academy to me meant shelter and protection. The harsh training, the punishing regime, the way they regulated our sleep, our diet, our activities – all this was a comfort. After growing up a Gurta slave I was used to strict order, and the idea of taking responsibility for myself terrified me. In my more introspective moments, I wondered whether it was fear, and not overwhelming gratitude, that had led me to swear myself into Bond to my rescuers. I put my life in the hands of others so easily.

Here at the Academy all I had to do was excel at the tasks they set me. Life was clean and simple. I never wanted to leave this place.

The complex was set on many levels, across steep slopes. Chthonomancers had sculpted it into an enormous rock garden, with the buildings of the Academy set amid great crystalline formations, fungal glades and arbours, ornamental pools and waterfalls. Light sources were artfully arranged, through phosphorescent stones and plants, lanterns and a single, squat shinehouse atop the circular Gathering Hall. It was always warm in the Academy. The cavern was set deep underground, heated by the fire at the heart of our moon.

I had many friends here, but the first was an older student called Rynn. He was assigned to orient me during my first few turns, and we took to each other immediately. At first, he treated me like a little sister. Even at thirteen years old, he was larger than most boys his age, and I enjoyed the feeling of being under his wing. New inductees were often bullied until they found their place, but nobody dared with Rynn looking out for me.

We had grown since then, and things had started to change. I had no idea how it happened, but there was an unspoken tension between us now. Glances, blushes, awkward silences. We would snap at each other, frustrated by something we didn't understand. He found excuses to touch me, and I wondered if he had always done that and if I was only now noticing it because of these new feelings. He would become sullen and moody, and resist my attempts to winkle him out of his shell; but still I tried, instead of leaving him to sulk as I used to.

It took me a while, but I eventually admitted it to myself. I was attracted to him. More of my time was spent considering him and his needs than my own. I invented reasons to hug him, making it seem like play. I started to have fantasies about him, and felt vaguely ashamed of them.

But his feelings were harder to read. I interpreted everything he did as possible flirtation. Every innocent comment was picked over for hidden meaning. Every time I thought that I had proof, unequivocal proof that he had similar feelings for me, he would confound me by being suddenly cold and distant. His behaviour had become uncharacteristically erratic, without rhyme or reason. He would seek me out and then seem resentful, as if I was forcing him to be with me. I'd cried myself silently to sleep in my dormitory more than once on account of his cruelty.

That was where we stood, when Master Allet announced we would be fighting each other on the sevenhour of that turn.

The news shook me. Combat training had always been one of the most ruthless and exacting areas of our regime, but while I was good at it I was far from the best in my age group. I was an accomplished meditator, and I outstripped everyone in feats of dexterity, stealth and the mental disciplines associated with spycraft. It was already decided where my talents lay, and I was being steadily narrowed towards them.

But Rynn was a consummate warrior. It was not only his size and strength, both of which were formidable, but his technique. He compensated for his slower speed with an uncanny ability to predict his opponent's next blow, and he had developed a natural fighting style that was quite unique and very effective. Fighting was his talent, and he was relentlessly competitive. He was generally recognised as the best in the Academy, even by the older students, many of whom he had beaten in the past.

When we first began to learn, we were limited to sparring and training with our Masters. But we had outgrown that now. Combat was full-contact, and it hurt like fuck when you lost.

I didn't want to fight Rynn for a lot of reasons, but foremost was that I was afraid of him.

The Masters had a tendency to randomly pull students out to fight each other, but so far we had escaped direct confrontation. Master Allet had come across us arguing in one of the communal glades the turn before. I don't know if he thought he was doing us a favour by letting us work out our aggression on one another, or if he was just being spiteful. Students were forbidden to indulge in relations with the opposite sex. It interfered with their studies, and led to situations just such as this. Master Allet was one of our more unpredictable teachers, whimsical and infuriating at times. I suspected that he had paired us up to see how we would react. He would know in the arena if something was going on between us.

The female students flocked to me at the news. They knew that this was more than just a particularly uneven match-up. Rumours had been flying about us for years.

'You can't go easy on him,' I was advised. 'It'll take everything you've got.'

'It's sick, what they're doing.'

'How could he bring himself to hit you, anyway? What a bastard!'

This was somewhat pre-emptive, I thought, but I let it pass.

'He can't refuse the Masters, though. He'll be thrown out of the Academy.'

'I don't see your problem.' This from Clisa, a particularly level-headed girl, whose advice was rarely welcome because she always spoke sense and usually I just wanted sympathy. 'On the battlefield nobody's going to care if you're a girl. If you can't beat a larger opponent you shouldn't be in the Cadre at all.'

'Shut up, Clisa,' snapped one of my comforters. 'Can't you see she's upset?'

'We're training to be the elite forces of our respective masters,' Clisa replied. 'It's supposed to be tough.'

She leaned in, past the disgusted tuts of the others, and addressed me. 'You know what you need to do, Orna? Think of everything you hate about him. Every time he's made you angry or sad. And then go and kick the shit out of him.'

It was good advice, and I took it. I excused myself from the other students and went to meditate. But I wasn't looking for calm as I sat in the Silent Room of the Academy's main building. I was running chants through my head, basic chua-kîn techniques for manipulating emotions. Taking my fury, my frustration, all the confusion and hurt I felt when I was around him, and screwing it up to a hard, bitter point. Teaching myself to be angry. It was a fine balancing act, because rage makes you sloppy, but I nailed it by the sixhour of the turn. Anger can be controlled. It can freeze instead of burning. When I left the Silent Room, I had convinced myself that I really *wanted* to hurt him.

The arena sat atop an elevated plateau on the floor of the cavern, overlooked by other buildings and gardens on the slope behind. It was little more than a gravelly circle, fringed by a wall of rocks that thrust upward like broken teeth. The stone was heavy with veins of bright minerals, rhodonite and clinoclase and celestine, their surfaces glittering faintly. There were three entrances to the arena, gaps in the rock leading to downward-sloping paths. Lanterns stood on poles to boost the natural light.

The other students ringed the arena, dressed in the plain grey robes of students. Several Masters were here to observe, clad in crimson and wearing the insignias of their station. I spotted Master Allet as I entered: head shaved, nose hooked, face heavily patterned. He was wearing a scowl, as ever.

Rynn was waiting for me. He was six spans high already, and still growing. His body was bulking out fast, and he was much heavier than I was. I was a little over five spans, and the only thing still growing on me were my breasts and hips, neither of which were going to do me much good in a fight.

But I didn't care about any of that. As soon as I laid eyes on him, I wanted to scratch his eyes out. I wanted revenge for the instability he had introduced into my nicely ordered life.

Don't you see what you're doing to me? Are you so stupid? I wanted to shout at him, but I held it back. Saved it. I'd deliver that message in pain.

The combat was unarmed. Later, we'd progress to mock weapons, and later still we would spar with real ones; but for now, it was hand-to-hand. I was faster, he was stronger.

Master Allet brought us to the centre of the arena, and there we faced each other. I could see the uncertainty on Rynn's face. Fighting a girl went against every instinct he had; fighting me was worse. I caught a flicker of shock as he found malice in my gaze. It took him back a little. Good. That was my advantage. But then his own gaze hardened in response, and I saw his pride reassert itself. The only thing worse than fighting a girl was losing to a girl.

'If I suspect either of you are fighting below the very best of your abilities,' Master Allet muttered, 'your training at the Academy will end here. Am I clear?'

'Clear,' we both said at the same time.

'I'll end the match when I see a winner,' he said. He stepped back, and we moved apart after hastily sketched and obligatory gestures of respect. The arena was silent. My senses crackled. I couldn't wait to be at him.

'Begin!'

I attacked in a flurry, hoping to overtake his defences with speed while he was still unsure of me. No good. Though his moves were slower than mine, he flowed backward to match my advance. Somehow my kicks and strikes hit only forearms and shins, and were knocked aside.

I sprung back before he could mount a counter-offensive, but he didn't. He was measuring me, maybe. We circled each other, searching for an opening. I was plotting my next strikes. Strike high and low and wide. Spread them all over so he's forced to move quick to stop them all.

I went in again, flashing a kick at his leg, jabbing at his forehead, turning an elbow towards his ribs. Each attack met only the meaty impact of a blocking limb. Then I felt something like a stone battering ram drive into the side of my face, and I staggered backward, dazzled by the pain. I tripped over my heels and went down in the centre of the arena, scraping the palms of my hands on the gravel.

Voids, I hadn't even seen that punch coming. My vision doubled for a moment then settled down. We were trained to deal with pain, but I was surprised he hadn't knocked me out.

Rynn was hanging back, not pressing the advantage. Letting me recover. I saw Master Allet watching him carefully. Rynn was concerned. He couldn't believe he'd hit me and he was afraid he'd hurt me badly. He never could hide a thing.

I got to my feet, rolling my jaw. He'd pulled that punch. Didn't put his shoulder into it.

I stanced again, ready for the next assault. He'd scored a point on me, but I'd scored a bigger one. He was afraid to hit me, whatever Master Allet's threats. There was my advantage.

We closed on each other again. He was watching me for signs of a lapse in my defenses. I gave him one, trying to lure him in, but he didn't take it. Master Allet coughed pointedly in the background. Rynn glanced at him for a fraction of a second, and I swung an elbow up into his jaw, rocking his head back and clacking his teeth together.

The surprise of the impact gave me a moment to press the attack, and I used it. I punched into a nerve-point on his inner thigh, paralysing his leg, and as he buckled I went for the spot where his shoulder joined his body. It would have put his arm out of commission, but somehow he pulled back, kept his balance, and the strike wasn't hard enough to do any damage. I rolled away as he chopped at me, the hard edge of his hand missing the side of my throat by a whisper.

Then I was back on my feet and we were stanced again, but now his leg was dragging and useless and the odds were stacked in my favour. He was angry. It would make him careless, but it also meant he wouldn't go easy on me again.

He waited for me to come to him. He had no choice but to play it defensively. The most obvious move would be to go for his other leg, but he knew I was smarter than that. So I went for the leg. I feinted at his face, ducked the counterstrike and kicked the side of his good knee, where it was weakest. The connection was solid, and he fell, but as he did I felt one huge hand snatch me around the back of the neck. He bore me down, flinging me to the floor and landing on top of me. His weight drove the breath from my lungs.

I tried to struggle but I couldn't seem to drag any air into my chest. Several moments of scrambling, and then he was over me, fist cocked, aimed at my face. His teeth clenched, eyes wild, ready to put me out.

But he didn't. And that tiny hesitation was all I needed to bring my knee up into his balls with all the force I could muster.

His face went white, eyes bulging, and he crumpled on top of me. I shoved him aside before he suffocated me completely, and he rolled over, curled up like a dying spider, clutching at himself. He wasn't getting up again. The fight was over.

I slowly rose to my feet, surveying the crowd. The boys wore pained expressions; the girls were emitting silent congratulations. Master Allet walked over to me and declared me the winner. I knelt down next to Rynn and put my hand on his shoulder, but he was alone in his private world of agony and didn't acknowledge me.

Probably better he didn't. I couldn't keep the grin down. I was going to be wearing a bruise over the side of my face for a week, but I couldn't stop smiling. Because even when he had me down, even when he was angry and his pride was at stake, he couldn't finish me.

There was only one explanation. Rynn was in love with me.

8

'Who exactly do you think you are, Orna?'

The temperature in Ledo's private chambers seems to drop a notch. Suddenly I become very aware of myself, of the room around me. Swirled marble everywhere, gems inlaid in patterns on the floor, crystal columns through which clear waters flow. Behind where my master sits a four-legged beast is pawing the air. It's one of the half dozen sculptures in the room, all of them woven from hardened sap spun thin as thread, glistening in the light of the hooded lanterns. Ledo only keeps lanterns in his chambers. He doesn't like shinestones: he says the light makes everything feel cold.

Ledo looks up from the letter which he's barely read. A letter from the Dean of Engineers of Bry Athka University. *This letter should open any doors that need opening*, he'd said. Not this one, apparently.

Liss and Casta stand together at their brother's side. It's been some time since I saw them last, but they haven't altered in the interim, which is a surprise in itself. Liss is still pale and ragged and waiflike, Casta black-skinned, red-eyed and flame-haired.

I swallow against a dry throat and speak. 'Magnate, I'm only trying to explain how Jai would be more useful to you if he were—'

'I know what you're saying,' he interrupts me. 'Shut up.' He's more direct than I remember him. He's bulked out and turned his hair and eyes black, in stark contrast to his white skin. Perhaps it's the fashion now.

I wait for him to speak again, and as I do I glance at the twins. Liss is wringing her hands. Casta looks grave. After we pulled into the Veya trainyards I went home to change and grab the letter from the Dean before going to see the twins. They were kind and understanding, and they promised to do the best they could. But their best obviously wasn't close to good enough. Suddenly I have the feeling that this was a lost battle from the start.

'You forget your place, Orna, and you forget your son's,' he says, his voice low and gravelly where it was previously high and soft. 'You are both in Bond to Clan Caracassa. The Bond is an obligation to submit to the will of your master, without question, without hesitation. Is that not so?'

'You didn't order Jai to join the Army—'

'Is that not so?' he barks.

'Yes,' I reply, bridling.

He sits back, satisfied that he has established his authority over me. As if it was ever in question. 'My sisters have explained your situation. I am not unsympathetic. Rynn was a great loss to us all. Your ordeal has been terrible indeed.' He taps his fingers on the stone armrest of the bench he sits on. 'But you forget your place. A Bondswoman does not lecture her master on how best to utilise those who serve him.'

'Magnate, I didn't presume to lecture, only to offer advice as to talents that may have escaped your notice. The letter in your hand testifies to his skill in engineering and invention. They're desperate to teach him. These are assets to the Clan that will be wasted if he is . . .' I can't bring myself to finish. 'I beg you.'

He sighs, but there's no real regret in it. 'Your motivations are transparent,' he says. 'If your concern for the Clan was so great, you would have raised this issue years ago.'

'That was my greatest mistake,' I reply, and the words taste bitter.

'The boy himself chose his path. He was allowed to join the Army because we prefer our people willing. He showed little enthusiasm for being an inventor, despite his talent.'

'That was because he wanted the approval of his—'

'Do you think you know better than your son what path his life should take?'

'I'm certain it's his wish as much as mine,' I reply, though I'm not at all certain. It's entirely possible he'll stick this course, even against his natural inclinations, out of loyalty to his father. I doubt it, but he might. The wishes of the dead become somehow sacred in a way they never were in life. That's why I want him to hear the news about Rynn from me, if he hasn't already found out. I want to talk to him, to persuade him to come back to what he values: to Reitha and the University.

'That is not an answer to my question,' Ledo says.

I phrase my reply carefully. 'I have fought for you and killed for you and watched my husband die for you, and I know my son. He doesn't have the temperament to survive it.'

'Perhaps he will surprise you.' Ledo smiles a little. He's toying with me, the fucker, and I have no option but to play his game, knowing I'm going to lose. He's enjoying making me sound like a wheedling, overprotective woman trying to gather her son back under her apron. But he's never seen battlefields full of people with half their heads gone, he's never seen someone's arm ripped off, he's never seen their manhood stripped away until they're just boys, screaming for their mothers as their blood runs unstoppably into the earth. He'll never understand that I *cannot* allow my son to be among those men.

'Where is your loyalty, Orna?' he asks. 'You had that boy because *I* permitted it. He exists because of me. You should be proud to give him up for the Clan. Your husband died a glorious death on the battlefield. You should be—'

'He died a *pointless* death on the battlefield!' I cry. I hear Liss's sharp intake of breath and know I shouldn't have raised my voice, but it's too late now and I can't stop myself anyway. It comes bursting out of me on a river of rage. 'He was killed in a miserable failure of an operation and one of our own people *sold us out*! Why do you want to waste my son's life that way?'

'*I will not be moved by the whims of a slave!*' he roars, with a volume that makes me back away. He surges to his feet. 'Your son will fight for me, and die if necessary, because it is *my* decision! Don't you understand, you idiot creature? I *don't care* about your maternal instincts. He is my property, as are you, and you will do what I tell you. You will not be told where he is. You will recuperate for as long as is deemed necessary and then return to my service and be as good as, if not better, than you were before. If you are not, I will have your son executed! Do you understand?'

I understand, all right. It crashes in on me like a landslide. I understand that all my effort has been for nothing, that I could have stayed in prison and died there and it would have made absolutely no difference to anything. I understand that my son is beyond my reach, and nothing I can do will prevent him being sent into combat against an enemy who could well be forewarned and forearmed. I came back to this life of service when I could have stayed free in the world above, and it was all for Jai; but now my hopes are dashed simply because Ledo doesn't feel like cooperating.

I finally realise how flimsy my plans were. Nereith was right. I've been clinging to hope and refusing to listen to sense. It was the only thing I had to drive me through the grief at Rynn's death. But in the end, everything had been leaning against this moment, the moment when I asked my master for this favour. I'd known how capricious he could be, and I'd chosen to ignore it. But now he's said no.

I feel betrayed. Rancour swirls into my thoughts like a black mist. I've given my fucking life to this man, *willingly*. I've murdered for him, cheated on my lover for him, lied for him, tortured for him and been tortured. And as if that wasn't enough, I gave him my son. And he can't grant me this? This sensible, logical thing that I ask of him? The frustration, the fury is enough to choke me. I just want to kill him. A single clean strike, punch the cartilage of his nose like a spear into his brain. It would be so easy . . .

'Do you understand?' he demands of me.

I nod, keeping back tears of rage. Liss rushes over and holds me protectively, shielding me from his wrath.

'If not for the fondness my sisters have for you, I would have you killed for speaking to me this way. It is your fortune that there is no one else here to witness this, or you would already be dead.'

Silence. Ledo sits down. The anger has flowed out of him, and he is almost serene. I wait for him to dismiss me, but he doesn't.

'You have been listening to the babble of the troops,' he says quietly. 'I will offer you this. There was no traitor. Your husband died because of poor planning and bad intelligence. He was not betrayed. *You* were not betrayed.' He shifts in his seat, becoming suddenly restless. He's tired of this now. 'I suggest you take a short vacation, Orna. I know you have suffered. Use the time to think about what it means to be a Bondswoman. Return to me when you are ready to act like one again.'

I raise my head. The tears are gone, conquered before they could fall.

'Magnate,' I say quietly, looking into his eyes. 'Do you know a man called Belek Aspa?'

A barely perceptible instant of surprise, and then hatred flickers across his face. His gaze darkens.

'Take her away,' he tells Liss. 'Before I have her tongue ripped out.'

I begin to shake uncontrollably in the carriage on the way to the club. Liss and Casta insisted that they take me out as their way of an apology for not swaying their brother enough. I didn't have the willpower left to refuse.

'Oh! She's shaking!' Liss says, because she's holding my hand. She becomes frantically solicitous, taking my temperature by laying her wrist against my forehead, looking into my averted eyes.

'Is she sick?' Casta asks.

'I don't know? Are you sick?' This addressed to me.

'You're not sick, are you?'

'I'm not sick,' I mutter, though I do suddenly feel queasy. But it's not sickness; it's the adrenaline comedown, the grief, the *rage*.

'It's our cruel brother, isn't it? He frightened you, didn't he?'

'Cruel,' Casta agrees.

'Oh, how I hate him! Don't listen to him. We'll protect you!'

I've never been so stupid in my life. I got out of control. I got riled, I got angry and frustrated, and I shouted at a man who could have me killed with a word. It's only now starting to sink in how close I was, how far I overstepped the line. I can't understand why he didn't do it. Maybe he was in an indulgent mood, or maybe he respected his sister's wishes too much, or maybe I'm of genuine value to him. The aristocracy are nothing if not unpredictable. But still . . . really, really fucking dumb.

I've burned my bridges with my outburst. He'll never go back on his decision now. I can taste the bitterness in my mouth. Abyss, I have to *do* something, but I have no idea what. I can barely concentrate through the haze of despair, anger, failure.

'You need a drink!' Liss prescribes, having run out of methods of diagnosis.

'Several, in fact,' Casta chimes in.

And right now that seems like the best idea in the world. Something to shut it out, something to make it go away. Something to keep me from tipping into this gaping hole that's opened inside me.

'Several,' I agree. Liss claps and even Casta looks pleased. It's like they've forgotten that I've just lost the only chance to save my son through any legal, honourable method. The only avenues left to me now are traitor's ways, going against my master's command, making my son a deserter. I can't think about them now. Those would be decisions I could never take back.

The twins take me to the Black Circlet, the club in the Tangles where I first talked to Liss about her upcoming marriage. We get their usual table, by a window that looks out over a garden of coloured rocks and waterfalls. The third seg has just begun but the club is largely empty. Handmaidens drift about like ghosts, lovers quarrel while trying not to be overheard, middlemen plot on their masters' behalf in the dim light. Through the windows on the far side the sound of the traffic can be heard.

'This place is dying,' Casta comments.

'I don't even know why we come here any more. Nobody's here. We should find a new place.'

'That's what everyone else did,' Casta replies. 'That's why we kept coming here.'

'Well, I'm sick of being different! I want to be the same!'

A handmaiden appears and I order hard liquor: spikevine, straight up. The twins exchange a glance and then order the same.

I barely say a word until the handmaiden returns. Then I take the cup, down it and order another, putting the empty back on the tray.

'Careful!' Liss warns me.

'She's grieving,' says Casta. 'It's Ledo's fault.'

'Bring more,' says Liss to the handmaiden, then necks her own drink and begins to choke, clawing at her throat as the liquor burns down into her chest. Casta ignores the drama, leaning over the table to take my wrist in her hand.

'We can keep at him,' says Casta conspiratorially. 'But you shouldn't have made him angry. He won't change his mind now.' She sighed. 'Ah, if only I were Magnate. *I* would have granted your plea, Orna. You know that, don't you? But I daren't go against his word, even to find out where—'

I'm barely listening. 'After all I went through, after everything . . . Abyss, he wasn't even willing to consider my request. What the fuck am I worth to him?' I snarl.

Casta is taken aback, not sure how to react. She's not used to hearing such a tone directed at her brother, and certainly not from a Bondswoman of the Clan. There's a warning in her eyes: *remember your place, Orna.* I glare back at her, too riled to submit.

'Oh, but Jai will be fine! I just know it!' Liss says, having abandoned her show now that nobody is paying attention to her. It defuses things just enough for us both to get away without a conflict.

'No,' says Casta, still watching me closely. 'There's the operation.'

'The operation?' Liss cries in horror.

'Operation Deadfall,' I say. Casta barely nods. 'You know about it?'

'I know it's not long now. A dozen turns. Maybe two.'

I don't want to ask, but I have to. 'What will happen?'

'They want to break the Gurta in the Borderlands, once and for all. They'll throw everything they've got at the enemy, and try to overwhelm them with weight of numbers at certain tactical points. But it's a risky strategy. It will leave them dangerously overstretched and committed. If it doesn't work, if we're forced to retreat, the Gurta will slaughter us.'

'It'll be carnage!' Liss whispers, scandalised. It's all so breathlessly exciting for her. She seems to have forgotten that *my fucking son* will be there. Sometimes I just want to punch her.

'What was that name you said to our brother?' Liss continues, off on a tangent. 'Brolicaspa or something?'

'Belek Aspa,' I correct her. 'Just a name I heard in prison. Someone asked me if I'd ever heard Ledo say it.'

She suddenly gets to her feet, losing interest. 'I need to piss!' she declares, apropos of nothing, and wanders off towards the toilets.

I'm faintly surprised that Casta has remained seated at the table with me.

'They intend to end the war in one stroke,' Casta says, returning to the previous subject. 'Many will die, but they think it will save lives in the long term.'

'And what do you think?' I ask. The spikevine has reached my brain now, and is soothing everything to a fuzz. The handmaiden returns with more, in bigger cups. Casta waits for the servant to leave before she answers.

'The operation is only good for Caracassa if we push and we fail. Otherwise, the war is over. The Clan is struggling to compete in the market anyway. We make our fortunes treating the wounded. Healers only turn a profit when there are people to heal.'

'It's in Clan Caracassa's interests to have this operation fail?'

'Exactly. When the war is over the Turnward Claw Alliance falls to pieces. Clan Caracassa loses its influence.'

She sees the suppressed feelings on my face. 'I know this is hard. Your son is there. But we have to think of the Clan.'

I drink my spikevine, and Casta sips at hers. She's never been as dizzy as her sister, but I've rarely heard her talk politics so confidently.

'What's Ledo up to?' I ask. Casta likes people to be direct. 'Why's he marrying Liss off to a family that manufactures textiles and luxury goods?'

'He won't say,' Casta replies. 'But I think he's hedging his bets. In case the push does succeed. If the war ends, Caracassa has good links to a peacetime industry.'

'We convert our factories to manufacture fine dyes and treatment agents for textiles—' I say.

'And they cut each other a mutually beneficial deal. Clan Caracassa and Clan Jerima go into business together.' She tuts and sits back, folding her arms. 'There's no real money in that. The reason we're being out-competed in the market is because he's dividing our resources.'

She takes out a cigarillo and lights it. I reach over and take one from the packet. She doesn't care enough to comment. Probably can't remember if I used to smoke or not.

'We made our money from war and we always have,' she says, blowing a plume of smoke into the air.

'I don't get it,' I say. 'Does Ledo want a war or doesn't he?'

'Clan Caracassa *needs* this war,' she says, then sneers. 'This sham of a marriage is his backup plan in case it all goes wrong.'

I watch Casta carefully. She seems to phase in and out of her moods. Sometimes she's sharp as a razor and other times she's as clueless and addled as her twin. Right now she's definitely the former.

I take a slug of spikevine. 'What do you think of Liss's fiancé?'

She holds my eyes steadily. 'I'd like to kill him,' she says. Then Liss comes back, Casta turns all sweetness, and everything is forgotten.

I can barely stand up by the time I get home. Liss and Casta have to get someone to help me to the door of my chambers in the Caracassa Mansions. I shut the door behind me and totter gingerly into the centre of the room. It's dark; only the lights of Veya beyond the huge circular window in our living-space provide any illumination.

I listen to the silence for a long time, knowing that it will never again be filled with my husband's laughter, that we will never eat as a family at that table again. I wonder if Jai will ever come home, but I can't believe he will. It feels so, so empty. A vacant nest is a terrible thing.

I sink to my knees and curl up on the floor. Lonely, scared, overwhelmed. Sniffles become sobs become great wracking whoops that score my throat, but I can't seem to cry it all out. At some point I stem the flow, and at some point I sleep; but I know that when I wake up in the morning, this shitty world will still be waiting for me.

7

I need to be active. Sitting in that graveyard of a home is killing me. So I send out a message to an old friend, and while I'm waiting for it to find him, I fulfil a promise I made to a dead man.

Spikevine hangovers are not the most pleasant of experiences, but I've invited the pain in and now I have to suffer it. Punishment for failure, and for my stupidity. Mouth dry and sticky, joints aching, I head into the seedier districts of Veya to deliver the letter entrusted to me by Juth before our escape from Farakza.

The address is in the Scornhold, on the poleways side of the city, just neath-backspin of the Flay and turnward of Marasca Springs. It's a run-down area in the process of revitalisation, all narrow, crumbling alleyways and graffiti. Far from the shinehouses that tower over the city, dimmer than the more wealthy areas. Lantern-posts dot the streets, some lit, some dark. Corners and alcoves are guarded by small groups of dangerously idle young men, eyeing passers-by.

I'm safe enough. Usually the Cadre symbol skinmarked on my shoulder is enough to deter anyone, but sometimes the thought of taking down a Cadre woman is too tempting. Thing is, anyone idiotic enough to try random violence against Cadre is almost certainly going to die for their trouble. Smart fighters, *disciplined* fighters, don't hang out on street corners desperate for someone to threaten in order to prove their masculinity. They're not that insecure.

The air rings with the blunt din of construction, adding to my already spectacular headache. Dirty arcades bristle with rootwood scaffolding and counterweighted crane jibs. Eskarans and Craggens work side-by-side here, the latter hauling great sleds of rock or applying their immense strength to huge pulleys. The air is dense with their language: a breathy, explosive mixture of glottal stops, swallowing noises and booming sounds. They hulk their way among their smaller companions, flat, spiked tails dragging behind them.

I've always had a bit of an affinity for Craggens. There's something alluring in their way of thinking, their lazy, gentle myths and simple yearnings. They don't hurry anywhere, and they seem unaffected by ambition or the traumatic complications of life.

As I watch them, I wonder what really goes on in the minds of these massive humanoids, with their small, tusked snouts and tiny black eyes. They're built to be unstoppable warriors: shambling mountains of red hide armour with a shaggy mane of quills running down their backs. But instead they're content to live their own slow lives, deep in the earth, where the pressure and heat is too great for us to follow.

It's a good system we've got, us and them. The males work in Veya to raise the money to build luxurious dens to attract females, who have to come nearer the surface to give birth. The young are more fragile than the adults. Eskaran craftsmen make the dens, which are far more elegant than Craggens can construct with their massive hands. The more elaborate the den, the more likely the male is to score a female.

When Craggens and Eskarans first came into contact, there wasn't a war. We just made a deal. Would that every meeting of cultures was so easy.

The address on Juth's envelope takes me down a dingy stairway, below street level, to an iron door with a viewing-slot. I hammer on it. Footsteps approach, and the shield on the slot slides back.

'What?' demands the girl on the other side. She's probably eighteen, twenty at most. Garish make-up, colourfully dyed hair. High cheekbones and bluish skin, giving away her Yurla bloodline.

'I've got a letter for you,' I say. 'From Juth.'

Surprise in her reaction. Then suspicion. 'So where is it?'

I hold it up.

'Put it through.'

I shove it through the slot, and she pulls the shield closed. I wait for a few moments, nonplussed, and then decide I can't be bothered with this and go back up the stairs. Promise fulfilled. I don't even really care what was in the letter.

I'm some way down the street when the girl comes running after me, followed by a dreadlocked scruff in his late twenties. 'Hoy! Hold up!' he shouts.

I stop and stare at them expectantly as they come to a halt in front of me. The man has the letter in his hand, now open.

'You knew Juth?' he asks, panting. It was only a short run. He might be wiry, but he's unfit and he smokes too much.

''Not well,' I say. 'He asked me to deliver that for him.'

'You were in a Gurta prison?'

'Farakza. Juth is still there.' I feel like doing something pointlessly vicious so I say: 'He's probably dead by now.'

It doesn't appear to bother them at all. The girl notes the Cadre sigil on my exposed shoulder for the first time, and she nudges the man with a pitiful lack of subtlety.

'You're Cadre?' he asks. He's nervous.

'That's right,' I say. 'And you two work for the Undercity Press, distributing subversive and illegal literature throughout Veya. You also have offices in Vect and Bry Athka and Lera, who handle distribution in those cities.' I look at the man steadily, whose jaw has dropped. 'I don't know who she is, but I'm guessing that you're Cherita Fal Barlan, the editor?'

He freezes up, guilt all over him. The girl looks like she's ready to run.

'Recognised the address,' I say, motioning at the envelope.

'You knew where we were?' Barlan gapes. 'How long?'

'Couple of years. Just never had cause to visit you.'

Still stunned. Doesn't know where to go next. I put him out of his misery.

'Listen, it's my business to know this stuff. You're not as secret as you'd like to believe. I'm sure you're wondering why Clan Caracassa haven't raided your premises and had you all arrested long ago, right?'

'Uh . . . it had crossed my mind,' he says. 'We publish some . . . pretty unfavourable books about the Plutarchs.'

'You want the truth?' I say, pinching the bridge of my nose, where my headache is sharpest. 'Nobody cares. The Plutarchs have bigger things to worry about. So do I.'

'Nobody cares?' the girl repeats, aghast.

'You're not half the thorn in the establishment's side that you think you are,' I tell her. I'm not in the mood to coddle anyone right now.

'Shit, that's a comedown,' says Barlan, deflating. 'Think I'd rather be arrested than ignored.'

'I can break your legs if you like. Would that make you feel better?'

It takes him a moment before he realises I'm not serious. He smiles uncertainly, then looks from me to the letter in his hand. 'You wanna come see?' he offers.

'Barlan!' the girl cries.

'She already knows, Pela,' he says. 'Besides, Juth trusted her.' He looks back at me. 'So? I'd like to talk to you.'

I have time to kill, and the old information-gathering instincts are still sharp. I motion to him to lead on.

Barlan hands me the letter from Juth and tells me I might as well read it, after all I went through to get it here. We head back to the stairs and through the iron door, into a short mould-speckled corridor that opens into a dim room cluttered with bales of broadsheets and boxes of books. Against one wall is a hand-cranked printing press. Two other men sit at makeshift desks, one reading mail, one scribbling furiously. Like Pela and Barlan, they're dressed scruffily, trying a little too hard to be malcontents. They react to my presence first with interest, then with alarm.

While Barlan is arguing with them I read the letter. It's short and to the point.

If this letter reaches you by some other hand, it is because I could not bring it myself and am likely dead. The bearer of this letter has escaped from Farakza, a Gurta prison where I am being held. Fortune took one masterpiece from my hands, but it may yet provide another. Stop at nothing to get the story from this person. We will show the people what their sons can expect if they are unlucky enough to face capture in our 'glorious' war. Consider it my final commission. Juth.

'Yeah, sorry about him,' says Barlan, as I fold up the letter and give it back to him. 'Juth was enthusiastic; you had to say that. But his judgement was all over the place. Always coming up with some shattering work of literature or another, always deeply average.'

'He was carrying this around in the hope of finding someone to give it to,' I say. 'I could have been anyone. He just caught me on my way out.'

'Don't suppose you fancy telling your story? Anonymous, of course. Can't really pay you, but y'know . . .'

He trails off. He knows by the expression on my face that it's not going to happen.

'Sorry,' I tell him. I'm not getting involved in their little revolutionary games. I respect their strength of belief and all that, but the simple fact is that if they ever became powerful enough to harm the Plutarchs or the Merchant Council, they'd be crushed flat. They exist only because they're beneath the notice of the powers that be.

'There's talk of a military push,' Barlan says, with affected nonchalance. 'Know anything about that?'

'I know they're not keeping it very secret.'

'They don't want to,' Pela interjects. 'They want to rally the troops and worry the Gurta. There've been enough false alarms though. Is this one real?'

'Your guess is as good as mine. I'm just a soldier.'

'You're Cadre,' she insists. 'You're inner circle with Caracassa. They trust you.'

'The aristocracy don't trust anyone, not even themselves,' I reply.

'There's a quote, right there!' Barlan cries. 'Can I use it?'

'No.'

'Anonymously?'

I sigh. 'My name turns up in print in any of your publications, I'll come find you.'

'Great!' he grins, and scribbles it down on a scrap of paper.

I look around the office. The other two are still watching me with undisguised suspicion and loathing. Difficult to decide if they're just playing revolutionary or if they have any muscle at all behind their politics.

'What's your take on the Korok thing?' I ask, wandering around the room, picking at this and that.

'Korok? Fucking whitewash, that's what that was,' Barlan mutters bitterly.

'I was there.'

He looks up, but it's Pela who exclaims: 'You were?'

'That's where I was captured. My husband was killed.' It's becoming easy to say now. I don't know if I should be pleased or saddened by that.

'Abyss! You're joking?'

'Does it sound like something I'd joke about?' I look at Barlan. 'You said it was a whitewash?'

He bursts into action all of a sudden, rummaging among the piles of paper scattered around the room. 'Look! If you're in any doubt that the Gurta knew our plans ahead of the attack, look at this.' He slaps a sheet onto a clear spot on one of the desks and smoothes it out. I recognise it immediately. It's a topographical map of the cavern where Korok lies, dominated by the lake in its centre. Coloured arrows and markers depict the movement of various forces around the landscape.

'How'd you get this?' I ask.

'We made it. It's compiled of eyewitness accounts from survivors, interviews with the soldiers who were there.' He catches the scepticism on my face. 'What, you think we can lift this stuff out of the Plutarch's records? We do what we can with what we have.'

'So what does this prove?' I ask, studying it.

'Just look at it. These here, this gang of Gurta bowmen? They were spotted moving towards this rise even before the soldiers they came to intercept were given the orders to go there. You see? They knew where the Eskarans were heading before our soldiers did.' He points to another spot on the map. 'Same thing happened here. There's just no way they could have reacted quick enough unless they already knew the attack was coming. You *ever* see Gurta this organised?'

I stare at the map. He makes a good point.

'They weren't even supposed to know you intended to take back Korok, but they'd placed explosives all over the port,' he says. 'They took out a ridge here and caused a landslide. Killed dozens of our people. And notice how they positioned the shard-cannon emplacements to overlook the areas where our troops were concentrated? That takes time to set up and supply. And look! Look how big the lake is! Think they could have got their ships from the other side that fast? Nah, they must have already had ships waiting in the lake even before Eskaran forces entered the cavern.'

I can feel something building inside me again as I gaze at the map: the anger, the frustration, the hate. I know the evidence is unreliable and yet I can't help but be convinced because I know how the game works and I know this is how it's played.

'Listen,' says Barlan, 'You swore your life to the high-ups and this may be hard to hear, but someone told the Gurta our plans. Someone important enough to know the tactics. That makes it a Warmaster at least, but most likely an aristo.' He shakes his head angrily. 'Someone sold us out. That's a fact. And you know what's worse? Someone could have told us *who*. But they got to him first.'

'Someone knew who the traitor was?'

'That was the rumour. Small-time merchant, he put out the word that he had evidence about some aristo dealing with the Gurta. But he was greedy. Wouldn't tell anyone until he got paid. He wanted to sell the evidence to the highest bidder, but he knew it was dangerous, so he tried to broker the deal through some crimelord out of Mal Eista. He got protection and a place to hide, and the crimelord was supposed to make the deal on his behalf in return for a cut of the money.' Barlan snarls. 'Fucking idiot. The traitor got to him, took him out before he could sell his little secret. All that stuff at Korok wouldn't have happened if that guy had just done the right thing.'

I can feel myself growing cold, and everything seems distant. My hangover has suddenly receded.

'What was his name?' I ask, but I already know his name.

'Gorak Jespyn,' Barlan replies.

Gorak Jespyn. The man I killed, quick and quiet, in his sleep, just like I was told to.

The traitor got to him.

6

I wait for Keren in a bar on a lantern-lit plaza, sipping blackspore cocktails to take the edge off my hangover. It's very late, and though Veya never sleeps it does have its rhythms. The streets are quiet, the plaza largely empty. The tall, severe buildings that overlook the area have their shutters drawn. Beyond the spattering of a nearby fountain and the stirring of the breeze, nothing moves.

I sit at my wrought-iron table out front of the bar, getting steadily wasted. Thinking the kind of thoughts I only dare think when I'm drunk.

I'm making ridiculous plans in my head. Plans to find my son, to steal him away. Plans to find a chthonomancer or a dweoming or someone powerful enough to remove the skinmarks that brand us. They were attached by a master: it'll take another master to remove them, one with no scruples or connection to the Clans. Someone who wouldn't just turn us in or kill us on the spot.

If it was just the sigil on my shoulder, maybe I could do it. Unlikely I'd get away with it for long, but it's a maybe. The problem is the Bond-mark on my face, and on my son's face. Even burning it off or cutting it away wouldn't work. As if anyone would believe that we had both been mutilated in the same place, exactly where the Bond-mark would lie. There's no hiding from it.

You can't save him.

Of course I've considered it before, but there were always so many variables in between that it seemed pointless to worry about it. No need to despair until hope is gone.

But maybe hope *is* gone, and I'm just refusing to accept it. If wild plans are all I have then I really don't have anything. Maybe I could find someone who could help, a chthonomancer who could help me lose the skinmarks . . . but the real problem is Jai.

Ledo has closed the door on me. While the possibility existed that our master would permit Jai to return to Veya, I had a chance. But now what's left, if I find him? Make my son a deserter? Dishonoured, reviled, hunted for the rest of his life. Prevented from ever seeing Reitha again.

He'll be in more danger if you try to save him than if you don't.

Of course. The rest of Ledo's Cadre will stop at nothing to find us if we run. I know most of them, and they'll be merciless and untiring in their pursuit. The agonies we face if they take us alive will be beyond imagining. We won't get away. He's safer taking his chances in the massacre to come.

I stare into nothingness. Reality is settling in like damp into the marrow of a building. It's the first time I've really squared up to the situation. The first time I've looked at it in the cold, clinical way that I should have been doing from the start. If you take out all emotion, if you forget about hope, you start to see things clearly.

Give it up. Leave it alone. Let things fall as they may.

It makes sense. To stop interfering where I'm not wanted. I'll only make things worse. For both of us. And maybe he's already dead. Maybe this was all finished before it began.

Let it go.

Can I? Can I really let it go? Can I accept that everything was for nothing?

No. Never. I can't just stand by and let this all happen. I have to find Jai. Even if only to warn him. Even if only because I can't go on not knowing if he's dead or alive. Because I can't bear the thought that he might have heard of his parents' deaths by now, and that he doesn't know I'm alive and searching for him. Even if only to tell him about the letter from the Dean of Engineers, because the Abyss knows Ledo might not be Magnate for ever, and Casta would be more sympathetic to my pleas.

All I want is to see my son. Even if I can't save him . . . just to *see* him . . .

I think of Ledo. My master. The head of Clan Caracassa, the man who owns my life and loyalty, the man I gave my only son to. Is he the one undermining the war effort? Is he the one who sold us out at Korok? Is he the one I owe for my husband's death? Did he really send me to kill Gorak Jespyn to preserve his secret, or was the story about the merchant only rumour and hearsay?

To try and escape the obligations of Bondsmanship is an almost inconceivable act. To turn on your master is even worse. It might be justifiable if Ledo's actions were putting Clan Caracassa in danger, but they're doing just the opposite. Sabotaging Operation Deadfall would be extremely profitable for the Clan. They don't want the war to end; Casta has already told me as much.

Could I go to the twins with my suspicions? No. That would be too much, even for the friendship that exists between us. I am a slave, as my master reminded me last turn. A slave's place is not to question the actions of her master.

Funny. I never thought of myself as a slave before last turn. It never seemed to really click. I saw Bondsmanship as a willing expression of loyalty, a matter of devotion. But in the end, I was rescued from forced slavery only to immediately volunteer for it again. I was ten years old, a stupid little girl, frightened of the world. I shouldn't have done it. They shouldn't have let me.

I catch myself, and take an extra large swig of my cocktail. The sour taste makes me wince, brings me back from maudlin reverie. Regrets are pointless. I was ten years old with no family and no relatives. If I hadn't sworn into Bond I would have starved or died in some forsaken orphanage. Caracassa not only saved my life, they gave me a life.

But how much more could I pay for it? How much more will they take?

I shake my head to clear it. I tell myself that there's nothing approaching proof here. Just a convenient theory that fits the facts. That makes me feel a little better.

Voids, there are dozens of Plutarchs who stand to benefit from the continuation of the war. Maybe they are dealing with the Gurta on matters I know nothing about. Stringing together a few unproven theories about a traitor is no reason to start suspecting your master of treason. I'm just angry at him because of Jai.

But then there's the matter of Gorak Jespyn. And there were the Magister's questions, back in Farakza. Why was he asking whether Ledo had ever spoken about a Gurta Minister?

Easy. He was asking me about Ledo because I'm affiliated with

Clan Caracassa. If I had been skinmarked with the sigil of Clan Jerima, he would have asked me about Vem. Maybe they just suspect Belek Aspa of consorting with the enemy. Maybe they're just fishing.

The more I think about it, the more it comes apart. Ledo? Involved in treason? There are many more likely candidates than him.

But what about the look on his face? I can't ignore that. The look on his face when I asked him if he knew Belek Aspa. Surprise. Hatred. The threat that he would have my tongue ripped out.

He *knows* something.

And that's when I realise what I'm considering. What I've been trying not to admit to myself ever since that meeting with Ledo. I *want* him to be the traitor. Because if he is, then I'll kill him, Bond or no Bond. And then Casta will be Magnate, and she'll let me go to Jai. She'll let me tell him about the letter from the Dean, and about his father, and maybe then he'll come home and be an inventor like he always wanted. He can be with Reitha. And he'll be safe from the slaughter to come.

This is dangerous ground. I'm afraid to believe I'm even capable of this. But the only thing that's important now is Jai.

I'll find out. I make that promise to myself, as I see my friend approaching. I'll find out if Ledo's the traitor.

Keren saunters up casually, smoking. He sits down without a word of greeting, orders a drink from a passing handmaiden and gets one for me too. He looks as grizzled and dishevelled as ever, as if he's hauled himself out of bed to get here and is ready to go back there.

'Welcome back,' he says. 'Missed you.'

'Got a cigarillo for me?'

'You don't smoke,' he observes, drawing one from a carven scratchwood case and handing it across the table.

'Been feeling self-destructive lately.'

'Ah. *There's* a story.' He lights me up. I draw the hot, aromatic smoke deep down into my lungs.

'You want to hear?'

He settles back in his chair. 'Course I do. We thought you bit it at Korok, Orna. We thought you died.'

'I did.' Shadow Death, I add silently.

'Then I'm talking to a ghost? Huh. I guess those Banchu corpse-worshippers were right after all.'

I tell him everything, from the assault on Korok until now. Usually I'm a little more cautious with Keren. I know he trades information with others. But I need him to understand. I need to tell someone. And if a few anonymous rumours are spread about my master, well, fuck him. The bastard should have let me go get my son.

When I'm done Keren is on his third drink and I'm on my fifth, and the inlaid silver ash-pan has been replaced and is refilling with butts. He's got a lot to chew over.

'You're in a situation,' he says.

'Right.'

'And I just bet you need something from me,' he grins.

'Little help, that's all. Nothing big. Nothing dangerous.'

'I wish I could get my hands on the classified records you need,' he says, spreading his hands, 'but my connections don't go that high.'

'I just need you to help me find someone. I'll owe you.'

'You're good for it. Who's the lucky target?'

'Josta Kayd Reitha. Jai's lover. She works for the University of Bry Athka. She's a naturalist, gets posted around a lot. Might even be up on the surface.'

'Not a problem. Mind if I ask why?' He scratches behind his ear.

'He might have sent her letters.'

'They censor those things.'

'There might be a clue. Anyway, I need to see her. To tell her some things, so she can tell Jai later, if something should happen to me.'

'What's going to happen to you?'

'I don't know, Keren. There might be some . . . It might get dangerous for me.' I look away, blow a jet of smoke, tap the ash. 'It's just in case.'

He stares at me hard. 'You're going after him, aren't you? Even though Ledo's forbidden it.'

'I've not decided that yet. I just want to know where he is.'

'Right,' he says, oozing scepticism. 'So how are you going to find out? No, wait, don't tell me. You can't ask the twins to help; they're too close to Ledo. So you're going to Silverfish, right?'

I look around the bar, wary of being overheard. We're the only ones here. 'Let's just say the proper channels aren't really working for me right now. And I don't have time to wait and see if Reitha can be found, and if she knows anything. That's an outside shot at best. So I need to investigate other options.'

Keren tuts, sits back, starts massaging the silver spikes in his lip with one knuckle. Body language for *this is a bad idea.* 'You get tangled with Silverfish, you might never get out.'

'Oh, fuck that. It's all bluster and smokescreens. Nobody knows for sure if Silverfish even exists.'

'But we've all seen his fingerprints. Can't deny it.'

'I'm just saying, right now there's more fear than substance. If he's as good as they say, he can find my son. If not, well . . .'

Keren looks doubtful, but in the end he shrugs. 'Your call,' he says. 'You were warned. Hey, I ran into an old friend of yours a while back. You remember Ekan?'

'He's hardly a friend, Keren. I cut his hand off.'

'Yeah, well. Anyway, since Caracassa pushed him out of the legitimate trade, he's started selling poisons. Word is, he's discovered something of a talent for it. Some of the right people have started to visit him. Just thought you might want to know.'

'Appreciate it,' I say.

He leans forward. 'Listen, you come to me any time you need help, okay? I've got your back.'

I put my hands over his and grip them. Keren is a good friend. Sure, he'll want repayment in kind; he's always tallying up favours like that. But for now, when I need him, he's here.

At least there's *one* person on my side.

I meet Nereith in a club in Coldwash, down among the alleys and lanes where the dockers work out their post-shift tensions in the bars and brothels. It's a shitty little dive, with peeling black walls and the air of an impending fight. Angry-looking men slouch in corners or sit hunched over drinks, conspiring with their companions. Everyone has blades, but nobody's showing them.

I'm wearing long sleeves to cover the emblem on my shoulder. Bond-marks don't attract too much attention, but announcing myself as Cadre would. When I arrive the Khaadu is already there, sitting at a table and watching the band play on the circular stage. Every man's eyes are on me as I walk across the half-empty room. It could be because they're all testosterone-swollen rapists-to-be and that anything with breasts would snare their attention in this dismal place, but I prefer to believe that I've still got it.

Nereith motions for me to sit and pushes a drink over. Naturally, he's picked my favourite. It's faintly worrying how much he seems to know about me.

The band are knocking out a bawdy version of an old work-song from my grandfather's generation, sung by two gravel-voiced women backed up by a calamity of percussion and a few strings. Nereith pays me no attention until they finish up. Making me wait. When they're done, he turns to me and gives me a fang-laden grin.

'Good, aren't they?'

'They're not bad,' I say.

'Do you play?'

'Used to. Gave it up. Bad memories.'

'That's a shame,' he commiserates unconvincingly.

'Yeah,' I reply with an equal lack of conviction.

'I assume the reason you're here is because your investigations haven't gone very well?'

'You made me an offer. I've come to take you up on it.'

'You want Silverfish to locate your son?'

'That's right.'

He looks me over casually. It's only been a few turns since I've seen him but he's a different person now. He has power. He's an operator. He knows I need him.

'There's a shipment going out in three turns' time,' Nereith says. 'Bonecane. Lots of it. Jerima Vem is leaking that he's got powder on the move, but it's a decoy to try and catch Silverfish.'

'Again?'

'Vem's never been particularly original. The real bonecane is being transported in secret on a Caracassa barge. A pre-nuptial favour from Ledo. Silverfish wants the name of that barge.'

'What's he going to do with it?'

'That's his business. Don't you concern yourself.'

I study him for a moment. 'A few turns isn't enough to get the name. They keep that information sewn tight. I'd need to dig.'

'We know that Vem sent instructions to Ledo. We think the letter still exists. It'll be among his personal correspondence, in his private quarters.'

'You want me break into my master's private quarters?'

'If anyone can, it's you. You're Cadre. Trusted. You can get in close.'

I drink my drink. This is betrayal. This is no going back. And it's awfully tempting.

If there's evidence to be found that my master is a traitor, it'll be in his private quarters. Before I can act on my suspicions, I need the proof. Until then, I can't be sure. And I can't make a move until the matter is beyond doubt.

In those rooms could be the answers I need to save Jai. If Ledo is the traitor, and I can take him out without anyone knowing, then Casta becomes Magnate and my son comes home.

If.

But what if he's *not* the traitor? What if I'm wrong? I'll be selling his secrets to an enemy. Breaking the oath of Bond.

This is a decision I don't want to face. Finding Jai is one thing, but to go directly against my master's interests is another thing entirely. I've been put to the question. Where do my loyalties lie?

And I find I'm not sure any more.

I sit back, drum my fingers on the table. The band is playing some awful swinging folk tune. Nereith just stares at me.

'This is about that Gurta Minister you mentioned to me, isn't it?' he says. 'Belek Aspa. You asked the wrong people the wrong questions.'

I don't answer that, but of course he's right. Ledo must have thought I had been threatening him with the name Belek Aspa, that I was implying there was something dangerous I could reveal about him. He must have thought I knew more than I did. But that reaction alone tells me there's something worth finding. 'You can speak for Silverfish? You can make deals on his behalf?'

'He trusts me implicitly.'

He's very confident. I get the impression that he was downplaying himself considerably when he made his little confession about being a mere information-gatherer. He's a lot more important than he let on.

'I want a guarantee.'

'No guarantees, except my word. If your son is alive, Silverfish will find him.' He looks down into his drink, contemplative. 'If he's dead, we'll still find him. But nothing will happen until you bring me the name of that barge. I'm sure you know that we'll have to verify that intelligence before we fulfil our end of the bargain.'

'Fair enough.'

'Then we have a deal?'

I don't say it for a long while, but I'm just delaying the inevitable. I'd made my decision before I even came here.

'Deal.'

I walk back through the Ashenpark to get to the mansions. It's not the smartest thing to do while drunk. The place is thick with den-runners at this hour, dealing bonecane to the addicts of the city. The joy of bonecane is that progressive use warps your limbs and eventually you end up a cripple. Everyone knows this, but there's no shortage of takers who can't resist trying it. Thinking that maybe they will be one of the infinitesimal minority who don't get hooked immediately. Thinking they can deal with it. Makes me wonder about people, sometimes.

The Ashenpark is near Veya's pole-turnward shinehouse, the Larimus. Its flat light pushes down on the stubby cliffs and slopes of volcanic ash, mingling uneasily with the deep red glow shining up from fenced-off cracks in the earth. I walk along paths that skirt bubbling mud-pools thick with bright fungi, past sullenly fuming geysers.

Suddenly it all wells up inside me again. The fear, the helplessness, the torment of conflicting loyalties. My husband is dead. My son may already be lost, and nothing I can do seems like enough. I left someone on the surface and part of me wants to go back to them, to throw everything up in the air and run, run, run, to a place where none of this matters. And my master, the man to whom I gave everything, may be the man I have to kill to save my son.

I feel something splinter inside me, and I feel like I could collapse. To lie down and never get up. Wouldn't that be sweet?

But I don't, because that's when they come for me.

They run in almost perfect silence, and that's how I know they're Ya'yeen. They attack from three directions: one along the path, one from behind, one springing down from an overhang. Long, slender needles in their long, slender hands.

Not just muggers. Assassins.

I'm drunk and out of practice, but the chua-kîn training is burned into every fibre. I'm still worth ten of any normal victim.

Their attacks are near-simultaneous, but not quite. That provides me opening enough to dodge them. I roll out of the path of the plunging assassin, taking me beyond the slash of the one coming from behind and inside the reach of the third. I grab at his arm and strike, but he bends in my grip and slips away, twisting in a fashion that would snap the bones of anyone but a Ya'yeen.

I drop and kick backwards, finding the leg of one of them, but again their flexible joints suck up the blow and the result is not what I had hoped for. A wet hiss tells me I hurt him, though. It's a start.

Block, kick, feint. For a few instants I'm on automatic, letting my instincts do what they do and trying not to override them with conscious thought. Then one of them makes a foolish double-thrust with his needles, and I pull him forward so that he's off-balance, seize his head and break his neck. Even these bastards can't flex *that* far.

The other two spring away as if burned, facing me on opposite sides. I let their companion drop to the ground and step away, stancing to receive both of them. They're wary. They thought this would be easy. Someone didn't prep them well enough.

Ya'yeen are tricky to fight. Unpredictable. Their skinny, double-jointed bodies and sinuous fighting style mean it's like trying to grab a bunch of eels. They're quick, and they shift techniques all the time, never settling on anything. Making bizarre choices, attacking when they should defend. Their randomness is their greatest strength and their greatest weakness. You never see them coming, but they're prone to mistakes.

I stare into the eyes of my enemy: large, tear-shaped black holes in a narrow grey face, which is given definition and individuality by bone ridges on the cheeks and brows or along the skull. These Ya'yeen are wearing battle garb, skintight outfits cut to some design that means nothing to me. Undoubtedly significant to them, though. One of them has strips of material like belts or ribbons hanging from his limbs that trail artistically behind him as he moves.

They close in slowly, sinister dancers on the hunt, needle points carving out shapes in the air. They're communicating their intentions to each other with their movements. Co-ordinating.

My senses sharpen hard under chua-kîn chants. Preparing me for battle, loosening muscles, switching my brain to a higher level of alertness. The sensation of drunkenness fades and disappears. I can sober up in less than a minute when I have to.

Shouldn't have given me breathing space, I tell them mentally. I won't be so easy to surprise this time.

They come at me together, needles darting, seeking to puncture and pierce. They go for the eyes, the heart, the back of the neck. I'm not there. I drop, twist, kick out. They're fast too: my kick hits air, and I only just avoid having my ankle pinned by a needle.

I roll backwards, but they're striking even as I find my feet. A flurry of blocking follows as I retreat from the thrust and stab of four needles. Then I spot the weakness on their flank, my battle-keen senses picking up possibilities where an ordinary warrior would see nothing. I twist aside as they strike, catch one of the needles between the flat palms of my hand, break it.

Then I'm away, running towards a low cliff that rises up to one side of the path. Drawing my SunChild shortblades as I go. With only three needles to deal with now, I can press the attack.

They're close behind me as I spring up against the cliff and launch myself off it. They've seen the move coming but they're wrongfooted by the angle. A needle misses my belly by a whisper but I get a solid swing at the arm that held it, and take it off at the elbow.

The Ya'yeen squeals. The pain and shock has focused him on nothing but his own mutilated arm, and his guard collapses. I've put him between me and the last assassin, so I have all the time in the world. I hit the ground, spin on the ball of my foot and hack his head off.

The final Ya'yeen is the one with the ribbons and straps. He's barefoot, as they all were, balancing on his toes. Doubly wary now, but showing no sign of giving up. Ya'yeen aren't afraid of dying. Which is good, because he's going to.

I'd try to take him alive if I thought there was any point, but there's a reason people hire Ya'yeen assassins. You can't trace them back to their employers. Even if they did talk, nobody would understand them.

Besides, I don't need him to tell me who's trying to kill me. There's only one person who could have sent them. One person who knows I'm back in Veya, who can afford assassins like this and who has reason to kill me anonymously. His only mistake is that he underestimated me.

He could have had me executed, but then questions might be asked, and he doesn't want those kind of questions. He could have sent his Cadre: at least they might have done the job right. But then, he couldn't take the risk that I'd beat them, and then I'd know what he was up to.

But I know, Ledo. I know.

The last assassin makes his move. I take the fight to him. It doesn't last long.

39

We'd never seen such wonders in all of our ten-year-old lives. I clutched at my best friend Aila and we stared and stared from the back of our wagon, dazzled by the dream we had stumbled into. Our master Chorik was indulgent, laughing and joking about the simplicity of our kind and how it did his heart good to see us lost in admiration at their great land. It proved how much more beautiful it was than the one we had been taken from.

They called it the Silverlight Caves, but the name lost something in the translation. It was a region which, I later learned, was situated just backspin of the Borderlands, a place long treasured by the Gurta until the war swallowed it. The Silverlight Caves had a steep and savage beauty unrivalled by anything I have seen since, but then the bombs and Blackwings and shard-cannons came. Now it only exists in my memory.

The train of wagons was crawling along a bridge of natural stone, a tentacle of scabrock that stretched impossibly across a massive chasm. The bridge was thick with luminous crystal formations, geometric prisms that burst in sprays like flowers. The walls of the cavern were striped with thick veins of some mineral, that reflected light like a silver mirror. Vines of multicoloured lichens hung from the cliffs, and fungi of varieties we had never imagined thrived here. At the bottom of the chasm a river of perfect blue churned and rushed, and giant insects ribboned through the air far below, paddling a dozen wings or more.

The light was white and blinding, and we feared we might lose our sight, but we had to look anyway. Besides, we trusted our masters. The Gurta were wise and they would protect us, their inferiors, like a man might protect his pet. We took comfort in that.

~ Did you ever think we should see something like this? ~ Aila asked, breathless. ~ Ever in our lives? ~

I shook my head. ~ Truly, I am grateful to our masters, for allowing us to behold such magnificence ~

~ Their kindness towards our lowly selves is beyond measure ~

I didn't remember how to speak Eskaran. My life before slavery was a vague and distant place, and I had no desire to return there. My thoughts and words were formed in ritualised Gurtan, shaped by years of harsh and painful teaching. But I accepted that I was ignorant, being of a lowly race, and so I thanked my tutors for their perseverance and apologised for my stupidity and promised to try harder. Languages were a weak point, but I took to their brainwashing like filings to a magnet.

We had been travelling for three turns now. The purpose of our journey had not been explained to us, but rumour among the slaves was that Chorik and several other important Administrators had been summoned by an Elder to help with a thorny supply problem in Dak, one of the mighty frontier cities of the Gurta.

Naturally, Aila and I were thrilled by the prospect. The idea that we would be allowed to meet an Elder was beyond comprehension and we dared not even hope for it. The sight of another great Gurta city would be enough for us. Our masters had a flair for architecture that overwhelmed us, and we were at the age when every new place was an adventure. Every city was wildly unique, further evidence of their superiority. It brought us comfort to know we were in the hands of such a people.

~ We will be stopping soon ~ said our master, from behind us. ~ Make ready ~

We turned back to where Chorik lounged amid the plush interior of the wagon. It was covered with patterned fabric stretched over an elaborate frame, carpeted in fur and strewn with cushions. He and two of his friends, whose professions were unclear but who entertained our master greatly, were lounging on settees laid against the sides of the wagon, drinking wine. We made sure the men's goblets were full before we set about our tasks of preparing evening clothes and perfumes.

Chorik gave me an indulgent swat on the arse as I glided past. I didn't really understand it, but there had been talk of 'duties' I would have to perform when I was older. Chorik had 'appetites'. At first I thought they were talking about cooking, but even at ten I sensed that there was more to it than that. Aila told me not to worry. Whatever it was, it was sure to be for my own good. Didn't I trust our masters?

Of course I did. Unquestioningly.

We came to an inn not long afterward. It stood just off the road, commanding a breathtaking view of the chasm, with a roaring waterfall nearby that plunged to the river below. The inn was built of cordwood, stone and ivory from gorth herds. It was circular in shape, all curves and points. A gazebo sat on the cliff edge, amid a small grove which shone eerily with its own luminescence. Bats fluttered between the dwarf mycora and lichen-trees, catching insects that were drawn to the light.

Aila and I scampered off with the other slaves to prepare our masters' rooms while the Gurta men drank and gossiped, and their masked women waited in a cluster nearby, silent. In public, they would not speak unless their husbands spoke to them. I thought them very elegant and dignified.

We made a game of it, as we always did, dividing up the tasks and racing each other to complete them first. Our strict training and our honest desire to please our masters prevented us from cutting corners, but I usually beat her by picking the least time-intensive jobs.

When we were done, the Gurta and their Entwined went to their rooms while we cleaned the interiors of the wagons, swiftly gobbled some food and then fed the chila. Even though I hated the smell of the bad-tempered beasts, we were eager workers, because we knew that soon there would be music, and music was our joy. When we were done, we asked our *zaze* for permission to get our instruments, and after she had checked our duties were complete we were allowed to take them and scamper to the gazebo.

The gazebo was built around a pool of water, which had to be heated from beneath with coals in the absence of a natural hot spring. Other slaves had already begun the process when we arrived. We picked a spot at the edge of the gazebo that gave us a good view down into the chasm, knelt down and began tuning and plucking our instruments. I played the *zhuk*, a nine-stringed instrument with a metal fingerboard and a trebly, cooing timbre. Aila played *oza*, a cube-shaped skin drum. I had been assured that it took many years of practice to truly learn the subtleties of *oza*, but secretly I thought it was a rather simple instrument.

I loved to play. With every note, I thanked my masters for allowing me that grace. Without them, I would never have been introduced to the art of music, would never even have laid my hands on a *zhuk*. But I had shown an aptitude while very young and they had recognised it and tutored me. I loved to play because I was better than anyone else at it, except the older slaves who had had more practice. But my tutor told me I would surpass them if I kept studying. He said he had never had such a talented pupil of such a young age.

The other two musicians turned up shortly after, and began tuning up their own instruments while Aila and I rehearsed. We knew many songs, from traditional Gurta lays to wild, rousing battle songs and mournful ballads. The Gurta music pierced me with its passion, stirred my blood and made me shiver. I thought what wonderful people these were to have made such music. I remembered snatches of tunes from my life before, verses of lullabies and a rowdy song my father used to sing with his friends. But they were rough and simple melodies, nothing like the counterpoint and harmony of Gurta compositions.

Our masters came to the gazebo in twos and threes. The other slaves served them food and wine while we played. Some of them stripped and lounged in the pool, because the women were being attended to elsewhere.

The conversation of the Gurta surrounded me, but I didn't understand much of what they were talking about and I concentrated on playing instead. They were powerful men, speaking of things beyond the knowledge of an Eskaran girl. Instead, I took private delight in my skill, marvelling at every trill and flourish, pleased that I was pleasing my masters.

And please them I did. After one particular ballad in which the *zhuk* took the lead – a favourite of mine – Chorik approached me with another man, whom I knew as one of the Administrators. He was broad and stocky for a Gurta, with small, sharp eyes and a knotted braid of a beard, even though he was still young. The musicians stood and we drew the Form Of Abject Subservience.

~ Didn't I tell you? ~ my master said to his companion. ~ She plays with such emotion for one so young ~

I positively glowed on the inside, but my pride was quickly snuffed.

~ An animal can imitate emotion ~ said the other man. ~ It is merely a matter of vibrato, tempo, volume. It can be faked ~

~ Oh, come now! You must admit that she has talent ~

~ I admit that much. But to suggest that these . . . *people* think and feel as we do? Ridiculous. Their emotions are as basic and rudimentary as the species we hunt for sport ~

Chorik laughed, but in his eyes was disappointment. His attempt to impress had failed. I felt terrible for having been the cause of that, and I bowed my head in shame.

~ You're right, of course ~ he said. ~ Foolish of me. To call them civilised when they're not even beholden to the Laws ~

~ Slavery is too good for these people ~ my master's companion said.

~ Belek Aspa, you're a man of impressive conviction ~ Chorik declared, leading him away. ~ Let us talk more on the subject ~

If there was anything more to be said, Chorik never had the chance to say it, because at that instant an arrow punched into his back and thrust its bloody tip through the centre of his chest.

Nobody reacted for a moment. There was only shock. Chorik had a surprised look on his face, and while he held it the rest of us were frozen, as if waiting to see what he would do next. Then he burped, and blood flowed over his lips. He tipped forward into the pool, and as he fell the shrieking began and the men panicked. Another Gurta, one of Chorik's friends from the wagon, was shot through the forehead as he clambered out of the water.

Then people were running everywhere. I was knocked aside, my *zhuk* falling to the floor with a discordant jangle of protest. As I gathered it up I heard the whip of more arrows, and one thudded into the rail of the balcony, close to my face. I screamed and recoiled, crashing into Aila who, like me, was caught between running away and trying to protect her instrument.

She clutched at me for safety as we heard our masters swear and curse and howl in fear, their voices high and raw. Our whole lives we had never seen a Gurta terrified. We had seen them in wild anger and deep despair; we saw them argue and bicker often. But to see them afraid? It cracked the foundations of our world.

~ Get up! ~ I said, scrambling to my feet and bringing Aila with me. ~ Run! ~

The men were scattering, heading for the inn or the wagons. The gazebo they left behind was defiled with corpses, the waters red. Several Gurta and one of the elder slaves lay impaled by arrows, their blood flowing steadily into the gaps between the floorboards.

We were the last to leave. The other slaves had been quicker, fleeing at the first signs of the attack. But as we went in pursuit of our masters, not knowing where else to go, we saw a dozen riders on crayl-back come racing out from behind the inn. Eskaran riders. The Gurta fled in all directions, shielding their heads with their hands, but they were easily outpaced.

We stumbled to a halt a half-dozen spans from the gazebo as they cut our masters down with swords. I felt my knees go weak. Some of the slaves were trying to put themselves between their kinfolk and the Gurta, making shields of their bodies. The soldiers pulled them aside and then slaughtered those they were protecting.

I tugged on Aila's arm, turning her away from that awful sight. As I did, I glimpsed a white face looking out at us from the undergrowth that surrounded the gazebo. It was the one who had criticised my playing. There was no other direction to go, so I ran towards him, and Aila came with me. He saw us coming, scowled and disappeared.

We ran into the undergrowth, searching for him. I didn't know what else to do. Our master was dead, and I couldn't think straight. I still saw his face, the surprise in his pale blue eyes, the arrow jutting from his chest. Someone had to look after us, protect us, keep us safe. Only the master he called Belek Aspa could do that now.

I dodged recklessly through the stems and branches and giant puffballs, panting, tugging Aila behind me. The Administrator was not where I thought he'd be, but I assumed it was my mistake. Why wouldn't he wait for us? He knew we were in trouble.

I saw movement to my left, and pushed through a tangle of vines in pursuit. But it was not a Gurta face that looked back at me.

He had his sword drawn, scrambling to a halt at the bottom of a small slope. His armour was hide and metal, alien and unfamiliar. He was thickset and stocky, features wide, black-bearded. An Eskaran soldier.

We stared at him, half-hidden in the vines, paralysed by the sight.

He relaxed. Sheathed his sword and knelt down.

'Just little girls,' he said, his voice deep and burred. 'Come on. Don't be afraid.'

The words made no sense to me, but his tone was reassuring. I was wary, not ready to trust him; and yet there was something about him that made me feel strangely secure. His hulking presence, the cadence of the words. An echo of the past.

Aila tugged at me, but I didn't go.

'Come on,' he said again, reaching his hand out. He wasn't approaching us, concerned that we would shy away and run. 'I'm a friend. You want to come home, hmm? Want to go home?'

Aila tugged again, but I just kept staring at him. Then I let go of Aila's hand, and I stepped out of the cover of the vines, and walked over to the soldier.

I didn't know why at the time, but I understood later. It was because he looked like my father. I've wondered since whether I would have done the same if it had been a clean-shaven, slender man who'd found us. I've wondered what my life would have been like if I hadn't gone to him.

'That's a good girl,' he said, gathering me gently within the circle of one big arm. I pressed myself into the crook of his shoulder, pushing my hands and cheek against his chest. The smell of sweat and hide and man. Gurta didn't smell that way; they were always perfumed and scrubbed. But I breathed it in, and it awakened memories, hazy sensations of comfort and sanctuary.

I looked back at Aila, who was still hovering where I left her. The soldier reached his other arm to her. She turned tail and fled. I cried out, and moved to run after her; but the soldier's arm tightened, and I couldn't go anywhere.

'Oh no,' he said, but it was with the benevolent strictness of a parent. 'I'm not letting go of you.'

I struggled and wept but he just held me, surrounding me with his arms, and it wasn't long before I was still. I sobbed and he held onto me and I knew I'd made a choice, but I didn't yet grasp the consequences. They were too much for a little girl to think about. He made me feel safe. That was enough.

He covered my eyes as he led me back. I knew what was beyond the hot dark of his hand. Blood. Death. The end of the slim, pale masters. What lay in the future, I wasn't sure. But I surrendered myself to it. I was powerless, as I had always been.

They captured eleven Eskaran slaves, all young like me. There were no Gurta. The men were all dead and I saw no sign of the women, but I knew what had become of them. They drank their poison vials rather than let the Eskarans take them. Elegant and dignified to the end.

Aila was not among the slaves. I hoped that she had found the Administrator who had been unimpressed by my music. He would protect her, I told myself. At least, that was what I believed then.

Maybe she did, maybe she didn't. I never saw her again.

5

Two turns later I meet the man who just tried to have me murdered and apologise to him. It doesn't rank among the easiest things I ever did.

The arrangements are made through the twins, and by their influence I manage to get an audience. They both seem relieved when I tell them my intentions, but Casta is cold and I get the impression that she's disappointed in me.

Ledo receives us in his chambers, dressed all in black, fingers and hair heavy with silver ornaments. Caydus is with him, maintaining a grim and brooding presence to one side of the room. Liss and Casta stand by their brother as I profess my sorrow at the way I behaved at our last meeting. Ledo listens stonily to my renewed promises of loyalty, my submission to his will in all things, my gratefulness for his mercy. I play the penitent well, chastened and brought to heel.

I wonder if he believes me. I wonder if he already knows that his assassins have failed, and he thinks I don't realise he sent them. Or maybe he thinks I *do* know. My coming back this way must seem very puzzling. He'll be wondering what my angle is.

That's good. Keep him guessing. In the end, it doesn't matter what he believes. The only reason I've apologised is to get inside his quarters.

'I am pleased that you have learned proper respect, Orna,' he says. 'But this does not change my decision regarding your son.'

'I do not ask you to change your decision, Magnate. It was just and fair.'

He regards me for a time. I have no idea what's going on behind those dark eyes.

'Very well, Orna. Your apology is accepted.'

I thank him humbly and he turns away, dismissing me without a word. I manage a weak smile at Liss, letting her glimpse the trembling vulnerability beneath my brave exterior. She swallows it, hurries to my side, arm round my shoulder. She leads me out, Casta trailing behind.

My fainting fit is pretty convincing, I like to think. We've barely left the room when I go boneless. Liss cries out for her sister, trying to hold me up.

'Oh! Oh! She's died!' Liss howls, as she struggles with my weight. Casta just watches, making no move to help.

'She's died? Are you sure she's not just sleeping?' She's mocking her sister, but Liss doesn't catch on.

'It must be that!' she declares desperately, patting my cheek. 'Wake up, Orna!'

My eyelids flutter and I find my feet again. I look around in mild confusion.

'You were asleep,' Casta says dryly.

'I don't feel well,' I tell them, and Liss's face sags in sympathy. 'I think I'm going to be sick.'

'Not here! Not here!' Liss panics, propelling me towards a door. We pass through several rooms before reaching Ledo's bathroom. I make lurching noises, threatening to vomit. Liss pushes me in but I hold out my hand when she tries to follow.

'Don't watch. I can't bear it.' And I close the door in her face.

Ledo's bathroom is all marble and gold and illuminated filaments of glow-glass, but I'm not interested in any of that. I'm interested in the window. It's made with a reinforced, ornamental frame that makes it practically impossible to get through from the outside. Not so hard if some careless person should leave it unlocked, however.

I do what I have to do, then I pretend to be sick.

An hour later I'm crawling up the side of the Caracassa Mansions, several hundred spans from the ground. I had to go down three stories to find a window that I could climb through unobserved.

The Caracassa Mansions are built into the root system of an ancient mycora, which presents a certain security flaw that I've long known but never needed to use. It may be a powerful status symbol to have such an unusual home, but it's also very easy to climb. The metal claws fixed over my hands and the bladed boots on my feet bite easily into the tough rootwood exterior. If this was stone, my job wouldn't have been half so simple.

I'm wearing black, and high up in the dark I'm invisible. Cool breezes rise from the city far below, slapping my clothes against my skin, flipping strands of hair. The climb uses muscles that have weakened through lack of use, but it's not far, and the curving surface of the colossal root makes things straightforward. I clamber up, avoiding the windows, an insect against the flanks of the Mansions. All of Veya is spread out beneath me, a complex pattern of lights delineating thoroughfares and riversides, pinned by its five tall shine-houses. In other times, I might have felt a deep peace in this moment. Now there's only the demanding pull of a job that needs to be done. Only the mission matters.

The bathroom window is still unlocked when I get to it. The locks are checked by handmaidens before Ledo goes to bed, but that will be some while yet. I'd like to have done this when he was asleep, but the windows would be locked again by then. So instead, I'll be sneaking through the chambers while Ledo is still up, and that means the Caydus and the handmaidens will be about, too.

I'll just have to be careful.

I creep through the window, into the bathroom, up to the door. Calm, collected. The best thieves are those that don't suffer from nerves. Their judgement stays good, they don't hesitate. Move quickly and decisively.

I open the door a crack and peer out. Ledo's chambers are sprawling and opulent, decorated with sculpture, ornamental weapons, ancient armour from far-off places. The lantern-light casts the kind of shadows you don't get with shinestones. Typical of one of the aristocracy, to be rich enough to afford shinestones and then to reject them in favour of firelight. They just have to be awkward.

The bathroom opens onto one of many sitting-rooms that appear to have no purpose other than to impress guests. Empty. I listen, but I can't hear a thing. Not that I'd hear a handmaiden even if she was right in the next room. Silence is their watchword.

I move quickly. A doorway at the end takes me into a many-mirrored corridor. I can hear voices at the end: Ledo and Caydus. I'm just about to step out when a handmaiden glides across my path. I pull back instinctively, a fraction too late. She stops, turns her red-veiled face my way. I hold my breath.

She goes on her way. I breathe out. Smart move, I tell her mentally. I don't want to be seen, but if I am I won't let myself be caught. If I'm cornered, I'll kill.

When the coast has cleared, I move up the corridor, heading from cover to cover. I've never been to Ledo's study, but I have a pretty good idea where it is. That's where he'll keep his correspondence. That's where I'll find the letter.

The voices get louder as I approach the room where I argued with Ledo. I hear Caydus' gravelly rumble but I don't catch the words.

At least I know where they are. That only leaves the handmaidens within the chambers themselves. There are usually two, and I just saw one of them go into the bedroom. The other one . . . what would she be doing now? Fetching his evening meal, most likely. That means she would be coming from the kitchen. Probably up this corridor.

Better be fast.

I peer into the room where Caydus and Ledo are. Ledo is pacing between the spun-sap statues and the crystal columns. Caydus has his back to me, immobile. Caydus is an even better fighter than Rynn was, but his senses aren't too sharp. I'm about to dart across the doorway and head up the corridor when I hear my name.

'And what is your opinion of Orna, then? In your experience.'

I stop and listen, briefly glancing up the corridor. I'm hiding in the shelter of a plinth. Too exposed for my liking, and I shouldn't loiter, but this I have to hear.

Caydus replies quickly. 'I've fought alongside her sometimes. Knew her a little in the Academy, but she was younger and we didn't speak much. I knew Rynn better. But Orna . . . she's solid, Magnate. I'd trust her with my life.'

'Do you think she might be . . . troublesome? Given the right incentive?'

'I think she was very upset when she spoke to you before. It's natural that she wants to be with her child after what she's been through.'

I always liked Caydus.

'You did not answer me,' Ledo says.

'I don't know, Magnate. Who knows what any of the Cadre are

capable of, if the incentive is strong enough? But I don't know of anything that would make Orna act against your interests. I believe her apology was genuine.'

Well, at least I fooled one of them.

Ledo is clearly unconvinced, even with Caydus' show of support. Maybe he's pondering what I meant by speaking of Belek Aspa. Maybe thinking it was an innocent question. Maybe considering calling off the assassins. Maybe not.

I decide I've heard enough. I can't risk staying in the corridor. When Ledo is turned away from the doorway I flit across it and move on.

I hit the study first time. Can't help a flush of self-congratulation at that.

It's a large room, with a bookcase and several tall cabinets against one wall. A broad desk at one end, neatly laid with writing equipment and stationery. Two lanterns on poles stand in opposite corners, their flames magnified by chthonomantically treated glass bulbs. Set into the long wall opposite the door is a window looking out over a park on the edge of the Tangles.

I'm high up here. The ambient glow from Veya's shinehouses bathes the tops of the lichen-trees in the park. Walking paths are lit with tracks of glowing dots.

I start with the desk, but the drawers are locked. I don't want to waste time, so I check the cabinets before I get into the fiddly stuff. Mostly bone scroll-cases, shipping manifestos and reports. I rummage through them, willing the evidence I need to reveal itself. Nothing does.

I scan the bookcase, then start on another cabinet. In here I find several leather-bound ledgers. I leaf through one, find it full of diagrams and sketches: military reports. Voids, I'd like to spend time reading this, find out what these bastards have planned for our Army. But none of this is what I need.

I draw out some tiny picks and get working at the lock of the uppermost desk drawer. Now I've got the right tools, taken from my chambers downstairs, it's somewhat easier than messing about with hairpins in Farakza. The thought of that place gives me a much-needed shot of confidence. I broke out of there, didn't I? This is easy by comparison.

The lock gives up and I slide the drawer open. Bundles of letters within. Some tied in little square stacks, some loose. I pick up the top one, skim-read it.

I can't believe my luck. First time, again. You couldn't *buy* fortune like that.

It's the letter from Jerima Vem, detailing the operation to be carried out. Name of the barge is the *Maid Of The Dark*. That's the name Silverfish needs. But it's not the evidence I want.

I'm putting the letter back when I see another one tucked among the others, and I stop. There's no way it would have caught my attention, but for one thing. That alphabet, comprised of arrangements of tiny triangles. It's written in Gurtan.

I pick it up. My breath is suddenly short, pulse pounding at my throat. Eyes wide as I start to read. My memory of written Gurtan has decayed faster than the speech, since I spent little time reading as a slave; but I start to decipher odd phrases.

Our meeting . . . success to our great enterprise . . . we two must . . . the appointed place . . . honoured Ledo . . .

A date. A location. And a name.

Belek Aspa.

Footsteps. I recognise the rhythm instinctively. Ledo.

My skin goes icy cold. I slide the letter back where it came from, check that everything is in place, shut the drawer. No time to lock it. Time becomes slippery, measured by the swift approach of boot heels.

Nowhere to hide. If he comes in here, I'm caught.

Kill him.

The thought surges up inside me, borne on a tide of rage like nothing I've ever felt before. My hatred of the Gurta is nothing to this: the hatred of the man I pledged my life to, the man who ordered me and my husband into a trap at Korok, who left us to die so he could turn a profit from prolonging a war.

Kill him. Rip his eyes out of his fucking skull.

No. No, I can't be sure.

You've seen the proof! He's conspiring with a Gurta Minister!

I know that, and yet I still can't do it. He's my master. His men saved me from slavery. He gave me a life and a living. I owe everything to him. My husband, my son. Twenty-nine years of utter and total loyalty can't be thrown away in an instant. It's ground in, rooted deep. I can't. I can't.

He's almost on me. No way out.

Then, inspiration. I hurry across the room, tilt the glass on one of the standing lanterns and blow it out. The study dims.

Ledo is outside the door now. A pause. Doing what? Admiring a sculpture? *Stay there. Just another moment.*

I flee back to the other corner of the room, raise the second lantern and blow on it. It gutters and holds. I blow again, and it dies.

Ledo pushes the door open just as the room falls into darkness. I freeze where I am, still holding the lantern glass. In the light that spills in from the park and the city I'm clearly visible. But the door stands between Ledo and me.

Go on, I think at him desperately. *There's no one in here. Those lazy handmaidens have let the lanterns go out. Fuck off and fetch them. Give them a piece of your mind, you treacherous bastard.*

He stays. For long, agonising moments he stays. I can feel the prickle of his suspicion. Then he steps back and the door closes, slowly. Perhaps he can't believe the handmaidens would let something like this happen. He knows how attentive they are. He knows something is amiss.

Then he's gone. I listen to his footsteps recede, and gently lower the lantern glass.

Too close. And the handmaidens will be here any second. I slip out of the study and head down the corridor, back towards the bathroom, where my escape route awaits. I've learned enough.

I've learned more than enough.

4

I go to ground in the dweoming-haunted slums of Grasp Hook, in the run-down neathways quarter of Veya. It's a far cry from the Tangles, or the elegant districts that line the river. Grasp Hook is a dark and dirty warren of narrow streets, its buildings tall and leaning drunkenly. The glow of the shinehouses is blocked by the clutter, plunging the district into shadow. Nobody comes to light the lanterns in Grasp Hook. The perfect place when you don't want to be found.

My chambers at the Caracassa Mansions are far too dangerous now. I can't take the risk that Ledo will try again. He won't fail twice. So I've let it be known that I'm travelling to the subsurface to take the vacation that Ledo suggested, to recuperate from my ordeal. It'll buy me a little time, and my absence won't seem suspicious.

Only Keren knows I'm here. He needs to be able to find me, in case he has information. But it's Nereith that I'm going to meet now. Several turns ago I gave him the name of a barge. I've come to hear whether Silverfish is satisfied. Whether he'll fulfil his part of the deal.

The streets of Grasp Hook are busy. Clusters of kneeling men throw dice at the foot of some steps. Hawkers sell food from their stalls, treats of meat and mycora pastry that smell so good because they're so bad for you. Dealers and tough guys lurk in gangs, sizing up passers-by. A dweoming stumbles past, blind on fireclaw, prophesying incoherently as he goes.

The air is dank and chill, redolent with grease and sweat and the washing that criss-crosses the street on lines overhead. I head towards our appointed meeting-place, my mind calm. Things are making sense to me now. I don't like the answers I've got, but it's better than having none at all. I feel like I've got a handle on matters. I feel like I'm in control, if only a little.

This is the way it goes. Ledo, through covert means, establishes a channel to the enemy: Belek Aspa, a powerful Gurta Minister. As a prominent member of the Turnward Claw Alliance, the pro-war faction of the Merchant Council of Plutarchs, he's privy to the highest information. The Turnward Claw Alliance works closely with the Eskaran Army, and they collaborate often on military matters. After all, the Eskaran Army is composed of forces provided by the Clans.

Clan Caracassa, as a manufacturer of battlefield medicines, has a vested interest in the continuation of the war. In fact, they're desperate that it *does* continue, as they're being beaten out of the market by other competitors and only a healthy turnover of wounded can prevent them from losing money and influence. So Ledo feeds his contact information about certain military events, like the one at Korok. Perhaps his contact returns the favour. It's not much, just enough to ensure that nobody ever gains the upper hand in the Borderlands. Enough to ensure the war keeps going.

What kind of profit are you making, Belek Aspa? I remember you now. You didn't like my music. You thought Eskarans were animals. What's your angle?

Then there's the impeding marriage of Liss to Jerima Dew, son of Jerima Vem and scion of Clan Jerima. Clan Jerima are textile manufacturers, peacetime profiteers who would benefit from the end of the war, because demand for their luxury goods would then increase. Marrying into that Clan provides Ledo with a back-up, the possibility of a merger if, despite his efforts, the war does come to a premature end.

But until the marriage is finalised he's not ready. If the military push succeeds, the war will be over. Clan Caracassa's position will be much less favourable; Clan Jerima might renegotiate the terms of the wedding or call it off altogether, leaving Caracassa high and dry in a world that doesn't want their medicines any more.

Ledo can't allow that. The push has to fail. The war can't be over until he's ready for it to be over, until he's set up the framework for a smooth shift into peacetime industry. He knows it's inevitable. Public opinion is growing against the war, and the time will come when the people are out of patience. Ledo is preparing for that moment. Casta thinks that by dividing himself he's showing a lack of dedication, but I think he's being canny. He senses the changing wind and tacks to meet it.

But the preparations aren't done yet. So he will betray us once again, like he did at Korok. He will meet with Belek Aspa and give him the plans for the great operation that our Army hopes will end the war. It will make him a huge profit, increase his influence, and buy him the time he needs to set up a solid exit strategy for when the conflict against the Gurta is no longer sustainable.

You were smart, Ledo. You made sure your own forces were involved in that little trick at Korok. You made sure you were wounded as badly as the other Clans, so suspicion would never fall on you. But you cost me my husband and you nearly took my life, and now there's a chance that you'll take my son's, too.

So I'll stop this. Somehow, I'll stop this. I'll kill you, and Casta will be Magnate then, and she'll use her influence to get Jai back, and maybe Operation Deadfall will still go ahead or maybe it will be aborted. All I know is, you have to die, Belek Aspa has to die, and nobody can know it was me who did it.

But I know where to find you, Ledo. I know where and when you're meeting up with the enemy. And I'll be coming for you then.

Nereith is waiting at a table, one of a dozen laid around the front of a rickety slop-house. The other tables are busy with garrulous men and the occasional couple. An untouched bowl of stew steams in front of him.

'Not hungry?' I ask as I sit, mustering a little humour for old times' sake.

He gazes at it distastefully. 'They made me buy something so I could sit here. How you barbarians eat the chopped-up and burnt corpses of dead creatures is beyond me. If you've never tasted the hot spurt of newly spilt blood as you tear out the throat of your meal, you've never lived.'

'I think I just became vegetarian. So what about the barge?'

'The information was good, of course,' he says. 'I knew Silverfish could trust you.'

I sit back, steeple my fingers and then let them cross into a clasp. 'So. I did what you asked.'

He shows his teeth. 'Silverfish was most impressed. He has agreed to locate your son for you.' A half-smile. 'I'm sure he would be happy to work with you again in the future.'

'Just you worry about finding Jai for me.'

'We're on it. Expect to hear from us soon.'

'I'm sure you can find me, if you need to,' I say, getting up.

'Oh, I'm certain of that,' he replies.

'Enjoy your meal,' I tell him, and I walk away.

I head over to the other side of Grasp Hook after that, to an anonymous doorway in the middle of a wreck of slums. There I knock and wait. The last time I visited this man, things were very different. He's fallen on hard times. When he opens the door, I see that he's lost weight, and not only because he's missing a hand.

'Hello, Ekan,' I say.

For the moment, I live in the upstairs room of a dweoming den. I'd originally intended to rent it, but one look at me sent the owner of this place shrieking into a corner, so I just walked in and stayed. Having a madwoman downstairs is a minor inconvenience, but she doesn't dare ask me for payment, so I don't pay. Whenever I go near her, she shrinks back and mutters that I have blood on my hands. No shit, sister.

Her name is Dust, and she's a scrawny thing with a haggard, tormented look that comes from years of bad fireclaw from shabby cut-joints. Dweomings use that stuff to get in touch with their chthonomantic powers, unlike real chthonomancers who are skilled or powerful enough to make magic without chemical assistance. But pure fireclaw is too expensive for these urban mystics, so they get it chopped with all kinds of crap, and it fucks up their brains in the end. Shame, really: sometimes the dweomings are the only recourse for the poor and destitute when they need healing or guidance or aid. Chthonomancers are all in the employ of the Clans.

After I've got what I need from Ekan, I make my way back to my room. I keep myself pretty covered up in Grasp Hook, so no one asks questions and no one knows I'm Cadre. But they still sense that I'm not someone to be messed with, so they let me be. A woman shouldn't last a turn here without protection, but they see I'm not afraid and they accept me as one of them. A fellow predator.

The den is run-down and dingy. It occupies the bottom two floors of a six-storey house, part of a terrace which collapses into rubble at the poleways end of the street. Grimy windows with time-warped frames glow with lantern-light. Small animals scuttle through the shadows.

I come in through the front door and Dust is there, her thatchy, multicoloured hair all over her face, tiny bones tangled in the knots. She's sitting on the bare floorboards in the middle of a chalk circle, surrounded by incense pots. A fireclaw pipe is loose in her hand, and she looks comatose, but somehow she's still in a slumped-yet-upright position. Her head hangs, chin resting on her breastbone.

I make my way across the room, picking through the strewn bits of arcane junk that she uses to connect with her inner force, or something. I'm almost at the stairs when her head snaps up and she gives me a filmy glare.

'Blood on your hands!' she screeches, then trembles and begins to sob. 'So much blood . . .'

I've heard it before, and I didn't care then. So I head upstairs, to my dim little room. I don't bother lighting the lantern. This place is cold and there's nothing here but a shabby bed that reeks of dust, and a chest of drawers, half of which don't open for reasons I frankly cannot fathom. I lie down and try to think of other things I could be doing, other leads I could follow. But I daren't expose myself for now, so all I can do is wait.

I'll find you, Jai. I just have to see you one more time. I'll tell you how much I love you and I'll explain everything. But first, oh please, just let me know you're safe. Because I should have fought your father harder, I shouldn't have been weak. You're where you are because of me. Maybe nothing can change that now. But at least I can say sorry. At least I can do that. At least . . .

I wake to the sound of a tread on the stairs, and I'm off the bed and across the room almost before I realise that I'd fallen asleep. My shortblades are out, held ready as I press myself against the wall to the left of the doorway. There's two of them, one lighter than the other, male and female.

They're coming up tentatively, the boards creaking beneath their shoes. Either they're trying to sneak, and making a bad job of it, or they've guessed I'm waiting for them. Both say assassin to me.

Closer. Almost at the top now. I keep my muscles loose, ready, blade pointed down to plunge into the collar of the foremost. Closer.

How did you find me, Ledo?

'Orna?'

I exhale. Keren steps through the doorway, scanning the empty room. He catches sight of me standing next to him in the dark and jumps out of his skin.

'Fuck me! Orna, you creepy bitch. What in the Abyss are you doing standing there?'

I sheathe my shortblades as I walk into the centre of the room. 'Thought you were someone else.' Then I catch sight of a frightened-looking face peering into the room from the stairway, and my relief becomes amazement. A beautiful girl, dark and intelligent. The girl my son loves.

'Reitha!'

'She was already in Veya,' Keren explains. 'Here for a conference that her master was attending. My man in Coldwash found her. Once I told her you were in the city, she demanded to see you. Wish all my jobs were so easy.'

'It's okay, Reitha,' I say, as she's clearly still alarmed by my reception. 'I'm so glad you could come.'

She hurries into the room and clutches me in a tight hug that takes me by surprise. There's desperation in it. Something dreadful makes its chill way towards my heart.

No. I won't think it.

She steps back, and holds out a letter to me. It's an official communication. High-quality paper, a broken Army seal, a postmark from three dozen turns ago. I don't look at it, but at her. Her lip is trembling, eyes filled with salt water.

No. Please, no.

My hand moves of its own accord, reaching out to take it from her, trembling. I swear I don't know whether I'm going to rip it up or read it, but it doesn't matter. My fingers are palsied, and it slips through my grip and on to the floor. Keren has worked out that something is really, really wrong. Reitha obviously hadn't told him. He doesn't have any idea.

'He heard what happened at Korok,' she said. 'He thought you were dead.' Her voice chokes off, throat swollen with grief.

'How?' I can barely manage the whisper.

'Poison,' she says. 'He took poison.' Tears spill down her cheeks and she has this look, this empty look of incomprehension. 'He thought you were dead,' she says again.

My legs go from under me. Suddenly they can't hold me up any more. Keren half-catches me, but he only succeeds in slowing my fall. My vision is swarming. I can't breathe properly.

He killed himself while I was in prison. All of this, everything, and I was too late all along. He took his own life. He took his own life because of what happened at Korok.

He killed himself because of what Ledo did.

I'm screaming, but I can't hear it over the roar of blood in my ears. I only know that if I don't let it out it will rip me apart. Keren and Reitha are trying to help me, to offer comfort or to stop me hurting myself, but they don't exist to me now. Only the screaming is left. Oblivion comes swiftly, but not fast enough.

My son is dead.

My son is dead.

My son . . .

40

Mama and Papa were kissing by the stove again. They had a game they used to play, in which he would creep up behind her while she was cooking, grab her round the waist and bite her neck, all the while making snarling noises like a monster. She would laugh in delight and pretend to fend him off.

Chada and I looked at each other across the table and wrinkled our noses in amused disgust. Papa often pretended to be a monster. He was a burly, hairy man who seemed impossibly huge to my five-year-old eyes. Dark hair, dark beard, dark eyes, dark complexion. In contrast, my mother was small, slender, light-skinned, her hair a wavy fall of tawny brown. Her voice was tiny bells and trickling water, my father's the rumble of the earth.

'Go and sit down,' she told him. 'It'll be ready in a moment.'

He nibbled her ear and she squealed and hit him with a wooden spoon. Chada and I laughed as he hurried over to the table with his hands over his head, mumming fear.

Our house was small, cosy and shadowy, with thick walls and small windows. The stove kept out the steady chill of the cavern outside, and lanterns brightened the corners. We had a couple of jinth bitches who slept at the foot of my bed, though Papa kicked them out at mealtimes because they got too frisky and knocked things over. They were hunting now, patrolling the farm for ground-bats and rackles.

Chada was swinging his little feet and kicking the underside of the table, tormented by the scent of Mama's cooking. I told him to stop, and he stuck his tongue out at me. Then Papa told him to stop and he did. Then I stuck my tongue out at him in snide triumph, and Papa caught me doing it and cuffed me.

'You're the older sister,' he said, as I rubbed my head and pouted sulkily. 'Set an example.'

Chada just looked smug. Only one year younger than me, but he was such a baby. He had Papa's look about him, while I was more like Mama. Sometimes he was fun to play with, like the time when we had gone down to the pool at the bottom of the grove and named all the fish and made up stories about them. But he could so easily throw a tantrum, and then I hated him. The tiniest thing would turn him into a scrunched ball of shrieking fury.

Mama started dishing up the food, and Papa had to glare at Chada to stop him grabbing at it before it was all served. There were roasted tubers, great hunks of basted fungus, spore-bread and a plateful of eels and crunchy arrow beetles. We were poised to eat the instant Mama sat down, but as usual she said: 'Ah! Ah!' and held up a finger the moment we dived for our plates. Then she made a great show of arranging herself, shuffling in her seat and flicking her hair, while we writhed in hungry agony. After she decided we had suffered enough, she kissed Papa on his bearded cheek and said: 'Eat.'

We went at it ravenously. We were always starving at the end of the turn, worn out from playing and from helping Papa and Mama with the farm chores. We helped them feed the lizards and collect the eggs. We followed them as they tended to our small herd of yoth. We went to the stream, checked the traps for crabs and then tottered back with buckets of fresh water.

Our farm was far from anywhere, and I wished for other girls to make friends with; but we were happy. I had no cares but the cares of a child, and there were no troubles so terrible that Papa couldn't deal with them. We had little money but our needs were small. Our lives were simple, slow, honest.

At the end of the turn, Papa would tell us tales while Mama dozed. Sometimes he frightened us with stories of the White-skins: those narrow-faced men, pale as pearl, who would steal children away if they were naughty. Then Chada clutched at me and I pretended not to be scared. Papa would crank up the tension and at some point he would lunge at us, yelling: '*The White-skins are coming!!!*' We would shriek and laugh and the fear would be gone. Then Papa would gather us up in his huge arms, we would snuggle into his chest, and he'd promise that the White-skins would never get us if we were good.

In that, at least, he was mistaken.

We all heard the jinths, their rapid, popping cries coming from somewhere down by the stream; but it was only Chada who thought that something was wrong, and nobody listened to him.

'They've found a rackle,' Papa said, head tilted as he listened. 'Sounds like it's leading them a good chase.'

One after the other, the jinths fell silent.

'See?' Papa said, settling back to his food. 'They got it. One less vermin to bore into my sweet-puffballs.'

Papa's sweet-puffballs were the pride of his crop. When dried and powdered, they made sugar, which we never grew tired of. Usually just the thought of it was enough to distract Chada, but not this time. He kept fidgeting, uneasy. He'd heard the warning in the jinths' cries that the rest of us hadn't.

'Don't worry, Chada,' said Mama. 'It was just a rackle.'

'Can I go see?'

'Finish your meal first.'

Chada knew it was useless to argue, so he began stuffing food into his mouth.

'Chew your food, dear,' Mama said patiently. 'You have to get one lot out of the way before the next lot goes in.'

Papa harrumphed and pushed back from the table, chair legs screeching noisily across the stone. 'I'll take a look.'

'Oh, leave it,' said Mama. 'The jinths are excited, that's all.'

Papa got up and went to the window. Chada watched him intently. I was more interested in my food, having been convinced that there was no cause for alarm, so I didn't witness Papa's reaction to what he saw. The first I knew of what was to come was when Papa turned away from the window, looked at Mama, and said, very calmly: 'Get the children out of here.'

She didn't question him. She got to her feet, pulled out Chada's chair, and lifted him. 'Come on. Out the back.'

'I'm not done!' I protested.

'Do as your father says,' Mama told me, holding out a hand for me to take. There was a briskness in her manner that barely concealed the terror beneath.

'What's happening?' I demanded, but I went with her towards the back door because I had picked up on her alarm.

Father had taken a long-hafted axe from the corner where it leaned.

He looked over at me, the hollows of his face shadowed by the lantern overhead.

'The White-skins are coming,' he said.

I'd never felt fear like I did in that moment, and I never did again. Some part of me, even then, had always thought that the White-skins were make-believe. They certainly hadn't stopped me misbehaving from time to time. The White-skins simply couldn't be. A life of such primal horrors was insupportable to a five-year-old.

But with those words, the White-skins came crashing into reality.

We hurried to the back door, which let out onto a little fenced garden patch. Mama had to put Chada down to open it up, and then she ushered us both through. At the same moment, the front door burst open and the White-skins rushed in.

I still see that frozen instant in my nightmares. The press of narrow faces, sharp and pale and cold, like a swarm of chi-rats. Those blank, dead eyes. I see the cruel tips of their blades. They were just as I had imagined them.

Papa roared and swung an axe into the chest of one of the invaders. Another pointed towards Mama and jabbered something in a horrible, piercing tongue. They'd seen her in the doorway, heading out back. But they hadn't seen us. She was blocking us from their sight with her body.

She looked at me with tragedy in her gaze, and I knew, before she shut the door in our faces, that she was saying goodbye. She thought she would never see us again.

How I wish that had been true.

My first instinct was to pull at the door, to get back into the house, but Mama had locked it. I couldn't understand why she'd abandoned us. I was bewildered, on the verge of tears. There were crashing noises and cries coming from inside. Indecision held me for a few heartbeats longer, then I grabbed Chada's hand and we ran.

The garden patch was too small to hide us, most of the plants having been pulled up recently. Only a few bulbroots and the aerial cups of burrow-vines were left among the neatly hoed rows. Papa had worked hard to get the soil right here, using compost full of bacteria that broke up the rock into a form that was kinder to plants. Only last turn I had helped him sow the seeds for a fresh batch.

Beyond was a copse of phosphorescent mycora, ten or twelve spans tall, that Papa had planted before I was born to provide light for another garden, where he grew those rare plants that needed it. We headed for that, Chada toddling fast to keep up. He was whimpering softly, but he was content to be led for now, putting himself into my care.

'You're the older sister,' I heard Papa say again, and for the first time I felt the weight of that. Chada was under my protection. He was my responsibility now.

We ran into the copse, dodging between the curved stems of the mycora, dazzled by the bluish-white light that radiated from the underside of their caps. But I knew from many games of hide-and-find that this was the first place a searcher would look, so I kept pulling Chada on, through the copse and out, up the slope towards a cluster of jagged rocks that thrust out of the ground. Papa had told us to stay away from them after Chada had cut his hand open on one of the edges, but I knew Papa wouldn't mind now.

Beyond the rocks was a thick wedge of scrub sandwiched between two sheer cliff walls. Tough lichen bushes and red web-fungus clustered around the grey humps of uneven boulders, rising over our heads. We plunged into it. The foliage resisted us, scratching and pushing; sticky tendrils tugged at our clothes and hair. I forged on, towing Chada behind me, until we reached the foot of the cliff. There, behind a spray of stiff, spiny fungi, was a narrow cave.

Chada shook his head, tugging at my hand, but I knelt down before him. 'It's safe,' I said. 'It's my secret place. I come here to hide when I want to be on my own.'

Reluctantly, he allowed himself to be reassured, and we went inside. The cave was shallow, little more than a scratch in the rock face, barely big enough for the two of us. It was dark and cold, but I had padded it with an ancient blanket that stank of mould. We squeezed in, and I let the fungi spring back into place to cover the entrance. We were invisible now. And so we waited.

Time passes slowly to a child. Later, I could sit still for a whole turn watching a doorway for the arrival of a target or observing the movements of guards around a house I was to penetrate. But to a five-year-old patience is not something that comes easily. We sat together on the blanket, my arms around my brother, and the only sound was our breathing.

My shocked thoughts unjammed gradually, and my imagination began to take over, offering suggestions and theories both hopeful and terrible. What if the White-skins had killed Mama and Papa, and were even now sniffing us out? Were the White-skins waiting silently, hoping to lure us out when we thought the coast was clear? Or had Papa slain them all with his axe, and was wondering where we had gone?

I realised suddenly that our jinths must have been killed by the White-skins, and that was the thing that set me crying at last. Chada joined in, and we sniffled and wept together as quietly as we could. Had it been our naughtiness and disobedience that had brought the White-skins down on us? Was it all our fault?

Still there was no sound from outside. No clue as to what had happened down at the house. Not knowing was the worst of it.

I peered out of the cave, but the scrub was too high to see through. Something rustled and I shrank back, fearing that the White-skins were stalking through the grass nearby. I looked back at Chada. He stared at me, seeking answers, seeking guidance. I felt his need, but I couldn't provide.

Then: the clattering of a door, the sound of their shrill voices, our Mama's screams.

Chada's breath quickened. He clutched at my arm, and I pressed him back against the wall of the cave. Mama was shrieking, hysterical, calling the White-skins names I had never heard before. I heard her struck, mid-sentence, and she began to wail. It was a sound of awful, wrenching despair, and it made me shrivel inside to hear it.

Where was Papa? I asked myself. Why wasn't Papa there to save her?

But of course I knew the answer to that.

They were squabbling between themselves. Mother's cries had quieted below audibility. I strained to hear, trying to learn what was happening down there; but all I could catch was nonsense.

It was no good. I had to know. Chada was depending on me. I have no idea where that stupid, suicidal courage came from. Maybe it was the desire to protect her in any way I could. Maybe I just wanted to be with my Mama, so she could make the decisions again, so she could somehow make it all right.

'I'm going to find Mama,' I said to Chada. 'You stay here.'

He shook his head, mute.

'Stay!' I hissed. 'You'll be safe. I'm just going to take a look.'

He just stood there. I took that as agreement, and headed into the scrub.

Now that I could hear the White-skins, I was less afraid of one of them lunging out of the undergrowth to snatch me up. But still I went slowly, hardly daring to breathe, until I came to the sharp rocks. From there, I could see glimpses of movement through the copse of luminous mycora. They were in the garden patch.

Mama began to scream anew. She was struggling. I knew there was nothing I could do to help her; but I couldn't just leave her, either.

Go back. Chada needs you.

But Mama was screaming.

I scanned the area and then slipped from the rocks, scuttling a short way to the safety of the mycora copse. There, drenched in light from above, I wriggled between the stems until I could peep out and see into the garden patch.

They were holding her down in the dirt. Three of them. Two others stood about, watching. Another was weeping over a corpse that lay half in and half out of the back door, belly opened to the air. I could see a little way into the house, enough to see other bodies. I couldn't tell if any of them were my father.

Mama was thrashing and spitting. Her clothes were torn and hanging off, her lips bloody where she had bitten her attackers, her face bruised. Despite their best efforts, they couldn't render her harmless. No matter how they pinned her, she used teeth and knees and elbows and nails. I thought they were trying to imprison her, to take her away. Mercifully, I didn't understand.

Fight, Mama! Fight! I willed her. I thought that there was still hope of a saviour. Maybe my father was only unconscious, and would revive any instant. Maybe one of our distant neighbours would come. Maybe the fabled Eskaran Army would save us.

Then Mama twisted, and got her arm free, and she plunged her thumb deep into the eye of one of her assailants. He recoiled with a high, ululating wail, gore leaking dreadfully from the socket. Mama had his eye in her hand, and with her teeth gritted she crushed it between her fingers and it burst like a spore pod.

The White-skins went into a frenzy. One of them hit Mama across the face, another went to aid his wounded companion. Then one of the bystanders walked over to where they were holding Mama, and in one quick movement he drew a dagger and thrust it into her neck.

'Mama!'

At first I thought it had come from my own throat, that the shock and horror had forced the cry from my lungs. But then I turned to my right and saw Chada behind me, his face slack, body trembling. He'd followed me.

The White-skins turned towards us, speared us with freezing gazes. I shrieked and ran, pulling Chada with me. We didn't get far. Irresistible hands swept us up and dragged us, howling, back to the garden patch.

Mama was watching us. The soil around her was sodden with her blood, and her tawny hair was black with it, but a flicker of life held within her as she lay there with the knife in her throat. Long enough to meet my tearful stare. Long enough to ask: *Why? Why did you come back?*

Then she relaxed, and her eyes went flat.

Chada and I were incoherent with fear, faces running with tears and snot. Two of the White-skins gripped our arms while the others argued about us. But the argument was a short one. One thing about the White-skins that Papa hadn't mentioned in his tales: they only took girl-children to be their slaves. Boys tended to grow up violent.

I could barely see through my hysterical grief as they pulled Chada away from me and one of them drew his sword. I screamed so hard I thought my throat would give, but nothing could stop what was to come.

That was the first time I failed to save someone I loved.

3

I break the surface with barely a ripple and climb up on to the bank, towing a waterproof sack behind me. Crouched small, dripping and naked, I search the mournful lichen-trees for signs of movement. A chill breeze, drawn through stony vents from the higher caverns, runs invisible fingers through the foliage. Beyond that, nothing moves.

Satisfied, I run silently into the undergrowth and hide at the feet of the shaggy green trees. There I open the sack, towel dry and dress. Soft black shoes, laced to the knee, where they meet the ends of my trousers. Long black gloves, sleeveless black top, black mask covering the lower half of my face.

I tie my hair up and then I lay out the remaining contents of the sack. Shortblades. Bow and quiver. Blowpipe and darts. Daggers. Garrotte. Flash bombs. Throwing knives. And finally, a couple of little treats concocted by Ekan. He was really pretty co-operative, once I told him what I was using it for.

I'm kitted out to kill, and I'm looking forward to it. All that's left to me is hate now. Cold, icy hate.

Ledo. I'm coming for you.

The mansion belongs to an eminent Plutarch of the Turnward Claw Alliance, a good friend of Ledo's who has presumably given him the use of it while he's away. I've watched the place for several turns now, from the roof of an apartment building in Lash Park. Finding a good vantage point has been the hardest part of the operation so far. Harder than getting through the underwater grate in the stream, anyway. A touch of acid paste and a swift kick was all it took. Someone should tell them it's no use building walls if you make it so easy to swim beneath them.

The staff were sent away a few hours ago. I watched them depart through my spyglass. Ledo doesn't want anyone but his Cadre to know what's going on here.

The exterior guards, six in all, are Caracassa men. There are two on the front door of the mansion, four patrolling the grounds. Two of them have leashed abris, to sniff out and disembowel intruders. The abris might have been a problem; it's not easy to hide from creatures with such a keen sense of smell. But I have ways and means.

Security is light, though that's to be expected. Too many men would only draw attention. Ledo's got no reason to think that anyone suspects what he's up to. He's protected by secrecy. Or so he believes.

Once dry, I splash myself in the first of Ekan's concoctions: a scent that imitates the smell of foliage, strong enough to mask my natural odour and hide me from the abris. I hesitate for the barest moment before applying it. It's not in my nature to trust an expert poisoner I've recently maimed. I'm running chants in expectation of a slow creep of deathly numbness where the formula touches my skin or hair, but there's nothing. I relax a little. It seems that Ekan is smart enough not to shoot the messenger, then. He knows who gave the order to cut his hand off. And he knows his only chance of retribution is through me.

Given the choice I wouldn't have used him at all. Risk is not something you take on lightly in an operation like this. But it's essential that I don't leave a trail, and that rules out any of my regulars. They'd never trace me to Ekan, and even if they did, Ekan won't say shit. Besides, there's a certain amount of poetic justice in it, and since there's little enough justice in the world, I might as well take the poetic kind while it's up for grabs.

Now, let's see if we're both as good as our reputations.

I sneak through the trees and come into sight of the mansion, across landscaped grounds cut through with narrow streams and spotted with copses of dwarf mycora. Shine-stacks – little ornamental cairns with shinestones hidden inside – cast their light across the lichen-fuzzed lawn. Something long-legged and thin moves with a startled gait in the distance, silhouetted against a shine-stack. It's just one of the grazing animals that the master of the house keeps, but it reminds me of the *scha'rak*, the lightning-fast steeds of the SunChild warriors.

I haven't thought of Feyn much since I left the caravan. I wonder if it's because I've been trying not to. Because I know if I think of him, I might want to go back to him; and there's a job to be done first.

The mansion is comprised of globular sections, like a cluster of unevenly sized bubbles that have crowded together and been petrified in ceramic. Irregular, round windows glow yellow, randomly scattered across the building's dark surface. A driveway leads from the front door to the entrance gate of the grounds. The two guards are standing to attention, liveried in formal Caracassa red and black. Dressed for ceremony rather than protection. I'll deal with them later.

Keeping to the shelter of the trees, I hunt down the first of the abris-handlers. I spot him walking in the open, his pet loping alongside with a sullen murderer's swing to its step. I've dealt with abris before, and I hate them. Their spiked carapaces make it hard to get a good hit on them. They're strong as three men and their claws and teeth can open you up to the bone. The best way to deal with an abris is to make sure it's dead before it realises you're there.

I use another of Ekan's little tricks to take them out. Poison powder, pungent and liberally scattered at knee-height among the foliage. It's not long before the abris notices the scent, and pulls its master over to investigate. He follows his pet warily into the copse, sword drawn.

'What have you found?' he asks. The abris is sniffing excitedly, sucking the deadly powder in through its sensitive muzzle. It slows, whines, sways a little, and then keels over. That's when I slip my garrotte over the guard's head and pull it tight. It takes him a while to die, but he does it silently, and that's what's important.

The death of the second handler isn't quite so elegant, but it's more straightforward. I hide out till they wander close to me, then shoot the abris through the neck with an arrow. It's a tricky shot, between the armour plates, but I make it well enough. Then I string and fire again before the surprised guard has time to react. Quick and sloppy, but I still get him through the lung so there's too much blood in his throat to scream.

The other two guards on patrol aren't a problem. Alone, unaware. Picking them off is child's play.

Bodies hidden, I creep closer to the mansion and wait. My timing is good. I'm there in time to see the carriage come rolling up the drive, pulled by a single crayl. Three figures get out, hooded and cowled, masked and gloved. Not a bit of flesh showing.

I feel a thrill of fury at the sight of them. Voids, the fucking audacity of that! To invite the Gurta into the heart of our capital city! And yet how easy it would be, travelling under Ledo's sanction. Nobody would dare to question or investigate. Less suspicious than a clandestine meeting on neutral ground, even. Ledo's leaving the city would raise eyebrows, but not this. Just a secret meeting, like dozens of others carried out by the Plutarchs every turn.

Just thinking about it makes me clench my teeth. For an instant, I see Jai: the same picture I've had in my mind since Reitha came to me. My son, sprawled dead on the floor of a barracks, an empty vial in his hand. Eyes closed, features still and lifeless. I stamp the images flat. Grief and sorrow come later. For now, there's only revenge.

The newcomers go inside, and the guards return to their posts. I give them a decent amount of time and then blowpipe them both with poison darts. The beauty of the blowpipe is that most people take several seconds to realise they're under attack. Several seconds is much more than I need.

I could have sneaked in, avoided the guards entirely. But that's not how I want to play this one. I'm taking no chances. I don't like the idea of one of the outside guards coming in and surprising me, and I don't want any witnesses.

That's the sensible and logical part of the reason. The irrational part is stronger. I *want* to kill them. I want them dead for just being *involved* with Clan Caracassa, with Ledo, with everything that's happened to me and my family. By dealing with the Gurta my master has become complicit in the deaths of everyone I ever lost. Even my parents and my brother. If he's working with the enemy, then he's condoning what was done to them. He's making my life meaningless. He's making a joke of it.

I'll never be able to kill enough to make this feeling go away, and I know that. But just these few. Just these.

I crack the door and look inside. The hall is polished rootwood and ivory, immaculate and predictable. Jewelled spiral steps lead up to a balcony on either side, and at the end is a wide staircase narrowing towards double doors at the top. There's nobody in here. If I'd thought there would be, I'd have gone up the side of the building, cut through a window. But I've counted who's been in and out. There are only seven people in this entire place. Three Gurta, three Cadre, and Ledo. If a single person spotted one of Ledo's visitors without their masks then the game would be up. He's keeping the numbers tight.

I head up the spiral steps to the balcony and pad along. Exquisite murals line the walls, but I only see their beauty, I don't feel it. Beauty exists no more. It's done and over, and it was useless anyway. Where's the reality in those fleeting moments of pleasure we leach from the sight of something that gladdens or puzzles us? I'm sick of these fucking illusions we create to make our bland lives that much more epic. I'm sick of trying to convince myself that life is not some horrific animal, into whose jaws we're thrown, to be tossed and rent in a brief and bloody struggle before being flung brokenly aside. Happiness is just the anaesthetic that delays the pain. If you don't think that, it's because you're too weak to face it.

Everyone's dead. I'm dead too. I just have too much hate to lie down.

At the end of the balcony is a door, leading to a corridor and rooms beyond. I'm used to the eerie emptiness of a sleeping mansion from a dozen infiltrations, but a deserted one has a uniquely forlorn air. It's an old, stately place, heavy with time. I pass through it, caring nothing for its charms.

They haven't gone far in. It takes me a little searching, but I find them. The room has the feel of a study about it, with a library gallery running around the top and a single double door. A heavy desk takes pride of place, flanked by a solid glass globe of Callespa, with the known lands suspended three-dimensionally inside, a complex cavern system of precious metals. The shinestones have been hooded and lanterns burn. Ledo always preferred firelight. It leaves the gallery in shadow. That suits me.

Having heard their voices through the door, I make my way to an upper level and through an attic crawlway to a trapdoor that opens on to the gallery. Blueprints were easy enough to acquire, for someone like Keren. I owe him a debt that is becoming colossal, but I think he sensed the finality of this and didn't complain. He even offered to act as lookout for me, to send up a signal if any unexpected guests should arrive at the mansion.

From the gallery, I can look down on them. The Gurta have shed their disguises. Two stand in ceremonial sap armour, pale and faintly iridescent, hands near their swords and bows on their backs. The third is standing before the desk, talking closely with Ledo. Even at this distance, I know him. I may have had trouble recalling the name, but I'll never forget the face of the man who told me I was an animal without passion. Close to thirty years have changed him, weathered him like bark; but he's still indisputably Belek Aspa.

Ledo has three Cadre with him. Caydus, Jyirt, and a chthonomancer known as Ashka. Jyirt and Caydus are two of a kind, massive brawlers who make deceptively subtle fighters, just like Rynn. The three of them were good friends, in their time. It bothers me a little that I'm going to have to kill them.

Caydus is heavily armoured, ruddy-faced and blond: he looks perpetually furious. Jyirt is bald-headed, grey-skinned and sunken-eyed, and wears a scornful expression which makes people instinctively mistrust him. He's clad in light blue leathers, designed for mobility. Ashka is a little more flamboyant by nature, long hair scraped back into a ponytail that dissolves into colourful extensions. His face is a symmetrical tapestry of skinmarks. He wears a tight black bodysuit beneath plates of light alloy, his arms folded across his chest.

There's a popular misconception that chthonomancers have the natural ability to sense things beyond the power of normal mortals, but I know their powers only work when they're trancing, and that drains them fast. Chthonomancers rely on meditation and focus to tap their inner power. They can get into it pretty fast, but it doesn't just turn on and off. Catch a chthonomancer in the street with a knife, and he's as helpless as anyone.

Nevertheless, I decide to kill him first. Because if he gets time to do what he does, then I don't stand a chance.

Below me, Ledo and Belek are leaning over something on the desk. A document. Ledo signs with a flourish, and then hands the pen to the Gurta, who does the same. I adjust my face mask carefully, scrutinising their body language. What kind of deal have they made? I'm thirsty to know the details of the betrayal. I want to understand everything about why my master has done what he's done.

Then they're clasping hands, Eskaran-style. Smiling. Like old comrades. It's a horrible sight, a mockery. Eskaran and Gurta together, wide grins on their faces, congratulating each other on the murder of their kinfolk. Then Belek turns away, motions to his bodyguards, and the three of them head for the door.

Voids, it's over already? I was only just in time. Once they're gone, they're gone for good.

No time to revise my plan. No time for second thoughts. It's now or not at all.

Goodbye Jai. Goodbye Rynn. Goodbye Mama, Papa, Chada. Goodbye Veya. Goodbye Orna.

Now!

2

The first they know of me is when Ashka gets an arrow through his forehead. Caydus and Jyirt react instantly, leaping towards their master to protect him with their bodies. It's what Cadre do. I know I'll never hit them on the move, so I fire at the spot where Jyirt is *going*, and he jumps right into the path of the arrow. It hits him in the nape of his neck, punching out through the front of his throat.

That's it for my free shots. The Gurta soldiers have their bows unloosed from their shoulders and they're tracking me as I bolt along the gallery. I dive and roll as arrows thump into the spines of the books behind me.

Caydus has Ledo covered with his body, backed into a corner. His enormous, curved sword is drawn, held defensively before them. Belek is making for the exit, under cover of his guards. Can't have that. I pull a metal sphere from a pouch at my belt and twist the two hemispheres in opposite directions. A loud crunch comes from within, and the two halves spring apart by a finger's width. I lob it over the balcony, and even before it's hit the study floor it's belching yellow, acrid smoke in great billows.

The Gurta soldiers yell and shy away from the missile as it bounces across the room. In seconds, we're all reduced to dirty silhouettes. Another arrow comes my way, but it's wild. They can't draw a bead on me now. Belek is still moving for the door, forging through blindly, a flailing shadow in the murk. I vault the balcony gallery and land in front of the Minister. He can't check his run fast enough. I sidestep, encircle his neck with my arm and spin him round. Before he knows where he is, I have a blade to his throat and we're standing, backs to the door, facing into the smoke-hazed room.

~ Put down your bows! ~ I shout. ~ Draw again and your Minister dies ~

The soldiers freeze. The flurry of chaos is abruptly at an end. It takes them a moment to find me, but the smoke is already thinning. The soldiers look uncertain, bows still half-drawn. They're not used to being ordered by a woman.

~ Do as she says! ~ Belek snaps at his soldiers. His skin has that oddly sterile feel of his kind. Just being near him brings back memories I'd rather not have.

The guards place their bows on the floor.

'Orna!'

It's Ledo. Pushing out from behind Caydus, walking towards me. Caydus sticks close to him.

'You too, Caydus. Drop the sword.'

'Not going to happen, Orna,' he replies, his voice dense with venom. I'm the traitor in his eyes, because I've broken my oath of Bond. Ironic, really. 'Kill him if you want. You won't get our master.'

'*Your* master,' I correct him.

'Orna, what is this?' Ledo hisses.

I adjust my grip on my hostage's neck, pushing the blade in hard enough to cut just out of spite. 'This? This is what happens when you betray your people, Ledo. When you consort with our sworn enemy.' I look up at him. 'This is what happens when you sell out your own kind.'

'Your loyalty is to me!' he cries. 'Don't presume to interfere in matters you don't understand!'

I shake my head slightly. No words could sway me now. 'I would have given my life for you,' I say, tight with anger. 'But instead you took my family.'

'Stop this now,' he snaps. He's not intimidated in the least. I don't think he even believes I'll do it. He still expects to be obeyed. 'Stop this now, and I'll let you leave this room with that life you seem so eager to throw away.'

~ Please ~ says Belek. ~ Listen to me. This is— ~

I push the dagger hard into his throat, and blood flows in a steady stream down his white neck, staining his collar. The soldiers twitch forward, but I stay them with a glare.

~ I'll bet you don't remember me, Belek Aspa ~ I murmur. ~ But I remember you. You once said that my kind were like animals. That we didn't have the same emotions as the Gurta did ~ I pull the knife along his neck a little, and he flinches and whimpers. ~ I'm feeling pretty emotional right now, Minister ~

'What do you gain, Orna?' Ledo calls. He's keeping a respectable distance, but he's not hiding from me, either. 'You'll die, and for what? You must know that even you don't stand a chance against Caydus. You'll kill one Gurta. Is it worth it? Leave now, and I may still be merciful.'

'I want to hear you say it!' I shout at him. 'I want to hear you say you betrayed us at Korok! I want to hear you say you were selling our troops out to this man!'

Ledo sneers. 'You don't make demands of me!'

There's a clacking of armour. Ledo looks over at the Gurta guard, who is picking himself unsteadily up from the ground. A moment later, the guard's balance deserts him again, and he drops dizzily to one knee.

I laugh softly through my mask. 'You actually think you have the upper hand, don't you? You arrogant aristo fuck. That smoke wasn't just for concealment, and nor is this mask. You've been dead for some while now.' As an afterthought, I add: 'Ekan the apothecary sends his compliments.'

The look on his face is perfect. If I could preserve just one thing in my memory for ever, it would be that. Then Caydus roars, and comes for me.

I shove my blade deep into Belek's neck and wrench it out in a jet of blood, then I shove him towards Caydus. He staggers, gargling, into the warrior's path, clawing at his wound. It slows Caydus long enough for me to fling a throwing knife across the room and into the eye of the Gurta soldier who's still standing. The last one is out of action, slipping and falling as he tries to get to his feet, nerves malfunctioning in a dreadful parody of a newborn animal.

I flit across the room, retreating from Caydus. He's the only one I have to worry about now. Ledo makes for the door, but his legs fail him for a moment and he goes over. The poison is beginning to make itself felt. Panicked, gasping, tears in his eyes, he tries again. He's too afraid to face the truth. All that aristo invulnerability and dignity is gone now. He's just a man, cowardly in the face of death.

He wrenches open the door and plunges through, calling for his guards. Nobody will come. I'd love to follow him and watch him die, but Caydus is blocking me. Loyal to the end.

Though he doesn't have long left, he's still got it in him to be dangerous. He takes a swing with his sword, but he's been slowed by the poison and I dart out of his reach. I back away a little. He makes an incoherent noise of rage, lunges clumsily towards me. I dance out of reach as he cuts air again. Teeth gritted, he tries a third time, but I'm way too quick for him. With each charge, he gets more tired and more angry.

'Don't do this,' I say, because I liked him, and this is embarrassing for both of us.

He stares at me with bloodshot eyes, sweating, hating. He tries to lift his sword and he can't. Slumps onto his arse, exhausted. He heaves a great sigh and raises his head.

'Bitch,' he says, and then his head lolls and he dies, just sitting there.

I step out into the corridor and find Ledo lying face down. He didn't get far. I take off my mask and unstrap the gas filter from around my nose and mouth. The poison in the air is long gone now.

I kneel down, turn Ledo over and stare at his lifeless corpse. I don't feel anything. No satisfaction. Compassionless as a child studying a beetle.

What did I expect? I don't know. I'm too fucking numb to know.

Listless, I wander back into the study. I'm waiting for some kind of closure and it hasn't come. Bodies everywhere, blood smeared across the floor. I walk over to the desk and look down at the document that Ledo and Belek were signing.

It's the signatures that draw my attention. The latest occupy pride of place at the bottom, as the authors and executors of the document; but there are many more. At a glance I can see over a dozen Plutarchs, all of the Folded Wing, with Ledo the only member of the Turnward Claw Alliance on there. A similar number of Gurta signatories have also put their names to it.

We, the undersigned, firm in our conviction, do hereby commit ourselves in whatever capacity we are able to sue for the cessation of hostilities between the two great nations of Eskara and Gurta . . .

I stop breathing. I snatch up the document, skim read.

. . . make all efforts to persuade our respective authorities . . . phased plan of withdrawal with negotiation of ceasefire to begin immediately . . .

Horror settles on me like a freezing fog. It's a peace accord. They were forging a truce.

They were trying to stop the war.

I

That's when it hits me. The one thing I never considered, the one possibility that never entered my head, because I never stopped seeing the Gurta as the enemy. I hated them too much to believe anything good of them. I was so accustomed to seeing them as monsters that I forgot that they were people. That they also had children who were being killed on the battlefields. I forgot that, just like us, they might not want to see their loved ones coming home in pieces. They wanted an end to the fighting as much as we did.

Ledo *was* dealing with the Gurta. But he wasn't selling us out. He was making peace. And knowing that, I understand everything.

Ledo saw the tide of public opinion turning and realised he was facing stiff competition in the field of battlefield medicine. Since all his interests were tied to the war, he needed to make a move into peacetime industries. So he agreed to marry off Liss to Clan Jerima, a successful textile manufacturer. He intended to use his workforce to make dyes instead of medicines, and he would go into business with Jerima. Probably he would also switch away from battlefield medicines to more commercial drugs like cold remedies. He knew the war was dying out, and he was gearing up for peace.

All this I'd learned from Casta, but I'd thought it was the backup plan in case his sabotage failed. I was wrong. He wanted to *prevent* Operation Deadfall, not sabotage it. He wanted to declare a truce.

As ever, it was all about the timing. If the other Plutarchs sensed the change coming, they would all start making similar plans. So Ledo went behind the Turnward Claw Alliance's back, and began gathering support among the Folded Wing for a truce with the Gurta. At the same time he contacted one of the Gurta, an influential Minister called Belek Aspa who was known to have the ear of the High Elder, and told him that he could get enough of the Plutarchs on his side to call a truce, if Belek could do the same.

His idea was to hamstring Operation Deadfall at the last moment, then defect to the Folded Wing, leaving him way ahead of his allies in the Turnward Claw Alliance, who had already committed themselves. Leaving them in the dust in the post-war era of peace. A smart and ruthless political move.

And I just fucked it all up.

Ledo wasn't the traitor. And that leaves only one person it could possibly be. One person who stands to profit by what I've done.

It's because I'm so overwhelmed by the realisation that I don't hear the arrow coming in time to avoid it. I move far too late, but at least I move, and that makes the difference between getting it square in the back and getting it through my side. The impact spins me off my feet and sends me crashing to the floor, gasping with shock.

Instinct kicks in. The chua-kîn chants that govern my metabolism start marching through the white emptiness in my head, and my body responds as best it can, but it doesn't have a lot left to give. I lie there, trembling and juddering, spitted. The arrow is sticking out of my ribs at an angle. At least the bastard went right through. It only delivered a small amount of the poison on the tip.

I've fallen facing the doorway, but I know who's done it even before my blurred vision resolves and the fuzzy blob stepping into the room takes on shape.

Nereith. Of course it's Nereith.

He walks slowly into the room, surveying the dead. He's wearing a scarlet trench coat, matching the skinmarked stripes on his bald skull. My heart is thumping in my ears, but I can't move. I'm paralysed.

'Reliable Orna,' he says. His bow is still trained on me, a new arrow nocked. 'You know, Silverfish had doubts as to whether you could pull it off or not, but I never lost faith. I was there when you got us out of Farakza. I knew you could do it.'

I've been used. I've been fucking *used.* I want to scream but I don't think I could take the agony. Because I know who Silverfish is now. Silverfish is the traitor. Silverfish is the one who's been playing me all along, who's deceived me over and over until, in the end, I killed my own innocent master.

Who was it who sent me to break into Ledo's quarters, where they could easily have put the letter from Belek Aspa in a place where I would find it? Who was it, apart from Ledo, that had the authority to send me to kill Gorak Jespyn, a man who knew the identity of the *real* traitor who sold us out at Korok? Who had reason to want Ledo dead, and needed an agent, a loyal member of his Cadre that could get close enough to him to do the job? Who had fucking well *told* me they wanted the war to continue, and that Operation Deadfall had to fail for the good of the Clan?

'Ah,' says Nereith, stepping closer. 'I see you get it now. A little late, perhaps, but congratulations all the same.'

'Casta,' I croak. 'Silverfish is Casta.'

'And you're just a fade, Orna. How does it feel?'

Casta. Casta, with her long absences from her lamenting twin. Casta, not half so dizzy as she pretended. With her connections in aristocratic society and the network she'd built up in the underworld as Silverfish, there was little that went on in the city that she didn't know. She hid her identity with the simple trick of always having her generals refer to her as male, but there were clues, if I'd have been smart enough to see them. I'd always wondered why Silverfish persecuted Clan Jerima in particular. Clan Jerima, the family that Liss was marrying into. The Clan that were going to take Casta's twin away from her.

It was her that had sent me to kill Gorak Jespyn, who really *did* have information that could compromise her. But she knew I'd suppose it was Ledo who'd given the order, and she made sure of it by sending me on a break with my family only to call me away the very first turn that I arrived. It didn't make sense for Casta to do that, so I assumed it was Ledo, and later that fitted in with the picture that was being presented to me. A picture in which Ledo was the traitor I was looking for.

'Fortunate, our meeting in Farakza,' Nereith says. 'And not only because you saved my life. Casta had been looking for a way to get rid of Ledo for quite some time. Ever since he'd decided to marry off Liss, actually. Ledo never really did understand the lengths she'd go to to keep her sister by her side.' He's still approaching, watching me for any sudden moves. 'But you were just too perfect. Grieving, desperate, so full of hate. You *wanted* someone to blame for it all. We just arranged things to make sure it was Ledo.'

And I gave them the instruments of my undoing. Casta had been there, at the sculpture graveyard in the Greyslopes, when I had professed that I would betray my master if he tried to take my son. I'd mentioned Belek Aspa to Nereith, hoping to learn something, and Nereith had worked out that I'd heard it in Farakza, in conjunction with Ledo's name. He'd worked out that I suspected Ledo of something.

I'd told him about the letter in my drawer, which would have given Casta plenty of time to find it and work out how to use it against me. I'd placed all my hopes in that letter.

'Casta . . . the letter . . .' I say, because I need to know. I need to be sure. I have to understand the whole of what's been done to me.

'We couldn't have Jai withdrawn from the front lines, Orna,' he says, a false apology in his tone. 'Then what reason would you have to kill Ledo? Casta had words with her brother, like you asked her to. But she made very sure he wouldn't grant your request. That wouldn't have suited her plans for you.'

Nereith must have had this in mind from the moment he met me. Once we got out, he sent word to Casta from Caralla. Then he waited there for me, knowing I'd turn up if I possibly could, because like an idiot I'd told him that was where Jai was stationed. Between what Casta knew of my past, and what I told Nereith, they had all the tools they needed to make me into their assassin. My family was always my weak spot.

The *scale* of the deception staggers me. They've had me in their hands from the start.

I have a thousand questions, but I ask only one, forced huskily from my resisting lungs.

'Is my son really dead?'

He walks carefully up to me, then loosens the tension on the bowstring. Obviously convinced I'm not a threat, and he's right. I don't have the strength to raise my head.

'I really don't know. If he is, it's news to me.' He picks up the document from the desk, runs his eyes over it briefly. 'Faking that letter from the Army was dirty, I'll admit. But we needed to be sure you'd kill Ledo. Otherwise it would all have been for nothing.' He shrugs. 'We knew you'd try to find Reitha. Better that the news came from her. Makes it seem less suspicious if it goes through a third party. Basic subterfuge, really. You should know that.'

The joy is enough to hurt my heart. It crushes in with the horror and the pain and the shock. It mingles with the disgust I feel at myself, curdles into the fury and the hope. I'm feeling too much at once and I can't handle it. Tears come and I'm trembling violently. I feel like I'm going to die, but it won't be from the poison.

He walks over to a lantern, rolls up the document and touches it to the flame.

'You'll get hero's honours,' he says. 'You were killed in defence of your master, trying to save him from these Gurta assassins.' He tips the peace treaty so that fire runs up its side, watching it with fascination. 'And so the war goes on, as it must. Too many people profiting from it to stop it now. It's not in Clan Caracassa's interests.'

He holds it until he can't hold it any more, then drops it to the floor. Worms of white and red writhe in the blackness of the scorched paper as it curls up.

'Operation Deadfall will fail,' he murmurs, looking down at the embers of Ledo's ambition. 'The humiliation will inspire such rage in the people of Eskara that they will redouble their efforts to wipe out the hated enemy.' His eyes flick away from the treaty, disinterested now. 'Caracassa does best during the really big slaughters. They have the manufacturing capacity to handle it.'

He comes over to me. I'm spasming pitifully, face streaked with tears. He bares his teeth and draws the bowstring. 'Be careful who you trust, Orna. If you don't pay attention, you're liable to get stabbed in the back.'

I hear the thud of an impact, and I flinch as his arrow fires into the floor and spins away. Nereith's face is puzzled. He looks down at me, for what seems a long time, and I can't help thinking that he seems betrayed, disappointed. *How could you?*

Then he groans and falls over sideways, a throwing knife buried to the hilt in between his shoulder blades.

'You got *that* right,' says Keren to the dead man, as he slopes into the room.

I just stare at the ceiling as he picks his way through the corpses and kneels down next to me. I can't do any more.

'Well,' he says helpfully. 'You're a mess.'

'You're late,' I tell him.

'You told me to keep watch on the gate in case anyone else arrived,' he replies. 'Didn't say anything about your Khaadu friend.'

'I didn't exactly see it coming, Keren, or I wouldn't be lying here. Why didn't you stop him?'

'Couldn't very well kill him until I knew whose side he was on, could I?'

'The arrow in my side makes things pretty fucking obvious on that score, wouldn't you say?'

Keren motions towards Nereith. 'Is he dead or isn't he?' he asks, exasperated. Then he pulls the knife out of Nereith's back and stabs him in the side of the neck. 'Anyway, now he definitely is.'

I'm struggling to get up. 'You think you can walk?' he says.

'Probably not.'

'I've got a guy who can fix you. Dweoming. Discreet. Not too insane.'

I nod slightly and cough. 'Just working off the poison. I don't think the arrow hit anything too major.'

'You're tough. You'll be okay.'

He helps me up. Every movement brings pain. I suck in the air through my gritted teeth and relish it.

'You owe me really, really big,' Keren says, as he helps me towards the door.

O

The outposts of Eskara are lonely, desolate places. Beyond the network of chthonomantically carved roadways and rivers, the world becomes hostile. Here, there are caverns that can only be reached by clambering up ancient gas vents or negotiating treacherous dust fields and fungal marshes that can swallow the unwary. Beasts roam, enormous insectile things with jaws strong enough to shear off a leg. Civilisation ends.

The people that choose to come here are the damaged, the exiled, the explorers. Those who don't mesh well with society, or who seek to live on its boundaries. They pay little attention to strangers, and they tend to keep to themselves. Most are occupied with the tough business of eking out a livelihood. That suits me well enough.

I've been all over the edges of Eskara this past season. I've stayed in outposts ranging from shanties to little towns. I've been put up in farms and slept in sheds with animals. I've used a dozen names and disguises.

It doesn't matter. They're still on my trail. The Cadre of Clan Caracassa, now under Casta's domination, as the elder of the twins by a few minutes. I've already killed two of them, but they keep coming.

I can't run any more.

The town of Scratch, where I find myself now, is a crude and empty place. They've planted luminous fungi where they can, but they haven't grown big enough yet, so the place is always dark. Lantern oil is always in short supply so none of the three streets are lit, and there's not a shinestone to be found. Small, square buildings hunker unevenly together, with stony paths winding between them. This place runs on little more than hope.

It's freezing cold here. The site is badly chosen: the cramped cavern is near enough to the surface to be far from the warmth at the core of our moon, but deep enough that hot air from outside doesn't reach this far. What money I had is almost gone, and only the most desperate would give me a job, fearing the retribution of my Bond-master. I could steal, but there's nothing to steal out here, and I daren't go back to a city.

It's a soulless, terrible place to spend a life. I've got better things to do with mine.

In a rented upper room of a house in Scratch, I write my letter. The walls are bare stone. A tatty bedroll lies on the floor behind me. In the lantern-light, I sit hunched over a desk so roughly carved that my hands are peppered with splinters. I'm wearing a fur cloak that I took from a man I found lying dead on a path, a few dozen turns ago. It doesn't keep me warm.

By next turn, this will all be over. Knowing that, I can endure anything.

Even so far away from Veya, I've heard the news. Casta is now Plutarch Nathka Caracassa Casta, Magnate of Clan Caracassa. And they're raking it in over the wounded and limbless and maimed that are left behind in the wake of the Eskaran Army's doomed attempt at a military breakthrough. Operation Deadfall was a failure, but they've painted it as a heroic attempt to stall a massive Gurta assault. A brave stand against overwhelming odds, thwarted by Gurta treachery. The populace are furious. Calling for an increase in the budget for the Eskaran Army. Calling for revenge. The Turnward Claw Alliance are back in the ascendant, and Clan Caracassa is at their head.

You have to hand it to her. That Casta, she's a piece of work.

And now the only loose end is me, and that's why I have Cadre on my tail. I'm the only one except Casta who knows what really happened. Well, except for Keren, but he'll never say a word. He knows better.

Keren still lives in Veya, I assume. I left him with enough tips, contacts and secrets to last him for years. The cream of a lifetime dealing in the Veyan underworld. My little reward for being a good friend to me.

I gave him a message to deliver to Reitha, too. To tell her that the letter from the Army was a lie. That if my son was dead, it wasn't because he took his own life. I needed her to know that. I couldn't have her believing that he'd give up that way.

I think of Jai, still and always. Is he alive, even now? Was he dead long ago, or did he become another victim of Casta's machinations, killed by the Gurta in the military catastrophe she engineered? I don't know, but I choose to believe. I believe he is alive.

And so I write my letter. A letter to Jai. The handwriting is disguised, the signature false, the content drab and typical. But it's what's underneath that counts. The code. The language that only he and I know.

It's a long letter, and in it I explain many things. I tell him how his father died, and I tell him about the letter from the Dean, and I tell him that I have to go away forever. I can never see him again, because there will always be people watching, waiting. People who would use him to draw me out, who would hurt him to get to me. I can't allow that. I tell him how dearly I love him, and how much I miss him, and how I hope he will be happy in his life.

But I say nothing about Casta, nor how she made me her fade, nor what I did to my master. These are things it's better that he doesn't know.

I've been cheated of the chance to see my son again, but at least I can make him understand. So I'll send this letter, borne on faith. I'll believe that it will get to him eventually, and he'll be alive and well. I'll believe that he'll read it in the end.

That'll do for me. That's enough.

When it's done and folded and sealed, I cry a little. But I've shed a thousand tears over this already, and there aren't many left in me. I've written many letters and burned them all, half-finished. It's only now, with time pressing, that I manage to reach the end. I'll put it in the post on my way out of this dreary place.

I glance at the pocket-watch lying on the desk, beneath the lantern. Not too long now. My guide will come for me on the sevenhour. The man who'll take me away from all of this, and from those that hunt me.

Even the Cadre won't follow me onto the surface.

I look down, at the skinmark on the inside of my wrist. Two chevrons pierced by three vertical lines. I hear the voice of a boy I knew once. *It means you are a friend to the SunChildren*, he says. *It means you belong to a coterie.*

I hear him again, asking me to stay with him. And I hear him telling me about a certain vine, that if burned in the right way would give off a smoke that could be smelt from afar. A smoke that would bring the SunChildren.

We will pass this way again, at the season's end.

Spore Season is drawing to a close and Swell Season is coming on. Up above, the Season of Nights is dying and the Season of Dust begins: a time of harsh winds and terrible storms. The coteries of the SunChildren will be on the move.

The nights are becoming short. More and more, Callespa will be ruled by the suns that scorched me. The surface is an alien world in which I'm not equipped to survive.

But I've been through the Shadow Death. I stood in the gaze of the suns and I lived. So I'm going. I'm heading to a place with no ceilings and no walls, where the sky keeps on forever and you could go mad with the freedom of it. Perhaps it will kill me, as sure as the Cadre on my tail would.

We'll see.